SAME, SAME BUT DIFFERENT

Monique de Ruiter

TALLWING
PRESS

*For Charlie and Logan, who never stopped asking,
"Are you still writing your book?"*

And for my dad, who is everything.

Chapter One

The air in the conference hall buzzed, like a sound just out of reach. By 3123, Earth had failed ten times, and in twenty-four hours, Earth's last hope would leave the ground. Grace waited offstage, one hand braced against the wall. Her stomach gave a slow, stubborn roll, not full panic, but close. Just the low, constant pressure of too many eyes waiting. Watching.

David leant close. "It's just another briefing," he whispered.

She gave him a look. "Sure," she said. "Just another briefing... with the fate of humanity attached."

He grinned, warm, easy, like he could take the edge off her nerves. It helped. A little.

From the wings, she could see them — officials, scientists, press — packed beneath chrome lights and floating drones. Some looked hopeful, others like they'd already given up. Grace wasn't sure which group unnerved her more, the ones who still believed, or the ones who'd already buried them.

The lighting shifted. A murmur rolled through the crowd. Commissioner Lin Tao stepped up to the mic, her black suit cutting a stark line against the gleaming backdrop.

"Before I introduce our mission leads," Lin said, "I want to acknowledge the agency I represent, The Australian Space Authority, and honour the ten missions that came before. Ten missions. Ten worlds. Ten chances. Every one of them, unsuccessful. Terraforming collapsed on Mars. Venus melted our probes. Titan cracked open beneath our feet. Each attempt cost lives. Years. Hope. EOS 11 is not another experiment. It's the last. The last mission that Earth will send."

She paused, letting the silence settle. "This isn't legacy-building. It's not a publicity stunt. It's what we have left. A single chance to begin again, not as conquerors, but as explorers." Her voice continued, calm but edged with clarity, the kind that made things feel official. "For those who've forgotten the names that built this mission, a reminder."

"Dr. Grace Virelli. Head Environmental Scientist at the Terra Pacific Centre for Environmental Sustainability. She holds a Bachelor of Environment, with majors in Climate Science and Environmental Earth Science. Although she's never travelled to space, she's spent the past eighteen months in intensive ASA training, preparing for survival, analysis, and mission operations."

She glanced down at her notes, then looked up again. "Dr. David Virelli. Lead Hydrogeologist at the Terra Pacific Applied Systems Division. He holds a Master of Science, with five years of experience at the ASA. Most recently, he flew aboard Pathfinder to oversee the installation of the final solar arrays on Terra Pacific's Orbital Research Station."

"Together, Drs. Grace and David Virelli have built a legacy of scientific achievement, and a marriage whose strength will be no less vital to this mission. They aren't just scientists, they're builders, problem-solvers, and thinkers who still believe humanity is worth saving. Now, please welcome the mission leads for EOS 11, Drs. Grace and David Virelli."

Grace stepped onto the stage, shoulders back, smile in place. The lights were blinding. Her stomach flipped. A slow roll of nausea stirred, settling low and refusing to ease.

Behind her, the screen lit up:

MISSION: EOS 11 - To Find Hope Among the Stars

David joined her, adjusting his collar with a subtle tug before stepping up to the microphone.

"Thank you for being here," he said. His voice landed smooth, practiced. "This is more than a mission. It's a promise. A promise to learn, to protect, and to lead with care. It's the continuation of everything we once believed humanity could be."

Polite applause followed, soft, restrained.

David looked at Grace. She gave a small nod and stepped forward. "I know what it looks like," she said. "Another launch. Another gamble. Another desperate reach for something better." She let the silence hang for a second, then continued, "EOS 11 is a mission of understanding, we'll be studying a world untouched. Where the climate works, the soil still breathes, the water runs clean. Our goal is to learn. To observe. To bring that knowledge home. That's the only way Earth gets a future."

Murmurs moved through the crowd. Someone near the middle raised a hand. "What's the destination? Where exactly is EOS 11 going?"

Grace stepped back slightly, and David leant in. "Veritas-9," he said. "Stable atmosphere, Earth-like gravity, no known civilization. It's the closest thing we've found to a fresh start."

Another voice called out, sharper this time. "How long will the mission take, Dr. Virelli?"

David didn't hesitate. "Engineers have fitted EOS 11 with advanced cryogenic fuel systems, sublight-speed propulsion, and deep-space shielding. We're expecting the journey to Veritas-9 to take roughly eighteen years one way. After a twelve-month surface study, the return trip will bring the total mission length to just over thirty years."

A voice rang out from the back, louder, skeptical. "Thirty years in deep space, and your lead scientist has never even left the planet? Who's flying this thing?"

A ripple of murmurs moved through the room.

David smiled, calm and sure. "That's a fair question," he said. "We're not alone on this mission. Alongside us is someone personally selected by Commissioner Lin herself."

"You may not see him today — he's never been one for the spotlight — but you might recognise his name. Commander Gareth Elderton. Seven ASA missions. Over seven hundred days in orbit. And yes, he's the reason the ASA had to ban roast beef sandwiches in space."

A ripple of laughter moved through the crowd.

David let out a soft laugh. "Turns out, smuggling deli meat into zero gravity leads to floating debris and some very unhappy engineers. But it also tells you everything you need to know about him — clever, bold, and not afraid to push boundaries. He's the best we've got."

Another voice called out. "And Veritas-9, you're sure this planet is uninhabited?"

David glanced at Grace, then back at the crowd. "There are no signs of advanced life. No communication, no infrastructure, nothing detectable by long-range scan. But we're not assuming. We're observing. EOS 11 is equipped with first-contact protocols. If there's life, we'll treat it with the respect it deserves."

A reporter in the third row stood up, voice cutting through the room. "EOS 2 melted on entry. EOS 8 suffered geothermal collapse, and EOS 6 vanished without a trace. What makes you think this crew won't be next?"

A quiet shift moved through the room, shoulders straightening, eyes narrowing, the collective weight of everyone waiting to see if they'd flinch.

Before anyone onstage could answer, Lin stepped forward. "Optimism did not guide our choice of this mission. It was built from necessity." She said. "If you came here for spectacle, find another war-zone."

The silence that followed didn't break.

Lin raised one hand. "One last question," she said. "Make it worth asking."

A woman near the front stood. "Dr. Virelli, as our lead environmental scientist, how can you justify leaving Earth now, when it's at its most fragile? Doesn't this feel like... giving up?"

Grace didn't flinch. "No," she said. "It feels like love. If your child were sick, wouldn't you do anything — everything — to save them? Even if it meant stepping away to find the cure?"

David reached for her hand. The motion was quiet, almost invisible. But she didn't let go. His fingers were warm. Grounding.

Together, they faced the waiting crowd. Camera lights flared. A low ripple of applause rose, swelling beneath the weight of a world watching.

— ✦ —

After the conference, the back corridors of the ASA felt like another world. Quiet, clinical, and scrubbed of emotion.

Grace and David turned the corner and found Gareth waiting, watching them approach. He leant against the wall, arms folded over his chest, dark canvas pants and a charcoal jacket with sleeves shoved to his elbows. He stood tall, all quiet strength and lean muscle, like a man who could fix a ship engine with one hand and silence a room with the other. His grey hair was tied neatly at the nape of his neck, and his slate-grey eyes studied Grace and David with the precision of someone who noticed everything and said almost nothing.

He watched them approach, he didn't smile, but he didn't have to. After five years of working side by side, they didn't need pleasantries to know where they stood. "That went better than expected," he said, pushing off the wall. "No one burst into tears. Always a win."

"I threw up in the conference suite beforehand," Grace said.

"Classy." He glanced at her. "Still feeling off?"

"It's nothing," she muttered. She kept walking. "Just nerves."

David's green eyes flicked to Gareth — bright, always a little too readable.

Gareth nodded his head toward the exit. "You still up for dinner then?"

"Oh please," Grace gave a faint smirk. "I'm getting in one last overpriced meal before we leave a planet where real honey costs more than the transport."

David chuckled. "Assuming the menu still has honey, and assuming it's even real. Bees died out over a hundred and fifty years ago. Whatever they're serving, it's closer to lab syrup than the real thing."

They stepped out into the soft hum of the city — all polished glass, clean lines, and silent calm. Auto-glides whispered past on fixed rails, sliding in perfect formation. They crossed into the main plaza, where pristine shopfronts lined the path, minimalist displays and backlit ads promising *The Choice Is In Your Hands* and *Progress Without Limits*.

The night breeze carried a faint bite of chlorine, laced with the sterile tang of processed air from the Skyfilters — sleek pillars tucked between buildings, pumping purified air into streets lined with climbing vines that never grew.

They paused at the kerb. Gareth glanced sideways. "Where to?"

"I made a reservation at The Preserve." David grinned.

Gareth let out a low whistle. "Going fancy."

David gave a half-shrug. "It's on the ASA tonight." He ran a hand through his copper-red hair, a habit he always fell back on when he felt a bit guilty.

"Nice." Gareth arched a brow. "Better use of our tax funds than air filters and algae control."

"Okay..." He gave a slow glance left, then right, and jerked his chin toward the street. "That way... then left at the Skyfilter tower."

Before either of them could answer, he stepped straight into the path of an approaching auto-glide. The sleek silver car slid to a dead stop without a sound.

"Gareth—" Grace hissed. Her bright blue eyes snapped wide. "Geez."

He kept walking, casual as ever. "What?" He flicked a hand toward the waiting auto-glide. "They've got collision control for a reason." He threw a glance back at them. "We all know the ad."

David caught up, shaking his head, and said it with him. "Safety! By popular demand."

Grace let out a short laugh, the kind that slipped out before you meant it to. She quickened her pace, then slowed sharply, her vision swimming for just a moment. She stopped, bracing her hands on her knees.

David turned. "Are you okay?"

Grace drew a breath, steadying. She straightened, sweeping her dark curls back from her face. "Yeah... they must've done a fresh chlorine flush in the harbour. The smell's stronger than usual."

David and Gareth exchanged a look, fast, subtle.

Grace caught it. "Stop doing that. I'm fine."

Gareth gave a quiet grunt but didn't press. They moved on, their steps syncing with the low hum of the city.

David gave a half-smile. "Here's a fun fact. Back in the 2050s, whales used to end up in this harbour. During migration season, some took a wrong turn and got stuck. Of course, that was before the global water chlorination programme. Obviously." He gave a soft laugh. "Some even say there were sharks in here. Real ones. Can you imagine?" He shook his head, smiling.

Gareth gave him a brief, unreadable look, then turned to Grace. "When was your last medical?"

Grace shrugged, tucking her hair behind her ear. "Two days ago. Same as you. Although they don't exactly roll out the gold standard for EOS crews anymore."

David snorted. "Gotta love those budget cuts."

"And the protocol cuts," Grace said dryly. "They took my blood pressure with a recycled cuff and asked if I felt emotionally stable on a scale from one to potato."

They passed beneath a glowing billboard mounted over the footpath. *Why be you, when you can be anyone?* The words pulsed in electric blue beneath a flawless model whose features shifted in slow, seamless cycles — a dozen perfect faces flickering across the same sculpted frame, each one smiling the exact same smile.

Grace shot Gareth a look. "Why don't you ever do the press conferences?"

Gareth gave a small shrug. "I don't do crowds... or lies." He glanced at her. "Besides, some of those questions were brutal," he said. "Especially the bit about disappearing into the stars."

Grace sighed. "They weren't wrong. We don't know what we're heading into. And I couldn't give them the comfort they wanted."

"You told them the truth," David said. "That's more than most leaders have done in the last... fifty years."

Gareth snorted. "Why would they? It's easier to let everyone have what they want and watch the world burn."

Grace gave a soft huff. "Truth stopped being part of the job description a long time ago. Remember what they said when the last of the trees came down?"

"Something like fewer allergies, and technology can do it better." David smirked.

Grace shook her head, soft and sharp. "Hard to argue with logic like that."

Gareth nodded slowly. "Still. That room was ready to tear you apart. Lucky Lin shut them down before they got the chance."

They reached the Skyfilter tower and turned down a quieter street, its low hum fading behind them.

"She always does," Grace said. "No one else could've pulled off the infamous 'last mission.'"

"She looked like she was carved from surgical steel," Gareth muttered. "I watched her dismantle half their objections with a look."

Grace smiled. "She told an ASA advisor, 'If you're offering opinions, you'll need evidence. Or a seat in the audience.'"

David winced. "Ouch."

"He excused himself," Grace added. "Came back three minutes later with red eyes and a revised briefing."

David gave a low whistle. "Damn. I'd follow her into battle." He paused. "But it's more than that. She believes in it."

Grace's smile faded. "That's what scares me. People who believe are dangerous."

No one spoke. There wasn't much left to say.

They reached The Preserve. The glow of its entryway cut a sharp, clinical line against the street. Smooth white walls wrapped the building like a sealed pod, its facade lined with towering glass panels. Inside, perfect rows of greenery shimmered behind the glass — clipped vines, sculpted trees, polished stones — all holographically rendered with surgical precision.

Above the door, a soft gold logo gleamed beneath scripted letters: A Taste of Nature.

Gareth gave a low whistle. "Subtle. Nature may be dead... but at least it's branded."

— ✦ —

The apartment was quiet, wrapped in the soft hum of the city and the slow, even breaths of David asleep behind her.

Grace sat at the desk tucked beneath the window, one knee drawn close, a soft blanket draped over her shoulders. Display light spilled across the desk and onto the window, mingling with the city's glow. Her fingers moved fluidly across the haptic surface, each motion echoing in silent flashes beneath her touch.

The system unlocked. Credentials accepted.

Her hands moved in measured rhythm, the surface flickering with each input.

Medical file located.

Her eyes tracked the scan results — each graph, each number — until she found it.

Grace sat back, blue light washing over her features.

She didn't move. Just stared.

Then, she pressed her palms to her face.

Her breath turned shallow, not quite panic, just pressure held at the edge.

She looked back to the display and leant in, her fingers moving with quiet precision across the lit surface.

She keyed in the sequence, slow and exact.

Her fingers trembled. She curled them into a fist, then forced them to move again.

She paused for a moment, then pressed confirm.

The marker blinked. Then vanished.

She ran the override.

Override accepted.

Grace let out a slow breath and shut the display down, her hands steady now. The light disappeared, leaving only the shape of her reflection in the dark glass.

She rose quietly, crossed to the bed, and slipped back beneath the covers.

David stirred briefly as she curled in beside him, tucking herself into the quiet warmth of his body. His arm reached out instinctively, finding her and pulling her close.

She leant in against his chest and let her eyes close.

Chapter Two

The morning sun threw long, sterile light across the city as the ASA-issued auto-glide hummed along its rail. Inside, Grace sat beside David, hands still in her lap, watching the world slide past in clinical perfection.

The city thinned quickly. Rows of apartments gave way to crisp housing estates, each one fronted by glass-panelled greenhouses, as common as bathrooms now. Inside each one, tidy rows of engineered crops grew in perfect symmetry. Her stomach shifted, not nerves exactly. Too much movement. Too little sleep. She steadied her gaze, keeping her eyes on the horizon.

The auto-glide moved onto its outbound rail. Factory districts took over fast, warehouses and harvest vaults packed shoulder to shoulder, grey and endless, each stamped with corporate branding and propaganda.

One banner loomed across a production complex: *Grow Your Own — Because Freedom Starts at Home.*

Another slid past: *GlideCore Transit — You're Always on the Right Track.*

Grace's gaze stayed fixed. Just more slogans. Clean fonts over crumbling promises.

David glanced over, voice low. "Did you leave the boilcore on?"

Grace stared out the window. "What?"

He hesitated. "The boilcore... you know, like... boiling over?"

She turned slightly, eyebrows drawn.

David sighed. "Oh, forget it. It was a joke."

Grace gave a barely there shake of her head, already looking ahead again.

David looked up. The sky was empty — clear, clean, not a single craft in sight. "Hard to believe they banned air travel just to stop clogging the Skyfilters," he said.

Grace hummed under her breath, dragging out the words like a bad jingle. "Clean air requires grounded travel," she sang.

He gave a quiet huff of laughter. "Yeah, exactly. Or at least that's what they told everyone."

Time was moving strangely — too fast, too slow, and before she could settle her thoughts, the factories were gone.

The launch bay rose ahead, sharp and gleaming, an open-air expanse of reinforced glass and clean-edged steel. Support beams towered over the platform, strung with high banners bearing the mission's latest motto:

Your Future. Your Freedom. Your Mission.

The auto-glide slowed, doors sliding open with a soft hiss. Gareth stood waiting at the edge of the platform, hands deep in his jacket pockets. He glanced up briefly as the door lifted.

Grace stepped out first. The air hit cool, sharp in her throat, laced with that faint chemical edge the world couldn't seem to scrub out anymore. She paused for a second, just long enough to breathe it in. Earth's last breath. She set her shoulders back and turned to see David swing out behind her.

Gareth stepped forward. Their eyes met. He gave a quiet smile, tired but true. She returned it without thinking, then reached out and gave his wrist a soft squeeze.

"How are you feeling?" he asked, voice low.

Grace nodded. "Never better."

He gave a small grunt, somewhere between disbelief and agreement, then glanced toward the launch chamber. Beyond the bay, the EOS 11 waited, sealed inside its launch chamber, shielded from public view. The press wasn't allowed, and no formal welcome was planned. What little fanfare the first EOS missions had enjoyed was long gone. By EOS 11, the grand celebrations were over, replaced by quiet efficiency and cargo loaders.

They moved together, three figures crossing a platform wide and echoing, the steel polished smooth beneath their boots. Grace walked between them, every step edged with purpose. The facility doors loomed ahead, smooth matte metal framed in glass. No checkpoints, just a silent scanner blinking green.

Gareth reached it first and pressed his thumb to the panel. The door slid open. The air changed instantly — cooler, thinner, the sharp tang of compressed air and metal settled in her throat. The door sealed behind them with a hush.

"We're really doing this," David said, his smile steady and sure.

Grace didn't answer. She let her eyes follow the corridor, white panels lined in surgical precision, silent as a sealed vault. Every step forward felt like a door locking behind them.

The hum beneath the floor deepened. She could feel the vibration now, faint and rhythmic. The pulse of launch systems coming online. Two staff members waited up ahead. Blank expressions. Clearance badges. The kind who didn't blink unless instructed.

"Final briefing's ready," one said.

Grace didn't slow. "Right on schedule," she said, breezing past without waiting for a response.

David gave a nod. Gareth grunted.

They stopped at the sealed door.

"Eighteen years," David said. "We'll be fifty-one when we land."

Grace raised a brow. "Speak for yourself. I'll be a sprightly forty-nine."

Gareth smirked. "And I'll be fifty-four. Practically a museum piece."

"Oh good," Grace said. "We'll have a seasoned antique onboard. That's bound to boost morale."

"You're welcome," Gareth muttered.

Grace's hand drifted to her stomach, a reflex, not a decision. She caught it, dropped it, stepped forward.

Behind the door, the mission waited.

And everything else — her doubts, her secrets, her fears — would have to wait.

The countdown had begun.

— ✦ —

The briefing room was all glass, white panels, and sharp-edged clarity — the kind of space designed for protocol, not sentiment.

Grace sat between David and Gareth at the long conference table, their reflections faint in the polished surface. Lin stood at the head, hands behind her back, her expression composed but edged with something close to respect.

"Eighteen months of preparation," she said, voice level. "I'd be surprised if any of you had questions at this stage, but a pre-launch debrief is protocol."

Her gaze moved to each of them in turn. "Are you all satisfied with the EOS 11's onboard systems? Life support, artificial gravity, maintenance automation?"

David gave a single nod. "All clear."

"Food storage and long-term sustainability, including onboard crop production?"

Gareth's arms folded across his chest. "Understood."

"Personal quarters, research facilities, access to medical supplies?"

Grace met Lin's eyes. "We're ready."

Lin gave a short nod. "Good."

She turned slightly, tapping the console beside her. The screen behind her lit up with their medical profiles — names, ID tags, health data rolling in silent precision. Grace kept her expression steady as her own profile flashed past. The flagged marker she'd cleared last night never appeared. A green status bar blinked at the base of the screen: **Cleared for launch.**

Lin glanced back at them. "Medical clearances confirmed."

Grace felt the tension drain from her shoulders, just a fraction. She turned and met Gareth's eyes. His brow creased slightly.

Lin tapped her comms. "The Prime Minister prepared a statement for you. I'll play it now."

The lights dimmed. Derick Carmichael's face filled the screen, carefully lit, the edges of his smile sharpened by too much practice.

"You represent Earth's hope. Our courage. Our freedom. For centuries, we've fought for a world without limits, where the right to choose defines us all."

Grace sat motionless, letting the words roll past her.

"You'll leave behind the planet that shaped you... but you'll carry its legacy. We move forward together. Because standing still is the greatest risk of all."

"Good luck. May your mission define a new era. For all of us."

The screen faded. In its place, the government's crest appeared, flanked by bold text: *We don't govern. We trust. We innovate.*

The lights came back on.

Lin's gaze swept the room. "You're cleared. Departure is on schedule. I'll see you at launch."

They rose together, no formal send-off, no last-minute reminders.

As they turned for the door, Gareth said, "That speech. Wow. I'm inspired. You guys inspired?"

Grace gave the faintest curve of a smile but said nothing.

Gareth stepped out first. "Alright. Show time."

Chapter Three

S pace was never quiet.

Grace had expected silence, something deep and endless, like the hush between stars. But space had a hum. A pulse. The ship gave off soft clicks and low murmurs, the quiet rhythm of systems in motion, steady and constant. Beyond the glass, space whispered in its own way. Not loud, but present — echoes of dust impacts, solar winds, and drifting debris, all captured by the ship and woven into its quiet song.

She paced beside the medical bed, gripping the railing as another wave of pain hit. Her breath came in short bursts. Her stomach clenched again, sharper this time. "David!" Her voice cut across the room. "Get Gareth!"

David's face appeared in the doorway, pale and stricken. "Now?"

"No," she snapped. "Let's schedule it for next week. Yes, now!"

He vanished in a scramble of footsteps. The next contraction hit. Deep, sharp, and mean. She braced against the support frame, trying to breathe through it.

"This wasn't in the manual," she moaned. Then, tighter, "Of all the places to give birth..."

No one answered. The ship murmured, indifferent.

She wasn't afraid. Not exactly. But everything felt too close. Too fast. The hum of the ship, the tension in her muscles, the strain behind her ribs — it all pressed inward, collapsing down to this one room, this one moment. And the pressure built. Nothing to stop it now. Ready or not.

Gareth arrived a minute later, surprisingly calm. David followed at his heels, wide-eyed. "You've done this before?"

"No," Gareth replied, pulling on gloves. "But I've read every file on childbirth — pre, post, and mid-orbital." He gave Grace a wry look. "And you've got a tough wife. We'll manage."

Grace half-laughed, half-moaned.

The ship's AI chimed in, voice calm and crisp with a British accent. "Bio-scans indicate crowning. Would you like mood lighting?"

"Turn it off!" all three of them shouted. The lights dimmed anyway.

Grace eased herself down onto the edge of the bed with a low breath. "AURA, seriously?" she growled. "I swear, if this baby comes out with a British accent—" Another contraction slammed through her. The joke didn't survive this one.

Gareth moved beside her, steady, like he'd trained for this his whole life. "Okay. You're doing great. Just one more. Maybe two."

David dropped to her side, gripping her hand too tightly, like panic could anchor her. "Grace, I—"

"Shut up, David," she panted.

Then the world narrowed. The ship, the stars, the mission — gone. Only breath, pressure and pain.

For a heartbeat, it felt like even the ship held still. And then... A sound. A cry.

Gareth's hands moved with care. "It's a girl." His voice cracked. Just for a second.

He looked down at her as if the moment might vanish if he blinked. "Hey, Pip," he whispered. "You made it." He held her, suspended in that first breath of life, eyes locked on a future no one could see yet. Then he moved quickly, wrapping her in a thermal blanket from the med shelf. Her tiny chest rose and fell against the soft-lined wrap, fists curled like she hadn't quite decided if she liked it here yet.

Grace slumped back against the metal, trembling. "Is she okay?"

"She's loud," Gareth said. "And she's yours." He turned and lowered her into Grace's arms.

David knelt next to his wife and baby daughter, and made a sound somewhere between a laugh and a sob. Grace pulled the baby closer, fingers trembling slightly as she touched her cheek. So small. So real. She'd carried her across the stars, and somehow, she was here.

The AI chimed in, far too pleased with itself. "Mood lighting is now appropriate. Initiating lullaby sequence."

"Oh, let him have it." Grace muttered, eyes barely open. The lullaby began — soft, ethereal, woven from threads of sound that barely touched the air.

AURA didn't miss.

The baby gave a wobbly little kick. Her cry was hoarse and stubborn. Grace exhaled, a soft smile tugging at her lips as she met her daughter's eyes. "She sounds furious," she murmured.

Gareth smiled. "She sounds like she belongs here." He placed a hand on Grace's shoulder and squeezed, then crossed the room to the console.

The screen blinked, waiting. Gareth didn't hesitate. His fingers moved with quiet precision, line by line, function by function, until the transmission queue dissolved into static. There was not a log left. No automated burst. No signature flare to say she'd arrived. AURA's voice didn't chime in, didn't object. Just continued to play its lullaby, as if the ship understood how to keep a secret.

Gareth stood there for a moment, hand hovering over the panel. Then he encrypted the logs, scrubbed the access trail. No trace. No record. Just a girl in her mother's arms — never officially born.

— ✦ —

Later, in the quiet hum of the dimmed ship, the baby slept curled against Grace's chest. Her tiny breaths rose and fell in rhythm with her mother's. Gareth sat nearby, calm but quiet. He kept looking at the newborn as if part of him still wasn't sure she was real.

The stars outside the viewport shimmered, cold and bright, clearer than any city sky. A child had been born in the silence between worlds. A soul with no planet to call home. No one knew what that would mean.

Grace looked down at the tiny weight on her chest, fingers brushing the soft red crown of hair across the baby's head. "Ivy," she whispered.

Gareth turned his head towards her.

"Her name is Ivy."

He nodded once. "Fitting."

Grace glanced at him.

Gareth looked at her, then down at the baby. "Ivy clings tight. Doesn't need light, just something to hold on to."

A pause stretched between them, heavy with meaning that didn't need to be said aloud. Deep somewhere in the ship, metal clanged faintly, followed by a frustrated mutter and the unmistakable thud of something being forced into place.

Grace exhaled a soft laugh. "He's building her a cot, isn't he?"

Gareth didn't smile, but his eyes warmed. "Looks that way."

Grace watched the stars for a while, her fingers drifting absently over Ivy's back. Then, softly, "I knew."

Gareth looked at her. "Yeah. I figured."

She didn't respond at first. Her breath slowed, soft and quiet. "He asked once. David. I lied." She glanced down. "I found out the night before the launch. I was scared. I didn't know what to do. I hacked the systems and changed my medical record."

Gareth shook his head slowly, voice low. "At the end... there really were no protocols in place."

"No," Grace said. "There weren't."

Gareth was silent for a moment, then looked at her. Thoughtful, worn. "So why did you do it? Why keep going?"

"I spent five years of my life on this mission." Grace's voice was steady but tired. "Earth was already failing. The ASA was cutting funding. If I'd pulled out, we never would've gotten another shot. No one would've taken my place." She glanced at the baby. "We were it."

Gareth didn't argue. He let the silence stretch.

"You didn't say anything to me," she said.

"Didn't need to. You'd already made the call."

She nodded. "You think I was wrong?"

"I think," he said slowly, "you made a choice most people couldn't."

Grace traced a small circle on Ivy's back. "She was born in the void. Do you think that... does something to a person?"

Gareth glanced at her. "What do you mean?"

"You know," Grace said, eyes still on Ivy, "the soul. Consciousness. All that stuff."

He raised an eyebrow. "You're a scientist. You're not exactly the type to entertain cosmic theories."

"I don't," she said. "Not usually. But out here... you get a lot of time to think." She hesitated, her voice softening. "I never expected to be a mum. Wasn't ready for the way it rewires your brain, how the fear just lodges in and stays. But it makes you wonder. If something like her — someone like her — might be different."

Ivy's fingers twitched, her breath catching slightly in sleep.

"She is so small. So delicate."

A rare smile tugged at Gareth's mouth — soft, proud. "Then she's exactly like ivy. Looks delicate... but strong as hell."

Grace tucked her in closer, fingers splayed protectively across her back. Somewhere in that breath, the universe shifted, just a little, to make space for her.

Chapter Four

At seventeen, Ivy moved like someone used to being watched, but rarely seen.

Her skin held a soft bronze glow, shaped by years spent in the ship's greenhouse beneath the artificial sun. Her eyes were a shock of blue — clear, watchful, and just a little too sharp for seventeen. She was a contradiction made whole, bold but unassuming, vibrant but quiet. Silence wrapped her like a second skin.

Her hair flared red in the corridor lights, a wild tangle she hadn't bothered to tame. Her boots landed softly, but her presence hit harder, like a quiet alarm you didn't notice until it was blaring. She crossed the lower corridor, ducking beneath a conduit line that ran low along the ceiling, part of the ship's skeletal frame always half-exposed in engineering sections. At this hour, the lights were still on a cool cycle, faint blue edging the walls, simulating early dawn.

The gym was located at the back, one level up from the engine room. Compact, like everything else on the ship, but functional. Foam-gripped bars stretched across one wall, padded mats covered most of the floor, and a half-sized treadmill blinked in standby mode in the corner. Gareth was already there, halfway through a workout, sweat clinging to his shoulders as he pulled against the resistance rig with steady force.

She leant in the doorway. "You know you're not twenty anymore, right?"

"Tell that to my joints," he said, not breaking rhythm. "They complain louder than you do. You're late."

"I'm early," Ivy shot back.

"For tomorrow, maybe."

She dropped her pack by the wall and stepped onto the mat. "What's the punishment? Extra laps or public shaming?"

"Both," he said. "But I'm too tired for theatrics. You get core circuits instead."

Ivy groaned, pulling on her wrist straps. "You're a monster."

"You'll thank me when we're breathing air that doesn't come from a panel," he said, tossing her a resistance band. "And if not, well, at least you'll have abs."

They moved through the warm-up in practiced silence. Gareth counted under his breath. Ivy's muscles ached in a good, earned way. There was comfort in the routine. In gravity that stayed steady. In company that didn't demand anything more.

Halfway through the second set, she paused, sweat beading at her hairline. "Why do we even need training? It's a research mission, not a rescue op."

Gareth didn't stop, lifting into another sit-up. "Because research missions go off-script. And I don't trust planets that look that perfect from orbit."

Ivy snorted. "That's optimistic."

Gareth looked over at her, his voice low. "Down there... we don't know what's waiting. Could be clean air and fresh water. Or it could be just good enough to fool you. You need to be ready."

"I'm not scared," Ivy said.

Gareth didn't answer. Instead, he reached over and checked the fit of her wrist strap.

"You don't have to be scared," he said finally, still focused on the strap. "Because I'll be right there." He didn't say it as a promise. He said it like a fact — solid, fixed, the same way he said things like *Check the seal* or *Don't touch that wire.*

She watched him. "You think something will go wrong?"

"I think hoping's not a plan." There wasn't fear in his voice, just calm certainty. Like he'd already run the numbers and didn't need luck to solve it.

She let the silence sit. The words lodged deep, heavier than she wanted to admit. She blew out a breath and dropped back into plank position, arms shaking. If Gareth had already done the math, then she didn't want to be the variable that failed the equation.

When the circuits ended, Ivy flopped onto her back, arms sprawled. "Remind me why I like you."

Gareth grinned. "Because I don't go easy on you."

"No, that's definitely not it."

He offered a hand and pulled her up. "Go shower. Then meet your parents in the greenhouse. They need help logging the new growth metrics."

She nodded, grabbed her pack and towel, and headed for the corridor, ponytail swinging behind her.

The moment the door hissed shut, Gareth exhaled and shook his head. "That girl's spark is going to burn through everything," he muttered.

— ✦ —

She stepped into the ship's greenhouse, a lush oasis tucked deep in the vessel's steel frame. The air folded around her as she crossed the threshold — warm, oxygen-rich, saturated with life. Tiered rows of vegetation spiralled around support beams, clustered along slim hydroponic trays. Near the back, an orange tree stood at the growbed's edge, its fruit gleaming faintly beneath the artificial sun. Thick greens pressed against the racks, their leaves glossy with moisture. Vines threaded through mist lines, flashing red where strawberries nestled in the leaves.

It wasn't just functional, it was thriving. Overflowing, like it didn't know when to stop. Overhead, the artificial amber sun adjusted in slow pulses, mimicking the rhythms of a planet she'd never known. With only starlight beyond the hull, it was the closest thing they had to time. Technically, the greenhouse was for oxygen cycling and food supply. But it was the only place on the ship that felt alive. Everything else was steel, circuits, and silence.

As she walked the rows, the leaves shimmered in her wake. A cluster of spinach leaves tilted toward her, a vine uncurled and brushed her wrist. She reached out, fingers gliding along its curve. Another tendril lifted from the rack beside her, curling around her arm like a greeting. She gently unwrapped it and moved on, her hand grazing the leaves as she passed.

Grace stood near the back, thumbing through readings on her datapad while David adjusted nutrient lines beneath the racks.

Both wore ASA-issue field suits, sleeves rolled, eyes focused. Neither looked up.

Ivy slipped in beside them, the herbs grazing her arm as she reached for the scanner. She kept her head down, fingers tapping in the readings with quiet precision, as if the numbers might offer safer conversation.

Grace looked over. "Log anything unusual. Root colour, fruiting variation, any stress indicators."

"Got it," Ivy said, kneeling beside a thick tangle of kale leaves.

David offered a nod, then went back to adjusting the pH regulator. "The patch near the orange tree is maturing faster than expected," he said. "Might be a lighting variance."

Ivy moved to the area. Sure enough, the growth was dense, clustered. She reached toward a young tendril, and it lifted, delicate, spiralling up to meet her touch.

Grace watched from the corner of her eye.

Ivy brushed the tendril aside and pivoted to the scanner. "I'll log it," she said, fingers already at work.

Grace tapped the edge of the datapad with her thumb. "You've been in here more than usual."

Ivy didn't look up. "It's quiet."

"It's controlled," Grace corrected.

"Same thing."

Grace's eyes softened as she adjusted the cuff of her sleeve. "Are you nervous about the descent?"

"No. Not really." Ivy kept her gaze on the scanner.

"If you want me to run through any protocols, just ask."

Ivy glanced up. "Thanks, Mum."

Grace's smile was faint but warm as she turned back to her readings.

David ducked out from under the rack, brushing off his hands. "Looks like good growth, and that's what we want. We'll need it thriving for another six months."

"Twelve," Grace said. "We planned for twelve."

He gave her a look. "You know the models are already trending short."

"And adjusting projections doesn't make the original mission window disappear," Grace replied evenly.

Ivy glanced between them, reading the coded edge in their voices. They weren't arguing. Not really. Just aligning, like they always did. Two minds, one mission. She ran her scanner over the overgrown patch. The readings flickered.

"It's responding to something," she said. "But it's not environmental. All metrics are stable."

Neither of them responded immediately. Grace typed something into her datapad. David shifted to the next rack.

The silence stretched.

Eventually, Grace said, "Submit a full analysis to AURA. Let him run the correlation logs."

"Sure," Ivy said. Her voice was smooth, practiced.

She crouched again, the scanner humming quietly beside her. A vine skimmed her ankle, curling loosely along her boot before slipping back into the leaves.

"It doesn't feel random," she muttered.

Grace glanced over. "What was that?"

"Nothing," Ivy said, already shifting focus.

The work settled into a rhythm. Data logged, samples noted, their movements fluid, habitual. Her parents locked in their routines — efficient, professional, quietly aligned. Like always.

But the leaves still reached for her.

— ✦ —

The greenhouse door slid shut behind her, sealing in the warmth and the soft hum of the oxygen system. Ivy padded barefoot down the corridor, the brushed metal floor cool beneath her feet. The air outside felt sharper, drier and thinner, a mechanical echo after the greenhouse's breath.

The ship always felt quieter at night. Less like a vessel and more like a waiting room orbiting the unknown.

She passed the kitchen and dining alcove; the lights dimmed to night mode, shadows long and heavy. Her parents were still back in the greenhouse, likely finishing the harvest alone. That was always the way — meetings, whispered theories, and plans from which they excluded her. Not out of malice, just habit. The quiet rhythm of two lives woven together long before Ivy was born. Ivy had offered to help, but they'd waved her off with matching smiles and murmurs about 'getting some rest.' That always meant they wanted to talk shop without her.

Ahead, the hallway branched. One path led to the lab, the other, to the crew quarters. She turned right.

Gareth's door was ajar, a soft glow spilling into the hallway. Tools hung neatly on the wall inside, worn handles paired with high-tech scanning heads. A coil of wire sat on the workbench beside a half-stripped panel from the greenhouse irrigation system. His bed was made, of course. Gareth didn't sleep much.

Further down were her parents' quarters. Door closed. No light from beneath. Silence, as always.

Ivy passed without slowing. The door to her room chimed softly as it slid open.

Ivy's room wasn't part of the original ship design. EOS 11 had been engineered for three adults — no nursery, no spare quarters, no child protocols. But she came anyway. So they carved out space.

A converted side bay, once used for supply overflow, now held a bed, a desk, and just enough floor to stretch out. The weld lines still showed on the walls, neat but visible, where Gareth had sealed the panels himself, shaping the room from scratch. The lighting was repurposed from old lab backups and ran a little warmer than the rest of the ship, casting a soft gold hue across the floor.

The mattress was a handmade twist of knotted canvas, stuffed with leftover buckwheat hulls from the early harvest years and stitched in loops. Grace had made it herself during a quiet week when Ivy was small. "It breathes better than foam," she said. The knots were uneven in places. Ivy loved that.

David had added a fold-down console shelf and stocked a cluster of potted plants from the greenhouse — a tiny citrus, a trailing lavender, and a sensitive fern whose leaves curled at the lightest touch. They always seemed to shift slightly when she was near. And Gareth had brought her blankets. Not ship-issued ones, these were heavy and soft, patch-worked from salvage fabric and faintly scented with greenhouse herbs. The kind meant for curling into. The kind that stayed warm long after you left them.

Her drawings were everywhere. Pinned to the matte walls, curled at the corners, drifting slightly when the air filters kicked on. Most were of plants, but the ones she returned to most were the leaf-shaped creatures. Always in motion, always half-fading into bark or vine. The protectors from Gareth's stories.

Near her pillow, one drawing stood out. A tiny figure with curly hair and bare feet, mid-step on a grassy hill, a pack slung over one shoulder. She'd drawn it after reading The Wanderer's Song, a story about a quiet traveler who left home with nothing but a satchel and an accidental map. It wasn't just the adventure she'd loved... it was the choice. The first step out the door.

The room wasn't big, but it was hers, shaped entirely by the people who loved her

She sat cross-legged on her bed, sliding a pencil behind her ear before opening the sketchbook in her lap. She was halfway through another drawing when a familiar knock tapped the doorframe.

"Are you drawing green things or flying things tonight?"

Gareth stood in the doorway, sleeves rolled, wiping his hands with a rag that looked like it had lost the battle hours ago.

"Both," Ivy said without looking up. "Sometimes the green things fly."

He stepped in, eyes scanning the wall, tucking the rag into his pocket. "You never stopped drawing them."

She glanced at him. "You never stopped telling the stories."

Gareth smiled softly.

"The glowing forests," Ivy said. "The creatures that appeared when someone was lost. You used to tell me they didn't save people, they just stayed until the person could save themselves."

"I always liked that story," Gareth said.

"I never forgot it." She glanced at the drawings, then back at him. "And the others too. The mini dragons with butterfly wings like stained glass? The glowing tiny firefly birds that changed colour depending on how someone was feeling?" She gave a half-smile. "I used to imagine one landing on my shoulder and glowing pink."

Gareth gave a low chuckle. "Right. You were obsessed with the idea that they could tell if someone was in love."

"And the ones that looked like leaves," she added, pointing to one of her sketches. "They could shift and melt into the background, camouflage like an octopus, vanishing into bark or branches when they needed to."

He crouched beside the bed, knees cracking faintly. "You remember more than I do."

She gave him a look. "I loved those stories, I remember everything you told me."

Gareth reached into his jacket and pulled out a small foil pouch, worn at the corners, like it had been handled too many times before. He offered it with a conspiratorial grin, the kind that always made Ivy feel like a co-conspirator in something important.

"Peanut butter pod," he said. "Last one. Figured it was time."

She blinked, then laughed. This had been their thing for years, peanut butter pods after greenhouse maintenance, back when she was little. Gareth used them to bribe her to clean seed trays. He'd always pretended they were rationed, a rare delicacy, and she'd played along, bartering chores for bites.

"No way," she breathed, taking the packet gently. "You saved this?"

"Some traditions are worth keeping." He passed it over, carefully folded like contraband.

She turned it in her fingers like it was treasure. "You're basically a hero," she said, smiling.

He shrugged. "A quiet, nut-based legacy. I'll take it."

Gareth's gaze stayed on her, quiet and steady. "Let's just say I know how to ration the important things."

She smiled down at the packet, voice soft. "Twelve years back home without these... I don't know how I'll survive."

His voice softened. "I know you spent your entire childhood on this ship. I know it probably felt small sometimes. But one thing you never had to carry was pain. Or heartbreak. Or fear. No bullying. No violence. That's something, Pip."

She looked up, the peanut butter pod forgotten in her hands. "Yeah," she said. "Caged and safe... or free and bleeding. I guess those are the options."

Gareth didn't correct her. He looked at the drawings again. "Did you ever name them?"

Ivy shrugged. "Not really. They just sort of... are."

Gareth studied one of the winged shapes. "Leafwings," he whispered, like the word had been waiting.

She tilted her head. "Yeah," she murmured. "That fits."

He stood slowly, then leant in and pressed a kiss to the top of her head. His voice was low and familiar. "Goodnight, Pip. Get some sleep. We're departing for Veritas in less than a week."

She nodded without looking back, her eyes on the sketchbook in her lap. His footsteps faded down the corridor. Then she set the sketchbook aside and picked up her datapad, watching the screen light up beneath her touch.

"AURA,"

"Yes, Ivy," the AI responded, his voice low, calm, and lightly British — as if he were permanently mid-lecture at a fancy university Ivy had never seen.

"Open my current read?"

The title flicked onto the screen in clean, black letters: The Stringbird's Song.

She'd read it before, a story about birds with strings tied to their wings. Delicate enough not to hurt. Just tight enough to control their flight. The villagers said it was to keep them safe, to stop them flying into predator territory. But one girl had cut the strings on a bird. It flew badly at first. Wild. Unsteady. Then it sang the most beautiful song anyone had ever heard. A song that hadn't existed... until it was free.

Ivy traced her thumb along the datapad's edge. "Freedom's messy," she said. "That's why it sounds different."

AURA stayed silent.

She leant back, exhaling. "Right. Back to the story."

But the words blurred. The bird flew wild, and its song followed — unbound, imperfect, beautiful.

Ivy shifted back, pulling the blanket over herself as she lay down, the datapad still cradled in her hands.

"When you're tethered in safety," she murmured into the quiet, "you'll never know how far you can fly."

Chapter Five

The week passed in soft rhythms — diagnostics, meal rotations, and the same checklists marked off without urgency. Ivy could feel the descent approaching now. Not just in data. In her chest. Like gravity was already reaching for her.

She wandered the upper corridor in slow, restless steps, the lights overhead shifting to simulate early evening. Her boots tapped softly against the metal floor, passing familiar junctions, low-slung pipes, and labelled compartments she could navigate in her sleep. She paused at the main access hall, the central spine of the ship where the mission plaques lined the wall like a museum exhibit no one ever visited. She'd passed them a hundred times. But today, they caught her eye. Eleven brushed steel plates. One for each EOS mission. EOS 1 through EOS 11. A lineage of hope, failure, desperation... and now hers. Each plate bore a launch date and destination.

Except for EOS 6. That one was just a number. A date, 2990, and a blank space where a mission destination should've been.

She stood there longer than she had meant to. Her hand hovered near the plaque, fingers grazing the cold edge of the metal. Something about it gnawed at her. EOS 6. The one no one mentioned. The one that didn't come back.

Ivy turned and headed for the archive room, a small research bay tucked beside the lab, mostly used for archival lookups and data syncs. The kind of place her parents barely glanced at anymore. There was history in here — quiet, overlooked. She liked it that way. The door hissed open, and she stepped inside.

No physical books, but still a library, digital archives stacked like invisible towers behind the walls. The lighting ran warmer than most modules, with adjustable overhead panels tuned to mimic old reading rooms. A low-slung console desk anchored the room's centre, paired with a cushioned chair that reclined just enough to feel like a choice. The glow from the console lit the space in soft blue, wrapping around the display. AURA's voice was always there, waiting, like breath behind glass.

A long, cushioned bench stretched beneath the viewport, layered in practical, scuff-resistant fabric. Ivy always curled up there, screen in her lap. A soft-textured blanket sat folded at one end, like it belonged to the space, not a person. Earth hadn't made many things overly comfortable on the EOS 11, but for a thirty-year round trip, they allowed a few soft edges. This room had them. It's why she came here to read, to think.

Ivy crossed the room, her steps unhurried. She settled into the chair, legs folded beneath her, fingers already moving. "AURA," she said. "Show me the EOS mission archive."

A soft chime answered. The interface glowed to life, populating the air with crisp, sterile history:

EOS 1: *MARS* — 2702
EOS 2: *VENUS* — 2715
EOS 3: *TITAN* — 2738
EOS 4: *EUROPA* — 2764
EOS 5: *KEPLER-442B* — 2801
EOS 6: [CLASSIFIED] — 2991
EOS 7: *TRAPPIST-1d* — 3010
EOS 8: *GLIESE-667Cc* — 3042
EOS 9: *GAIA-4* — 3077
EOS 10: *MIRA-6* — 3105
EOS 11: *VERITAS-9* — 3123

Every few decades, another shot in the dark. Every few decades, another failure. One last mission. Hers.

But EOS 6 kept whispering. It wasn't just redacted. It had been erased, deliberately and cleanly, like someone didn't want it remembered.

She shifted forward, voice low. "AURA... why is EOS 6 classified?"

AURA responded with calm precision. "Mission EOS 6 is restricted to Command Tier Five."

She leant closer. "Has it always been?"

"Yes."

Her gaze didn't leave the display. "Were there casualties?"

"I'm sorry. That information is not available."

The quiet settled, heavier now. Even the ship's usual hum seemed to thin out, edged out by the weight of what wasn't being said.

"Did my mother go on that mission?"

"No, Grace Virelli was not assigned to EOS 6. It launched one hundred and fifty-one years ago."

"Oh." She tapped her fingers against the console. "What was their destination planet?"

"Mission trajectory and endpoint are also classified."

"Did it ever make contact?"

"That information is not available."

"So let me get this straight. No records. No location. No status update. Just a name in a file and a warning label?"

The screen didn't move. The red classification bar pulsed like a silent alarm. She eased back into the chair, voice smooth and casual. "AURA, override. Change my access level to Command Tier Five."

A half-second pause.

"Nice try," AURA replied. "Would you like me to play soothing forest sounds instead?"

"I'll soothe-sound you right out the airlock." Ivy muttered. She stared at the blinking alert for a few seconds longer. EOS 6. A ghost mission. No return. No wreckage. Nothing. Earth had never officially mourned. Just... absence. She closed the data feed, fingers tapping on the console's edge, each beat marking the questions she wasn't done asking.

She stood in one fluid motion, smooth and certain. The answers weren't here. Crossing to the door, her steps picked up, quick and deliberate, matching the sharp edge in her thoughts. Her pulse kept pace. Faster now. Focused.

Something had gone before them.

And someone had made sure the world forgot.

— ✦ —

Dinner carried a weight, like the descent was already pressing in around them. Every conversation faded before it began. The rehydrated stew was lumpy and barely warm. Nutrient-dense, engineered to last, and depressing as ever. Next to it sat a bright salad of fresh lettuce, shaved carrot, and cherry tomatoes, and a bowl of ripe strawberries and blueberries so perfect they looked like props. Gareth made a comment about the strawberries. David muttered something about crop rotation. Grace answered with a nod. Ivy picked at a tomato with her fork, then let it fall.

The scrape of David's spoon and the creak of Gareth leaning back in his seat filled the quiet gaps. They were all pretending things were normal. Ivy was done pretending.

"What happened to EOS 6?" she asked, like she was asking for the salt.

The silence that followed didn't settle. It sliced.

David's spoon froze midair. Grace didn't flinch, but she stopped chewing. Gareth looked at Ivy straight on.

"You found the mission logs," he said. Not a question.

"They're not exactly hidden," Ivy said. "Except one. EOS 6's locked down tighter than the med bay liquor cabinet."

"Ivy," Grace said, carefully. "That's not something you need to worry about."

Ivy tilted her head. "Why not? What is it? Some ancient training run?"

No one answered.

"Was it a test flight? A cosmic screw-up?" Her voice stayed light, but the surrounding air didn't. She leant back, eyes flicking between them. "Did someone input the wrong coordinates and slingshot themselves into deep space?"

No one laughed.

She set her spoon down with a soft clink. "Because all I've got is a locked file and three people suddenly very interested in their lentils."

Gareth exhaled, slow and deliberate, eyes shifting to Grace. "She deserves to know," he said.

David lowered his bowl. "EOS 6 launched decades ago. The official report says it was lost in transit. Jump error. Never arrived."

"Where were they going?"

Grace and David exchanged a glance. The pause that followed told her more than their words ever could.

"Veritas-9," Gareth said.

"Veritas?" Her spoon stilled as her eyebrows lifted. She looked at each of them. "But that's where we're going."

David nodded. "Same coordinates. Same planet."

Ivy's eyebrows lifted. Her voice stayed steady, but sharper now. "And no one thought that was worth mentioning?"

Silence. She let it stretch, then leant forward. "What happened to them?"

"We don't know," Gareth said. "No signal. No return. No debris. The ship was just... gone. And by the time anyone started asking questions, the files had already been erased."

Ivy stared at him. Her fingers curled into fists against her thighs. "And we're just... doing it again?" she said. "Same planet. Same risk. And everyone's fine with that?"

Her knee bounced under the table as the words came faster. "You say they vanished. But how? What if it wasn't a glitch? What if something down there took them? What if we're walking into it? Same trap, new crew, and we're still pretending we're different?"

Grace's voice stayed level. "Earth ran out of time, Ivy. Crops are failing, coastlines are vanishing, and no one's funding another launch. EOS 11 was the last mission approved before the collapse. One ship, one crew. One chance to find a future."

David set his spoon down. "It was the only target where the ship and crew weren't outright destroyed. Every other viable planet chewed through them."

Grace nodded. "Veritas-9 had a breathable atmosphere. Stable gravity. Potential for water. It was this or nothing."

"There are no more chances, Ivy," Gareth said. "Earth's exhausted its reach. Every viable planet in our system is either lifeless or lethal." He looked at her, steady. "Every reachable star is fading, and the universe isn't making new ones."

Grace met Ivy's eyes. "We knew the risks. But we came anyway."

Ivy sat back slowly, the truth pressing against her chest. She didn't speak. Didn't move. Just let it settle.

"Then why wipe the data?" Ivy asked. "Why bury it?"

No one spoke. The ship's hum filled the space where the truth should've gone.

Ivy pushed her bowl away and stared at her hands. "They weren't just numbers," she said. "They were people. And they vanished."

Grace's gaze softened, but she didn't reach for her.

It was Gareth who finally spoke. "We're not them, Ivy. We're writing a different story."

Ivy stood, the chair sliding back with a soft scrape. "I hope so," she said. "Because someone already deleted the last one."

She walked out, her footsteps fading down the corridor.

— ✦ —

Ivy knelt beside a patch of flowering mint, watching the soft simulation of moonlight glide over the leaves while the ship's low hum pressed into the silence. It was technically her turn to help clear after dinner, but she'd needed out, away from clipped tones and unfinished sentences. At least here, among the vines, everything was soft. Predictable. No one asked questions. No one expected her to be mission-ready. Just her, the mint, and the only other crew member who never slept, AURA.

AURA — Autonomous Utility for Research and Assistance — wasn't just an assistant. He'd been designed for a London-based science mission decades before the EOS 11 launch, then quietly recycled when the ASA couldn't afford a new AI. Budget cuts, meet space exploration. Now he ran the ship's environmental systems, handled all non-pilot diagnostics, and responded to most voice commands. He was calm, British, and far too competent for something Australia got on clearance. Ivy had grown up with his voice in her ear like background static — always there, always polite.

She lingered among the vines a moment longer before reaching into her pack. The datapad was warm in her hands, humming faintly as it booted. She crossed to the bench beneath the orange tree, its low branches rustling as she passed. Pale light filtered through the leaves, casting a shifting pattern across the seat, the edges worn smooth from time and use. Ivy curled into the corner, tucking one leg beneath her. A vine trailed lazily across the armrest, brushing her elbow like a cat. She reached for it absentmindedly, curling the soft fronds around her fingers.

She opened the datapad in her lap, fingers hovering above the screen as if the question was still forming. "Hey AURA," she said, "can you show me the Amazon? Before it burned."

The device flickered to life, casting a soft glow across Ivy's lap. AURA responded instantly, projecting the image upward in a translucent arc. Green burst across it in near-holographic clarity — dense trees layered beneath mist-draped treetops, rivers winding like veins through the undergrowth. Birds erupted from the branches like sparks.

Ivy watched the birds vanish into the mist. "Did it really look like this?"

"Approximately," AURA replied. "Imagery reconstructed from pre-collapse scans and environmental models."

"I wish I could have gone there," she said. "What happened to it?"

"Illegal mining. Logging. Government deregulation. Climate feedback loops. Fires, both natural and accelerated."

"A climate feedback loop, what's that?" she asked, eyes on the tangled green forest.

"A loop, one disaster nudges another, until it doesn't matter where it started. The system collapses under its own weight."

"So we just... let it die?"

There was a pause, long enough that Ivy thought maybe the system hadn't heard.

Then AURA spoke. "Not all at once. Not with malice. With indifference and delay. Enough to be irreversible."

She glanced down, lips pressed together. "Were there others? Places like this? Things we ruined?"

"Yes," AURA said. "Many."

"Show me another place. Something beautiful. Something no one talks about."

AURA responded without hesitation. "The Great Barrier Reef, off the northeastern coast of Australia. Once the largest living structure on the planet, visible from space. Home to thousands of marine species. A cathedral of coral and light."

Colour burst across the projection, a living mosaic of coral in brilliant reds, golds, and vivid purples. Towers of branching coral reached skyward, tangled with soft anemones swaying in invisible currents. Schools of fish flashed like scattered gemstones — electric blues, sunburst yellows, streaks of silver darting through labyrinths of reef.

"It's beautiful," she said. "And I'm assuming now it's gone?"

"Mass coral bleaching," AURA replied. "As ocean temperatures rose, the reef expelled its symbiotic algae. Without them, the coral turned white and died. Much of it is now skeletal remains."

Ivy was quiet for a moment. "Did we ruin everything that used to glow?"

"We dimmed more than we preserved." AURA said. "We controlled what we could. Until we couldn't."

Ivy frowned. "But that's the opposite of control."

"No," AURA said. "That is what happens when control is removed. Systems degrade. Harmony collapses. Entropy increases."

She watched as the reef paled and crumbled, the colours draining into a ghost-white husk.

AURA continued, almost gently. "Entropy is not evil. It is inevitable. It's the law of all things. Without balance, systems fray. Even the strongest structures unravel."

Ivy's jaw tightened. "Earth wasn't the problem. The people were."

The AI paused. "Perhaps. But their choices made the outcome clear. There was no pretending. Only truth in what they allowed to happen."

A soft sound stirred near the back racks, someone passing by, pausing mid-step. Ivy glanced up to see David just beyond the archway.

He stepped into view, posture unsure, giving her a small, awkward wave.

Ivy smiled. "Hey."

David's voice was soft. "You always come here when you're upset."

"Am I upset?" Ivy's tone didn't give anything away.

He hesitated. "You left dinner early."

"I finished early." She twirled the vine between her fingers.

David shifted tactics. "It's okay to be scared. About the mission. About EOS 6…"

She finally looked up. "I'm not scared, Dad. I'm just thinking."

"They could've gotten lost. Doesn't mean we will."

Ivy nodded once. "Sure." She pointed towards the projection. "Did you know about the Reef?"

David hesitated. "I read the reports. It was in one of the early collapse briefings. They logged it, filed it, and kept going."

"Why didn't they care?" Ivy asked, voice low. "It was alive. It was beautiful. Why wasn't that enough?"

David came over and took a seat beside her.

She tapped the datapad again. The rainforest bloomed back into view — green, dense, untamed. "Did you know about the Amazon too? Before it burned?"

David exhaled, slow. "Yeah. That one hurt. It was called the lungs of the planet. We cut it down as if it didn't matter. Sometimes people stop noticing beauty when it gets in the way of profit."

Ivy finally looked at him. "Then why are you doing this mission? Why try again if no one ever learns?"

He met her eyes. Something in his face shifted, like he'd remembered something too big to say out loud. "Because someone has to," he said. "Maybe if we get it right, we'll finally understand how to fix what we broke."

She stared at him for a long moment, as if trying to read between the lines. "Do you really believe it's possible to fix Earth?"

David didn't answer immediately. His gaze drifted toward the swaying greenery, like the plants might offer something gentler than the truth.

"Not everyone on Earth was bad, Ivy. But sometimes the ones who are — the greedy ones, the cruel ones — they're the ones who climb to the top. They make the rules. Burn the forests. Promise the public whatever they want, just to win votes. Even if it means speeding up the collapse."

He glanced at her again, softer now. "But the good ones? The quiet ones, the ones who try to rebuild, who tell the truth and still believe in something better. They deserve a future too."

He raised an eyebrow at the vine. "They seem to like you."

The vine coiled tighter around her finger, slow and soft. Ivy watched it curl, a quiet smile touching her lips.

David reached out to touch the same plant. Nothing. The leaves stilled. He tried again. Still nothing.

"I guess I don't have the touch," he said, smiling like it didn't bother him.

Ivy glanced at him. "Don't worry. It's not normal. But AURA ran the tests. I'm not a mutant or anything special."

David chuckled softly. "I wasn't worried."

Ivy hesitated. The vine curled gently around her wrist again, soft and deliberate.

"Then why hasn't Mum ever said anything?" she asked, quiet but sharp. "She's seen it. The way the plants react when I walk in. The scans. The footage. How they move."

David looked down, as if the answer might be hiding in the seams of his uniform. "I don't know."

"Yes, you do." Her voice stayed even, but her jaw had tightened. "She's one of the top environmental scientists on Earth. If anyone could explain it, it'd be her."

David exhaled slowly. "That's just it," he said. "She can't explain it."

Ivy's chest prickled. "So she ignores it?"

"She doesn't ignore it, Ivy. She just... files it away. That's what scientists do when the data doesn't make sense. They file it under outliers and wait for more evidence."

Ivy looked away. "Except I'm not a data set. I'm her daughter."

David opened his mouth. Closed it again. He looked gutted for a second, like someone had said the one thing he wasn't ready to hear. "I think it unsettles her," he said finally. "Not because it's wrong. But because it's beyond her."

Before she could answer, the door slid open.

Grace entered like a file being slammed shut, arms folded tight. Her eyes swept the greenhouse, then landed on Ivy. Cool. Clinical.

David turned. "She's fine. We had a good chat about it."

Ivy raised a brow. "We did?"

Grace's sigh cut through the air. "I'm sorry we didn't tell you Ivy, but you spiral. You get emotional. You jump to worst-case scenarios. And that, this, is exactly what I was trying to avoid."

Ivy met her mother's gaze, her voice flat but quiet. "Sorry, Mum. Didn't mean to be in the way. It's not like I can go outside and play. Bit explodie out there."

Grace's jaw tightened. "I don't know where you get that from, Ivy, but it's not me."

David, still prodding at the stubborn vine, snorted. "Oh, it's definitely not you."

He looked up just in time to catch Grace's stare.

Ivy smirked. David blinked, clearly registering the mistake a second too late.

"Lights out in twenty." Grace didn't wait for a response, she just walked out.

Their eyes met. Ivy let out a dry laugh first, small, surprised. David gave a quiet chuckle in return. For once, the silence between them didn't feel like distance. Just a truce. David stood and kissed Ivy gently on the top of the head. "Don't lose sleep over things you can't control," he said, and walked out of the greenhouse.

She watched him leave, his hand grazing a vine on the way out — the leaves didn't move.

Ivy uncrossed her legs and pushed slowly to her feet, heading for the workstation at the back of the greenhouse. It had a desk and console for logging data, but it also had a quiet viewport, tucked far enough back that the stars felt like they belonged only to her. She climbed into the chair, legs tucked close, and stared out at the velvet dark.

Veritas-9 loomed like a jewel in the void, cloud-ringed and silent. They were only a few days away from entering its orbit. Her reflection hovered in the glass, faint and unfamiliar, like she was watching someone else drift through space. She sat in silence, chin propped on her hand, watching the clouds ripple across the planet's surface — calm, slow, unbothered.

"AURA," she said. "Veritas has twin suns and two moons, right?"

"Correct."

"So, would that change how plants grow? Like, would photosynthesis work the same? Or could it make things... different? Bigger? Weirder?"

"Enhanced solar exposure may impact growth patterns, though biological responses would depend on the native species' evolutionary adaptations. However, Veritas-9's twin suns are each approximately half the diameter of Earth's sun, resulting in a combined solar output comparable to a single terrestrial sun."

She nodded absently. "Right. And what about the moons? Does that much reflected light at night do anything?"

"Possibly. With two moons, even though they both vary in size, the combined reflected light may elevate nocturnal photoreactivity. Some flora on Earth respond to moonlight, the same may hold true for Veritas-9."

She sat back, thoughtful. "I wonder what kind of food grows there. What it tastes like."

Her fingers tapped lightly on the edge of the console. "AURA," she hesitated. "Why do plants respond to me?"

"In what way?"

She curled her fingers tighter, tracing the console's edge. "The vines lean in when I'm near. Sometimes they wrap around my wrist. Branches shift toward me, leaves part to show fruit. It happens in the greenhouse. Even in my room. It's like they... know me."

Another pause.

"They don't do that for anyone else," she added. "It's not just weird, right? But it has to mean something."

AURA answered, voice soft. "It may be less about what you do, and more about what you are."

Ivy raised an eyebrow. "Okay, cryptic much?"

"You were born in deep space," AURA said. "Away from Earth's atmosphere, its interference, its constant signals. No magnetic field. No cultural noise. No shaping inputs."

She blinked. "So?"

"You developed in stillness," he said. "Which means your brain, your body, is tuned differently. More purely. You are not separate from nature, Ivy. Humanity is composed of the same matter. The same atomic structure. The same energetic patterns. Some theories even suggest a shared field of consciousness."

Ivy tilted her head.

AURA continued, "If consciousness is not created, but shared. Then everything that grows, moves, breathes, or forms is part of the same original thread. Plants. People. Even planets."

She looked out the viewport. "So I'm not doing anything to them?"

"No," he said. "You're just clearer than most. And they respond to that clarity. Not because you command them, but because you're vibrating on the same signal."

She let out a breath. "Like a tuning fork."

"Precisely."

She thought for a moment. "So I'm not magic."

"No," AURA said. "You're attuned."

"So they are... aware?" She said. "They listen to emotion the way we listen to music."

AURA paused. "Your phrasing is not scientifically precise, but contextually plausible. There were a series of early Earth experiments suggesting that water could respond to human emotion."

Ivy lifted her head. "Seriously?"

"Visual evidence was inconclusive. But the work of one Temari Saye, specifically her crystalline water photography, remains archived under both scientific and pseudoscientific tags."

A few soft clicks, then a quiet flicker lit the console beside her. Grainy images rotated across the screen, jagged, fractured crystals labelled hate, fear, greed. Then delicate, snowflake-perfect forms appeared, marked love, gratitude, hope. Ivy stared at the shifting display, elbows braced on the desk as if grounding herself against the weight of what she was seeing.

AURA spoke gently, his tone low and precise. "The coherence of emotional intention appears to influence structure. At least under some conditions."

She leant back slowly, her gaze still fixed on the swirling patterns. "So even something as simple as water... listens."

"It does not listen," AURA said. "It reflects."

She turned toward the viewport, where the curve of Veritas-9 drifted in the black, cloud-wrapped and luminous. "Emotion shapes form," she murmured. "Even water remembers the shape of love."

The projection flickered softly. "That phrasing aligns with Dr. Saye's poetic interpretations."

Something in her chest loosened. Not all at once, but enough to notice. She wasn't causing anything. She wasn't magical or chosen or marked. She was just... part of the rhythm. A clear note in the same song.

The display flickered subtly as the ship shifted, a near-silent recalibration that AURA would've described in technical terms, stabilising orbit and adjusting for optimal descent, but Ivy didn't look away.

Her focus stayed locked on the planet below, watching as it turned beneath its veil of cloud, slow and silent and impossibly vast.

Chapter Six

The following afternoon, Grace, David, and Gareth gathered on the command deck, ringed by the soft glow of the main display. Grace stood at the console, her gaze locked on line after line of scrolling code.

AURA's voice filled the space with calm precision. "Surface conditions in the equatorial zone remain stable. Atmospheric oxygen falls within human tolerance. No detectable lifeforms. No active transmissions."

David looked up from the scans. "Which is what we want. Stable and predictable."

AURA continued. "The northern continent registers elevated heat signatures. Geometric symmetry is consistent with designed structures. One formation reflects a near-perfect octagonal array. Power grid residuals detected beneath the surface, inactive but present."

Gareth frowned. "I thought earlier scans ruled out infrastructure."

Grace tapped a few keys, calling up the image. "I went back over it. The first sweep missed it, buried too deep, camouflaged under growth. But the energy signature doesn't match anything natural."

Gareth's eyebrows lifted. "So... a city?"

"Maybe," Grace said carefully. "Or ruins. Or an automated system that outlived its creators."

"And no sign of life?" David asked.

"None that we can detect," AURA said. "But absence of evidence does not confirm absence."

"EOS 6 lost contact somewhere in this region," David said. "We never confirmed descent, but this is close to where the trail went cold."

Gareth's gaze tracked the scan. "Could be something. Could be nothing. Data's not confirming either way."

A soft chime sounded, Grace's head snapped toward the doorway. "Where is Ivy?"

"Zero gravity chamber," AURA answered. "She has been gliding for twenty-four minutes and fourteen seconds."

Grace's shoulders eased. "Good," she said. "Keep her there."

The hum of the console filled the silence, steady and detached. Lights blinked. Data streamed. The mission kept moving.

Grace broke the silence first. "We knew the risks. This doesn't change the objective."

"It could," David said. "If there's intelligent life, if EOS 6 encountered something, we need to consider the possibility of contact."

Gareth crossed his arms. "Or conflict."

AURA offered no comfort. "Human error under duress remains the leading cause of mission failure."

Grace's voice was steady. "We're still going. But with eyes wide open."

David refocused. "The structures could be geological. Or they might be remnants. Abandoned. Old."

"We won't know until we land," Gareth said. "But from orbit, the southern ridge near the anomaly zone looks promising — elevated, dry, minimal vegetation."

Grace nodded. "We'll establish base camp there. David, you'll start the environmental scans. Air, water, soil. Gareth, power grid and safety perimeter. I'll log the terrain and begin surface analysis if anything reads unusual."

A long silence settled between them, the kind that only came when no one wanted to say what they were really thinking. Grace kept her eyes on the console, watching the orbit path shift by fractions.

"So it's not just scans and soil anymore," she said. "There's a risk, something real. It might not be safe."

David nodded slowly. "Or it could be nothing," he said. "Like you said, we go in careful, eyes open."

Her jaw set with quiet resolve. "Yes, we will," she said calmly. "But we've trained for this."

David studied her. "So what are you getting at Grace?"

Grace looked down, her expression unreadable. "There's still time to leave Ivy aboard the ship."

David winced. "No." The words came too fast, too certain. A reflex. "She deserves to go," he said. "She's earned that."

Grace's voice dropped. "That's not the point."

"It is the point," he said. "We trained her. She's capable. You saw her last rotation, she handled that systems glitch faster than Gareth."

"She's seventeen, David."

"She's ready."

Grace turned, finally meeting his eyes. "Ready doesn't mean safe. You said it yourself, if EOS 6 encountered something down there..."

David faltered. His hands found the edge of the console, gripping hard. "We can't lock her out. Not after everything we promised."

Grace's voice softened, practical but firm. "If she stays, it's twelve months. That's all. We'll have comms. She'll have AURA. She can maintain the greenhouse, and you saw the last output logs. The models are already trending short. It's not a demotion, David. It's a safeguard."

David's shoulders dropped. "I know." He glanced toward the viewport, jaw tightening. "It just feels like breaking a promise."

David met Grace's gaze. Something passed between them, not agreement exactly, just a shared understanding of what had to be done.

Gareth's head lifted.

Grace looked at him, one brow arched. "Gareth—"

"She goes," he said.

David exhaled. "We just want to keep her safe."

Gareth didn't move. His gaze locked on David, unreadable. "Then we take her. She's safer with us than alone."

Grace shook her head, jaw tight. "You've seen how she is — impulsive, emotional. She reacts on instinct."

Gareth glanced at them both. "She goes."

He turned and walked out, not waiting for an answer.

— ✦ —

The zero-gravity chamber stretched out, vast and silent. To Ivy, it felt endless.

The lights were dimmed. Above her, a wide arc of reinforced glass revealed the stars in full — bright, sharp, and infinite. They scattered across the black like spilled diamonds, real and raw in a way projections could never match. The chamber stretched around her like a hollowed dome, curved and expansive, almost cathedral-like in its quiet scale. Handholds lined the silver walls in gentle curves, and a mesh net floated near the comm panel, swaying softly in the still air. Straps, velcro loops, an old patch of padding near one corner, the signs of training long past. The room was quiet but not silent, the creak of the hull adjusting to pressure, the faint, rhythmic thump of her heartbeat in her ears.

She floated through the centre, arms outstretched, body relaxed into the gentle drift of motion. The straps she used to rely on dangled from the wall, forgotten, she hadn't needed them in years. She let herself drift backwards, catching the wall gently with her palms, then pushed off again — slow, smooth, unhurried. Her curls floated around her face in a loose red cloud, catching soft light from above. This was the only place that ever felt effortless. She didn't have to hold herself upright. Didn't have to pretend she wasn't different. Here, the silence felt easy. The weightlessness, familiar. Existing without gravity had never felt strange to her. It felt right. Back then, she'd thought she was training for life on other worlds. Preparing for something beyond Earth. Now, looking back... she realised she'd been learning how to just... be. Floating. Turning. Moving without force.

Ivy floated out from the wall, arms wide, drifting slowly through the centre of the room like a leaf caught in a breeze. This was the only place on the ship that asked nothing of her. No equations. No questions. No experiments or protocols. Just floating, and motion. Just the soft hum of engines far beneath her feet, or they would've been her feet, if direction mattered in here. She hovered a while longer, then kicked off from the ceiling with a gentle nudge and launched herself into a slow, lazy cartwheel through the air.

"Hey, AURA?" she called.

A soft chime resonated through the comm system. "Yes, Ivy?"

"Can you play something?" she said. "Something good."

"I have a library of over sixty thousand historical musical tracks. Would you like a random selection?"

She grinned. "Hit me with whatever used to make people dance in their bedrooms."

A moment later, a low beat filled the chamber, warm and pulsing.

A smooth voice followed, easy and low.

"Out past the lights, where the silence calls...
I'll find you drifting where the lost stars fall...
Weightless hearts don't break, they burn,
Pulled by the tide where the echoes turn.
Say my name where the sky runs deep,
I'll meet you there in the in-between."

She sang along as she drifted, arms splayed, the music wrapping around her like warmth. Out of every track she always came back to, this was one of her favourites. Like it was playing from somewhere buried in her blood. Ivy let out a small breath, spun once, and closed her eyes.

"There's a place where the night won't end,
Where the stars still shine like they did back then.
I'd wait a hundred years or two,
Just to find my way back to you."

She didn't get to have a bedroom. Or walk the city streets. Or go to house parties with a bunch of friends. But this? This was her dance floor. Her place. Her beat. And for these few minutes, she wasn't preparing for scans or duties or environmental suits.

"Float with me, forget the ground,
Love, like gravity, can't be found.
You and me — untethered, true,
I'd orbit every life, waiting for you."

She was just a girl. Spinning to an old Earth song in a weightless room no one else used.

Free.

She let herself coast gently across the chamber, bumping softly against the padded wall with a small smile. Then she stretched out again, catching a breath and tucking her knees just for the fun of the flip. Her record was eight rotations before hitting anything. She was going for nine.

"Three," she whispered to herself, twisting in midair, "four… five…"

The room spun around her like a galaxy, all soft amber lights and silver panels. In here, she wasn't a stowaway kid or the ship's almost-adult. In here, she was a comet.

"Six… sev—"

The door hissed open.

Gareth leant into the doorway, arms crossed, one brow raised. "Practicing for a circus career or just trying to give AURA a panic attack?"

"I'm working on my core strength," Ivy said, still floating upside down. "It's very scientific."

Gareth rolled his eyes but stepped inside, grabbing one of the overhead grips to keep himself steady. "Well, your mum wants you suited up in ten. Environmental scans need cross-checking before entry protocols."

She groaned. "Fine. But tell her my gravitational artistry deserves appreciation."

"Consider it logged."

She stretched out, trailing one hand across the ceiling as if she could trace constellations there. She gave herself one last spin before drifting toward the exit, grinning like she'd invented flight. For a second, she wished she could stay suspended like this forever — weightless, in-between, untouched by whatever waited on the surface below.

But then again, something about falling was starting to feel kind of thrilling too.

CHAPTER SEVEN

The POD sat low within the ship's docking bay, its oval dome gleaming under the overhead lights. The matte hull curved seamlessly into the docking clamps, panelled with embedded systems, every surface serving a purpose. Large enough to house crew quarters, a compact lab, and months of supplies, it was designed for planetfall, not a joyride.

Engineers had carefully arranged the space inside, building it to handle long-term surface deployment. An airlock decontamination zone marked the entry. A compact utility area lined with suits, boots, lockers, and gear hooks. Just beyond, the main chamber opened up: an open-plan kitchen along one wall, with bench space, built-in storage, and compact appliances. A lab bench and dining table took up the centre, with supply cabinets tucked neatly into recessed compartments. Everything was labelled, accessible, efficient.

A narrow corridor ran off the main area, leading to two compact crew rooms — each with a built-in bed, a narrow strip of floor, and metal compartments set into the wall for personal gear. Grace and David shared one. Gareth had quietly claimed the other. Ivy's space was a converted storage alcove at the corridor's end, wide enough for her handmade mattress, which Grace and David had carried over from her room and layered with extra blankets. Gareth had mounted a soft light panel overhead, and there was still space on the floor for her to sit. The remaining alcoves were stacked with strapped-down storage crates: sealed food packs, water canisters, and mission gear. Screens blinked in standby mode, displaying ship vitals and surface approach diagnostics. A pale lightstrip traced the curve of the ceiling, mimicking dawn. And at the heart of it all, the AURA interface pulsed faint blue from its table mount, waiting.

The air held a faint synthetic tang, edged with the sterile crispness of sealed environments. But it was clean. Balanced. A reminder that this wasn't a fallback shelter. It was a lifeboat, a field lab, a home in miniature.

They were almost ready. The morning unfolding in a steady rhythm as they loaded vacuum-sealed rations, portable water filters, soil testers, and data cores. Containment-grade bags of dried grains, flours, and compressed protein blocks were stacked in neat rows, waiting for the next run. Everything was sealed, tagged, and packed to avoid contamination. Ivy handed over containers near the side hatch, mostly getting in the way. Grace moved through the chaos, firing off orders that cracked through the air like whipcord. "Ivy, don't just stand there. Help Gareth with the bio-sensors and double-check the medkit seal."

David's voice followed from behind a stack of crates. "Once we land, you stay within visual range. No wandering. You follow protocols."

"Is that clear?"

Ivy let out a breath. "So I'm meant to go from seventeen years on a ship, to twelve months in a tin can, and then twelve more going back to Earth?"

David straightened. "It's not a tin can. It's a Planetary Operations Dropcraft."

She raised an eyebrow. "Which is definitely what someone would name a tin can to make it sound better."

David's jaw shifted as his fingers tightened on the panel. "We don't know what's waiting down there. The biosphere is unverifiable. AURA's scans are promising, but until we're on the ground, we're still guessing. There could be pathogens. Or worse."

Ivy's eyes widened in mock alarm. "Worse than pathogens?"

Grace snapped a crate closed harder than necessary. "If there were another option, Ivy, we'd take it. But I can't leave you alone on the EOS, and I don't have the luxury of assigning someone to babysit you."

"Oh, thank the stars for protocol," Ivy muttered.

Grace turned sharply. "This is a science mission. Not a vacation. You assist when asked. You don't improvise. You do as you're told."

Ivy's jaw tightened. "Right. Because thinking for myself would be chaos."

David rubbed his brow, the motion slow and deliberate. "This isn't about control. It's about risk. The terrain's unstable, and the last scans picked up something... unusual. Structures, maybe. Two rotations ago, we saw geometry that didn't look natural. But the atmosphere's minerals are interfering with AURA's imaging."

Ivy frowned. "You think there's something down there."

"We don't have enough data to identify it," Grace said. "And we can't jump to conclusions."

"You didn't want *me* jumping to conclusions," Ivy said flatly.

Grace didn't argue. She just looked away.

Ivy folded her arms. "So I'm only here because protocol says you can't leave me behind. You don't think I'm useful. And you're scared, but none of you will admit it."

Silence followed — which, in Ivy's book, counted as confirmation.

Across the POD, Gareth zipped the final hatch shut and muttered, "Well. This is going to be a fun year."

AURA's voice crackled overhead. "Departure countdown: forty-four minutes. Quadrant Twelve scan, anomaly unchanged. Geometry remains irregular and may be artificial."

Grace's head lifted. "Confirmed?"

"Unconfirmed," AURA replied. "Reflective minerals are still obstructing imaging. Structures could be natural formations... or remnants."

Ivy looked from face to face. They'd clearly been talking about this without her.

"So when exactly were you planning to tell me?" Ivy said. "When I was hosting afternoon tea for the alien invasion committee?"

David's jaw flexed. "Ivy," he said, clipped. "Nothing is confirmed."

Grace lifted the medscanner from the counter and began packing it into its case with clipped precision. "Preliminary scans don't justify a mission-level alert. We wait for confirmation."

Ivy tilted her head, eyes narrowing. "So what's the plan? Keep me boxed up like spare equipment until it's safe to let me out? Or am I just here in case you need someone to blame when it all goes wrong?"

Grace slammed the medscanner into its port with more force than necessary. "That's enough, Ivy."

Her voice wasn't loud, but it cut clean. "We are hours from touching down on an unverified planet, half our equipment could fail in the atmosphere, and you're standing here acting like this is some personal punishment. You are not the only one under pressure."

Ivy flinched.

"You want to be treated like a member of this crew?" Grace's eyes locked onto hers. "Then act like one."

Silence swelled until the POD's low hum was the only thing pushing through the static between them.

Gareth caught Ivy's eye and tipped his head toward the open hatch. "Come on. I need to grab something."

They left the noise of the POD behind, stepping into the corridor linking it to the ship. The systems pulsed softer here, the air cooler. Gareth leant against the wall, pulling a thin bronze chain with a pendant from his pocket and letting it dangle between them.

The pendant caught the light — bronze, small enough to fit neatly in her palm, shaped like a teardrop formed from overlapping leaves. The metal was etched with fine branching veins, delicate but worn. It looked old. Simple yet timeless.

Ivy's eyes widened, a flicker of wonder breaking through. "It's beautiful. What is it?"

Gareth didn't answer right away. His gaze lingered on her, proud and searching, as though her reaction was the only answer he needed.

"Did you make it?" she asked.

He shook his head. "No. It was passed down to me. A long time ago."

She took it gently, letting the weight settle into her palm.

"It belonged to my mother," he said. "She gave it to me when I was six."

Ivy's thumb traced the groove of a leaf, the bronze warm against her skin.

"She said it would keep me safe. That even when I felt alone, I wouldn't be."

Her fingers stilled. Her gaze lifted from the pendant to meet his. "I'm sorry you didn't get more time with them. With your parents."

Gareth's expression barely shifted, but something in his voice softened. "Yeah. Me too." His gaze lingered on the pendant in her hand, as if measuring its place with her. "I want you to hold on to it."

"Not because I think anything will go wrong," he added quickly, "but because I trust you to keep it safe. I don't want to have it on me if I'm out scouting or collecting samples."

Her throat tightened. "Gareth…"

He held her gaze. "You've got spirit, Pip. Fierce, curious. Always a little too brave for your own good."

He let the words hang between them before adding softly, "And I think of you as my own. Not by blood. But by bond."

The silence that followed didn't need filling. Ivy stepped forward and wrapped her arms around him. He held her tighter, his grip a silent promise.

"Are you scared, Gareth?" Ivy asked.

He pulled back just enough to meet her eyes. "No, Pip."

She hesitated. "Should I be?"

His gaze held steady. "Would a star be afraid of the dark?"

— ✦ —

The POD vibrated faintly, systems humming steadily as they closed the distance to Veritas-9. Ivy stood in the observation nook near the console, fingers tapping a quiet rhythm against the metal wall, heart thudding harder than the engines. Outside the viewport, the planet loomed. A swirl of blue and green smudged by clouds, haloed in the gold light of its suns. Peaceful on the surface, but shadows stirred beneath.

"Ten minutes until atmospheric breach," AURA's voice came through steady and clear.

Ivy pushed away from the wall and crossed to her seat. She sat back slow, though her fingers trembled against the armrest. Gareth was already there, adjusting the harness before she even settled in. The restraints clicked into place, the padded seat pressing firmly against her shoulders.

"Don't overthink it," he said.

"I'm not."

He raised an eyebrow. "You're vibrating."

She glanced down, the subtle bounce of her knee a quiet pulse against the floor.

Gareth stood after securing Ivy's harness, crossing to the forward panels and adjusting readings with calm precision. Grace slid into the co-pilot's seat, her gaze flicking over the secondary displays. At the rear console, David's eyes fixed on the descent velocity. He stayed on his feet, having given up the third seat for Ivy, and watched as the main screen flared with shifting data.

"Still no change in the structures," he said. "They're holding formation. We're picking up organic sprawl near Quadrant Twelve... but it's unnaturally still."

"Define 'unnaturally,'" Gareth said.

"No heat movement. No wind disruption. The atmosphere's reading stable, too stable. It's like the whole quadrant's frozen in place."

Gareth kept his gaze on the screen. "Stable doesn't mean safe." His eyes flicked over the instrument cluster, reading streams of data with practiced calm.

Grace leant in, jaw tight. David's eyes skimmed the readings, then flicked to Ivy, a subtle crease pulling between his brows. The same unsettling thought, shared but unspoken.

Ivy's fingers curled hard around the armrests, her shoulders locked against the seatback.

AURA's voice softened, as if trying not to interrupt. "Five minutes to descent. Cloaking system remains stable. Visual signature and energy output are within stealth parameters."

The POD would vanish upon entry. A ghost slipping into the atmosphere. Calm, soundless, like a secret.

A sharp jolt rocked the POD. Ivy's breath hitched.

"Stabilisers adjusting for gravitational shift," AURA said. "Remain seated."

Her fingers tightened on the armrests.

Gareth settled into the pilot seat beside her, adjusting his harness without a word.

"You good?" he asked, voice low.

"I've never not been on a ship before," she whispered. "Not since... ever."

His hand closed gently over hers, warm and solid. "You're still on one. Just a small one with worse toilets."

Ivy let out a shaky breath that might've been a laugh.

"Three minutes."

Gareth tapped a button on the console, sending a quiet signal through the ship's systems.

The POD tilted. Veritas-9 surged into view, an entire world unrolling beneath them like a secret kept too long. Twin suns hung just off the horizon, casting long, overlapping shadows that shimmered as the POD shifted. Forests stretched endlessly, wild and lush, threaded with veins of silver riverlight that glimmered faintly beneath the treetops. Mountains rose like fractured bone, jagged and raw, their peaks dusted in lavender ice. Below, not far from their descent path, the coastline unfolded. A crescent of pale, silken sand cradled water that shifted hues as it moved — sapphire, teal, then a green lit from within, carrying a quiet luminescent glow. The clouds didn't drift, they curled and flexed, trailing a luminescent shimmer through the sky.

Something fluttered in Ivy's chest. Not fear. Not excitement. Something she didn't have a word for.

"Two minutes."

Grace spoke softly into her comms, cross-checking systems. David shifted his stance, bracing against the console. Gareth gave Ivy's harness one last check, then leant back, drawing a deep breath as he glanced toward the viewport.

"One minute."

Gareth ran a final check across the controls, his slight nod signalling they were ready.

The POD shifted as systems locked into place. The air thickened. Ivy pressed back into the seat, every muscle braced for the drop. A storm of green and blue spun beneath them now, not like a planet, but like something waiting. Slow. Sleeping. About to be disturbed.

"Descent initiated," AURA announced.

The POD dropped.

Sound became pressure. Air became weight. Ivy's breath caught in her throat as the world outside became a motion blur. Her stomach lurched so hard it forgot whose body it belonged to. The frame shuddered around her, a low vibration rattled through her chest.

Branches whipped past the viewport. Close now. Too close. Then a flare of colour. Birds? No. Something else.

The POD curved hard to the right, skimming low over a clearing washed in strange light, just flashes of colour and movement, impossible to pin down. Something below gleamed. Shapes blurred. The trees rippled, like wind moving through water instead of leaves.

The straps bit in. Her pulse thundered in her ears. She squeezed her eyes shut, like that might stop the spiral.

Then — the POD pulled up hard, her stomach lurching as gravity caught.

A soft jolt. Ground beneath. They were down.

A hush fell...

Ivy opened her eyes.

Outside the viewport, the trees beyond the clearing began to shift. Not swaying, but glowing faintly beneath their bark, light pulsing in a slow rhythm. Pale spores rose from their bases in a soft burst, catching sunlight like dust in a cathedral. Ivy leant closer.

Then something small emerged, a creature no bigger than a rabbit, woven from moss and iridescent fur. It stepped to the edge of the clearing, ears twitching. As Ivy watched, the soft tips of its ears shimmered blue, then gold, then pink, pulsing. It lingered for a moment, then moved off slowly, fading back into the forest.

Ivy exhaled, not realising she'd been holding her breath. "What is this place?" She whispered.

Her limbs felt grounded, like gravity had grown thicker. For the first time in her life, the floor beneath her was solid, anchored to a world, not drifting through space. A flicker of nerves rose in her chest, fast and fluttering. There was a hum beneath her skin, not fear. Just... awareness, sharp and new.

Across from her, Grace was already unstrapping, focused and calm.

"Everyone intact?" Gareth asked, his voice low and steady. He turned to glance at Ivy. Just a quick check — her breathing, her eyes — before his attention snapped back to the controls. No room for anything else. Not now.

"Nicely done, Gareth," David said, easing his grip on the console. "Smoothest landing I've had in years of simulations."

Ivy glanced around, the rush in her ears fading as her heartbeat steadied.

"Environmental systems are down," Grace said. "AURA, initiate atmospheric scan."

The AI's voice came online smoothly, a slight delay the only sign of transition. "Scanning… composition 21% oxygen… trace nitrogen… unrecognised organics present. Recommend manual confirmation."

David reached into a wall compartment and pulled out the portable scanner. "Backup it is."

They waited in tense silence as he calibrated the device. A long beep. Then another. He held up the screen. "Looks clean. O2, CO2, nitrogen all within tolerable ranges. No airborne toxins or corrosives. At least not in the immediate vicinity."

Ivy leant forward, staring out the small viewport. The world outside was impossibly green and still. Towering trees rose high above the forest floor, their massive square leaves hanging in heavy folds from a thick central stalk. Each one was broad as a blanket and textured like fleece, with a mossy shimmer that caught the light. Overhead, the upper branches shifted in a slow, soundless sway. Nothing rushed, but everything felt… alert.

"We need a field test," Grace said. "Full exposure protocol. No improvisation. No mistakes."

"Agreed," David said, already preparing the first-stage gear.

Gareth glanced back at Ivy. "Get some rest if you can. We'll run every check, and then some, before anyone steps outside."

Ivy didn't answer. Her gaze stayed fixed on the treeline. The pull was magnetic. Like gravity, but older, carried in the slow reach of the branches and the hush beneath them.

Chapter Eight

They didn't step out right away.

The first two days passed sealed inside the POD. Even with the scanners showing safe levels, even with AURA's readouts cleared and cross-checked, no one moved toward the open air.

David paced the length of the POD, helmet in hand. "We test it the right way. Gradual exposure." He was already suited up—not full EVA gear, but a reinforced environmental suit, the fabric laced with dermal sensors and the faint hiss of its internal air feed. "I'll step out, stay ten minutes. Grace, you monitor vitals. Gareth, you're on hatch. Ivy..."

"I'm watching," she said, already at the viewport, fingers unconsciously pressed to the glass.

David took a breath, pulled on his gloves, and locked the helmet in place. The seals clicked with a soft hiss. He stepped into the airlock decontamination zone, a chamber sealed for atmosphere adjustment and contaminant checks. The inner door slid shut behind him, cutting him off from the POD. A burst of pressure hit as the system equalised for exit. The outer door opened.

He started down the ramp. The light struck him in a wash of gold, spilling over his suit like liquid, like a song with no sound. The moment his boots touched solid ground, his stance shifted, shoulders settling as if the air had taken on a different weight. The stillness deepened, the forest steady and slow around him.

The clearing was ringed with tall, silver-barked trees whose leaves sparkled in waves of blue and green. Moss grew in soft whorls underfoot, glowing faintly beneath the trees. Petal-like growths opened as he passed, releasing particles of something fragrant into the air. Plants swayed with a slow, instinctive rhythm. Gentle, patterned, like breath through leaves.

High above, a flicker of movement caught the light, not a bird, but something gliding. It twisted through the upper branches with weightless ease, its limbs outstretched like a flying squirrel, but draped in long, ribbon-like threads that shimmered like translucent silk. As it drifted overhead, a faint trail of glowing pollen spiralled behind it, then faded. Its call was soft, a fluttery chime, like wind stirring the strings of a distant harp.

"Vitals stable," Grace said from the console. "No stress indicators. No dermal inflammation. Heart rate elevated, expected."

"I feel fine," David reported. "Actually... better than fine." He swept the scanner slowly in a circle, taking in the clearing. "Humidity's high but within tolerance. No airborne particulates outside expected range."

He walked slowly, circling the POD. The forest didn't press in; it opened wide and quiet, each breath matched by the hush around him. Every leaf seemed to glow, its veins catching the light in a steady rhythm. Another bird, smaller this time, fluttered through a shaft of sun like a living ember. It hovered for a moment near a flowering vine, then vanished into the light.

"Environmental readings match projections. No immediate anomalies."

"Alright," Gareth said, hand still resting on the manual override. "Let's bring you in."

David crossed the clearing and stepped onto the short ramp leading up to the decontamination zone. The outer door slid open with a soft hiss as he reached the top. He stepped inside, the outer seal closing behind him. A faint mist sprayed over him as the internal sensors ran their sweep. Then the inner door unlocked with a soft tone, releasing him back into the POD. He peeled off the helmet and gloves, flexing his fingers.

"Air feels humid. Dense. But clean." He turned to Grace. "We could probably open the hatch fully."

"Not until we run a secondary exposure," Grace said firmly.

She glanced at Ivy, who was still watching the trees. The vines above shifted slightly, their movement slow and fluid, like leaves caught in a rhythm she couldn't name.

Gareth looked up, brow furrowing. "Wind's changing," he muttered.

But there was no wind.

Ivy stayed at the viewport, heart racing now, like something in her already knew the shape of the world beyond the glass.

She just wanted out.

Chapter Nine

The air felt different here.

It wasn't just the scent, though that was strange enough. Earthy, but not like soil. Sweet, but not like flowers. Something in between, a note she didn't have a name for yet. It hit her the moment she stepped off the ramp and hadn't faded since. Not artificial. Not ship-clean. Just... real. So real it scraped her lungs, like her body didn't know what to do with it. Ivy moved carefully, the way you might in someone else's dream — slow, wide-eyed, half-waiting to be kicked out. She'd wandered past the edge of the clearing, beyond the buzz of equipment and the echo of Grace's last call. The air shifted the further she went. Thicker. Warmer. Threaded with a low vibration she could feel more than hear.

The trees stood taller than anything she'd imagined. Smooth and spiralling, their leaves thin and glinting, colours rolling from deep green to teal in the shifting light. Light filtered down in pale beams, warm gold laced with silver, casting rippling patterns across the moss as if the entire forest swayed underwater.

Just ahead, the ground fell into a gentle slope where the trees thinned and the sky opened out. A wide ledge of grass spread between the trunks, edged with silverleaf and soft patches of moss. It felt held somehow, like the forest had stepped back just enough to let the light in. She followed the slope down, light spilling over her as the earth dropped away into a sweep of open air, wide and endless, the faint shimmer of water far below catching the sun.

She heard no engines. No clicks from AURA. No metallic hum of recycled air. Just wind. Birds. A faint rustle. The sounds didn't compete, they blended. Like an orchestra tuning itself. A branch creaked above. Ivy looked up.

Perched on a curved limb, a slender bird watched in stillness. Wings arched like folded crystal, its feathers scattering light in soft, shifting rainbows. Long tail-feathers trailed beneath it like ribbons, trailing on the air with every tiny shift. Its wings unfolded in a slow, fluid sweep, catching the sunslight until they flared with colour. It rose in an unhurried spiral, each beat scattering a wash of prism-light across the clearing before it glided out over the open air. Ivy's gaze followed until it was only light and sky, the image lingering like something she might dream about later.

She crouched near a patch of moss. It gave softly under her fingertips, damp with the trace of rain, each tiny frond springing back as she pressed. Warmth travelled up her arms, grounding, unfamiliar. The ship had been all metal and hum. This... was alive. A hush folded over the clearing, the wind slipping into stillness. A low rustle behind her, tension rippled through her shoulders.

A soft flicker caught the edge of her eye, a flash of movement low to the ground. Ivy turned just in time to catch a thick, candyfloss-pink tail tipped with a swirl of white as it slipped into the undergrowth, vanishing with a ripple of branches. She stared at the spot, heart hitching somewhere between wonder and disbelief. A giggle escaped before she could stop it, half breath, half spark of something that felt dangerously close to joy.

She moved through the clearing, brushing past a cluster of tall, glass-pale stalks. They swayed toward her touch, scattering a fine mist of pollen into the light before easing upright again. Her heartbeat thumped in her ears. Every part of her felt awake. Too awake.

A flying insect drifted into view, its wings shaped like leaves, edges frayed, the surface textured like bark. It hovered for a moment, impossibly familiar. Its body glowed with hues, turning slowly, as if studying her just as closely. Then — slowly, delicately — it landed on her arm.

Ivy held her breath.

For a moment, it stayed still, then its colour shifted. From golden-violet shimmer to the muted green of her jacket until it vanished completely against her sleeve. Like a chameleon. Like instinct. Camouflaging to her, adapting hue until it was part of her. Then it lifted off again, slow and graceful, circling her once before darting up into the trees. A quiet laugh slipped out — soft, startled, almost weightless.

"Hi," she whispered. Nothing answered, but the air felt bright with welcome.

She let her hand trail over the moss again, slower this time. Not testing it. Just feeling it. And Ivy, for the first time, didn't feel like an intruder.

She felt like the beginning of a story.

Chapter Ten

It had been five days since landing.

The camp was up and running. Solar panels stretched toward the filtered light, charging banks buried beneath soft dirt. They had assembled prefabricated modules for lab work, water purification, and storage. There were no fences, no walls — just clean zones marked by portable beacons and an unspoken agreement not to wander.

Ivy had claimed a hammock near the edge of the clearing, slung between two silver-leaved trees, just far enough from the others to feel like her own space. Her morning tasks were basic — water checks, food inventory, soil readings — things AURA could've done faster, but Grace insisted on "hands-on discipline."

Grace was always moving between the readouts and her notes, carrying the same charged energy she'd had since touchdown — the rush of landing, the thrill of setting up camp, all of it pulling her deeper into the mission. David kept giving her that soft, worn smile. The one that said they loved her, but loved the mission too, and wished they didn't have to keep watching out for both.

Gareth had been strangely upbeat. He helped her calibrate the sensors, taught her how to recognise heat signatures on the scans, and once spent twenty minutes explaining why moss growth patterns could help predict local water flow. Ivy had caught him watching the treeline more than once, eyes tracking something he wouldn't name.

The twin suns, identical in every way, rose and set in perfect sync, casting crisp double shadows across the treetops. Their light was unwavering, balanced so precisely it felt staged, as if the sky itself were caught in a loop. Mornings arrived all at once in golden clarity, and dusk fell with sharp precision. It was breathtaking. And unnerving.

The two moons, by contrast, seemed to obey no law at all. One was pale silver, vast and cold, hanging high above like a watchful eye. The other loomed large and cratered, glowing a deep molten gold that bathed the treetops in soft firelight. They never appeared together, never moved the same way twice, like siblings who refused to speak to each other.

And the beauty, the kind that clung to you long after you'd looked away, was all they could talk about. They'd catalogued over thirty plant species so far, two dozen insects, and six mammals. All gentle, all disarmingly beautiful. The water was clean. The air, breathable. Gravity just low enough to make movement feel like memory.

But it was the silence that stayed with her. Not the absence of sound — the air carried calls, buzzes, the restless rustle of leaves — but beneath it all, something deeper waited. A quiet stretched thin, held in perfect suspension. Tension layered into the stillness.

They hadn't talked about the structures AURA had picked up before the landing. Not openly. Which was strange, considering how much focus they'd given them during descent. Ivy had overheard Gareth mention it a few days ago, just a quiet comment while checking the heat signatures with David. Something about angles that didn't match erosion patterns. About shadows that stayed fixed too long. He'd suggested a scouting loop beyond the ridge — subtle, careful, nothing official. Grace had shut it down instantly. David hadn't even looked up.

Now, Ivy stood in the clearing, sensor pad warm in her hands. Her job this morning was flora pattern mapping. Boring, repetitive, and oddly calming. She moved from tree to tree, logging species type, leaf variance, and pollen count. Behind her, the POD sat in the clearing, all clean lines and dull metal, a fragment of another world dropped into this one. Around it, colour and light moved with effortless grace, the craft's stillness almost jarring against the living backdrop. A soft-winged insect drifted into view, pulsing with blue light. It hovered for a moment at her shoulder before gliding away, vanishing into the shimmer of leaves.

She glanced down at her scanner, then up again as the leaves brushed her arm. The touch was soft, reactive, like the vines in the greenhouse used to do. She hadn't said anything then, and she wouldn't now. Grace would call it a sensor glitch. David would frown and change the subject.

But the plants were moving. Just slightly. Just around her.

She adjusted the sensor range and kept walking.

— ✦ —

That night, Ivy sat by the fading fire, knees hugged to her chest, chin resting on them as she stared up at the stars spilling across the open sky. Her back rested against one of the logs Gareth had set in place around the flames.

The sky above didn't just glitter, it blazed. Not with heat, but with depth. Layers upon layers of starlight, sharp and endless, stretched across the black, like the universe had cracked, just enough to spill its secrets. Galaxies curled like smoke trails in the dark, quiet spirals of blue and violet, scattered between constellations Ivy didn't recognise. One bright star pulsed low near the horizon, steady and soft, like a signal waiting for someone to notice. She'd never seen a sky like this. Not from behind the glass of the ship. Not from orbit. Not even something her imagination would have thought to shape.

Out there among the stars, everything was measured. Filtered through sensors and metal and routine. Beautiful, but clinical. Detached. But here, lying under them, watching from the quiet dark, it felt different. Real. Like seeing the stars as they were meant to be seen. From a distance, they shimmered more. The scale made them infinite. Honest. Out there, she was inside the machine. But here... here, she could feel the whole universe turning above her.

The fire popped in slow, uneven bursts, seeping warmth into the unmoving air. Grace joined her quietly, settling on a log with a soft exhale. Not from effort, just the kind of tired that came from thinking too much. She didn't speak at first. Just pulled her sleeves over her hands and rubbed them together.

"Ivy," she said eventually, her voice soft, "there's something I should've told you earlier."

Ivy kept her gaze on the flames, the quiet settling as she waited for her to continue.

Grace hesitated. Her mouth opened like she was about to offer a technical update, something clinical and safe, but instead she said, "We think there are people here."

That pulled her focus. Ivy turned, the firelight catching in her eyes, sharpening them. "People?"

Grace nodded. "We haven't seen them directly. No contact. But David picked up faint energy signatures last night. Structured patterns. And I... I found traces of an old footpath this morning. Overgrown, but deliberate."

Ivy tilted her head, studying her. "You think they're close?"

Grace met her eye. "Close enough to leave traces. Far enough to stay hidden."

Her mind spun through the possibilities. "Who are they?" She met Grace's eyes. "Are they human... like us?"

"We don't know yet. What we do know, is we're pretty sure they don't know we're here." Grace hesitated, then added, "We've kept the lights low. Monitored transmissions. But if they're out there... they're quiet. Careful. And we don't know if that's ignorance or caution."

"And you weren't going to tell me?" The words came low, almost careful, but they landed between them like a dropped stone.

Grace looked down at her hands. "I was trying to give you time. Time to adjust. Time to be safe."

Ivy stared back out into the dark. The two moons cast dueling light across the trees. One was dim and unsteady, like a thought trying to stay alive. The other, bold and molten gold, drew slow-moving shadows across the ground.

The quiet stretched, unbroken but for the slow pop and sigh of the fire. Her hands pressed into the earth beside her, steadying her breath. On the outside, she looked calm. But inside, her thoughts spun wild.

What were they like, the people here? Did they have stories, songs, books? Would any of them look like her?

Were there girls her age? Someone to talk to. Laugh with. Someone who hadn't read the same Earth novels over and over, who hadn't lived on protein shakes and filtered air.

Her grip on her knees tightened, the rush of thoughts thinning to a single, steady ache. Someone real.

Of course Grace hadn't told her.

Because this — this quiet flicker of hope, this ache for something more — was dangerous.

Grace knew it. And Ivy knew it too.

But still... she couldn't help wondering.

Somewhere beyond the trees, someone might be sitting beside a different fire. Looking up at the same moons.

Wondering if someone else out there had ever looked up and wanted more.

A soft crunch of footsteps broke the quiet.

Ivy turned at the sound behind her. David was walking towards them, carrying a vacuum-sealed ration pouch and two metal cups. Gareth followed with a thermal pack tucked under one arm, another pair of cups hooked through his fingers. He gave a small nod, like this was the most natural thing in the world, sitting under alien stars on an even stranger planet.

"Figured stargazing pairs better with something sweet," David said, lowering himself onto the grass beside her. "Dessert?"

Ivy squinted at the pouch. "That says apple crumble."

"And I choose to believe it."

She cracked the seal and sniffed. It didn't smell like apples. Or crumble. Or food, really. But it was warm, and vaguely sweet, and that was enough. Gareth handed her a cup without a word, then settled beside Grace on the log.

They sat in silence, hands curled around cups of lukewarm cocoa, staring at the sky as if waiting for it to answer.

And for a minute, the night felt still. But her thoughts refused to be.

She swallowed a bite and said, "So... the people."

David nodded slowly. "We're not making contact."

"Not yet, or not at all?"

Gareth answered this time. "Not at all."

That landed with a thud. "Why?"

Grace straightened. "Because we don't know who they are or what they're capable of. Or what they've seen. We landed undetected, at least we think so. That's a major advantage. We keep it."

"If they're advanced enough for you to pick up on a scan," Ivy pushed, "they probably already—"

"We're not debating this," Grace said, firmer now. She gave Ivy a sharp look, the kind that warned this wasn't a discussion. "We observe. That's what the mission is."

Ivy held her ground, the silence stretching a moment before she spoke again. "And me?" Her voice was quiet. "What if I see them?"

"You walk away," Grace said.

Ivy looked at David. "You agree with this?"

He hesitated. "I think… we came here to study. Not to interfere."

Ivy let the cup settle on her lap, her hand curling lightly around the pendant at her neck. "You don't think I can decide for myself?"

Grace met her eyes. "No. But you're still our responsibility, not just because you're part of this mission… but because we care about you."

She looked down at the pouch in her hand. The food felt heavier than it should have.

"What if they're good?" she whispered. "What if we miss the only chance to find out?"

"And what if they're not?" Gareth said. "What if the next time you go wandering, someone doesn't let you go?"

Ivy didn't answer.

The fire crackled between them. The stars blazed on, indifferent.

David nudged her shoulder gently. "Let's focus on what we can control. We gave up everything to be here. Let's not forget to enjoy it."

Ivy didn't smile. But she looked up anyway.

Above her, galaxies stretched in every direction, silent and unknowable. It felt less like looking up and more like falling in.

Chapter Eleven

By the second week, Ivy knew the forest's rhythms better than her own. She lay back in her hammock, toes nudging the ground, each push sending it into a slow, steady sway. Above her, silver leaves shifted in soft waves, scattering light that flickered across her skin. The air was rich with damp earth and clean sunslight — fresh, golden, impossibly perfect.

Across the clearing, Grace and David were arguing again, something about soil enzymes and fungal root networks. Gareth adjusted a solar array near the slope, methodical as always. Same as yesterday. And the day before that. Ivy pushed off harder, sending the hammock swinging.

She wanted more than filtered wonder and polite discoveries. More than rehydrated lentils and daily logs. She wanted something that wasn't on the checklist. Something alive. Unpredictable. Even if it meant consequences.

Ivy let the hammock slow, then swung her legs over and stepped onto the ground. She lingered for a moment, boot soles firm against the packed earth, before drifting toward the edge of the clearing. Sunslight thinned in the spaces between the trees, drawing her in. She slipped into the underbrush without a sound. Grace and David didn't notice. They never did.

The forest didn't resist. Branches gave way like paths worn into habit. Light dappled the ground in gold and green. She moved fast, quiet. Her boots knew the way before her thoughts caught up. Just a glimpse. Just a breath of something different.

After a while, she reached the ridge and then, there it was. She dropped low, branches brushing her shoulders. The valley spread out below like a secret she was starting to memorise. Homes built from living wood and pale stone curled together like they'd grown there. Soft light glowed from their seams. The whole town moved like breath — steady, rhythmic, alive.

The people moved in the same way. Effortless, beautiful, their colours shimmering in quiet harmony. Skin, hair, and eyes all drawn from the same base tone within each person, every feature matched in colour, only shifting in shade. A girl in sea-tones walked barefoot beside an elder in jade. A pair of children chased light through the grass. One had deep gold-threaded hair, pale golden skin, and bright eyes, the other was flushed in coral-pink, her whole palette glowing as she darted between the trees. Every set felt unified, yet no two were exactly alike, like each colour spun through a hundred shades. And their presence, that was the part Ivy couldn't explain. They moved as if the planet itself carried them, not with wires, or engines, or sound. Just life, folded effortlessly into the world around them.

She lingered until the shadows pressed in, holding the scene in her mind like a photograph. Then she turned for the forest, moving slower now, her mind heavy.

By the time she pushed through the clearing, her boots were damp, the forest's stillness clinging to her. Gareth was crouched over a tether line, testing its tension before knotting it off again. He glanced up as she stepped out of the trees, one eyebrow lifting. She met it with the barest flick of her eyes and crossed the clearing to him. Gareth stood, dusted his hands on his pants, and they headed inside together.

In the cramped kitchen, Grace was portioning out ration trays with precise, practised movements. David sat at the table, eyes on his datapad, one hand idly spinning his cup. Gareth headed for the wash station, rinsing his hands before taking his seat at the far end. Ivy slid into the nearest chair, keeping her head down.

Grace glanced over her shoulder. "Where have you been all afternoon?"

"Fell asleep in my hammock," she said, reaching for a cup and filling it from the water canister.

Grace set a tray in front of her without comment, but the silence was heavy enough to count.

"Thanks," Ivy said, picking up her spoon and giving the lentils a slow stir.

Grace took her seat, the chair legs scraping softly against the floor.

Ivy drew in a slow, measured breath. "The people in the valley," she started.

"No, Ivy," Grace cut in. "We've already discussed this."

"I want to meet them."

David's spoon slipped from his hand and clinked against his tray. "Are you crazy? Absolutely not."

"But Mum said they're peaceful—"

"When did I say that?" Grace snapped sharper than usual. "We don't know what they are, and we don't know how they'll react. The mission wasn't to make contact. It's gathering samples, collecting data, taking environmental readings. We observe. We report. Nothing more."

"We keep hidden." She met Ivy's eyes now, gaze steady. "All of us."

Ivy leant back, letting the heat pass. No point pushing when the wall is up. Her eyes drifted toward the small viewport. The stars hadn't quite broken through the deepening blue. "Do you know if they have kids?" she asked. "Teenagers?"

Grace didn't answer.

"Important details," Ivy said lightly, "if we're reporting everything."

Gareth's eyes flicked to her from across the table. He hadn't said a word all evening. He rarely did. But he was listening, keeping some score no one else could see.

"Do you know about them?" she asked him.

Gareth picked up his cup and took a sip, leaving the question hanging between them.

Grace glanced up. "Don't."

"I was just asking—"

"He's not your shortcut, Ivy."

Ivy clenched her jaw and looked down, poking at her lentils like they might become something else if she stirred long enough.

"But—"

"Ivy, stop!" Grace stood, her spoon falling to the floor. "This isn't a game. We didn't cross half the galaxy so you could run off and insert yourself into a society we don't understand. You don't belong with those people. Their biology, their behaviour, their entire evolutionary path, it's not human. You are." Her voice sharpened. "Why do you have to make everything so difficult? Why can't you ever just follow the rules?"

"Okay." Gareth's voice cut through the tension, low and steady. "Let's calm down." He set his cup down with quiet precision. He looked at Grace, then at Ivy.

"She has the right to ask questions. But she also needs to listen." His eyes locked on Ivy. "No contact. You follow your mother's lead. Understood?"

She swallowed hard, her gaze dropping as she nodded stiffly.

He went back to eating, the argument left exactly where he'd set it down. The line had been drawn.

Her spoon hovered over her tray, unmoving. She wasn't hungry anymore. Her mind filled with them. The girl with sea-coloured hair. A boy her age in rust-red tones. Someone who might teach her to braid vines into shelter. Someone who might laugh with her under twin suns.

Grace had seen it in her. That ache to connect. The draw toward danger wrapped in wonder.

That's why she hadn't told her.

Curiosity was Ivy's gravity.

And she was already falling.

Chapter Twelve

The sun was high and bright, slanting through the trees in warm patches as Ivy scrubbed moss from a soil sensor with a fibre cloth.

"Let me get this straight," she said, "we travel halfway across the galaxy so I can... clean?" She glanced over her shoulder. Grace didn't answer, just stood by the solar panels, inspecting something on her scanner as if Ivy hadn't said a word.

"Great way to harness my curiosity. Can't wait to log algae stats." Ivy murmured.

The chores weren't hard, just insultingly pointless. Yesterday, it was sorting sample vials by chemical code. The day before? Scanning the inside of the storage lockers for fungal growth. "Glamorous mission work," she'd joked to Gareth. He hadn't laughed.

But that morning, he'd shown her a rogue data file. Quietly, like a secret between them. Blurry images auto-logged on descent: the outline of a building half-swallowed by vines. Clearly artificial. Clearly real. Grace and David hadn't mentioned it. Hadn't even hinted. Now she was stuck wiping moss off equipment they barely used.

They all saw them. She knew they did.

She dumped the cloth in the rinse bin and stood, wiping her hands down her pants as she glanced toward the treeline. Beyond the last line of solar panels, the forest glinted gold and green, deep and alive. Somewhere out there was not only the village she'd been watching at night, but the structures from the scans. Real places, real stories. And no one wanted to go near them.

Ivy drifted toward the trees, slow at first, tracing the edge of the clearing with her gaze. The sunlight shifted across the leaves, drawing her deeper, until her boots reached the line where grass gave way to undergrowth.

"Stay within range of the scanners," Grace called, not even looking up.

Ivy didn't answer. She stepped past the last of the prefabricated modules and into the trees, slow and casual, like she was just wandering. Like her feet didn't already know where they were going. The clearing's brightness fell away, replaced by mottled light and the cool scent of moss. Leaves whispered overhead. She pushed a low branch aside, taking another few steps deeper.

A flicker of movement caught her eye. She sank into a crouch, scanning the underbrush. A creature — mouse-small, with silken fur in soft shades of lilac and cream — darted between the stems. It had long lashes, tufted ears, and delicate paws that made no sound at all. For a heartbeat, it paused, eyes like glinting pearls, curious and still. The creature tilted its head.

Then vanished beneath a fern, no more than a whisper in the grass.

She stayed there a moment longer, her pulse still skimming too fast. Behind her, the camp lay muted and distant. Around her, it felt like the forest waited, a trail of shifting light threading between the trunks, just far enough to make her wonder. She stood slowly.

They could ignore the truth if they wanted.

She wasn't going to.

— ✦ —

Late that night, Ivy stood at the edge of camp, gaze turned toward the darkness beyond the trees — the same stretch she'd been watching for nights now, where she knew the town waited, hidden but pulling at her all the same.

The camp behind her was quiet. Grace and David had finally gone to sleep, the lights in their room dimmed to night mode. Gareth had stayed up late, hunched over the filtration system muttering to himself as he swapped parts in and out. She had listened to him for a while from her room, leaning against the cool wall beside the door, counting each clink of metal and click of a seal locking into place. When his footsteps had finally reached his room and the door had shut behind him, she had stayed where she was. Still, listening, until the camp had settled into complete silence.

She slipped on her boots and stepped into the trees.

With each step, the camp fell away, swallowed by shadow and moonlight glinting off bark. Here and there, pale threads of light curled through the moss at her feet, shifting in soft, organic patterns as she passed. The air was thick with something unspoken, a quiet dare pulling her deeper. Branches wove overhead, dimming the stars, while leaves grazed her shoulders as if marking her passing.

She passed the familiar ridge and kept going, pushing through the undergrowth until the trees began to thin. The ground opened onto a narrow ledge, and beyond it, there it was. The town. Alive, shifting with light beneath the two moons. A living painting of light and motion and colour.

She squinted, watching for something new. A laugh, a slip, a secret, something human. Her hand lifted, absently turning the pendant at her neck.

A girl who looked her age walked across one of the vine-strung bridges, golden-yellow from head to toe. Skin like ripe peaches, hair like spun sun, and a dress the colour of sunflower petals. She turned mid-step and smiled at someone Ivy couldn't see.

Ivy leant toward her, aching to close the distance. Who are you? Do you laugh with your friends? Get into stupid fights? Or is that not allowed here?

She stayed until her knees hurt, until the cold crept in, until her breath fogged in the air and the town dimmed. Then she rose slowly, quietly, and turned back through the forest — heart loud, thoughts louder.

She was done watching. She was done waiting.

Chapter Thirteen

The next night, it felt like the forest's rhythm had changed. Temperature fluctuations triggered new bioluminescent patterns in the moss, and the forest's hum dipped into a slow, steady pulse. Overhead, the planet's moons hung in the sky — never in sync, always shifting positions like dancers in separate routines. Their off-balance rise bathed the forest in a strange, wavering glow.

Ivy crept through the silver-lit underbrush, silent as Gareth had taught her. Her boots brushed moss that glowed faintly under her step. She kept low, breath steady, each heartbeat thudding through the stillness. This was reckless. But the kind of reckless that made her feel alive.

She reached the ridge above the valley and paused, scanning. Empty... Then movement, a figure alone, walking a narrow forest path below. Tall. Broad shoulders. Moving like the forest belonged to him.

She drew a breath. Now or never. She slipped down a slope and cut through a line of glowing ferns, circling until she reached a clearing ahead of him. She pressed her back against a tree, its bark holding a low, steady warmth.

Steps crunched through the undergrowth. She stepped into view.

The boy stilled, his stride breaking mid-step. He didn't flinch, like someone raised in a world where danger was just theory, not experience.

His gaze locked on hers. She met it, steady.

Up close, he looked even taller. Lean, with a quiet strength that settled under his skin instead of demanding attention. His tousled dark hair caught the light like wind-ruffled bark, soft but unruly. His bronze-toned skin reflected the gold of one moon and the silver of the other, as if the sky itself had cast him in its light. His eyes, dark amber and steady, met hers. Focused, unguarded. Just... awake. Like he was used to seeing things that didn't fit.

"Who are you?" he asked.

"You speak English?" She blurted.

"I don't know what that is." His voice was calm. "I'm speaking my language."

She hesitated. "But I understand you."

He tilted his head slightly, studying her. "Then maybe you were meant to."

The quiet stretched between them. Not awkward exactly, just charged, like the air before a storm.

His eyes swept over her — the curls, the mismatched tones, the nervous way her fingers twitched at her sides. "You don't match," he said, like he was stating a law of physics.

Her brow arched. "That's your opening line?"

He shrugged. "It's true."

"Well, sorry I didn't consult the local dress code."

"You're not from here."

She gave a nervous half-laugh. "I live nearby."

"Nearby?" he repeated, unconvinced.

She pointed vaguely toward the trees. "Yeah, nearby. You know. Just... around the mossy bend."

He didn't move, but something in his posture said he wasn't buying it. He let a small grin slip. "You're not dangerous, are you?"

"No," Ivy tilted her head, all mock innocence. "Are you?"

He smiled, crooked and cautious, like it hadn't been used in a while. "No."

Something flickered across his face. "I'm Ambry," he said.

She smiled. "Ivy."

He paused, still watching her. "Where is your family?"

"Nearby."

His expression softened, just slightly. He lifted his chin, a quiet challenge in the gesture. "All right, keep your secrets."

Ivy stared at him too long and only snapped out of it when she realised her face had twisted into a weird grin all on its own. Her brain screamed, abort. Her mouth naturally ignored it.

She yanked her gaze toward the nearest tree. Tall, with broad square leaves hanging in heavy folds from a thick central stalk. They looked like moss-green blankets strung high in the air, their surfaces catching a faint shimmer as they swayed. "Cool trees," she blurted. "Big fan of the moss drapes. Very... interior design-forward."

Ambry watched her, his crooked smile giving way to a low laugh. "Do you always sneak out late at night?" he asked.

"Only when the moons look interesting."

He glanced up. "They do tonight."

"I thought so."

Silence again. Not uncomfortable, just... full. Like neither wanted to move in case the moment shattered.

Ivy's fingers toyed with the pendant at her neck. "So... I'm new here. And I was just wondering, I mean, not wondering, more like... asking? Do you think you might, maybe, sometime... want to show me around? Or not. That's... fine too."

He studied her for a long second. "Why?"

She frowned. "Why?"

"You don't look like someone who follows."

She opened her mouth. Closed it. Then said, "Okay, rude. But fair."

She shifted her weight, trying to sound breezy. "I don't really know how anything works yet." The pitch of her voice betrayed her.

He looked at her again. Longer this time. Then said, "Okay.... Tomorrow. Meet here."

Ivy nodded.

He turned and then glanced over his shoulder. "You'll come back, right?" The words weren't teasing. Just quiet. Like he wasn't used to asking.

Ivy nodded quickly. "Yeah. Totally. I mean, yes. Obviously. Unless I, like... fall into a moss pit or get eaten by tree fungus. But otherwise? Yep."

"You are strange." He shook his head, laughing like he meant it as a good thing.

Then he turned without another word and headed into the trees, his silhouette fading slowly between trunk and shadow. She watched him disappear into the silvered dark of the forest.

Ivy stood there, the echo of his words buzzing in her chest. Her cheeks hurt from smiling. It wasn't just the novelty of it, it was the fact that someone had looked at her and seen her. Really seen her. After months of silence, of parents speaking only in soft science and soft steps, that crooked smile had cracked something open. It felt like sunlight on the skin after too many winters.

She had met someone new. A real someone. Her age. And she hadn't exploded, fainted, or totally humiliated herself.

... Well. Not completely.

— ✦ —

They met again. And again. And over the next three weeks, it slipped into a rhythm neither of them broke. Always at night. Always in the forest, halfway between her hidden world and his.

Ambry taught her how to move through the trees — how to place her steps, how to watch the ground — and the names of the plants and insects they passed along the way. He called the planet Spero, not just its name, but something deeper. Like it wasn't a place they'd discovered, but one he belonged to.

Ivy had always thought of it as Veritas-9, the mission. The target. But hearing him say it like that... it landed differently. Like the name itself had roots.

She hadn't told him the truth, not all of it. Just the version that sounded safe. That her parents were explorers, and they were here to map the region and study its ecosystems. That her uncle handled their supplies and helped with the fieldwork. She'd never been to school, always travelling, always learning on the move. And her parents were strict about strangers, which is why she kept their meetings secret.

She said she'd grown up in distant regions, far from this part of Spero. If she ever slipped and mentioned something from Earth, she brushed it off as stories from another region, one he'd never heard of.

Ambry never questioned her stories. He took each word like it was the truth, no suspicion, no hesitation. Which somehow made it worse. Every time she left something out, it felt like a crack she was putting in the middle of something solid.

Still, she brought pieces of her old life. A freeze-dried ice cream cube once — chalky, crunchy, and deeply offensive to Ambry's food sensibilities. She nearly cried laughing at his face. Sarcasm, stories that sounded too strange for Spero. She even sang once, quietly and off-key, a line from a song Ambry would never know. 'Just a small-town girl...' He'd tilted his head, confused. She didn't explain.

"You're... loud," he said once, after she made fun of a glowing beetle.

She laughed. "That's what we call having a personality."

He smiled, that sideways, hesitant smile that made her chest ache. "It's not a bad thing. Just different."

The forest settled into stillness again. Ivy crouched beside a low-slung fern, its curled fronds lit from within — faint threads of violet and copper winding through the dark, dusted in silver pollen that shimmered like stars on velvet. The quiet here wasn't empty. It sparkled, full of breath and waiting.

Soft night-chirps threaded through the undergrowth. Not quite insect. Not quite bird. Somewhere between a trill and a fluttering hum. Overhead, a squirrel-possum hybrid darted along a branch, its tail curling like smoke behind it. A sweet, spicy scent drifted from a broken vine above, the kind of smell that made your lungs ache from breathing too deep.

Glowing creatures, firefly-small, drifted low near the roots. Their feather-lined bodies pulsed between soft pink and gold, the glow rising and fading, slow-moving, delicate. They hovered in spirals, like thoughts you hadn't quite finished thinking.

Ivy's gaze lifted, drawn to the movement. "What are those?"

Ambry knelt beside her. "Lumibugs," he said.

She watched one drift past. "They look like they're glowing."

"They are." He paused. "They'll match you."

Ivy turned toward him. "What do you mean?"

He didn't answer. Just lifted a hand to her shoulder. "Hold still," he said.

Something light shifted against her back. A moment later, his hand came into view, a small creature clinging to his fingers.

The same leaflike butterfly that had landed on her when she first arrived in Spero now held still on his hand, its veined wings catching the light, almost too perfect to be real.

"They usually camouflage against the trees," Ambry said softly. "But they've been landing on you all night."

Ivy leant closer. "I've seen these before," she said. "What is it called?"

"A Leafwing." He said.

"Leafwing..." Ivy echoed, the sound of it tugging at her memory. "That name sounds familiar..."

"It looks like your pendant," Ambry said, "the wings."

Ivy raised an eyebrow. "My necklace is spying on me?"

He rolled his eyes. "I'm being serious."

She examined the creature, then glanced at the pendant. "Okay... yeah. That's mildly creepy."

"Maybe," he said. "Or maybe you're more local than you want to admit."

She laughed, soft and brief. The Leafwing lifted off, drifting into the dark, and both of them followed its flight. Just beneath their gaze, the pendant pulsed, electric-blue light threading the veins of its bronze leaves for the briefest heartbeat. Neither of them noticed.

Ambry lowered his hand. "They listen for what's true," he said. "Resonance, my grandmother called it. Like the planet responds to people who are... aligned."

Ivy frowned. "Aligned with what?"

Ambry shrugged. "I don't know. My grandma said a lot of strange things."

She gave him a look. "That's helpful."

He smirked, not offering more.

A few of the gold-specked firefly creatures looped between them again, hovering low near her hands. Ivy watched, not moving.

"They really do like you," Ambry said.

She glanced at him. "That's... not normal, is it?"

"You're not," he said gently. "Not in a bad way. Just... you glow sometimes. Not light. Something else. It's like the forest leans toward you."

Ivy gave him a slow, teasing smile. "You've been watching me?"

"I've been trying not to," he said.

They held each other's gaze.

The hush between them settled, easy and unhurried. High above, leaves drifted in a slow, soundless sway, moonlight brushing their faces in pale, shifting patterns. A low hum shimmered through the branches, faint and rhythmic, echoing in her chest like the beat of something shared.

And Ivy felt grounded. In the sound, in the light, in him.

Chapter Fourteen

Over the next few weeks, their connection grew like roots beneath the forest floor. Slow, quiet, inevitable.

Ivy didn't notice it at first. A conversation that ran late. A silence that felt like music. A glance that lingered longer than it should've. Then one night, she found herself waiting for the sound of his steps. Half breathless, half angry at herself for needing it.

She craved the calm in his presence, how he never filled the silence with questions. He just let her be. He didn't flinch when she was sarcastic or strange or asked three questions before he could answer the first. With him, there was no urge to fix her. He didn't seem to think she needed fixing.

He didn't stare at her like a problem to solve.

He just... saw her.

But the truth pressed against her ribs like a blade she couldn't dislodge. She hadn't told him who she really was. Not where she came from, not why she was here, not the truth about her family. Every time his gaze met hers, open and steady, it made the secret heavier. She wanted to tell him. The words formed behind her lips sometimes, pressing forward like they had weight of their own. But she couldn't risk it. Not yet. The moment she spoke the truth out loud, the world would split into before and after, and she wasn't ready for that crack to form.

One night, they sat beside a still forest pool, its surface catching glints of moonlight through the trees. A thin waterfall trickled from a rock shelf nearby, soft as a breath, threading sound into the quiet. A few tiny insects hovered over the water, their wings catching the shimmer like glass shards. Ivy watched the light ripple across Ambry's face — not bright, but enough to make everything feel suspended, weightless. Ambry reached for a glowing pebble and rolled it between his fingers. "You like the dark, huh?"

"Not really," she said. "It's just... easier."

"Easier to hide?" His voice was gentle, his eyes still on the pebble.

He set it down with care.

She didn't answer.

Ambry rubbed his thumb against the heel of his hand, a small, absent motion she had noticed before. Like he was trying to calm something inside him without letting it show. Ivy's gaze caught on it, softening. It was the tiniest tell, but somehow it made him feel even more real. Not flawless. Just trying. Just... honest. "There's a place I want to show you. It's called the Singing Vale."

She turned to him. "That's... dramatic."

"It's earned," he said with a crooked smile. "You've never heard the wind move like this. The vines gleam with sound. The whole grove vibrates."

"Sounds... beautiful."

"It is." His voice eased into fondness. "We used to go all the time when I was a kid."

She glanced over. "Family trip?"

He nodded, a quiet warmth in his eyes. "One time, my parents took us, all of us. My little brother Riven spent the trip climbing everything he wasn't supposed to, laughing because Dad had to chase him. My little sister Mirae tried to talk to the vines, and Thess got her foot stuck in a glowing puddle and screamed like it was lava. My mum laughed so hard she cried."

The memory softened his features. "The light there... it comes through in layers. Gold on green, like the whole place is always in motion. And the sound—" He gave a small shake of his head. "It hums. Low and soulful, like music your body already knows."

He turned to her. "But it doesn't sing at night."

Ivy's chest tightened. "Ambry..."

"I know," he said before she could finish. "I'm not trying to push. I just—" He glanced at her, something raw flickering in his eyes. "I want to show you my world. Not just these quiet slivers in the dark. The real parts. The places that shine when both suns are awake."

She looked down, curling her fingers into her palms. She hated how much she wanted that. How badly she wanted to say yes. How close she was to tearing down everything her parents had warned her about just to hear him say her name in daylight.

But she couldn't. Not yet.

Still, she didn't move away when he reached for her hand. He didn't take it, just let his fingers rest near hers, like an offer she could accept or ignore.

Her hand stayed still, but her whole body felt like it was humming. Like the space between their fingers was charged, waiting to close. She didn't dare breathe.

Maybe this was what belonging really was. Not roots, not blood, not history. Just this. Someone seeing you and waiting. Not demanding, not explaining. Just... there.

And maybe, for the first time, she wanted to reach back.

Even if her hand wasn't steady enough to close the distance yet.

CHAPTER FIFTEEN

The morning air inside the POD was warm and stale, laced with the familiar scent of sterilised gear and metal. Ivy stepped out of her alcove, yawning as she pulled her hair into a loose ponytail.

Grace didn't look up from the bench. "You slept in."

"Morning to you too," Ivy said, tugging on her boots.

"You missed the morning check-in."

"I'll survive." Ivy yawned again. "Assuming the local fungi haven't unionised overnight."

"Ivy, this is not a joke. We are on an unknown planet with unknown dangers. We don't know the pathogens, the predators, or what kind of ecosystem we've landed in. You don't get to treat this like you're on some sort of school holiday."

"Oh no, not the pathogens again," Ivy groaned. "I swear, if I had a dollar for every time you and Dad said that word, I could buy my own planet and catch diseases in peace."

"You're still my daughter." Grace said. "And this isn't Earth."

"I noticed." Ivy moved to the counter and started sorting sample flasks without asking what Grace wanted. The silence between them thickened, growing heavier with every clink of glass, so brittle it felt like one more breath might crack it.

She didn't say it, but the message was still clear. Grace controlled every part of this mission, and Ivy's life was no exception.

A shadow passed the small viewport. Gareth.

Ivy glanced toward the door, then back at Grace. No reaction.

She slipped outside, quiet as a thought.

The light was already strong, casting long shadows across the packed dirt. Gareth sat on a crate near the edge of the clearing, adjusting the straps on a sensor pack. His back was to her, but he looked up as she approached.

"Escaped the lab, huh?" he said.

"Mum was setting up for another pathogen monologue," Ivy said, brushing a stray curl behind her ear.

Ivy sat beside him, fingers toying absently with the chain around her neck. The metal was cool against her skin, the familiar weight of the pendant resting there.

She lifted it gently, the chain sliding through her fingers as the pendant caught a flicker of sun. It felt heavier than she remembered, or maybe she was only noticing the weight now.

"Do you know where your mother got this?"

Gareth didn't answer right away. His fingers stilled on the pack, then resumed, slower.

"Not exactly."

She let the pendant swing gently between her fingers. "It looks like it belongs here."

That got him. For just a second, his mouth twitched, almost a smile. Almost. "Maybe it does," he said.

She hesitated, then said, "There are creatures here, small, with wings like leaves. They land on me sometimes."

Gareth turned. "You've seen them?"

She nodded. "Their wings look just like this. Like it was modelled after them."

"Interesting," he mumbled, but didn't offer anything more.

She hesitated. "Gareth... I have to tell you something."

He looked up again, eyebrows raised.

"And I don't want you getting mad."

She twisted the pendant chain tighter around her finger. "I went near the village. And I met someone."

"A boy," she said after a breath, quieter now. "Ambry."

Gareth didn't flinch. Didn't even blink. Just kept watching her, his face unreadable.

Ivy stared at him. "Wait — Gareth? You knew?"

He stayed silent, turning back to the sensor pack.

"Oh, my god. You totally knew." Her voice pitched up. "How long? How long have you known? Does Mum know? Does Dad?"

A low chuckle escaped him. "If your parents knew, Ivy, they'd have launched you back to the EOS before you finished your first conversation with him."

She let out a shaky breath — half laugh, half relief. "So... that's a no?"

"They don't know. But you're not exactly subtle."

"Oh," she said, then looked down at her hands.

"I didn't mean for it to happen. I wasn't... looking."

She pressed her hands into her lap. "But he's just... there. And real. And kind. And I think part of me was waiting for someone like him, even if I didn't know it."

Gareth's focus shifted to her, his expression unreadable.

"I don't want to just watch this planet through a viewport," she said, the words spilling faster now. "We're only here for a year. That's it. And then twelve more years in transit. I'll be middle-aged by the time we get back to Earth."

Her voice cracked. "Gareth, I just want to feel something real while I still can. I want to see the places Ambry's been telling me about. I want to feel sunlight without hiding."

He didn't answer right away. Just kept looking at her, like he was trying to see past the words. Past the guilt and the need and the hope behind her eyes.

"You're asking me to go against your mother," he said finally. "To break protocol. To cover for you."

Ivy nodded. "Yes."

He leant forward, eyes narrowing. "Okay," he said, nodding thoughtfully. "I'll help you. But carefully. Quietly. And only when I tell you."

Ivy exhaled, her shoulders dropping with relief. "Thank you."

For a few moments, they just sat there, the only sounds the hum of insects and the soft creak of the trees overhead. The air was warm. Still.

"You look like them, you know," she said. "The people here."

Gareth gave a faint smile, but it didn't reach his eyes. "Oh?"

She nudged his knee. "It's true. Grey hair, slate eyes, old-man skin tone — you're basically a monochrome art piece."

"Charming," he said dryly.

Her laughter faded into a thoughtful hum. "No, really. You do look like them. Isn't that weird?"

He didn't respond. He bent over the pack again, securing a clamp with fingers too steady to be casual.

For the first time, Ivy saw the silence he wore, not just a habit, but armour.

Maybe she'd only ever known the parts he let her see.

And maybe the rest wasn't meant for her.

Chapter Sixteen

Grace wasn't thrilled. That much was obvious from the way she didn't even look up, just tightened her grip on the stylus like it had personally insulted her.

"This isn't a sightseeing trip," she said, her voice clipped. "We have protocols."

"I'm aware," Gareth said evenly. He stood beside the lab's central console, arms folded, close enough for his voice to carry but leaving her space to work. "But we're running out of viable sample zones near base camp. The next ridge has a completely different microclimate. It's worth investigating."

Grace still didn't look at him. "You mean the one Ivy's been suspiciously curious about?"

Ivy looked up, glancing around like she'd just been name-dropped in a trial. "It's called being observant," she muttered, then cleared her throat and tried again. "I've just... noticed things. The ground, I think? It echoes weirdly when you stand near it. Like, the sound kind of bounces, not normal bounce, but weird bounce. Like there's... layers? Or maybe a tunnel? Or... I don't know, maybe a giant sleeping worm."

She winced. "Not an actual worm. That was a metaphor. Sort of."

Gareth said nothing, but his mouth twitched as if he were holding back a smile. "It's a high-probability biome split. If the terrain readings are right, and that ridge is layered beneath the surface, we could find new species. Possibly edible flora. Or resistance-grade compounds."

David looked up from the console, tilting his head toward the data stream. "He's not wrong. That patch has weird interference, the last scan came back scrambled. No terrain map. Just heat, echoes and static."

Grace finally looked up, fixing Gareth with a stare sharp enough to cut wire. "And you think it's a good idea to take a teenager into unscanned territory?"

"I think," Gareth said calmly, "it's better than having her sneak off to explore it alone."

That landed. Hard.

The air in the POD changed, subtle, but sharp. David turned toward Ivy, as if he was trying to decide if she'd already done it.

Ivy froze, then picked up a flask and began repositioning it like its angle would save lives. She didn't say anything. But she definitely didn't not look guilty.

David's mouth twitched. Not quite a smile, but close.

"She won't be alone," Gareth added. "I'll be with her. We go in with full sample gear, monitor the environment, and log everything. No stunts. No deviations. One week, max."

Grace's expression didn't change. But the pause said plenty.

"Controlled variables. Measured risk. Your rules, remember?" Gareth said, his voice softening. "We can either lead the expedition... or get left behind by it."

Grace exhaled slowly, as if she could blow the whole argument away with breath alone. Her fingers loosened on the stylus. Just slightly.

"One week," she said finally. "Keep your comms open. If you hit anything suspicious, you come back. No stunts."

Ivy tried to look grateful. Mature. Responsible.

But her mouth betrayed her.

"Yes, mother," she muttered under her breath. The second it left her lips, she squeezed her eyes shut, bracing for the fallout and wondering if she'd just nuked her own permission slip.

Grace's jaw flexed.

David coughed, definitely a laugh this time, and went back to his scans. Grace ignored him. Gareth arched a brow at Ivy as if to say, really?

Ivy lingered a moment, then turned toward the hatch. Heat prickled at the back of her neck, and her stomach pitched in that twisty, nervous way that always came right before something really good or really stupid.

Permission granted. Now she just had to make it count.

And wait until dark, so she could sneak out and tell Ambry before she exploded.

CHAPTER SEVENTEEN

The next morning, Ivy and Gareth set out with full packs and fabricated gear. The path was narrow but clear, curving along the edge of a moss-lined ridge before dipping into low, sun-dappled undergrowth. Ivy followed just behind, her boots brushing loose bark and fallen leaves. For a while, neither of them spoke. The air held that strange early hush — not silence, exactly, but a kind of waiting.

She caught up beside him. "Hey," she said quietly. "Thank you. Thank you for doing this for me."

Gareth didn't look over, but the line of his jaw had softened, just enough to take the edge off his words. "You'd have done it without me."

"Maybe," Ivy admitted. "But I'd rather not."

They walked on in step until the trail widened, opening to a break in the trees. At the bend, Ivy spotted Ambry waiting just beyond the treeline, one hand resting casually on a tall, vine-covered stone.

She turned towards Gareth. "That's him," she said, pulse skipping. Not from surprise, but from a rush of something warmer. She hadn't realised just how much she'd wanted this moment, Ambry here, meeting Gareth.

Gareth squinted. "Looks like he's been waiting."

Ivy didn't answer right away. She caught his eye across the clearing. He straightened slightly, like the moment mattered to him too.

When they reached him, Ivy nodded toward Ambry. "This is Ambry," she said, her voice lighter than expected. "Ambry, this is Gareth."

Gareth didn't offer his hand, just gave him a long look. "So you're the one she keeps meeting out here."

Ambry met his gaze evenly. "Only when she asked."

Ivy's eyebrows lifted slightly at that. Her cheeks warmed.

Gareth folded his arms. "So this is the spot?"

Ambry glanced around, then tipped his head toward the clearing behind him. "Yep, figured it might suit for setting up your camp."

Gareth's brow lifted slightly.

"High ground, suitable cover, and there's a spring about fifty steps that way." Ambry nodded to the east. "Safe enough for the week."

The tension in Gareth's shoulders eased by a fraction. "Is your village far from here?"

Ambry held steady. "Treliv," he said, "not far, just over the ridge."

Gareth studied him for another second.

Ambry tilted his head. "What about you? Where are you from?"

Gareth's expression didn't shift. "Nearby."

Ambry gave a single nod, like he'd expected that.

Ivy bit back a grin. It was like watching two wild animals circle, cautious but curious.

Gareth turned, but before stepping away, he pulled Ivy aside.

"I need to check something," he said. "There's something I've been looking for, and today feels right. I'll need a few hours. You good here with him?"

Ivy gave him a look. "You're not just here for samples."

He didn't confirm or deny. "Are you good with him?"

Her gaze drifted to Ambry. He wasn't pretending to be charming or helpful. Just... present.

"I'm fine," she said.

Gareth's eyes lingered on Ambry a moment longer. "He so much as looks at you sideways, I'll plant him so deep in the forest his brown tones'll blend right in with the soil." The words were pitched straight at Ambry.

Ivy smothered a laugh. Ambry, to his credit, just blinked.

"Noted," he said.

With that, Gareth turned and walked into the trees without another word.

Ambry came to stand beside her, voice low. "He doesn't like me."

Ivy raised a brow. "What are you talking about? That was practically a hug and a fruit basket."

Ambry's smile softened. "He's comfortable here."

Ivy shot him a quick look. "How can you tell?"

He glanced after Gareth. "He moves like he's used to walking where paths aren't marked."

A quiet moment passed.

Ivy looked up at him. "Thanks for coming."

He met her gaze. "Thanks for asking."

She tried not to smile. Failed.

Ambry turned toward her, a spark of interest in his voice. "I really want to see this place. 'Nearby' sounds fascinating."

Ivy tilted her head, feigning thoughtfulness. "Maybe one day. But today we need to set up this camp. Make it nice and comfy. A whole week away from my parents."

His smile curved. "A whole week."

She gave a mock-serious nod. "With adult supervision, don't worry."

Ambry laughed under his breath. "Terrifying."

He eyed the gear Ivy had dropped beside a low-branched tree. "That's what you're sleeping in?"

She followed his gaze. "It opens up," she said, lifting one corner. "Promise it's less tragic once it's standing."

"If you say so." He stepped closer, curiosity winning over caution. "What's it made of?"

Ivy hesitated, then shrugged. "Multi-layered polymer mesh with embedded solar weave. Breathable. Self-insulating."

Ambry nodded slowly. "Huh."

"You say that like it's impressive," she teased.

"It is," he said, still studying the way the material caught the light. "We use woven barkcloth or pressed shimmervine mats back home. Strong, flexible. But this..." He crouched and ran two fingers gently over the fabric. "It looks like water and light got stitched together."

Ivy watched him, something warm tugging at her chest. It was the way he noticed things — how he moved like everything deserved his full attention.

"Can I help?" he asked, standing.

She glanced toward her gear, then back at him. "Oh, yeah. That'd be great."

He helped her unfurl the dome, and when it sprang open with a smooth shffft, Ambry stepped back surprised. "You'll live in that?"

"Only for a week," she said with a laugh. "We've got beds, climate mesh, heat regulation. The usual."

Ambry gave her a long look. "You're not like anyone I've met before."

Ivy reached for the rope. "Good different?"

He grinned. "Still figuring that out."

They got to work with the kind of quiet ease that surprised her. Ambry moved confidently, showing her where the slope leveled off best, where tree limbs interwove just right for anchoring a rain tarp. He handed her rope and stakes, and Ivy fell into rhythm, pretending she totally knew how to do this.

"So," he said casually, looping twine around a branch like he'd done it a hundred times, "you set up camp like this often?"

Ivy smirked. "Oh yeah. Me and my tragic dome skills go way back."

He raised an eyebrow.

"We move around a lot," she added quickly. "I've... picked up a few things."

He nodded, smiling. And Ivy felt it, how easy it was with him. She could hold things back and still feel understood. She drove a stake into the ground with more force than necessary, trying to shove down the flutter in her chest.

They finished the tarp, cleared a patch of soft earth beneath it, and ringed a fire circle. When they were done, Ivy stood back and nodded approvingly.

"Well," she said, brushing dirt off her knees, "that definitely counts as survival."

Ambry tilted his head. "One tent?"

Ivy smiled. "Gareth's just making sure I don't go sneaking off after dark. Which is... fair."

Ambry stood back, eyes scanning the camp. "Come with me," he said simply. "I have an idea."

She followed him through the trees, the air soft, brushed with shifting light. The path opened into a towering grove — Kavari trees, Ambry had called them — their broad, square leaves hanging in layered tiers high above. Each one hung from a single thick stalk fixed at the very centre of its surface, the weight pulling the surrounding leaf forward until the heavy folds draped in slow, deliberate curves. The surface shimmered faintly with mossy light, the kind of sheen that shifted as the tiers swayed overhead. Beneath, the air felt warmer, the ground patterned with deep green shadows.

Ambry paused beneath a lower branch, scanning the tiers overhead. "These are ready."

"For what?" Ivy asked.

His smile crept in, slow and deliberate. "Interior design, obviously."

She snorted. "Right. And actually?"

"Sleeping, mostly."

With practiced ease, he pulled himself onto the branch. His hand found the thick stalk where it joined the centre of the first leaf, fingers curling around the base. He eased it upward, then gave a firm, clean pull. The stalk came free with a muffled snap, the surrounding leaf sagging into his grip before he let it drop. It fell in a slow, deliberate descent, the heavy folds swaying just enough to catch the light before settling at Ivy's feet.

He reached for another, twisting it free with the same clean motion, and let it fall beside the first.

"They hold warmth better than anything else," he said, landing beside her. He gave each stalk a quick twist, snapping them free from their thick central joints and leaving a round scar in the middle of both leaves. Folding them over his arm, he added, "You'll sleep better with one, Gareth too."

Back at the camp, they laid the Kavari leaves inside the dome. Ivy smoothed hers out, surprised by how soft it felt beneath her fingers, almost like fleece, but cool to the touch.

Ambry adjusted the second leaf neatly at the far end of the tent and stepped back.

"It's like the forest grows its own bedding," she murmured.

Ambry laughed, soft and genuine. "Are you hungry?"

"Kind of. Why?"

"Come on." He held the tent screen open, letting the mild afternoon air drift in. They stepped out into the clearing, the open ground warmed in soft sunslight. Ambry crossed to one of the short, worn logs around the fire pit and dropped onto it, nodding to the space beside him.

He reached into his bag — it looked to be handwoven from thick green vines, rough and practical — and pulled out two tightly wrapped leaf parcels. "Glowroot flatbread stuffed with emberroot."

She took the offering, surprised, and sat on the log beside him. "You brought food?"

Ambry shrugged. "Didn't know what you'd have. Thought it made sense to bring something for both of us."

Her gaze flicked to him, the weight of it catching her off guard. Not just the food, but the way he said it, like it was obvious. Like caring for someone was as ordinary as breathing.

The bread was still warm, soft and springy between her fingers. The first bite hit her with layers of flavour she wasn't ready for — toasted grain, something citrusy-sweet, and a hint of spice that warmed the back of her throat.

Ivy took another bite, chewing slowly. It tasted real. Like something grown in sunlight, not rehydrated in a foil pack.

They sat quietly together, watching the light shift through the trees. A few glass-winged insects flickered overhead, catching sparks of blue as they drifted in lazy loops.

Ivy tilted her head. "Those always show up when things feel... clear."

Ambry followed her gaze. "Yeah. I've noticed that too."

She studied his profile, the way the soft light edged his jaw, how relaxed he looked here. Like the forest recognised him.

"This is going to sound weird," she said quietly, "but sometimes... it feels like this place makes more sense than anywhere I've been."

Ambry turned toward her, one brow raised. "That's not weird."

"No?"

He shook his head. "Maybe it just feels like home?"

Something caught in her chest at that.

Before she could answer, movement stirred in the trees. Ivy glanced up and spotted Gareth's shape returning, slower now, moving with a different kind of focus, a small bundle of moss and vine samples slung across one shoulder.

"Your shadow's back," Ambry murmured.

Ivy smiled faintly. "Mm, let's not encourage him."

They both stood. Gareth said nothing, just glanced around camp, then gave a brief nod. Not quite approval, but maybe the closest he'd offer.

"You built this?" he asked.

Ambry tipped his chin toward Ivy. "Team effort."

Gareth's gaze moved from the tarp, to the fire circle, to Ambry. "Sturdy."

Ivy bit the inside of her cheek, hiding her grin.

"Good," he said at last, like the word had earned its way out. "I'll get the gear."

As he moved toward his pack, Ivy glanced at Ambry.

"Tomorrow," he said quietly, "I'll take you to the Singing Vale."

A quick thrill shot through her.

"Okay." She couldn't stop the grin that followed. "But if it's a cave full of glowing spiders, I'm leaving you there."

Chapter Eighteen

The next morning, Ivy walked along the forest's edge, the twin suns casting long shadows behind her. The air smelled of citrus and ashwood, warm and oddly clean. She moved in silence, each step pulling her further from camp... and further from Grace's rules.

A rush of energy tightened through her, sharp, like she knew something was about to change. This wasn't her first time out with Ambry, but it felt like the start of something. Like she was on the edge of a story she hadn't been told yet. She glanced down at her boots. Too dirty. Then smoothed her braid. Too neat? Ugh.

She was halfway through debating whether or not to undo it when she spotted him through the trees, leaning against a low branch like he'd been born waiting.

"You're late," he said, grinning.

"I'm early. You're just weirdly punctual."

He handed her a fist-sized fruit, its skin dappled and smooth like riverstone, the colour somewhere between peach and firelight. "Eat."

"What is it?"

"Sweet. And keeps your voice from cracking in the valley wind."

"You're making that up."

"Only a little."

Ivy bit into it. The flesh gave easily — tart at first, then honey-smooth, like citrus with better manners.

"Okay. Not bad." She licked juice from her thumb. "What's it called?"

"Talli fruit."

She gave a slow nod. "Right. Talli. That clears nothing up."

He grinned, already moving. "Come on, the best part's just ahead."

They moved quickly, ducking between bark-smooth trees and fields of nodding stalks that chimed when brushed. The ground grew firmer as they descended. One moment, they were moving through dense undergrowth — ducking under looped vines, skirting fern-wrapped roots — and then suddenly, it was gone. No last branch to push through. No obvious line of transition. Just stillness, like the trees had collectively decided to stop existing for a while.

The valley opened below them, and her gaze locked on it, unable to take in enough at once.

The Singing Vale stretched wide before her, shallow and soft-edged, ringed in layered hills and haloed in mist. Pale green spilled across the grass like velvet. The suns hung low in the sky, casting long shadows and pulling streaks of colour through the upper air. Ribbons of light shimmered overhead in quiet waves. Not quite aurora, not quite storm, soft and slow, like the sky was breathing. Light swept across the moss in soft strokes, scattering through mist and pooling in the stone basins like liquid dawn.

Everything in her body stilled. Then came the sound.

Not music. Not exactly. But something vibrated in the air, a layered hum that curled behind her ribs.

She turned slowly, taking it in. The ground sloped gently into a basin, where a scatter of upright stones stood like sentinels. Some were smooth and rounded, others jagged, weatherworn, all of them towering taller than a person. And each one had narrow, oval hollows, smoothed by wind and time until light passed through.

Wind moved in waves, soft then sudden, and every time it shifted a new note emerged. Not a whistle. Not a moan. Something finer, hollow and harmonic, like glass tuned in a cathedral. The stones didn't echo each other; they layered, weaving into one steady, unbroken chord. Vines along the far rock wall rippled in slow, tidal pulses, their leaves glowing faintly. Even the ground beneath her boots gave off a tone so low it barely registered, more feeling than sound.

Harmonious. Like a hundred instruments tuning themselves in secret.

A narrow stream wound through the centre of the vale. Its water was impossibly clear, soft stones, tangled roots, the curve of light shifting as if the world had nothing to hide. When it pooled in shallow stone basins, it made a sound she didn't have words for.

A chime maybe, but cleaner. Like the idea of a bell before the bell even existed.

Ambry stood beside her, just outside the light, his arms folded loosely over his chest. But his eyes never left her.

Ivy turned in place slowly, taking it in. "This is… unreal."

Ambry's gaze drifted to the vale. "Yeah. It sneaks up on you."

"It feels like I remember this place," she said. "Like I'm catching up to a memory I haven't made yet."

He didn't answer, but that crooked half-smile appeared. Quiet, lopsided, familiar. And just like that, her heart betrayed her again, a soft skip like it wanted to admit something she wasn't ready to say.

They walked in silence; the stream glinting ahead, weaving its soft rhythm through the trees. When they reached the bank, Ivy settled on a broad, flat boulder, brushing her fingers over its sun-warmed surface. The stone was smooth under her palm. Something shifted in her chest, not loud, but there. Like a note she almost recognised.

Ambry watched her. "You feel it, don't you?" he asked.

"It's like I'm in rhythm with everything. Like… for once, I'm not two beats off from everyone else." The words came out low, more honest than she meant. "Does it always do this?"

He shook his head. "No. Some days it's just wind and rocks. But other times…" He glanced around the vale, then back at her. "Other times it leaves a mark."

The words were rooted somewhere deep.

She looked around again, slower this time. The vale wasn't just beautiful, it moved like it was part of one whole rhythm, just… resonating. And somehow, Ivy felt like she matched it.

Ambry dropped onto the broad, flat boulder beside her, leaning back on his hands like he belonged there. The silence stretched. When he finally spoke, his voice had dropped, softer now, like the quiet had settled over him too.

He glanced at her. "It sounds different with you here."

Ivy didn't answer. She didn't trust her voice. Or maybe she just didn't want to break whatever spell was holding them. She turned away before her face could betray her.

She tilted her head back, eyes half-closed, letting the sunslight slide across her skin like water.

Beside her, Ambry was quiet, watching her like he was memorising the shape of her in this light.

She turned, caught his gaze. The space between them tightened, pulling her in before she could think. His eyes held hers, steady and warm, and for a breath it felt like the air had its own gravity — drawing them closer, waiting for the smallest movement to close the rest.

Suddenly, a noise unlike anything Ivy had ever heard before shattered the silence. A deep, guttural bark cut through the vale. Branches cracked, followed by the heavy thump of paws tearing through undergrowth.

Ivy shot to her feet, heart jerking into her throat.

Something barreled from the trees. The size of a dog, but stockier, rounder, with thick, soil-dark fur streaked in mossy greens and warm, forest browns. Its paws were massive, stone-like, skidding through the mist like a boulder off its leash. Bioluminescent freckles shimmered faintly along its sides, soft green pinpricks that pulsed as it moved. Its tail curled over its back like a thick fern-frond, and its wide, intelligent eyes locked on Ivy as it let out a bark more thunder than sound.

Ivy stumbled back, breath caught somewhere too high in her throat. Her boot slipped on the edge of the stream, arms flailing for balance. The thing kept coming. Paws pounding. Eyes locked. She barely had time to blink before—

"Brax!" Ambry's voice cut through the clearing, firm and sharp.

Ivy staggered back as the creature barreled into her legs, all mossy fur and thumping tail. Brax let out a pleased, rumbling huff, nuzzling against her like she was the best surprise he'd smelled all week.

For a second, the only sound was Ivy's breath punching out of her chest. The creature tilted its head, then let out a softer huff — less bark, more grunt — and sat.

Like it had just remembered it had manners.

A high-pitched voice squealed from behind the trees.

"Brax! You're not supposed to tackle people unless they smell bad!"

Ivy turned at the sound of footsteps and saw a little girl — six or seven, barefoot — charging in from the tree line. Her curls bounced wildly, deep bronze in the shifting light, and her eyes sparked amber-bright beneath messy lashes.

She didn't slow down.

The girl launched herself straight at the creature, flinging her arms around its neck and burying her face in its mossy fur like it was a long-lost teddy.

Brax whuffed softly, then nuzzled her with the gentlest brush of his bark-textured nose.

Ivy caught her breath. "What even is that? A mini bear?"

Ambry squinted. "A mini what?"

"Big, furry thing. You know, nature's worst roommate for campers?"

Ambry squinted. "Roommate?"

Ivy waved a hand. "Forget it." She looked over at Brax. "He's... friendly?"

"Mostly, he's a Muruun. He's good at reading moods," Ambry said. "But he still tackles Laz when he laughs too loud."

Then a splash. A yelp. A triumphant squeal.

The little girl was knee-deep in the stream, chasing something small and fast that darted under the roots. Brax bounded in after her with all the grace of a boulder, sending water everywhere. Ambry didn't even flinch, he just stepped in and caught her by the back of her tunic before she went under.

"You're supposed to observe, remember?" he said, the words already wearing a smile.

She beamed. "I am. I'm observing it go really, really fast."

Ambry lifted Thess with both hands, and set her down squarely in front of Ivy, ruffling the girl's curls. "Ivy, this is Thess. My little sister. She's usually less feral."

"Hi, Thess. I like your... bear dog," Ivy said, smiling.

Brax shook out his fur, soaking all three of them. Ivy gasped, laughing despite herself as cold droplets hit her arms and neck.

Ambry handed Thess a talli fruit from his pouch. "Bribe him out of the water. Otherwise, he'll eat anything that glows in there."

"He's got taste," Thess said proudly.

The moment hadn't vanished, not really. It had just... shifted. Domestic. Real. A different kind of harmony. She followed Ambry up the slope from the stream and settled beside him, the grass cool under her palms.

Thess offered Brax the fruit with both hands. He took it delicately between his teeth, then flopped onto the grass with a grunt that sounded suspiciously like satisfaction.

Ambry turned as a second girl padded into the clearing. She looked about nine, with golden-yellow skin, sun-honey eyes, and a halo of soft curls the colour of blooming daffodils. She carried a jar of something pink and fizzing, and her expression held the kind of dreamy calm Ivy had only ever seen in sleepwalkers or prophets.

"You dragged Mirae into this too?" Ambry gave Thess a look.

"Technically, Brax brought us," Thess said, all innocence. "But only after we asked him to track you."

Mirae sighed. "She bribed him with solari paste."

"Worked, didn't it?" Thess beamed.

Ambry turned back to Ivy. "Thess," he said, "is our chaos elemental. And this," he nodded to the newcomer, "is Mirae."

Mirae tilted her head. "You're not like the others."

Ivy scratched the side of her head. "Um.... Is that... a good thing?"

The girl smiled, like she already knew the answer. "I think Brax likes you."

Thess pointed, grinning. "He ran straight up to her like he knew her."

"Exactly," Mirae said, reaching out to scratch Brax's fur. "And now he's humming."

Mirae came forward and sat beside Ivy as if it were the most normal thing in the world. She uncorked her jar and offered it to her.

"It's a skyvine pod," she said. "Makes your tongue tingle."

Ivy took a pink fruit, hesitated, then bit into it.

Zing — like pop rocks on her tongue, but brighter. She jerked back with a muffled yelp, hand flying to her mouth as the fizz lit up her tongue. "Okay... wasn't ready for that."

Thess burst out laughing from the water. "Your face! Ivy, you should've seen your face!"

Ivy wiped juice off her mouth, trying to look unimpressed. "You could've warned me. That was more than a tingle."

"That's the best part!" Thess yelled, already splashing again. The girls exchanged grins.

Ambry nudged her arm. "You survived your first Thess encounter. That earns you points."

She snorted. "Bit aggressive for a welcome party." Her voice softened. "Your sisters are amazing."

Ambry's smile came slow, crooked and warm, the kind that slid under your skin and made thinking optional.

Ivy looked away before she did something stupid. Like smiling back too hard. And for the first time in her life, Ivy didn't feel like she was borrowing space. She felt... included. And the shock of it settled like weight across her chest. She didn't know it could feel like this. That she could fit.

She closed her eyes.

And in the middle of a planet she didn't understand, beside a boy who wasn't asking for anything, Ivy felt something she hadn't even known she was missing. And the Vale sang, a low hum held steady, like the world had hit the right pitch and wasn't ready to let go.

She opened her eyes and cleared her throat. "So..." She glanced sideways at him. "What exactly is solari paste?"

Chapter Nineteen

The climb wasn't dangerous. That's what Ambry said anyway, right before she nearly lost her boot to a clingvine.

"It likes warm ankles," he said, tugging her up. "You've got to move fast or it'll snuggle in."

Ivy yanked her foot free, then looked up. The treetops parted just enough for light to spill through in slow, golden ribbons, and nestled in the branches above were swollen, bulbous hives, textured like knotted wood and honeycombed stone.

"There," Ambry said, pointing. "Velmiir hives. They only open in the morning light."

Above them, the buzz grew louder. Not aggressive, just constant, like the steady hum of a shared workload. Dozens of tiny winged insects wove in and out of the hive, their translucent bodies catching the light. They moved more like pollinators than guards, their wings a blur of motion, their legs dusted with amber pollen. One hovered near Ivy, pausing mid-air as if registering her, then zipped away again.

"Velmiir bees," Ambry said. "They make the solari. Harvest from sap vines and cave blooms."

Ivy watched them for a moment, wide-eyed. "You have cave bloom bees. That feels important."

The nearest hive caught her eye just as a seam peeled open like a yawning mouth, revealing a swirl of thick, golden paste. It shimmered faintly, catching the light like melted glass. She leant in, the sweet, nutty warmth already flooding her nose.

"Oh, my god. Is that—" She slipped past Ambry, clambering up the branch like it owed her answers. "Is that peanut butter?"

"Peanut what?" Ambry said. "That is solari."

"It smells like peanut butter." She dipped a finger into the glistening hive and tasted it. Her eyes widened. "Oh, my god. This is peanut butter! But better, like it was made by forest gods with culinary degrees."

Ambry laughed. "You always say weird things when you like something."

She swirled another finger through the hive. "Tell my family I love them... but I live here now."

She licked the paste off her finger. "Oh! We should bring some back to your siblings."

"We could try," Ambry said. "But Mirae will hoard it in her sock drawer. Thess will try to bathe in it."

His grin widened. "Riven complains when there's none left, but always saves the last bit for Thess."

Ivy smiled. The buzz of wings eased, and the leaves slowed their sway, like the moment held still, just for them.

Ambry didn't say anything, but he lingered beside her, one hand resting lightly on the branch. His usual alertness, that scan-the-horizon kind of calm, had softened. He just balanced there, watching her scrape another dollop of solari out of the hive like it was the best thing she'd ever discovered.

The quiet stretched. Not awkward, just full. Like the pause between words you don't want to break.

She met his gaze. "What?"

He shrugged. "You're just... really into solari paste."

"It's a core memory now," she said, mouth full. "There's a before-solari Ivy and an after-solari Ivy. Totally different species."

Ambry chuckled, low and warm. He didn't climb higher. Didn't remind her to be careful. Just stayed, like this was exactly where he wanted to be. His fingers brushed the bark absently, but his gaze never drifted, like if he looked away, the moment might change.

When she turned back, he was still watching her, like she was something worth noticing. Just calm. Present. Like something had settled behind his eyes.

She offered him a bit on a leaf. "Forest diplomacy?"

He accepted it with a grin, the edges of his fingers brushing hers as he took it.

"This is ridiculous," she said. "How are you not up here every single day?"

Ambry tilted his head slightly. "Did they not have this in your part of Spero?"

She froze for a moment. The kind of question someone wouldn't think twice about. But it hit like a dropped stone. She knew he didn't mean anything by it. He wasn't accusing. Just curious. But it cracked something anyway, a quiet line between belonging and pretending.

She fumbled for the hive again, scraping her finger along the edge like it suddenly demanded all her attention. "We... didn't really have trees like this," she said. "It was more... industrial. You know, less golden peanut goo hanging from the trees, more... steel and noise and metal and... Bolts! Lots of bolts. Super thrilling."

Ambry wiped his fingers on his pant leg. "How many siblings do you have?"

The question also caught her off guard. "Me? Just... none. Only child." She hesitated, then tacked on, "Spoiled rotten. Practically raised by algorithms."

He squinted. "Algorithms?"

"Never mind," she said quickly. "It's a really boring village thing."

She scrambled for a new subject. "That clingvine, how it grabs for you. Do all plants do that, or is that one special?"

"What do you mean?"

"You know," she said. "Grass leaning toward people. Flowers opening when people get close, leaves curling around your leg. That kind of thing."

He tilted his head. "Only the clingvine I think. It only grows around the Velmiir trees, protects the hives."

"So nothing else does that for you?"

Ambry's brow furrowed. "Not that I've noticed."

She nodded like it didn't matter. Even though it did.

"Mirae talks to them sometimes," he added after a beat. "Swears the Kavari near the grove lean in when she sings. She says the old vines by the crystal spring only bloom if she tells them a story first." His mouth curved into a smile, fond but guarded. "Maybe they just like kids better."

Ivy gave a laugh and looked away before it turned into something real. "She sounds like my kind of person."

She leant back into the crook of the tree, wiping her hand on her pant leg, wishing she could wipe the last few moments just as easily.

Her gaze drifted upward, fixed on the treetops, like she wasn't quite ready to meet his eyes.

They stayed a little longer, feet swinging. The forest below was still, the hive's hum filling the space where the truth should have been.

CHAPTER TWENTY

T he forest buzzed with soft, hidden life — rustles, chirps, and the steady pulse of wings. Somewhere behind them, a flock of green-bellied shrieks — tiny forest birds with piercing calls — flitted between the high branches, calling to each other in irregular bursts. Ivy stood barefoot in the shallow creek, cool water curling around her ankles as she scooped a handful over the back of her neck. Ambry sat nearby on a sun-warmed rock, legs stretched out, gaze following the shrieks drifting through the trees.

Gareth knelt beside his supply bag, pretending not to listen, but the tilt of his head gave him away.

They were gathering enough samples to make it look official. Just enough for Grace to believe this week-long 'expedition' hadn't been a total detour.

Ivy dipped a sample vial into the creek, scooping up a frond of riverweed, slippery and pale green, like translucent ribbons. As she sealed the lid, she flicked a bead of water at Ambry, smirking.

He didn't smirk back.

"Did you ever think you were different?" he asked, not looking at her.

Ivy stared at him. "Me? Constantly."

"No, I mean—" He scratched at the back of his neck. "When you were a kid. Did you feel things that didn't match what was around you?"

She tilted her head. "I think I just... never fit right. I was the weird one no one could figure out."

Ambry gave a slow nod, his gaze fixed on the ripples in the creek. "Same. I just didn't know it wasn't normal."

Gareth stilled, his hands hovering over the supply bag.

"When I was younger, there was this boy," Ambry said. "Toven. He cried when his sister got sick. Got angry when he failed a test. Nothing huge. Then one day, I saw him in the markets, yelling at his mum for not buying him something, and the guards came. Two of them. They didn't say anything. Just took him. The next day, he didn't show up at school."

She straightened, water dripping off the sample vial. "You lost a kid for shouting?"

"They said he got moved. For support." Ambry's voice was flat. "He came back a few days later, calm, quiet, 'normal.'" He glanced at her. "Everyone acted as if that was good. Like it meant the support worked."

He looked down. "Part of me thought maybe I needed that too... help. Except I couldn't stop seeing the guards, the way they looked at him before he left. I was eight. They scared the hell out of me."

He rubbed his thumb against the heel of his hand. She'd seen the habit before, but it seemed sharper somehow now.

"I watched that happen and thought... I can't let that be me. So I copied the others. Smiled when I was supposed to. Laughed on cue. Made my voice soft. My hands still. My face calm."

Ivy moved to sit beside him, saying nothing. She just watched the way his shoulders stayed tight, like even now, he wasn't sure if he was allowed to say it.

"I thought I was the broken one," he said. "Because I couldn't let go of how I felt. So I buried it."

He met her eyes. "Then you crashed into my life and felt everything out loud. Like it was okay. Like maybe it's okay that I felt it too."

Ivy didn't move. Something in her wanted to reach for him. Something else wanted to hide.

Gareth glanced between them, then back to his samples. A hush settled around them, forest sounds soft and scattered, like everything had paused to listen.

"You're not broken," Ivy said softly. She let the words sit for a second, then added, "It's normal to cry when someone's sick, or to yell when things feel wrong. That's human. That's sane. Honestly, if you're not terrified pathogens might steal your children in the night, that's when I worry."

Ambry huffed a laugh, shaking his head. "You haven't seen what I have."

Gareth rose and slung the pack over his shoulder. "Ambry, you were never broken," he said. "You felt what others couldn't. Or wouldn't. That doesn't make you wrong, it makes you real."

"Just... awake in a world that teaches sleep."

Ivy tilted her head. "That's... a strange way to put it."

Gareth shrugged. "Just something I overheard." He adjusted the strap on his shoulder as if that might explain the weight behind the words.

But Ivy wasn't sure he meant it that way.

Ambry exhaled. Ivy brushed her fingers against his. His skin was warm. He didn't pull away. Instead, he turned his hand and laced his fingers with hers.

Ivy glanced up at him with a small smile.

"You know," she said, "you're my favourite kind of not-normal."

Ambry looked at her, a smile tugging at his mouth. "Is that supposed to be romantic?"

"Extremely," she said. "It ranks just under 'guy who brings snacks' and slightly above 'guy who doesn't get weirded out when I say stuff like this.'"

He chuckled. "Well, I did bring the snacks."

"Exactly." She gave his hand a gentle squeeze.

CHAPTER TWENTY-ONE

The next day, Ambry took Ivy to explore the local markets. The air smelled of citrus and smoke, and something sweet she couldn't place. Not just any kind of sweetness, something rich and sticky and warm, like roasted nectar. Stall after stall lined the winding stone paths, canopies stretched high above in patchwork hues, casting jewel-toned shadows over the crowd. Vines twisted around every post. Bioluminescent fruits glowed faintly in bowls of water. Nothing was static. Light pulsed. Colour shifted. Music swirled through the air like mist — not loud, but ever-present, stitched into the rhythm of footsteps and laughter.

Ivy stuck close to Ambry. He took it all in stride. No sighs, no sarcasm, just quiet patience as she peppered him with questions and marvelled at the glowing produce like a tourist. But today, his usual calm felt thinner, like a thread stretched too far. His smile still flicked up at the right moments. He still gave polite nods and a soft smile as he tapped a silver card against the counter, a chime marking the payment. From behind the man's leg, a little girl peered out, watching him with wide eyes. The vendor slid over a small notebook, its cover softened and scuffed, bound in a strip of waxed cloth. Ambry handed it to Ivy with a quick grin, and she couldn't help smiling back.

But Ivy had learned to read silences, and Ambry's were suddenly louder.

A pair of guards turned the corner. Not marching, just walking, unhurried. They wore sleek charcoal uniforms, the fabric close-fitted and seamless, reinforced with black plating across the chest and shoulders. The matte finish caught no light, engineered for silence. Each suit bore a high collar fitted with a narrow receiver loop, and stamped dead-centre on the chest plate, the red emblem of the Order:

a circle encasing a single vertical line and a downward-pointed triangle. No one spared them a glance.

Except Ambry.

He didn't panic, he just... changed. His shoulders curved in. His gaze dropped. One hand casually brushed Ivy's arm, like he meant to guide her toward a stall, but it was too smooth. Too careful.

She glanced around. A child nearby watched the guards with curious eyes, but no fear. A vendor joked as they passed. Someone else waved. Ivy stared, trying to decide if this was normal... or just normal here.

"Are you still hungry?" She asked him, trying to keep it light. "That starfruit thing looks edible... maybe."

Ambry didn't answer, just waited until the guards were well past. His hand brushed the stall counter like he needed to ground himself. Ivy reached for him, fingers brushing his lightly, but he let go almost immediately. "We should go," he said, eyes tracking the guards.

The quiet held as they left the ridge and crossed into the valley, the sweep of grass bowing in the breeze around them. Sunslight pooled in the low ground, warm on their backs, until the first dark line of forest began to rise ahead. They were halfway down the trail when she said, "Is that what you meant? About controlling yourself?"

Ambry didn't respond right away, leaves crunching under his boots.

He gave a dry exhale. "Yeah. But a lot of people are scared of the guards," he said finally.

She shook her head. "No, they're not."

He looked at her.

"They smiled at the guards," she said slowly. "They waved. They barely looked twice. It's like... the guards are part of the scenery. Like no one even thinks about them."

She stepped in front of him, stopping them both. The air between them tightened, like something unspoken had finally caught up. "You don't have to do that," she said quietly. "They're not going to hurt you for having feelings."

His jaw shifted, holding back the words before they formed.

Then, without looking at her, he said, "You don't know that." His voice was steady, but low. Flat in a way that didn't match the breeze or the path or the calm of anything else around them. "You don't know how many people I've seen get taken," he went on. "Dragged in for a conversation, and when they came back, they weren't the same."

Ivy's chest pinched. She knew he was scared, that whatever he'd lived through had left old wounds behind. She just wasn't sure the world shifted the way he saw it. But she could still feel the weight of what it meant to him.

Ambry finally looked at her. "You don't know what they're doing. You haven't seen it."

Behind them, the valley grass shifted in the wind. Gold, quiet, untouched. Just ahead, a flicker of orange light drifted into view. One of the prism-winged creatures. It pulsed once as it passed between them, then veered off and vanished into the dusk.

She knew that look, the ache underneath it. She'd spent her whole life trying to be the right version of herself, bending around expectations, chasing approval she wasn't sure she wanted. And now here was Ambry, doing the same thing with every step, every breath. Not careless, not cold. Just trying to fit in enough to stay invisible. It broke something in her, because she understood it too well. The weight of always performing. The loneliness of never feeling safe to just... be.

Some hurts didn't have answers, so she found his hand in the quiet, and together they continued down the trail.

And this time, he didn't let go.

— ✦ —

Ambry's village felt like nothing Ivy had ever seen — not in books, not in archived footage, not in any of the old movies she'd grown up watching.

Weeks ago, she'd crouched in the treetops, spying on this very town with a racing heart and dirt under her nails. Even then, it had felt like something out of a story. Up close, it was no less magical. Homes built from living bark and crystal-veined stone flowed in spirals and curves, tucked into a sun-dappled valley where everything moved in quiet rhythm. Roofs shimmered with sun-fed moss. Children played barefoot near a spiraling water structure that sang as it turned. There were no machines, only organic constructs shaped by knowledge Ivy couldn't begin to understand.

And the people.

They moved like dancers. Graceful, fluid, all of them hued in harmonious colour sets. A woman with deep green skin and kelp-coloured hair passed by, her eyes gleaming the same bright green. A pair of siblings, both sun-bright orange with coppery curls, laughed and tossed floating seeds between them. It was… beautiful. Effortless. A chorus of colour, every note in a different tune.

Ambry glanced at her. "People might notice you don't fit the pattern," he said, voice low. "Don't let it get to you."

She looked down at her pale bronze skin, fiery red curls, and blue eyes. Yep, she didn't just stand out, she glitched the whole aesthetic.

"That's my house," Ambry said softly, nodding toward a wide, woven structure nestled at the base of several Kavari trees. Their thick trunks rose straight through the roof, branches layered with broad square leaves hanging in slow, heavy folds, the mossy surfaces softening the late-afternoon light. The walls were formed from living wood, coaxed into shape without severing life, curved and weathered smooth by time, not tools. A stone chimney rose off one side, smoke curling gently above the treetops. A wide porch wrapped the front, draped in woven mats and strung with wind chimes that tinkled softly in the breeze.

"But we've got a little hideout nearby," he added with a quiet grin.

They continued along a winding stone path, its surface set with smooth, iridescent rocks that caught the light like riverglass, and passed beneath a woven arch tangled with pale blossoms. Beyond it, a grove opened up, bathed in golden light. Lantern orbs hung between trees, strung like stars across the branches. Hammocks swayed gently between trunks, some scattered with woven blankets and small bowls of strange fruits Ivy couldn't name. The ground was layered with moss and softwoven mats, dappled in filtered sun. Everything felt carefully grown rather than built, as if the grove had shaped itself to be lived in.

Two boys lounged in hammocks braided from silken vines, legs dangling lazily. One straightened instantly, blue-toned skin gleaming like polished steel, dark spiked hair, eyes sharp as frost. "Ambry," he called. "You brought the outsider."

"Be nice, Riven." Ambry gave him a look. "Ivy, this is my little brother."

Ivy offered a smile. "So you're the infamous sibling," she said. "Ambry didn't mention you were so much cooler than him."

That earned a skeptical huff from Riven, but he looked her over again, curiosity sharpening.

"Don't fall for it," said the other boy, grinning. "She's trying to recruit you."

"Recruit me?"

"For the rebellion of weirdos," Ivy said, perfectly straight-faced. "We meet at lunch. Bring snacks."

"Laz," Ambry added, gesturing to the second boy. "This is Ivy."

The boy had skin like rose quartz, with tousled magenta-pink hair and bright fuchsia eyes that flicked like sparks. He wore loose, soft-woven pants rolled to the calf and a half-buttoned tunic, its sleeves faintly smudged with oil. A loop of fine wiring circled his wrist like a bracelet, delicate coils of copper and crystal-fibre, braided with tiny tech components like jewellery made from spare parts. His grin was pure mischief, like he was one bad idea away from brilliance.

"We were starting to think you made her up," Laz said, giving a lazy salute from the hammock, halfway between mockery and charm.

Seated beside them on a bench that seemed to grow directly from the trunk of the largest Kavari tree — its curves shaped by nature into smooth, inviting arcs — sat a girl Ivy hadn't noticed at first. Legs tucked neatly beneath her, poised and watching. Ambry followed Ivy's gaze and offered a faint smile. "That's Nyra," he said, then turned to the girl on the bench. "Nyra, this is Ivy. She's... new here."

Her amethyst skin gleamed in the sunslight, every line of her posture poised and deliberate. Deep-plum hair spilled over her shoulder in perfect waves, catching stray beams of light like strands of silk. Her silver-lavender eyes were locked on Ivy, cool and unreadable. A small, knowing smile curved her lips, the kind that said she'd already decided things about you that you hadn't said aloud. She was stunning, regal without trying. Perfect in a way that felt practiced.

"Ambry's new project," Nyra said smoothly, voice soft and cool.

"I'm not a project," Ivy replied. "I'm more of a challenge."

That earned a smirk from Laz and a surprised snort from Riven.

Ivy and Ambry settled onto a softwoven mat near a cluster of glowing stones that pulsed faintly with warmth. Riven tossed her a piece of fruit carved into a flower, and she caught it with a grin.

She glanced between them. "So... are you all from here? I mean, this village?"

Laz's expression shifted slightly — fond, wistful. "I used to live here, actually. Near Ambry. We were the terror twins of the village. My dad got a job in the city when I was ten, so we moved to Domaris. But Ambry and I reconnected during civic rotation, tech archives. He broke things, I fixed them."

"I broke nothing," Ambry said.

"Sure you didn't," Laz said, grinning.

Ivy looked toward Nyra. "And you, Nyra?"

"Domaris," Nyra said — crisp, cool, clipped. "Like Laz. Just... higher."

Ivy tilted her head. "How'd you meet these two, then? Laz and Ambry?"

Nyra's expression didn't shift. "During civic rotation. Same assignment."

Ivy studied her. "So what's Domaris like?"

Nyra paused, then said in a voice smoothed to neutrality, "Efficient. Structured."

Laz leant closer to Ivy and stage-whispered, "Translation, cold and boring."

Nyra didn't look at him, but her lips curved. Just barely. Like maybe, despite herself, she didn't completely disagree.

A small voice broke the moment. "Nyra! Are you coming to braid with us later? You promised."

Ivy turned to see Thess bounding over from the house, her bronze curls bouncing as she ran.

Nyra's features softened a fraction. "Of course, Thess. I never break a promise."

The girl beamed and ran off again, barefoot and humming. As she passed Ivy, she waved enthusiastically. "Hi!"

Ivy smiled and waved, caught off guard by the warmth.

Laz smirked. "She likes Nyra better than me. Not that I'm bitter."

Nyra didn't respond, but a faint warmth lingered in her posture.

"Where's Mirae?" Ivy asked Ambry.

He nodded towards the trees. Mirae sat beneath a tall Kavari, a pair of leaf-shaped insects balanced on her fingers, their wings shifting in slow colour. She whispered to them, her movements unhurried, as if she kept time to a rhythm no one else could hear. A gentle light warmed her eyes, soft with curiosity.

Laz added, "She once told me a tree sang her a lullaby. I believe her. Honestly, she's probably half-spirit."

They lingered in the grove, surrounded by neighbours who moved with an easy joy. It wasn't a festival, not officially, but something in the air felt like a celebration. People shared food in woven bowls, music drifted between homes, and laughter echoed through the trees. They talked, laughed, and swapped stories about strange school rituals and awkward village festivals.

Ivy picked at the fruit in her hand. "Do you all go to school together? Like actual classes?"

Laz grinned. "We used to. Learning groves, holograms, elder guides, civic rotation. You know, the usual."

"We finished earlier this season," Ambry added. "School ends at eighteen out here."

Nyra's voice slipped in, soft and dry. "Though some of us graduated with more distinctions than others."

Laz gasped in mock offence. "I brought a leaf to class once and called it a thesis. They passed me out of pity. Or concern..."

Nyra rolled her eyes.

Ivy tilted her head. "So... do you all have jobs now? Or like, what happens after school?"

"We will," Ambry said. "But not yet. Most people take time after school ends. Reflect, rest, spend time with family."

"We all still live at home," Laz added with a shrug. "No rush. You're not kicked out the second you graduate."

"So what kind of jobs are there?" Ivy asked.

"In the outer villages, pretty much anything," Ambry said. "You choose your civic role based on what you're good at. Growers, techs, carers, cultivators. No applications. No interviews. Just... figure out how you want to contribute and show up."

He glanced toward Nyra. "Roles in Domaris are a little more regulated."

Nyra offered a condescending smile, small and polished.

Ivy laughed, then shifted slightly. "So what do you want to do? I mean... when you start."

Ambry glanced out toward the trees, where light filtered through layers of Kavari leaves. "I want to shape new villages," he said. "Design places that fit into the land, not overtake it. Homes that feel like belonging. Like peace. Somewhere people walk into and think... yes. This is home."

Ivy smiled at him. "That's... beautiful."

She turned to Nyra. "What about you, Nyra?"

Nyra's posture stayed flawless, her tone clipped. "I've been offered a position within The Order. A strategic role in my father's division. High placement. High credits."

"Oh," Ivy said, "That sounds... sensible."

Nyra's eyes drifted, just slightly, toward Thess and Mirae, where they sat braiding vines in the amber light, Mirae giggling as Thess proudly wove in a flower. "Sometimes I think..." she said softly, "I'd like to go into education. Work with the learning groves. Help shape the younger ones." Her voice held a rare warmth. Almost wistful.

Then, as if snapping a thread, she straightened. "But The Order is important. Structure matters. And the credits are unmatched."

Ivy said nothing. The warmth in Nyra's voice had vanished so quickly, it almost didn't feel real.

"I'm going into tech," Laz said cheerfully. "All day, every day. Tech."

Ivy laughed. "Yeah. That definitely suits you."

He shrugged. "Give me something broken, I'll make it better. Or explode it. Either way, fun."

Riven snorted. "He wired a glowvine runner into a stump once and called it a mood player. It lit up and whistled every time someone walked past."

"You're welcome," Laz said, leaning back with a smug little grin.

"And you get paid in...?"

"Credits," Ambry said. "They load to your card at the end of each day, based on the work you've done."

Laz tugged a smooth metal card from his pocket and handed it over without ceremony.

Ivy turned it in her hand. It was smooth and solid — a sleek, rectangular slab of layered metal, its surface shifting subtly between silver, bronze, and black depending on the angle. A faint etched symbol curled near the corner, like a crest.

Ivy handed it back to Laz.

Laz took it. "Belongs to my dad. I don't have my own yet." He grinned. "But it still buys snacks, though."

"And if you lose it?"

Laz shot her a look. "Why are you looking at me when you say that?"

Ivy didn't answer, just shrugged with a grin.

"Wow," Laz muttered, tucking the card away.

"Then you lose your credits," Ambry said. "The council can give you a new card, but it starts empty."

Ivy nodded, picking at an invisible mark on her sleeve. "And your language... has it always, I mean, was it always, like this?" She glanced up, quick and a little uncertain.

Nyra tilted her head slightly. "What an odd question."

Ambry shrugged. "So the story is, it was brought here a long time ago, by a man from the stars. He taught our people how to speak, how to write. The first Lightbringer."

"Some called him the Skyfounder," Laz added. "Old story, brought language, knowledge, then vanished into the trees or something."

Ivy's brow lifted. "Conveniently dramatic."

Ambry gave a half-smile. "You know how history is, half fact, half story."

She stared across the grove. The traditions, the rituals, they were so similar to Earth's in spirit, and yet entirely different. It was like being dropped into a dream stitched from things she half-remembered.

Riven squinted at her. "Didn't you go to school?"

"I was homeschooled," Ivy said smoothly. "My parents are travelers. Scientists. We were never in the same place for very long."

Riven leant toward Laz and whispered, "What's a scientist?"

Laz gave a tiny shrug.

Then Nyra leant forward, eyes fixed on Ivy. "You ask a lot of questions," she said, polished, sharpened. "But you don't answer many."

"I'm just... curious," Ivy said.

"A little too curious, I'd say."

Nyra's voice didn't rise. If anything, it softened, which somehow made it worse.

"And where are you from?"

Ivy hesitated. "Nowhere in particular. We moved around a lot. My parents are explorers. We never stayed in one place for very long."

"Funny," Nyra said dryly. "Earlier you said they were scientists. Now it's explorers. Which is it?"

"B–both," Ivy said, the word catching slightly. "They're both."

"So where were you before here?"

"Just... travelling," Ivy said carefully.

"Travelling where?"

Nyra's tone stayed light, almost curious, but her gaze didn't move. "Which regions? What cities?"

Ivy hesitated. "Mostly isolated work zones. Research sites. I don't always know the names." Her throat felt dry. She hated how rehearsed it sounded, because it wasn't.

Nyra studied her like a complex equation. "Your colours, your eyes, your hair, they don't match. No ancestral blend I've seen would result in that."

Ivy's hand drifted up, brushing her curls back from her face without thinking.

"Who are your parents? Where are they now?"

Ivy's shoulders tensed. "That's a lot of questions."

"And I haven't even started."

Ambry leant slightly toward her. "Nyra. Ease up."

Nyra stared a moment longer, then sat back with cool grace. "Just watching out for my friends."

"Nyra! We're ready!" Thess called from across the grove.

Nyra turned toward the girls with a quiet smile, smoothing her sleeves as she stood. "Mirae, come on. Let's go braid before Thess explodes."

Mirae looked up instantly, her face brightening. She jogged over barefoot, insects forgotten, and Nyra bent to meet her, arms open without hesitation. Mirae leapt into them, wrapping herself around Nyra's waist like her place had always been right there, no permission needed.

Nyra moved with steady, fluid grace and offered a hand to Thess, who grabbed it with a squeal. The three of them disappeared into the house, warm light spilling from its open doorway, laughter and ease trailing behind.

The moment they were gone, Ivy let out a slow breath. "What was that about?" she asked.

"Nyra's smart," Ambry said. "Too smart. She's not out to get you, just… raised to notice everything. Her dad is head of The Order."

Ivy frowned. "What's The Order?"

"They control everything — Domaris, government, education, civic records. Everything official traces back to them." Ambry said.

Ivy's chest tightened. "And Nyra's dad is… in charge?"

"More like owns it," Laz muttered. "And probably half the city too."

"But that wasn't curiosity," Ivy said. "That was… something else."

Ambry didn't argue. He just watched the house where they'd disappeared, brows drawn low.

Laz nudged a stone with his foot. "She means well. But sometimes it's like she's playing five moves ahead of the rest of us. Always has been."

Ivy played with a loose curl. Something about the way Nyra had looked at her — sharp, measured, almost protective — was sticking in her chest like a pin.

Ambry stretched his legs out and leant back on his elbows. "There's a festival tomorrow," he said. "Aeylan Grounds. Food, music, dancing."

Ivy raised an eyebrow. "Should I be nervous?"

"Only if you're scared of fun," Laz said, tossing a pebble into a nearby bowl like it was a game he'd invented. "Oh, and hate crowds, noise, dancing, and enough food to question your life choices."

Riven perked up. "Glowfruit pies the size of your face. That's the real reason we go."

Laz grinned. "He ate a whole one last year and threw up in the river."

"Worth it," Riven muttered.

Ambry rolled his eyes. "It's tradition. A way of marking the shift between seasons."

"It's also the best time to swipe extra skyvine fizz while everyone's too busy dancing to notice," Laz added. "Not that we would ever do that."

His expression was so pure, Ivy almost believed him. "Sounds… kind of fun."

Ambry smiled. "You'll see."

"Tomorrow's a spectacle," Laz said, stretching like a cat. "Hope you're ready."

Ivy watched the trees sway above them, the glow of the grove settling into her bones.

She wasn't sure if she was ready for any of this.

But miss it? Not a chance.

— ✦ —

Ivy crouched by the fire circle at camp, poking at a small pot nestled in the coals. The air smelled earthy and rich — dried lentils and powdered potato from their ration kits, simmered with a small bunch of crushed green leaf Ambry had brought her from the markets that morning. It tasted as if pepper and mint had decided to team up.

The pot bubbled as she stirred, brow furrowed in concentration. Behind her, footsteps crunched through the undergrowth. "Took you long enough," she said without turning.

Gareth stepped into view, dirt streaking his boots, his pack slung low on one shoulder. "Didn't know I was on a timer."

"You weren't," she said, pointing her spoon at him. "But the food was. You're lucky I didn't start without you."

He dropped his pack beside a log at the fire pit and peered into the pot. "Smells like something died in there."

She grinned. "That's the rations. The green stuff's new. Ambry swears it's edible."

Gareth raised a brow, but didn't argue. Just settled onto the log and watched the pot steam.

After a moment, she said, "So where do you go?"

Gareth adjusted the strap on his boot without looking up. "When?"

"When I'm out with Ambry," she said. "Most days you're gone before I get back."

He rubbed his jaw. "Thought that was the deal. You get your Spero time, I stay out of the way."

"You vanish completely," she said. "What, do you have a moss-woven stealth cloak and a tragic backstory?"

That got a small smirk. "If I did, I'd use it to disappear mid-conversation."

"Wow. Hurtful. And here I was, stirring your questionable dinner with love." She narrowed her eyes. "Are you off whispering to trees or just doing weird Gareth things?"

"Depends on your definition of weird."

Ivy rolled her eyes. "Okay, be mysterious. But I'm serious. What are you doing out there?"

He was quiet long enough that she almost let it go.

"I'm tracking something old."

"Where?"

Gareth dug into his pack and pulled out the comms unit. "Some places on this planet hold on to their history, if you know where to look." He turned it over in his hands. "We'll have to touch base with your parents after dinner."

Ivy slowed. "That's not an answer."

"It's the best I've got."

"You're looking for something."

He gave a half-nod. "I'm following something."

Ivy ladled stew into two metal bowls and passed one to Gareth. "Don't burn your mouth," she said, settling across from him.

He gave it a cautious sniff. "Smells... complex."

"That's the mint-pepper-leaf thing," she said. "Shouldn't kill us."

"Comforting." Gareth took a tentative bite.

Then, as he set the bowl down, Ivy hit him with that look again. "So, what are you looking for?"

His expression didn't change. "You've got a real talent for pestering, you know that?" he said. "Supposed to be 'feeling the sunlight without hiding', remember?"

Ivy just smiled at him and took another bite of stew.

He looked at her, really looked. Something flickered in his eyes. He tapped against the rim of his bowl. "This place used to be ruled by what looks like a royal family," he said. "A long time ago. Then they vanished or were erased. I'm trying to find more information about them."

Ivy stilled, spoon halfway to her mouth.

"For the mission," he added.

She stared at him. "That's some theory for a few days of wandering around."

He took another bite of stew. "It started with the structures we saw in orbit. They look to be an old palace. It's overgrown now. But a lot of it's still intact. Like the place hasn't quite let go."

Her eyebrow lifted. "That's a lot of focus on ruins for a planet full of living, breathing people."

Gareth didn't flinch. "The people matter. But so does what came before them."

"Because of the old family?" Ivy asked, tilting her head.

A breeze stirred the trees around them. The fire crackled softly.

"You don't have to believe me," Gareth said, quieter now. "But something happened here. Something big enough to bury. And I need to know what it was."

Ivy didn't answer right away. Just watched him over the rim of her bowl.

Gareth set his stew aside, quiet for a moment. "Just promise me something."

She lifted an eyebrow.

"If things start to feel... off, like something under the surface is shifting, pay attention."

She hesitated. Then nodded once.

He gave a small, satisfied nod back.

A moment passed. Then Ivy said, "Ambry invited us to a festival tomorrow. Can we go?"

CHAPTER TWENTY-TWO

Set between the city and the villages — a symbol of equalism, Ivy guessed — the Aeylan Grounds gleamed like a cut gemstone nestled in the forest. Vast and open, every path curved in perfect symmetry, the gathering space stretching across a natural clearing ringed by smooth stone markers etched with old symbols, and panels that gleamed with captured moonlight.

At the far edge, a low platform rose from the clearing, slender posts marking each corner. Between them, banners of light-reactive silk drifted gently, glowing as soft as dusk. Low, rhythmic tones pulsed from hidden speakers, syncing with the crowd's slow, unified breaths.

Scattered throughout, tucked between pathways and set out beneath the open sky, were signs of celebration. Tables crowded with fruit carved into flower shapes. Woven baskets stacked high with glowing bread rolls. Garlands strung with living petals that shimmered softly as people passed. Children darted between adults, chasing one another in spirals, their lightpetal hoops flashing with soft bursts. Even the firebowls, perfectly placed along the paths, released plumes of scented mist instead of smoke, curling into the air like the festival itself was breathing.

The air buzzed with a quiet, waiting tension. It looked like a festival, but felt like a performance.

Ivy stood at the edge of it all, shoulder to shoulder with Ambry, Gareth, Nyra, and Laz.

A hush swept the ground as the platform lit up. From it, a projection unfurled. Not a person, but a figure of radiant white, faceless and tall. Its arms spread as if blessing the crowd.

"There was once wildness," the voice intoned — warm, sonorous, reverent. "The land was rich. The people lived in peace, scattered across the wilds, speaking in many tongues, guided by their own traditions. Beauty thrived, but without unity, there was no certainty." A slow bloom of golden light illuminated the figure's hands.

"Then came the Lightbringer. He offered alignment. A shared language. A shared vision. He spoke of preservation, harmony through structure, peace through design. Tools to sustain what was already perfect. Technology woven gently with nature, never in opposition."

The figure lifted its head. "And so, balance was refined. And through balance, order. A world where growth could thrive with certainty, and all hearts could beat in time."

Just below the platform, a line of figures stepped forward. Robes sleek, posture identical. The heads of The Order. At the centre stood one man, tall and composed, his deep red robes gleaming under the lights. He looked carved from fire and earth — copper-toned skin, ember-red hair, eyes steady and sharp. The others mirrored his posture, forming a silent arc like statues watching over the crowd.

Laz leant closer to Ivy. "That's Nyra's dad, Solen. The friendly neighbourhood overlord."

Ivy gave a soft snort, eyes darting from Laz back to the red-robed figure.

Nyra didn't deny it. Just exhaled softly.

Ivy tilted toward Nyra. "Is all of this true?"

"Parts of it," Nyra said, her gaze fixed on the projection. "The Lightbringer came from somewhere, that much is true. But every cycle, they sand it down. Erase the pieces that don't fit the message."

She gave a faint smile, but her eyes stayed sharp. "My father told me once, the Lightbringer was mismatched. Skin, eyes, hair — like you." Her voice stayed light, almost careless. "I guess that's why they blur him out now. Easier to hide the parts they didn't want seen."

Gareth watched, jaw tight, eyes sharp beneath a calm that looked brittle around the edges. There was no reverence in his stare, only contempt, quiet and simmering. It wasn't rage, and it wasn't grief. It was colder, the kind of silence that forms when you've lost something you can never get back, and learned to keep breathing anyway. He let out a low scoff. "Right. Harmony."

Laz, on the other hand, grinned. "Bet he was just a control freak who figured out how to sell matching robes," he whispered loudly.

Ambry let out a quiet laugh, arms loosely folded, his shoulders angled toward Laz. Ivy remembered what he'd told her, how crowds made him cautious, how he'd trained himself to stay still. But something in him had eased. He was still watching, still aware, but the tension had softened. Just enough to let the laugh out.

A child's cry broke the harmony. It sliced through the hum like glass — high, sharp, unmistakably human. The sound cut across the clearing and left a jagged silence behind it. Ivy turned, her eyes searching for the source. Two guards moved swiftly, gentle but sure, guiding the child and their parent toward the outer edge. No shouting. No force. Just the smooth, quiet removal of a disruption. Ivy's chest tightened. Above, a flicker of motion caught her eye, a tiny creature darting through the air, its feather-lined belly glinting in the light. It shimmered as it passed. Gold. Then blue. Then... black.

She felt it like a drop of cold water between her shoulder blades. The creature vanished into the trees. She turned toward Ambry, but his expression had settled back into that familiar stillness, mouth tilted in a faint smile, eyes reflecting the light but showing nothing. Whatever had softened a moment ago was gone. Or hidden.

On stage, the figure lifted its hands. A chorus of voices rose in perfect unison, praising the Lightbringer, vowing allegiance to harmony. And Ivy stood in the middle of it all, throat dry, pulse thudding in her ears. The sound washed over her, but her skin prickled. Tension had knotted through her fingers, slow and tight.

"Okay," Laz said, already scanning the crowd. "Creepy myth complete. Where's the snack tables?"

Ivy let the tightness in her fists ease slightly. She might not trust the story. But she could follow the smell of spiced bread.

Laz was already walking. "If they've got honey-glazed shimmer bulbs again, I'm elbowing a toddler. Fair warning."

Nyra fell in beside him. "There's usually solari paste on solarbread too. The diplomats pretend not to like it, but they always eat it first."

Ivy turned to catch up. "What's solarbread?"

Ambry tilted his head. "It's a grain that only grows under moonlight. The crust glows a little. You'll see."

Laz threw her a wink. "You're not officially a Spero citizen until you've cried over your first bite. Come on, newbie. Let's corrupt you properly."

As the others wandered toward the food stalls, Gareth caught Ivy's arm, a gentle touch, his eyes still fixed on the red-robed figures.

"I'll meet you back at camp," he said quietly.

She turned — but he was already walking the other way, slipping into the edge of the trees like a shadow peeled from the crowd.

CHAPTER TWENTY-THREE

The next day, late in the afternoon, Ivy walked to meet Ambry, bare feet sinking slightly into the soft earth, the scent of moss and sun-warmed bark thick in the air. She had spent the morning collecting samples with Gareth, knowing that tomorrow they'd be packing up camp and returning to the POD, back to Grace and David, and everything waiting there. Ambry hadn't said much, only that there was a gathering tonight, part of something called the Moonrise Pull. A yearly tradition when the two moons began their ascent and the ocean tides grew wild and luminous. Ivy didn't know what to expect, but she was determined to enjoy what might be her last taste of freedom.

Ambry had told her to bring something she could swim in. The thought alone had made her stomach twist. She'd never been in actual water, nothing untamed. Only filtered mist showers and sterilised water streams, controlled and lukewarm, surrounded by steel. She didn't even know what counted as swimwear here.

Eventually, she'd pulled on a simple tank and tight-fitting shorts from her sleep stash. The kind of thing that clung when damp, but wouldn't float away if she moved wrong. Not exactly graceful. But it worked. She'd thrown pants and a loose T-shirt over the top and tried not to think about it too much.

He was bringing her into his life completely now, showing her his people, his home, and she hadn't even told him where she was born. She was excited to see him, more than she wanted to admit, but her lies sat heavier with every step. They didn't belong here. And maybe... neither did she.

When she rounded a bend in the trail, Ambry was already waiting. He leaned casually against a ribbed tree, hair damp like he had just come from a quick swim, water still trailing down his neck.

His shirt stuck in darker patches to the lean strength of his shoulders. He looked completely at home here, like the forest had grown him from its own soil.

"There you are," he said, eyes lighting up like he'd been waiting all day just to see her.

She smiled despite herself, the nerves in her chest loosening just a little.

He pushed off the tree with an easy stretch. "Come on. We have somewhere to be."

They walked in companionable silence, the kind that didn't demand words but spoke volumes. Her heart raced, a cocktail of excitement and nerves. Ivy noticed the trees bending subtly toward their path, the grass thickening with every step she took, like the path was remembering their rhythm. Somewhere between her heartbeat and the rustling leaves, an unspoken thread of connection pulled taut between them.

The trail wound through glowing reeds, narrow enough for just one of them to pass. Ambry moved silently ahead, and Ivy followed, buzzing with anticipation, nerves sparking in her chest like static. She had met Ambry's friends, his family, but tonight was different. Tonight, she'd be stepping into a crowd, her first real social gathering since the day she was born. When they reached the final ridge, the forest fell away, and the world opened.

Below them, a crescent beach unfurled in the last golden light of day. The twin suns sat low over the treeline behind them, their shared glow stretched long across the sand in mirrored ribbons of gold and flame. The ocean lay flat and glassy, a seamless pane of turquoise shot through with luminous blue, holding the sky's reflection like a secret. It didn't glow yet, but the promise shimmered on its surface. Along the far edge of the bay, dark stone outcrops jutted from the shore, cradling shallow pools left behind by the tide. They glittered like scattered mirrors, catching fragments of sky and sun in their glassy surfaces. Tall strands of seagrass swayed gently in the salt-kissed breeze, tracing lazy arcs through the air.

At the centre of the beach, a steady bonfire crackled, its flames catching the driftwood with bursts of gold and green. Smooth-cut logs and woven mats formed a loose circle around it where Ambry's friends — Laz, magenta hair gleaming, and Nyra, regal and watchful

— laughed and moved through the fading light, their silhouettes shifting like part of the tide itself.

There were others too, at least twenty more, clustered in little groups. Some with musical instruments that seemed grown from crystal and wood, others weaving bioluminescent reeds into glowing strands that wrapped around their arms. The air was filled with music, laughter, and the scent of roasted fruit. Ambry turned, offering his hand. Ivy didn't think, she just moved, sliding her fingers into his like it was the most natural thing in the world. Together, they stepped onto the sand, casting gold across their skin in waves that flickered with the flames.

A girl greeted them first, dressed in a sea-glass green bathing wrap that clung to her figure like flowing tidewater. Her skin was a soft jade tone that shone faintly in the firelight, with eyes like pale green quartz and curls the colour of fresh moss pinned up with delicate crystal clips.

Ambry smiled. "Ivy, this is Sela. She's one of the Gatherers. If you've ever tasted anything good around here, it probably came from her."

"First Pull?" Sela asked.

Ivy nodded, and Sela's expression softened. "Then start with this." She pressed a delicate leafcup into Ivy's hand.

Ivy took a sip, it fizzed on her tongue like tasting sunlight. Bright, electric, unforgettable.

"It's fizzing up my nose," Ivy spluttered, laughing.

Ambry grinned. "Skyvine Fizz, Moonrise tradition. First time's the best, because you don't know what to expect."

Ivy squinted at the drink. "Wait — is this from the same fruit Mirae gave me?"

"Yeah," Ambry said, tipping back the rest of his cup. "Mirae eats them raw like a dare. This is the fermented version, with a few wildflower additives to make it sing."

Ambry took her hand and guided her past the firepit. "Come on, do you know how to dance?"

"Dance?" Ivy asked nervously.

They moved between groups of teens sprawled on sun-warmed sand and woven mats, stepping around half-finished sand sculptures that glowed faintly with embedded crystal shards. Ambry pointed out a boy balancing empty skyvine leafcups in a wobbly tower, daring passersby to knock it over, or beat his record.

Near the fire, music spilled from a trio. One plucking a harp made of curved wood strung with crystal-thread, another tapping a drum carved from glowing bark that lit with each strike, and a third whistling through a flute grown from sun-dried seaweed. The sounds layered into a rhythm that felt born from the sand itself.

Another group of teens danced barefoot in the shallows, their feet stirring light from the water. Ambry tugged her gently toward the music. "Come on," he said with a grin. "You can't just stand there and sip fizz forever."

"I can if I sip dramatically," Ivy replied, lifting her leafcup like a toast. Ambry laughed, took the cup from her hands, and set it on a nearby log. Then he spun her around and pulled her toward the dancers in the shallows.

The moment her feet touched the wet sand, the shallows shimmered in response, sending ripples of light beneath every step. The rhythm picked up — crystal-thread harp, glowbark drum, sea-flute weaving between the beats — and Ivy moved without thinking.

Ambry matched her easily, his movements playful, loose, hands flicking water at her when she got too serious.

"You call that dancing?" she teased.

"Bold words from someone doing the wiggle-hop," he shot back.

"I'm pioneering a style."

She skidded and nearly fell, caught only by his arm looping instinctively around her waist. For a breath, they didn't move. His fingers rested against her lower back, her palms on his chest.

"Careful," he said, voice low.

Her breath caught. "Guess I needed a steady hand."

His smile was warm. "You're in luck. I've got two."

Before the moment could stretch too long, Ambry caught her hand again. "You're not getting out of it that easy."

They spun once more beneath the fading suns, laughter rising like sparks in the salt-bright air. Every corner of the beach pulsed with movement, light, and easy laughter.

Ivy couldn't stop smiling. The whole beach felt alive. Like the universe had decided, just for tonight, to let teenagers run the world.

Then, without warning, the atmosphere shifted. The last golden edge of the twin suns slipped behind the trees, casting long violet shadows that bled slowly across the sand. For a moment, everything held — quiet, dim, suspended between light and dark. A hush swept across the beach like a breeze. She looked toward the horizon, out across the sea.

Then the sky shifted. The first moon crested the edge of the sea, a molten gold disc rising slow and heavy. Its smaller echo followed, silver-bright, their glow climbing together through the darkening sky until their light spilled across the water in braided shimmer. Ivy had seen them before, but never like this. Never this close, their reflections met across the water. Two rippling lights converging into one.

A ripple of voices stirred across the beach. "They're almost touching," someone said.

A few teens scrambled closer to the water, pointing skyward.

"Hold me," Laz whispered. "It's too beautiful. I'm emotionally compromised."

That broke the spell. Laughter burst across the crowd, loud and real, like the whole beach had been holding its breath.

Ambry stepped beside Ivy, his hand brushing hers. "Look," he said, eyes fixed on the water.

She followed his gaze — and saw it. The tide had begun to pull. Gently at first, then stronger, waves rising in rhythmic swells, glowing faintly as they crashed against the shore. The ocean shimmered brighter with each crest, as if the moons themselves were calling it to life.

"That's why it's called the Moonrise Pull," he grinned.

Something stirred deep inside her. A quiet weight, full and electric. Awe, sharp and real. All around them, teens drifted toward the water, peeling off wraps and tumbling down the sand in messy, laughing groups. The first few splashed into the surf with wild whoops, sending glowing foam arcing into the air, as the moons climbed steadily on the horizon.

Laz sprinted past at full tilt, shedding a tunic as he went. "Last one in gets hexed by the tide gods!"

Ambry laughed and peeled off his shirt in one smooth motion, tucking it into a driftwood hollow. Ivy hesitated, then tugged off her tee and pants, leaving her in just the tank and shorts beneath.

They reached the water's edge, where the surf pulsed with moonlight — a soft rhythm, bright and alive. Ambry stepped in first, and the bioluminescent coils rose to meet him, twining around his ankles like liquid silk. Ivy hesitated. Her toes sank into the cool, damp sand. The water looked alive. Not dangerous, just impossibly vast. Wild in a way she'd never felt before.

"I've never done this," she said.

Ambry turned, already waist-deep. "Then let's fix that." He held out a hand.

The tide lapped at her feet, glowing softly. Her breath came uneven. Everything about this felt too big, too wild, too... alive.

Ambry didn't let his hand drop. "Hey," he said, voice steady. "I've got you."

She looked up and took it. The first touch of the ocean was like velvet, warm and thick with light. As she moved deeper, soft light shimmered around her legs, each ripple tracing luminous patterns on her skin. Her breath caught as a wave lifted her, saltwater rising beneath her like it had been waiting. At first, her movements were unsure, testing, but soon she found a rhythm. Her limbs drifted with the current like she already knew how. It wasn't swimming, it was... gliding, every shift of the tide folding around her with ease.

She let go of Ambry's hand and rolled onto her back, arms stretched wide, carried by the tide. It rocked beneath her like a lullaby, gentle and endless, holding her in its rhythm. Ambry floated next to her, close enough that their shoulders touched whenever the current shifted. He reached over, trailing his fingers through her hair where it fanned like flames. The strands shimmered red in the sea-glow, curling at his knuckles. Their hands brushed, then their fingers curled together, slow and certain, like the rest of the world could wait.

Ivy let her head fall back and felt his thumb graze her knuckles. The waves, the beach, the noise... For once, she didn't feel like the girl born between worlds. She just felt real.

Then she turned and smirked. "You're still gonna owe me if a sea monster eats my leg."

Ambry grinned. "Only if it's the good leg."

She splashed him.

He dove under with a yell, disappearing into glowing bubbles, then popped up behind her and tickled her side, catching her off guard.

She shrieked, twisting. But instead of fighting back, threw her arms around his neck in a laughing, breathless hug. He held her easily, light dancing in the water between them. Then she pushed off, and they chased each other into deeper water, spirals of light spinning with their movements.

When they finally climbed ashore, breathless and soaked, Ivy's hair clung to her shoulders in fiery strands. Ambry picked up a folded towel from the bundle waiting on the shore — thick and fleece-soft, woven from Kavari leaves — and handed it to her, his smile quiet, full of something unspoken.

They walked back to the fire, side by side, the sand glowing faintly beneath their feet. As they reached the circle, Ambry dropped onto one of the sun-bleached logs, shifting to make room for her. Ivy sank down next to him, towel still wrapped around her shoulders, warmth radiating from both the fire and his quiet presence.

Nyra shifted closer, her elbow brushing Ambry's arm with deliberate ease. He glanced at her and smiled.

Ivy kept her expression neutral, but something bitter twisted in her chest. Nyra was beautiful. Polished. She moved like the wind bowed to her. And worse, she belonged here.

A burst of laughter rang out as a boy launched a glowing splash from a hollowed glowfruit husk and nailed Laz square in the chest.

Laz froze, gasped, and stared down like he'd been personally betrayed. "Oh no. Water. On the beach. How will I ever recover?"

His eyes narrowed. "You realise what you've done." He snatched a husk from a passing girl, dunked it in the surf with dramatic flair, and rose like a soggy avenger.

"You've declared war," he said. "And I accept." He launched the glowing payload overhead. "Justice!"

The boy shrieked, dodged and someone else took the hit. Chaos erupted. Shouts, splashes, glowing puddles everywhere.

"He's in chaos mode," Nyra said, looking bored.

"Is this normal for him?" Ivy asked. "Or is this a moon thing?"

"That's just Laz," Ambry replied. "Wait for the dramatic monologue."

Sure enough, seconds later, Laz popped up, dripping and grinning. "Ambry!" he called, flinging water dramatically from his hair. "You dare leave me to handle the logistics of joy alone? This is a two-man operation! Now get in here before I file an official complaint with the Ministry of Fun!"

Ambry shook his head, grinning. "No way man, you started it."

"I defended myself!" Laz called back. "Did you not witness the first act of unprovoked aggression? A direct hit! To the chest!" He pointed dramatically. "There are laws about this, Ambry. Laws!"

Ambry cupped a hand to his ear. "Sorry, can't hear you over all that soggy righteousness."

"Traitor!" Laz shouted, then ducked another blast of water and flung himself into a roll that kicked up a wave of sand. He popped up grinning, soaked and triumphant. Then he jogged back to the fire, shaking out his hair like a drenched puppy. He flopped dramatically beside Ivy and leant in.

"You enjoying your first official induction into Spero's teen cult of soggy regret?" Laz asked, grinning.

Ivy's eyes sparked with mischief. "Are we all getting robes later or...?" She eyed him. "And you're absolutely soaked."

Laz spread his arms with mock solemnity. "I'm a very complex puddle."

A platter of glowing solarbread passed through the circle. Ivy bit into a warm slice. It was slightly sweet, with a softness that melted in her mouth.

Laz handed her a pink skyvine pod next. "Just don't eat more than three or your eyebrows start vibrating." he said.

She bit in and sputtered with laughter, the fizz still catching her by surprise.

Next came a platter of cakes — small, golden rounds crisp at the edges, their surface flecked with toasted seeds and glistening threads of glaze. They smelled faintly of roasted nuts and saltwind, and steam curled from the cracks like they'd just come off the fire. Sela passed one to Ivy on a broad leaf. "Try this," she said, grinning. "Velmiir hive solari, folded into sungrain flour."

Ivy's eyes lit up. "Oh! Solari! Ambry and I climbed halfway up a velmiir tree to find a hive. He said it would be worth it, and it so was. I've thought about it every day since."

Ambry gave her a lopsided smile.

She took a bite and practically melted. The cake was warm, nutty, and just sweet enough, with that same rich, earthy flavour she remembered. Comfort wrapped in crunch. "Still perfect," she murmured around the mouthful.

Ambry nudged her gently with his shoulder. "It's fun watching you try things. You look... happy."

Laz grinned. "And a little high on solari."

Sela winked. "Best batch I've ever made. Moonrise always deserves the good stuff."

Nyra, who had been quiet until then, arched a brow, her voice smooth but edged. "I can have it whenever I want. In Domaris, we have an endless supply." She didn't look at Ivy when she said it, her gaze lingered on Ambry instead, just long enough to register the sting.

Laz raised an eyebrow. "Subtle, Nyra," he murmured under his breath.

Beside her, Ambry shifted slightly, like he felt it too. But he didn't move away.

Across the circle, someone split open a songfruit. A low, clear note drifted out, threading through the air until every voice faded. Ambry's voice was barely above a whisper. "No one speaks while it hums."

The sound brushed through Ivy's chest, light as a breath against glass, lingering until she wasn't sure where it ended and the night began. The branches above rippled, leaves shifting to reveal stars choreographed by unseen hands. Tiny bugs drifted up, glowing rings spinning like living constellations.

She leant into Ambry's warmth. He slid an arm around her shoulders, pulling her gently closer. "I could stay like this forever," she said.

He gently tucked a loose strand of hair behind her ear, his fingers trailing warm against her skin. "Me too," he said, a faint smile tugging at his mouth.

Ivy glanced around the circle and soaked it all in — the firelight, the moons, the easy laughter, the saltwater and solari, and something softer that warmed through her chest every time Ambry looked at her like that. This world had crept under her skin. Not just the beauty of it, but the rightness, like the pieces of her had finally lined up with something real.

Tomorrow was a question she couldn't answer. But tonight, here, beneath the two moons and watchful stars, she wasn't just surviving. She belonged.

And it felt like home.

— ✦ —

The fire had burned low by the time they pulled themselves away. Ambry offered to walk her back, and Ivy didn't hesitate.

They followed the winding path through the forest, soft light flickering between the trees as the last of the Spero fireflies danced upward. The silence between them held its own kind of ease. Comfortable. Something unspoken curled between their footsteps.

"So…" Ambry said after a while. "You're really going home tomorrow?"

Ivy nodded, tugging her towel tighter around her shoulders. "Yeah. My parents want me home again. Gareth, too. They think we've been out here long enough."

"To… nearby?" he asked with a crooked grin.

She laughed. "Yes."

Ambry smiled, like he didn't believe her but didn't mind. "But we'll still meet up? Like before? Even if it's just at night?"

"I'll try," she said. "I might be able to sneak out during the day. My parents are… intense. But Gareth might cover for me."

Ambry walked a little slower, then glanced over. "Would it help if they met me?"

Ivy stopped. "Met you?"

He gave a little shrug, like it wasn't a big deal. "Might ease them up a bit. If they knew who I was."

She stared at the ground, toes scuffing the path. "Oh. They just have this stupid rule. No dating until I'm eighteen."

Ambry's smile tilted. "Wait… are we dating?"

Her brain short-circuited. "No! I mean — no, no one's dating. Definitely not. I mean, unless — are you? I mean, am I—?"

He laughed, the warm kind that curled into her chest. "I'm just walking you home, Ivy."

"Oh, right." She tucked her hair behind her ear. "Casual walk. Totally casual."

"But," he said, softer now, "if we were dating... I don't think I'd mind."

She looked up at him, heart hammering so loud it felt unfair. "Yeah?"

"Yeah."

She didn't know what to say, so she didn't say anything. They kept walking, slower now, like the path had softened beneath them. She stepped closer — close enough for their hands to brush, then linger, until her fingers slid into his like they'd always belonged there. Ahead, the soft outline of the camp came into view, the tent lit dimly from within, casting a warm spill of light across the clearing.

He stopped slowly, then looked at her, really looked. His eyes searched hers as if he were trying to memorize something, some unspoken truth between them. Then his gaze flicked down to her lips, lingered, just long enough to make the air stretch, to make her heart skip.

Ivy's breath caught. The pause had weight, thick enough to feel between heartbeats. She thought he might close the distance. She wanted him to.

His gaze held hers. "Please try," he said, barely above a whisper.

Ivy nodded, her throat tight.

And then—

He looked away, the moment folding in on itself like a wave that never broke. "I should get back," he said softly.

The silence stretched.

Still holding her hand, he stepped backward, just one step, his eyes never leaving hers. Then another, slower this time, like the distance was something he could undo if he changed his mind.

Finally, his fingers slipped free.

Ivy stayed inside that moment, the almost. The breath they never took.

And she knew, without question, that she'd do whatever it took to keep seeing him.

CHAPTER TWENTY-FOUR

The morning after Moonrise Pull was quiet. The forest stood still, its edges softened by dawn.

Ivy crouched beside a shallow stream, splashing her face with cold water, the last traces of salt still clinging to her skin. Her body felt heavy, not from exhaustion, but from leaving something behind. The firelight, the tide, the laughter. Ambry's almost-kiss.

Gareth was already up, rolling sleeping mats and repacking their field gear with a focus that felt too sharp for how soft the morning was. The tarp rustled under his hands as Ivy approached.

"Morning," she said.

"Morning," he echoed, looking up. "Sleep alright?"

"Eventually."

He gave her a sidelong glance. "You were out late."

"Moonrise Pull. I got the full experience."

Gareth hummed, neutral, unreadable. But he didn't push.

They worked side by side for a while, quietly. Securing the gear. Packing away the leftover supplies. Stowing the root and leaf samples she and Gareth had collected the day before.

"Grace will want us logging all of this the second we get back," Gareth said, breaking the silence.

Ivy nodded, fastening a latch. "Are we staying at the POD from now on?"

"That's the idea. They're worried we've been out here too long."

She stared at the treetops above them, swaying gently with the breeze. "We haven't been long enough."

He paused, just for a moment. And that was all she needed.

"If I wanted to see someone again," she said, "hypothetically speaking... how much trouble would that cause?"

Gareth looked almost amused. "Depends. Are we talking casual curiosity or coordinated escape plan?"

She hesitated. "Not casual."

He leant back and gave her a long look. "Ivy."

"I know," she said quickly. "I know what I'm supposed to say. But this isn't some random crush. It doesn't feel temporary. And I don't want to pretend it didn't happen just because it's inconvenient now."

Gareth dragged both hands through his hair, letting out a slow breath before he answered. "Let's just get through today."

"I'm serious," she said. "I want to see him again."

"I'll think about it." He turned back to the gear, cinching a strap tight. "No promises."

She didn't push, but something in her chest eased, just a little.

Gareth slung the last pack over his shoulder and glanced toward the trail. "Maybe it's time your parents saw something else besides the POD," he said. "David and Grace have barely left camp. They haven't even seen the real Spero. Show them something real."

Ivy straightened, slipping her arms through her pack straps. "What about the place Ambry took us to collect samples? The one with the waterfalls?"

He gave a quick nod. "Could work. Show them it's not all risk out here... maybe they'll loosen the leash a bit.

That sparked something bolder. Ivy lit up. "What if they met some of the people?"

Gareth's answer came fast. "Absolutely not." He didn't raise his voice, but the words landed firm.

"You never tell them you've made contact without permission. That's how you end up grounded for life — or worse, sorting pathogens."

— ✦ —

By midday, they stepped into the clearing, and the forest gave way to the POD's steel panels and hard edges. A jarring break in Spero's seamless green.

Ivy's stomach gave a slow, unwelcome turn the moment she saw it. Sharp metal, perfect symmetry, all wrong against the forest's slow-breathing wild. It didn't belong here. Maybe neither of them did.

The camp sat quiet. Grace knelt beside a sample tray, sorting shards of pale crystals into sterile tubes, their surfaces catching the sunslight in brief, glassy flares. David worked nearby, recalibrating a scanner, fingers moving in sharp, efficient motions.

"There you are," Grace said, standing up. "Cutting it a bit close, aren't you? We were waiting on you for lunch."

Ivy dropped her pack to the ground. "We lost track of time. The forest's hard to walk away from."

"All good, might've been something useful out there." She gave Ivy a brief smile. "Either way... good to have you back. You know how your dad worries."

Ivy managed a small smile in return.

David glanced over his shoulder. "There she is. Hi, sweetheart." He crossed over, pressing a kiss to her temple. "Hope you brought back some good samples. Still plenty to catalogue, but we'll get there."

He gave her a once-over, casual but sharp. "So... how was it out there? See anything unusual? See any of the local wildlife?" He grinned. "I hope they all kept their distance."

The wildlife hadn't stayed away. They'd watched her, moved with her, like she'd stepped into a story no one else could see.

She kept her voice light. "Nothing too wild. Just... different."

David nodded, already half-turning back to his scanner. "Well. That's something."

Gareth passed behind her — a steady, silent presence.

The moment stretched too long.

Grace dusted her hands against her pants and met Ivy's gaze, her face softening, but only just. "We'll need to debrief soon. And help tagging samples. I imagine you brought back quite a lot." She held up a sliver of translucent crystal, the edges catching light like ice. "You should've seen what we found this morning. Some of these samples show regenerative lattice structures. Self-correcting. We've never seen anything like it."

David looked up. "And the mineral density? Off the charts. If these readings hold, this place could tell us more about natural resilience than anything we've ever studied."

Grace smiled, the edge of real excitement creeping in. "This could change everything, Ivy. If we document it right... if we present it clearly... Earth might finally listen."

Ivy stood still, jaw tight. "If they come here, they'll ruin it."

Grace's tone stayed calm, too calm. "No one said they're coming here. These samples," she lifted the crystal again, "could reshape how we think about sustainability. Crop growth. Water filtration. Atmospheric repair. This is bigger than colonisation."

Her gaze flicked back to Ivy's. "And if Earth ever does need a new home, it'll be a last resort. But that doesn't mean we stop learning. Or stop preparing."

"Right." The word slipped out, small, flat, heavier than it should've been.

No one spoke. Then, with the quiet still hanging in the air, they eased back into their work. Ivy turned to the POD. Its door hung slightly ajar, the air around it sharper, harder, like she'd stepped out of rhythm.

She slipped inside. The space felt smaller than she remembered. The hum of recycled air pressed in, filtered, scrubbed, stripped of everything living. Every surface gleamed with that too-clean brightness, untouched and untouchable.

"Hi AURA," she said, her voice low.

"Welcome back, Ivy," the AI replied, smooth and unbothered. "You've returned intact. Statistically, that was likely."

She pressed her hand flat against the console. The metal stayed cool beneath her skin. Steady. Predictable. Exactly what it had always been.

She drew in a breath that smelled like nothing.

She already missed the forest.

— ✦ —

The table wasn't anything special. Just a collapsible surface with metal edges and foldout legs, set up under the silver-leafed trees. But someone had gone to the trouble of laying out actual bowls and heating the food properly. David, probably. Ivy doubted Grace would bother, and Gareth was more the type to hand you something and say, *Eat this*, without explaining what it was.

Steam curled off the lentil stew. The bread was warm, baked fresh, and it smelled like something real. Ivy sat opposite her parents, elbows on the table, her back still stiff from the camping trip.

"Any surprises while we were gone?" Gareth asked as he slid into the seat across from Ivy, settling beside Grace. He didn't say anything, but the move felt deliberate. Not just joining the table, but shielding it a little. Gareth was the buffer now, just in case Ivy said something that might light the fuse.

"All as expected," Grace said. "One of the filters flagged trace particulates we hadn't seen before, might be a mineral compound leaching from the soil. And the comms array spiked again, but diagnostics show it's stabilised."

David leant forward slightly. "And you two? Everything alright out there?"

"Uneventful," Gareth said at the same time Ivy said, "Not really."

They both paused.

Grace's eyes narrowed slightly. "Not really?"

Ivy took a bite of stew to stall. "I saw the trees start to change. That silver-barked one's shifting, and the light beneath its roots is brighter than it was a week ago."

David perked up, grabbing his datapad from where it rested on the corner. "That lines up with the early readings. We might be entering a seasonal shift."

Ivy raised an eyebrow. "You mean autumn?"

"Sort of," he said. "Veritas doesn't have seasons in the Earth sense, no axial tilt means no cold or heat cycles. But it has other patterns. Lunar resonance, bio-rhythmic shifts. It's all tied to light and magnetic pulses."

Grace added, "The flora here aren't reacting to temperature. They're reacting to time. You can't see the pattern unless you're paying attention."

"I was paying attention," Ivy said.

David looked up at her, warmth in his eyes. "I know."

Gareth's expression softened as he tore a piece of bread in half.

Ivy sat back, then reached under the table and pulled out a small woven pouch Ambry had given her. It was made of Kavari fibres and tied with vine twine.

"We brought something back," she said.

Grace froze. "Ivy, please tell me you didn't eat anything you found out there."

"I didn't," Ivy said quickly.

She untied the pouch and tipped it forward. Three small, orange-glowing pods rolled onto the table, each pulsing faintly with internal light.

David leant in instantly, eyes wide. "Where did you find these?"

"Near the ridge," Gareth said, unfazed. "Low vines, shaded beneath the trees. No signs of rot, no fungal traces. I ran full scans—checked for protein chains, cross-reactivity, mineral content. They match a few of the nutrient profiles we logged from earlier samples. I wouldn't have let her touch them if I hadn't double-checked."

Grace still looked horrified. "That doesn't mean they're safe."

"No," Gareth agreed. "But it means they're not immediately dangerous. And since we're planning to be here longer than six months, we'll need to start identifying viable flora."

David was already poking one of the pods with the back of his fork. "They're bio-reactive. The glow shifts when touched. That suggests some kind of defence or communication mechanism."

"They unravel, like petals folding back," Ivy added helpfully. "Smells kind of like mint and burnt sugar."

Grace pressed a hand to her temple. "I'm going to need another week's worth of bloodwork from you both."

Gareth nodded. "Add it to the list." He leant toward Ivy with a low murmur only she could hear. "Better hold off telling them about the Velmiir hives."

Something shimmered overhead, catching Ivy's eye. Ambry had told her the name, Tallwings. Their glasslike wings refracted the sunslight into spectral colours as they drifted silently past the clearing.

David glanced up too, mesmerised. "I wonder if they're migrating, if they migrate?"

"They nested near our camp," Ivy said, watching the birds disappear beyond the trees. "You could hear them at night. Like wind chimes."

Grace murmured, "It's early. Could be tied to the resonance pulse we logged last cycle."

David made a note on his datapad. "Or something bigger's at play. Maybe it's tied to lunar light patterns. Could be a whole environmental trigger we're not seeing."

He glanced back at Ivy, his eyes lighting with remembered excitement. "I did spot something new this morning, by the way. Out past the southern rise, I logged a reptilian species we hadn't seen before. Compact body, burnished bronze scales, curling tail. But the wings, blue-green with golden specks, like stained glass come alive. Antennae too, long and twitchy. Looked straight at me like it understood."

Grace looked up. "That's not in the existing database."

"Exactly," David said. "Which means we're still scratching the surface here."

He rubbed the back of his neck, eyes gleaming. "I didn't know what to call it. Looked like a cross between a dragon and a butterfly, so... I called it a dragonfly. Bit on the nose, I know."

Ivy smiled. "Better than 'weird six-legged flappy lizard'."

Grace let out a soft laugh, and David shook his head, a grin tugging at his mouth.

Beyond the edge of the clearing, the trees swayed, soft and rhythmic, their light shifting in gentle waves.

Ivy glanced across the table. Her parents were leaning in, trading notes, chasing ideas. Smiling. They were always like this, lit by the same spark, speaking in sync without even trying.

They had their belonging, and it wrapped around them like warmth. She wanted hers, and she wasn't convinced it waited for her here.

Chapter Twenty-Five

Sunslight slipped through the overhanging branches in soft waves as Ivy adjusted the strap on her pack. Behind her, the others were lagging. Not out of fatigue, out of fascination. Grace had stopped again, speaking into her field comm while gesturing toward a vine that pulsed faintly from within. David knelt beside a root cluster, fingers brushing the glowing edge of a bulb like he was coaxing it open.

"Between the bioluminescence and the symbiosis, this forest's rewriting my entire thesis," David said as a beetle landed on his arm. It paused, then sprang into a neat backflip, landing farther up his sleeve. David grinned. "Guess I'm part of the local transportation network now."

Ivy smiled over her shoulder. "Come on, it's not much further." She led them around another bend, ducking beneath a low arch of foliage. Then she stepped out of the trees into the heart of it.

The sound came first, not just water, but music woven into motion. A waterfall spilled down a crystal-veined rockface, refracting sunslight into liquid shards that danced across the surface below. The pool rippled gently beneath the falls, but farther out, it stilled — smooth as glass, with greens and blues drifting beneath the surface in slow, hypnotic swirls. Around the water's edge, a sunslit meadow opened wide, its grass dappled with wildflowers that shimmered with the shifting light from the falls.

Grace stepped past her, silent. David followed. Even Gareth paused at the edge, letting the moment breathe.

"I didn't want to tell you," Ivy said softly, "because I wanted you to feel it first."

Grace stepped forward, drawn toward the water. She crouched near the bank, her hand reaching toward the surface. When her fingers dipped through, the ripples spread, slow and wide, ringed in soft gold.

David let out a slow breath. "This is unbelievable."

Around them, the clearing hushed, the air caught in a brief, weightless pause.

Then, a soft rustle from the underbrush.

A creature slipped from the treeline, quiet as dawn. It moved with the grace of a small deer, long-limbed and slender, its steps so smooth they barely stirred the ground. Its coat lay as sleek as pressed velvet, catching the dappled light with a pearly opalescence, like moonlight caught in motion. Underneath, its base colouring was a soft dun, golden-brown with shadowy undertones, but veiled with an ethereal sheen of pink, silver, and pale green. Its face was graceful and fox-like, with luminous amber eyes and gently tapered ears that flicked with quiet alertness. Long lashes framed its gaze, giving it a curious softness. A thick, curling tail, almost wolf-like, swayed behind it. Every step was fluid, unhurried, like it had always been part of this place.

Grace froze. David lowered his field comm slowly, heavy with disbelief. The creature stepped closer, calm, poised... present.

It paused beside Grace and lowered its head. The movement was deliberate, almost reverent. A soft exhale fluttered from its nostrils, and the air shifted with it, warmer, heavier. Grace lifted her hand, brushing her fingers along the smooth curve of its head. The creature leaned into the touch, eyes half-lidded, breath slow.

Ivy watched, heart still, throat tight.

The moment held.

Then, just as slowly, the creature stepped back. Another rustle echoed across the clearing.

From the trees beyond, more shapes emerged. A small herd of the same species, each one unique in colour but unified in earth-toned hues. There was a rich bay with a silver sheen, a deep chocolate veiled in soft gold, a pale dappled cream like morning fog. Their opaline overlays shimmered faintly, like sunlight through dew.

The first creature lingered a moment, its luminous eyes holding Grace's gaze, before turning to follow the others. They moved past, unhurried, their hooves barely disturbing the grass and shallow water as they crossed the meadow toward the far bank. With a final flick of their tails, they vanished into the opposite treeline.

And they were gone. As if they'd never been there.

Grace stayed kneeling at the edge, still staring at her open hand like it didn't belong to her, as if the creature's touch still lingered there.

"That's what I mean," Ivy said, easing down beside her. "The magic here, you can't chart it."

The rush of the falls filled the air, soft beneath the hum of insects. From somewhere deep in the trees, a single bird called, then another. The sounds of the forest stirred back to life. The clearing didn't feel empty after the creatures had left. It felt fuller somehow. Like the space they'd taken up was still echoing with something warm.

"You don't have to see it like I do," Ivy said. "I just want you to feel it, not record it, not measure it. Just let yourself experience it."

Grace stayed quiet for a long moment. Then, slowly, she let her hand fall to her lap.

"We would never understand this from inside a lab," she said. "We would've catalogued it. Studied it. Put it in a file. And missed… all of it."

She looked up at Ivy, really looked, and something in her expression shifted. Not just softened. Opened.

"Thank you," Grace said quietly. "For showing me this."

Ivy blinked, caught off guard. The air felt too big for words, so she just gave a small nod.

Grace's gaze lingered on the water. A smile touched her lips, small, but steady.

Gareth met Ivy's eyes across the clearing, tipping his chin in a small, steady acknowledgement.

— ✦ —

The hollow tree stood near the clearing where they'd first met. Knotted, wide-trunked, draped in a curtain of vines. It had become their unspoken place.

Tucked inside a crevice near its base, barely visible unless you knew exactly where to look, sat a small weatherworn notebook wrapped in waxed fabric. Ivy crouched low and slipped it free. Her fingers traced the faint impressions on the book's cover, Ambry's carvings, barely more than scratches in the waxed fabric. A crescent moon. A spiral. A leaf turned sideways. Beside them, her own, the sweep of Leafwing's, a small heart tucked beneath. Their private code. Their secret.

They'd only managed to meet three times in the past two weeks. Once when Gareth had covered for her. Another time, when Grace and David were buried in environmental analysis. And a third when she'd lied, said she needed solitude to process data, when really, she just needed him.

But this notebook, this little book tucked in a tree, had become their heartbeat. A tether. Pages passed back and forth like a touch stretched across distance.

Some notes were practical. *"Tide's high, watch the sand path."* *"Stick to the south trail. The guards walk the upper ridge."*

But most weren't.

"Still thinking about your laugh at Moonpull. You snorted. Best part of the night."

"Did you see the twin blooms today? One opened late. Definitely you."

"Every trail feels longer without you on it."

"Sat on the moss rock by the stream today. Kept wishing you were there."

Once, Ivy had left a silver-petal flower pressed between the pages, the scent still lingering faintly days later. Another time, Ambry had left a small polished crystal, smooth and sun-warmed, as if he'd carried it in his hand all day before parting with it. A note was wrapped around it: *"I didn't know missing someone could feel like this."*

He never wrote long entries. But Ivy could read between the pencil lines. She was learning the shape of him in silence, in restraint, in the way his handwriting tilted more when he missed her. And when it didn't tilt at all, she knew he'd written it fast, like he couldn't get the words out quick enough.

She opened it now, the page catching the last gold of the day. A fresh message waited inside, simple but breathless.

"Can you get out? Do I get to see you for the whole day?"

Her chest ached at the sight of his handwriting, familiar and new, all at once. She ran her thumb over it as if it might still be warm.

Beneath it, she added: *"Tomorrow. Just after suns-rise. The western overlook."*

Gareth had finally convinced Grace and David to let them out together for the whole day. A research day, he'd called it.

She paused, then added one more line: *"Excited to see you. A little. Okay... a lot."*

She folded the notebook closed and placed it back in the hollow, careful to wrap it tight again. Not much by Earth standards. Nothing by ship standards. But out here? It was magic. Paper, smudged graphite, and longing.

It was how they'd stayed close when everything else pulled them apart.

She glanced toward the direction of his village, the first place they'd met, cloaked in shadow and half-truths. That night, they'd been strangers circling curiosity. Now?

Now the silence between them held meaning. Now the notes weren't just messages, they were proof.

Proof that even in hiding, something real could grow.

The tree would carry their words until tomorrow, when, just maybe, her world would feel whole again.

Chapter Twenty-Six

They slipped through the crystal-threaded corridor just as the guard's shadow glided past, like a ripple across still water. Ivy pressed her back against the stone, stifling a laugh.

Ambry leant in close, eyes sparkling. "You're terrible at sneaking."

Ivy tipped her head a little closer, voice low. "And you're too smug for someone who just walked face-first into a vine."

They grinned and ran again.

The halls wound deeper with each turn. Half palace, half dream. This was no ruin. It was the ancient heart of something sacred, the old royal stronghold of Spero, hidden beneath the tangle of the forest and preserved in stillness. Arches rose in perfect symmetry, wrapped in quiet ivy. Mosaic ceilings scattered sunslight into kaleidoscopic shards. They ducked into echoing chambers, down stairwells etched with forgotten symbols that gleamed faintly as they passed. Ambry pulled her into the shadow of a hollow arch, their shoulders brushing in the narrow space. His presence pressed in, warm and steady, and she found herself holding still, wishing the moment would stretch.

When the guard's footsteps faded, they slipped back into the open, following the curve of the passage until it widened into a long hallway of murals, vast floor-to-ceiling panels that stretched like woven memory down the corridor. Each portrait was rendered in swirling, luminous pigment. Amethyst kings with starlight in their robes, ruby queens whose eyes seemed to follow Ivy as she passed, golden-eyed children laughing mid-spin in scenes of joy. The colours weren't flat, but layered. Alive with motion and depth, as if the paint remembered the people it once captured. Every figure was painted in a single palette, but shaded with such delicate contrast that they shimmered with identity. It was less a gallery than a living archive, a memory held in glass and pigment.

Ivy's gaze traced the murals. "Who were they?" she whispered. "They look… beautiful. Not just in their faces, in the way they moved, the way they lived. Like… artists."

She lingered before the image of a dark-skinned boy with cropped hair, caught mid-stride through a spray of painted rain, his laughter etched in bright, fluid strokes.

"What happened to them?" she asked. "All these people?"

Ambry looked up at the portraits. "No one knows for sure. Some say there was a betrayal. Others say they were overthrown quietly. There was no war, no uprising. Just… silence. The palace was sealed, and The Order took control."

He stepped along the corridor, eyes tracing the length of the mural. "My dad used to say the royal line wasn't just a government. It was a rhythm we all lived by. And when they fell, everything shifted."

"What did they teach you about it in school?" Ivy asked.

"They didn't," Ambry said. "None of this is in the learning groves. No one talks about it. Not really." He glanced down the hallway behind them. "We're not even supposed to be here. It's forbidden."

Her eyebrows lifted. "And yet…"

He grinned. "Laz and I snuck in a couple of years ago. He spotted a crack in the outer wall and said, 'If the universe leaves a door open, you don't ask questions… you open it and hope for snacks.' Then he went straight through before I could tell him it wasn't even a door." He gave a soft laugh.

"We found a room buried deep in the west wing, the most beautiful place I've ever been. I've wanted to come back ever since."

"Come on. I want to show you." Ambry reached for her hand, his fingers brushing hers, warm and steady. She curled her hand into his like it had always belonged there. They walked in silence, the corridor narrowing and rising with each turn. Their footsteps echoed softly beneath the stained-glass windows above, painting them in fleeting bands of colour.

Then the hall opened, and they slipped into a grand chamber. Her steps stalled mid-stride.

The chamber stretched wide and circular, a sun-caught dome of glass and life. Ivy stepped in slowly, her gaze tracing the sweep of colour. Every wall shimmered with stained glass, no two panels alike. Crimson bled into sapphire, gold into jade, soft rose into violet, each one humming with quiet light. As the suns shifted outside, the colours rippled across the floor like moving water.

Her eyes lifted. Above, the ceiling soared in a dome of bioglass laced with golden-veined vines. Not wild, but woven, shaped with purpose. Sunslight slipped through patterned gaps in twin beams, scattering motes of dust that drifted like tiny dancers in the air. Coils of skyvine looped from the lattice, their fizz-shaped bulbs glimmering with nectar. It felt sacred, as if the chamber didn't just shelter life, it was life.

Ambry laced his fingers through hers as they walked the edge, his free hand trailing along the wall as he spoke, soft, like it wasn't meant to be a lesson. "Kavari saplings," he said, touching one of the pale roots. "They only grow in places that are meant to last. If they take hold, they'll outlive us all." Their small, square leaves fanned against the stone, edges lifting in the breeze as if they knew what they'd become.

He pointed ahead. "Duskthorn. The petals shift colours when the light moves. Always chasing it." She watched the glass-stemmed spires as they leant toward a golden patch, indigo fading to amber as they turned.

Beside the walkway, faint glimmers pulsed along the cracks. "Shimmer bulbs and mossfronds," Ambry said. "They drink in the day's light, storing it to shine through the night. By dawn, the glow thins to nothing, and they start filling again." Ivy tracked the glow threading through the stone, soft and scattered, like a reflection slipping across water.

At the chamber's heart rose a single, breathtaking bloom. Grand and luminous, spiralling up from a thick vine that wrapped a carved pedestal bearing a leafwing crest. Its stem shimmered with silver veining, a faint pulse running in time with the light. Broad petals bloomed outward like crystallised flame, translucent, radiant, each veined with threads of opaline glow. Dozens of fine filaments unfurled from the base, winding across the floor and wall, disappearing into the surrounding growth as if woven into the chamber itself. At its centre, a soft blue light glowed beneath broad green leaves, their curled edges guarding the flower's heart.

Her hand slipped from Ambry's as she stepped closer, every sense sharpened by the stillness pressing in. She moved toward the centre, the bloom rising taller with each slow step, until she could feel the faint stir of air and see the silver-veined stem pulse with a soft glow. A thin vine lifted from the stem — delicate, trembling — and hovered in the space between them, close enough for her to feel the air stir. She lifted her hand, slow and steady, until the space between closed.

The moment held. Then the vine found her palm, feather-light, cool at first. Warmth unfurled in its wake, spilling through her hand in a slow tide. She leant closer, as though the bloom had shared a secret meant for her alone. The vine curled once around her fingers, tender and sure, then slowly retreated, satisfied.

A single leaf curled outward in a slow, fluid stretch. Another followed. Then the rest loosened, folding back in a seamless, unhurried motion. At the flower's heart, its core emerged. A smooth sphere of crystal, glowing from within. Blue light spilled in delicate pulses, steady and alive, like a heartbeat made visible.

Beneath her collar, the pendant resting against her chest gave a faint pulse, a single flicker of matching blue.

Ambry watched her from the archway, breath held as though the moment might break. The colours danced across her skin, catching in her hair like firelight. Reds and golds flared across her cheeks, blues glinted in her eyes, until she looked less like a girl and more like something painted. Alive with colour and light. She didn't just belong, she clicked into place, like a piece that had been missing.

He crossed the room in three long strides and kissed her.

One hand caught her jaw, the other resting at her waist, grounding them both. She lifted into him without thinking, her fingers curling in the fabric of his shirt. The kiss unfolded slow, unsure, then deepened, like a breath after too long underwater. There was no hesitation, no uncertainty… just gravity. The kind of kiss that didn't ask permission, because every breath leading up to it had already answered.

When they finally pulled apart, the moment stretched between them, quiet, impossible to undo.

Her lips parted in a breathless, startled smile. "Well," she said. "That complicates things."

Ambry looked at her like he'd just seen the world tilt, like something he hadn't dared hope for had just stepped into the light. "I'm not sure I want things simple."

She laughed, light and breathless.

Then they heard it. Footsteps. Voices. Close.

Ivy grabbed his hand. "Come on."

They ran again, through the rainbow-lit chamber and out into the shadowed maze beyond. Hearts pounding, fingers laced, the moment clinging to them like a promise not yet spoken.

— ✦ —

Their boots struck stone in rhythm, quick, light, like gravity had let go. Ambry's laugh drifted ahead as he reached for Ivy's hand and spun her beneath a twisting arch of vines. She giggled, stumbling into him as the world blurred around them.

"Do you even know where we're going?" she asked, breath catching between laughs.

"Not a clue," he said and tugged her close. His mouth finding hers, warm and breathless and full of that impossible grin.

They moved through echoing halls where stained glass spilled fractured light across the floor, bruised and faded, like forgotten jewels. Ivy ducked behind a carved pillar, then jumped out just as Ambry passed. He stumbled, startled, jolting sideways into a low stone shelf. A carved bowl hit the ground with a hollow thud and rolled once before settling.

She pressed her fingers to his lips, trying to look serious, but her grin ruined it. "You trying to get us caught?" She whispered, then leant in for a quick, soft kiss that lingered just long enough to make her heart skip.

He mouthed a sheepish sorry, then caught her hand and tugged. She stumbled forward with a laugh of her own, gripping tight as he pulled her along. Their steps stayed soft, but her heart kicked up, like the whole world had narrowed to just this. The thrill, the quiet, and his hand wrapped in hers.

They rounded a corner where the stained glass gave way to bare stone, older and unlit, the colour bleeding out of the world around them. The hallway ahead narrowed, darker than the others, its arch lined with cracks that reached like veins through the ceiling. Their steps slowed. The air shifted, just slightly, like sound had thinned.

The walls were different here. The stone was etched with shallow carvings. Small leafwing crests. Dozens of them scattered across the surface like a quiet warning.

Ambry moved forward, eyes scanning the dark. He reached his hand back toward her, steady, sure. Ivy slipped her hand into his, her chest tightening.

Two guards stood in the next hall, stationed on either side of a passage where the stone turned smoother, more precise — its edges too sharp, the angles too clean to match the palace's old aesthetics. One leant against the wall, arms crossed, muttering something under his breath. The other gave a short, sharp laugh. The kind that didn't sound amused.

A faint shimmer clung to the doorway between them, not from light, but from within, like the stone was responding to something deeper.

Something stirred against her chest, a faint twitch like a pulse that wasn't hers. She reached down, fingers finding the pendant. The metal shifted beneath her touch. With a soft mechanical click, it unfurled, bronze wings spreading slowly, etched veins glowing blue. Warm beneath her palm, the light deepened with each pulse. She closed her fingers around it instinctively, steadying it. The glow softened, still pulsing, like it was aware of something she wasn't. Then, slowly, the bronze wings folded back into place, sealing the light inside.

Ambry stared at it, brows drawn tight. "What was that?" he whispered.

Ivy looked down at the pendant, still warm on her chest. "I don't know. It just... moved."

A flicker caught Ivy's eye.

Along the wall ahead, a small cluster of what looked like Leafwings clung to the stone, their wings folded flat, nearly indistinguishable from the carvings around them. For a breath, nothing moved. Then, one by one, they stirred. Wings parted gently, unfolding with a slow flicker of light. They lifted into the air, silent and synchronised, gliding toward a side corridor and disappearing into the dark.

Ivy looked at Ambry. "We're following them, right?" she whispered.

His eyes met hers, and he shrugged.

Ivy took Ambry's hand and kept low as they slipped past the hall. The guards were still talking, one with his back to the corridor, the other halfway through a rant about supply rotations. Their voices echoed down the stone, sharp and careless. They didn't even glance toward the passage Ivy and Ambry disappeared into.

The Leafwings moved ahead in a loose, gliding pattern, hugging the walls, wings barely stirring the air. At the next junction, a few paused mid-hover before veering right, guiding Ivy and Ambry into a narrower passage that wound deeper. Behind them, the guards' voices faded. Only their breath and footsteps echoed now.

The air felt strangely warm, almost pulsing with quiet energy. At the end of the corridor, the Leafwings slowed, some clinging to the walls, others hovering just ahead. Her pendant pulsed, blue light running down the etched veins of its bronze wings, steady and silent.

Ambry stepped forward, his gaze tracking the wall as he reached out to touch it. "Where have they taken us?" he murmured, fingers brushing along the stone.

Ivy followed his gaze. A smooth section of wall stood out, slightly recessed, with seams so fine they almost vanished into the stonework. Beside it sat a small panel, tapered and elegant, its surface barely etched. It didn't look mechanical, but it didn't feel natural either.

Ivy's fingers found the pendant at her collarbone, eyes tracing the etched wings as if seeing them for the first time. Then she reached up, unclasped the chain, and slipped it from around her neck.

As her fingers curled around the metal, it began to open. With a soft click, the two sweeping front leaves slid outward and tipped upward, uncurling like wings caught in slow flight. Beneath them, a second set — smaller, more delicate — rose to follow, folding back to uncover the heart of the pendant. At its centre, a crystal core flared to life, blue light spilling through the etched veins until every leaf glowed in a quiet, rhythmic wave.

It pulsed again, blue light spilling from the crystal core in soft, rhythmic waves. As she brought it closer, the panel answered, a bloom of light unfurling beneath the surface, tracing the faint outline of a leafwing-shaped recess. Ivy pressed the pendant into the hollow, the form fitting cleanly into place.

A low vibration stirred in the wall. The recessed door clicked, then shifted, edges sliding back with quiet precision. A narrow gap appeared, just wide enough to slip through. Ivy and Ambry exchanged a look. He reached for her hand as they stepped through together.

They stepped into a chamber that looked more grown than built, as if the planet had dreamt it into being, then sealed it away. A wide, curved window took up the far wall. Not looking out into the sky, but inward, into a vast tangle of glowing golden root structures. They pulsed gently, light shimmering through the humid air.

A console stood at the centre, sleek and wide, shaped like a half-unfurled petal. The bronze surface caught the light with a soft gleam, its etched veins curling outward in delicate symmetry. At its heart sat a socket, leaf-shaped and inlaid with a crystal identical to the one in Ivy's pendant. It glowed with a soft, steady blue, layered and luminous. It didn't feel manufactured, but alive, a softness under the metal, like warmth hidden beneath stone. Crystalline roots coiled outward from its base, spiralling beneath the floor in quiet rhythm. The stone beneath their feet was etched in sweeping rings that caught the glow where the roots passed underneath, like the whole chamber was breathing through them.

The room held a quiet magic, something ancient and still, as if it had been waiting. But beneath that wonder, the space felt disturbed. A doorway stood ahead of them, stark and out of place, its sharp edges didn't match the chamber's organic symmetry. Pale light from the corridor spilled through a small square window in the door, cutting across the floor in a hard, clinical line. Scuff marks streaked the stone near the doorway, not from age, but from boots. Too modern. Too careless. They paused just inside the threshold, eyes adjusting to the soft, layered glow.

Ambry moved slowly along the edge of the room, gaze sweeping over the floor, then up to the far wall. He stopped in front of the squared-off doorway, frowning. "This looks like the same corridor the guards were watching," he said quietly. "Must connect to the main hall."

Ivy gave a small nod, but her focus had already shifted. The console stood in the centre of the room like it was waiting. The glow from the crystal deepened as she drew closer, soft light stirring beneath the bronze. Her pendant pulsed once against her palm. It stayed warm, not urgent, just... ready. Like it knew where it was.

She turned it slowly in her hand, the bronze casing felt heavier now. The etched wings remained closed, but when her thumb found the groove between them, the same soft click answered her touch. The wings unfolded with deliberate grace, revealing the core inside. Her gaze flicked from the pendant to the socket. The crystal was identical, that same luminous depth, the same soft hum beneath the surface. It also reminded her of the spectacular bloom in the greenhouse, at the chamber's heart — the glow, the rhythm, the quiet pull beneath it all. She couldn't explain how she knew, only that they were connected. The bloom, the pendant, the console. All pieces of something larger. The same design. The same thread.

Ambry stepped up beside her. His hand brushed her arm, a light, grounding touch. "What do you think it is?" he asked.

She didn't look away from the glow. "I don't know," she murmured. "But it feels like... like it's waiting."

She stepped closer, the pendant open in her palm, wings unfurled and glowing. The glow deepened as she neared the console, the pendant flickering in perfect rhythm with the socket's quiet hum. Without fully meaning to, her fingers shifted. The pendant tilted, and the wings seemed to guide it, angling with delicate precision. It aligned with the socket as if by memory, like it had always known where it belonged. It slid into place against the crystal with a soft, final click. For a suspended breath, nothing moved.

Then, the console flared to life. Light pulsed outward from the socket, catching in the bronze grooves, veins of blue racing across the surface like lightning threading through water. A low harmonic tone resonated through the chamber, quiet and deep, like a memory waking up. Glyphs organised across the panel, some shifting into alignment, others emerging from the surface in soft layers. Above the console, a faint shimmer took shape, hazy projections sharpening, then holding steady in the air.

Ambry's eyes tracked the shifting projections. "What is this?"

Ivy stepped backwards, glancing from the console to the shifting light overhead. "I'm not sure..." she whispered.

New shapes bloomed into the space, seemingly formed of light and memory. Floating screens hovered in slow arcs around them.

Diagrams. Webs of shifting lines. Patterns in constant, quiet motion. There were no labels. No instructions. Just a quiet, clinical precision. A system running — efficient, active.

"I think…" Ivy's voice dropped. "I really think we're not supposed to be here."

Ambry didn't answer. He was staring at a floating diagram. Two figures, side by side. Their outlines glowed faintly, marked with looping neural patterns and shifting overlays. It looked medical, maybe diagnostic. But something about the second figure made him frown. Its map was quieter. Dimmer. Certain pathways looked simplified. Others were just… missing. There were no labels. Just a line of unfamiliar glyphs that pulsed once, then dissolved.

Ambry stepped back, jaw tight. "I don't like this," he said. "It looks like a control system. Like it's changing people."

The glyphs kept shifting, realigning across the console's surface, waiting.

In the silence, unease pooled low in Ivy's chest. This wasn't old. It was awake.

A burst of laughter echoed down the corridor. Footsteps followed. Sharp, uneven, one pair dragged slightly. Another voice chimed in, louder, half annoyed.

Ivy froze. She met Ambry's eyes.

He touched her arm. A quick, warning nudge. Ivy reached for the pendant and gently removed it from the console. The wings folded shut, the light dimming as it nestled into her palm. The glyphs across the console faded in retreat, the harmonic tone falling silent. Above, the projections wavered, thinning into haze before vanishing. The panel stilled. She closed her fingers around the pendant and lifted the chain to her neck, the metal settling cool against her skin as she fastened it.

They moved quickly, feet light on the stone. At the wall, the hidden door slid open, silent, seamless. Ivy slipped through first, Ambry close behind. They slipped out of the chamber, the door sealing behind them with a soft click. The Leafwings were gone. Ivy tightened her grip on Ambry's hand, and they broke into a run, their pace steady but urgent. The corridor curved again before narrowing, the air still charged with the same quiet energy that had clung to the chamber. At the next junction, Ambry slowed, pressing close to the wall as he peered around the corner.

Clear. The guards were still heading for the chamber.

He gave a quick nod, and they ran. Stone corridors twisted around them like a memory unraveling. Ivy's boots hit uneven tile and she stumbled, but Ambry caught her without missing a step, steadying her as they kept moving. "Left," Ambry whispered. "Then up."

They ran low, breath sharp in their chests, the sound of quick, quiet footsteps against stone. Corridors blurred past, long and silent, perfectly carved. The space around her blurred. Light, colour, detail lost in the push forward. Only the next turn. The next corner. The way out.

Ambry reached the gap first, pushing aside the climbing leaves. Cool air spilled through the narrow gap in the outer wall. He glanced back once. Ivy didn't. She slipped through the crack in the stone and turned, pressing her back to the outer wall. Her lungs burned. The stone felt cool against her spine. Ambry leant beside her, breath catching in his throat.

"What was that?" Ivy asked, voice low.

"I don't know," he said, eyes still on the wall behind them. "But it has The Order written all over it."

She turned toward him. "What did you see? In the files?"

He shook his head. "I'm not sure. It looked like... a control system. Or an experiment. Something designed to change people I think."

The pendant rested warm against her chest, chain looped around her neck. Ivy lifted it carefully, letting it settle in her palm. It pulsed once, like it was answering something she hadn't asked aloud.

Ambry watched the pendant, eyes narrowing. "Where did you get that?"

Ivy closed her fingers around it. "Gareth gave it to me."

His expression shifted. "Gareth?"

She nodded. "Not long ago, back on the..." She hesitated, "Back when I was scared. He said it would protect me. Help me feel safe."

Ambry glanced toward the palace. "Well, it's more than that. That thing's a key. And whatever it opens... The Order's guarding it."

They stood in silence, the sound of distant footsteps long gone.

Ivy met his eyes. "We need to know what it's doing, and why they're hiding it."

Ambry nodded slowly. "We should talk to Gareth." His eyes glanced down to her neck. "About that pendant."

Chapter Twenty-Seven

They followed the narrow path along the tree line, the castle's shadow fading behind them. Ivy flexed her hands, trying to shake off the strange energy humming under her skin.

Gareth would be waiting, right where they'd agreed, before suns-set so they could head back to the POD together. The cover story was that they were recalibrating the environmental sensors on the ridge. Safe. Accounted for. This... wasn't exactly in the calibration manual.

"Do you think it was some kind of tech hub?" she asked.

Ambry shook his head. "I don't know. It didn't feel like tech. Not in the way The Order uses it. It felt... older. Like it was built for something else."

They reached the edge of a small clearing, half-ringed by tall ferns and the angled trunks of two Kavari trees. Near the centre, Gareth sat on a broad, flat stone, hunched over a length of cord and a cracked sensor panel. He looped the wire carefully, knotting it around the housing with the kind of quiet focus that always meant his mind was running ahead of his hands. He glanced up as they stepped closer, and his expression shifted.

"What's wrong?" he asked, already on alert. His eyes moved between Ivy's face and Ambry's, narrowing slightly. "Did he do something?"

Ivy shook her head, too keyed up to even smirk. "It's not that. It's... something else. We found a chamber."

Ambry looked like he might object but stayed quiet.

Ivy reached for the pendant, unclasped the chain, and slipped it from around her neck. It had cooled again, small, almost ordinary against her palm. Then she held it out to Gareth, her grip shaky, but tight.

"This opened a door," she blurted. "We found a sealed chamber. There was this panel, and a door, and the pendant just… fit. I didn't even press anything, it clicked, and the door opened." She took a breath. "Inside, there was a console. And the pendant, it opened up. Like a key. And something activated. A system."

Gareth's hands stilled. The sensor panel forgotten. "What kind of system?"

Ambry answered. "Some kind of control system. We only caught fragments, overlays of neural patterns, like something was being changed." He met Gareth's eyes. "The before and after, it wasn't natural. The after looked… dulled. Muted. Like whoever it was didn't feel the same anymore."

Gareth's hands stilled, his expression tightening just enough for Ivy to catch.

"It felt… like it was waiting," Ivy added, her voice slower now. "But I didn't know what to do. I didn't even know what I was looking at."

A bird called in the distance. One long note, then quiet.

Then Gareth said, "Where?"

"Beneath the abandoned castle," Ambry said. "We got in through a break in the outer wall. Laz and I used to explore it when we were kids."

He caught Gareth's eye and rushed on, "We didn't touch anything. And it's safe. Mostly. I mean… safe enough."

"Well… except for the guards," Ambry muttered.

Ivy gave him a look. A sharp, silent *stop talking*. Ambry's mouth snapped shut.

Gareth finally took the pendant, turning it over slowly in his hand. His voice was low. "So this opened for you?"

"Yeah… but I didn't touch anything. Promise. It just, did it on its own."

She glanced at Ambry and then turned back to Gareth. "You said your mother gave it to you?"

Gareth nodded, eyes still on the pendant. He turned it over once more. Opening his hand, he let it rest flat against his palm. The etched leaves caught the sunslight, a soft gleam along their fine-cut edges. Slowly, he lifted it closer, his thumb brushing over the edges, careful… almost expectant.

He stayed like that, head slightly bowed, eyes narrowed. His breath low and held, the pendant cradled in his palm. The suns threw a soft glow across his face, shadows cutting sharply across his features.

Ivy reached out and gently touched his arm. Gareth blinked, his gaze snapping up as if surfacing from somewhere deep.

"Gareth... what do you know?"

He met her eyes, his jaw set. "Not here. Not now. Grace will be furious if we're not back before suns-set."

Ivy's eyes flared. "I don't care. This is more important."

"I know it is," he said gently. "But we can't draw attention. Not yet. The more normal we act, the more time we'll buy."

Gareth stood, looping the pendant's cord gently around Ivy's neck, letting it settle against her chest.

"Keep it close," he whispered. Then he turned to Ambry. "We need more information. I've been trying to get into The Order's headquarters, but it's sealed tighter than a vault. Is there anyone who could help us? Someone good with systems?"

Ambry nodded. "Laz. He's — well, he acts like an idiot, but he's brilliant with tech. If anyone can get us inside, it's him."

"Good," Gareth said. "Two days. We meet again then. Here, in the morning. I need to get her back now, or I'll never get her out again."

That last line was aimed at Ambry, and Ivy didn't miss it.

"Gareth, seriously—"

"Two days," he repeated. "No more. No less."

Ambry looked like he wanted to argue but only nodded. "I'll bring Laz."

Ivy took a step toward him, brows drawn, but Gareth was already guiding her away with a firm hand.

"Pip," Gareth said softly. "Go ahead. I'll catch up."

Ivy stopped mid-step. "What? Why?"

"I just need a word with Ambry."

She frowned. "Gareth—"

"It'll only take a second," he said, tone calm but firm. "I'll be right behind you."

Her eyes flicked between the two of them. Ambry gave a subtle shrug. He didn't look worried. Ivy rolled her eyes and turned to go. As she passed, she glanced back over her shoulder and mouthed, *Sorry*, before slipping into the trees.

Gareth waited until Ivy's footsteps faded.

Then he turned. "She likes you."

Ambry gave a small shrug. "I like her too."

Gareth's expression didn't shift. "Is that going to be enough?"

Ambry met his eyes.

"She's stronger than she knows," Gareth said. "And she's always had us. Her parents, me. People who would never leave her by choice."

He held Ambry's gaze. "You're not here because you have to be."

Ambry's jaw shifted, but he didn't look away.

"And if this pendant really responds to her... if she's the one who can activate it... then she's heading straight for something hard. And when it hits, she's going to need someone who won't disappear."

"I'm not planning on leaving," Ambry said.

Gareth gave a slight nod. "Good. Because when it gets hard. When she pushes you away, or pulls you in so close it starts to tear you apart. You don't get to vanish."

Ambry met his eyes. "It was never a question. I'm not going anywhere."

Gareth held his gaze a beat longer. "Then we understand each other."

He tipped his head toward the trees. "Go on. Before she comes storming back."

Ambry started to turn away, then stopped. "Gareth?"

"I'd burn the world down before I let anything happen to her."

Gareth met his stare. He gave a single firm nod.

By the time Ambry stepped away, Gareth was gone.

Chapter Twenty-Eight

The storm came without warning. One minute the sky was clear, suns casting soft amber light through the trees. The next, the wind turned sharp and electric.

Ivy watched from the edge of the POD, eyes fixed on the world outside as deep clouds coiled over the crowns of the trees. It wasn't grey or angry, but rich and strange. Like smoke swirling through ink. Flashes of turquoise and violet lit the sky in silent bursts. No thunder. Just light and pressure. Static that raised the hairs on her arms. Spero storms didn't rage. They unfolded. Grace and David were working in the shelter of the forward prefab, voices overlapping, hands darting between gear.

"David, look at this!" Grace called, eyes fixed on her scanner. "Ion saturation's spiking at ground level. It's not just following the storm. It's riding it!"

David flicked his sensor across the rainlit air, a grin flashing sharp. "I've never seen readings like this. It's not residual. It's active."

Grace turned in a quick pivot, dragging a corded data lead behind her. "Get the topography overlay. If this surge tracks with the pressure lines, we might be seeing a migratory pattern. In weather!"

David laughed under his breath, half in disbelief. "A migratory storm system? That's insane."

"That's brilliant," Grace shot back, breathless with it. "We could be looking at a self-regulating biosphere. Weather that moves with the ecosystem."

They circled past the field kits, working in tight, fluid sync. Grace logging, David recalibrating, both grinning like kids chasing fireflies at dusk.

Ivy just watched them, the storm flashing behind, her parents alive in a way she only ever saw when discovery was close. She understood their excitement; on Earth, storms tore things down. But here, storms nurtured instead of destroyed, migrating like herds to deliver nutrients, clear toxins, trigger blooming cycles. They stirred root systems, woke the soil, told whole forests it was time to grow. Weather with purpose, written right into the ecosystem. It was... kind of brilliant. No wonder her parents were obsessed.

She stepped back inside. The quiet inside the POD felt heavier now.

Gareth hadn't gone with them to catalogue the storm. He'd shut himself in his alcove when it had rolled in, door sealed, no explanation offered. Since the moment Ivy and Ambry discovered the core, he'd barely said a word to her. Every question she asked, about the core, about the pendant, met the same answer.

In time.

He claimed he didn't know much yet. That the pieces would fall into place when they were meant to. But the weight in his eyes said otherwise.

She crossed to the console and tapped the screen. The EOS 11 flickered into view, her greenhouse bay, still sealed and intact in orbit. Rows of plants bloomed in artificial light. The strawberries were climbing well. The kale had bolted again. The orange tree was heavy with fruit.

"I hope you're not bored without me," she murmured to the screen.

AURA's voice responded, smooth and dry. "They've logged 1.6% more growth since your departure. It's possible they prefer the solitude."

Ivy gave a weak snort. "Harsh."

Propping her chin in one hand, she leaned on the console, gaze tracking a single droplet sliding down the viewport glass. "AURA... can I ask you something else?"

"You usually do," he said, his British accent showing no sign of sarcasm.

She looked at the storm. The light outside flared soft and strange, washed in pinks and pale green, like a dream trying to bloom. "The plants here... they respond to me. Like the ones on the ship."

She hesitated. "The animals too... mostly insects."

There was a pause, calibrated but thoughtful. "This planet's biosphere may have a higher reactive threshold. Your presence may trigger instinctive response patterns, resonance within its native lifeforms."

Ivy frowned. "So basically, I'm just a walking mood antenna."

"In essence."

She touched the pendant, hesitating. "And my pendant? Do your scans show anything unusual about it?"

"Hold still."

A brief pause. Then AURA spoke again, calm and measured. "My scans show the pendant emits low-level bioelectric feedback when in contact with you. However, I detect no internal mechanics, no power source, no known circuitry."

Ivy blinked. "So... it just opens?"

"Essentially."

She raised an eyebrow. "By itself."

"Essentially."

"But it's not magic."

"That classification would be inaccurate."

"And you still don't know what it is."

"I cannot match the signature to known parameters."

She sighed. "So I'm not special... just unusually functional."

Another pause. "It is statistically improbable that this is chance."

Ivy jabbed at the console, then slumped back in her chair. "Might as well ask the rehydrator, at least it pretends to be useful."

The storm flickered again, casting a pale light across the POD walls. "AURA, how good are you with advice?"

AURA replied, smooth as ever, "I am an advanced AI programmed for strategic analysis, crisis management... and, apparently, teenage heart-to-hearts."

Ivy snorted. "So... about as good as a horoscope app."

"If the app came with superior logic processors and an impeccable British accent — yes."

She shook her head and gave a small laugh. "Good enough." She wrapped her arms around herself. "I met someone down here."

AURA replied in that same neutral, too-polite way. "Has there been confirmed contact with intelligent life in your vicinity?"

Ivy's stomach flipped, her mind scrambling. "Oh. Oh, no… it's—" She cleared her throat. "It's a Pegasus."

There was a pause.

AURA responded perfectly polite. "That would indeed be noteworthy. Would you like me to catalogue its physical description for mission records?"

"Describe the Pegasus?" She let her gaze drift toward the storm. "He's strong… but not in a loud way. The kind of strong you only notice when everything else goes quiet, like he was made for both sunlight and storms. His face is the kind you don't forget, serious one second, then split wide by this crooked smile that feels like it's meant only for me."

She gave a soft, almost breathless laugh. "His wings… dark brown, curling at the edges. Like wind-caught silk. And his eyes…" Her voice dropped. "Brown, but lit through with honey, like sunlight trapped inside. The kind you could fall into and forget how to find your way back."

Another pause. "Quite the Pegasus."

Ivy gave a quiet, helpless laugh. "Yeah. Quite."

"I care about him. Probably more than I should. And I know I have to leave when the twelve months are up." Her fingers traced a slow, restless circle on the console. "How am I supposed to leave… when I've finally found something real?" Her voice dropped even lower. "When I finally let myself want it?"

She sat back, the storm's reflection glimmering faint in the glass. "They are my family," she whispered. "Dad. Mum… Gareth."

Her throat tightened. "Gareth… He's—" She shook her head slightly. "He's the one who's always been there. The one who made it feel like I wasn't some mistake born on a ship. He gave me… normal."

Her next words barely rose above a breath. "I can't walk away from that. From them. Even if it means walking away from this."

AURA's voice was soft. "The choice will define you. But it will not diminish you."

She dropped her head. "Is that your way of saying I won't break?"

"I'm saying you already made your choice. Long before you asked the question."

Ivy let the words settle. For once, she didn't argue.

Outside, the storm deepened. The rain glowed softly, pooling in the grass and flickering as flashes of turquoise lit the air. Rhythmic, like the storm was unfolding in its own sequence. Grace and David moved through the rain, their jackets soaked, hoods half-blown back by the wind. Grace laughed as David fumbled a sensor, her voice sharp and bright against the storm's low hum. David laughed with her, bumping her shoulder as he caught it, shaking his head like he couldn't believe they got to do this. Storm-chasing, side by side, under the strange skies of an alien world. They didn't just chase answers. They chased them together. Always together.

Ivy watched them through the glass. She didn't need to hear their words to know how they worked, how they fit. How they met each other in the middle of every storm, every mission, every impossible choice... and held on. And in that quiet space between heartbeats, Ivy realised it wasn't just Ambry she was afraid of losing. It was this. The kind of love that caught you. And never let go.

Ivy stared through the glass. Something in her felt pulled, stretched between two homes. She didn't know where she belonged. But here... in this storm, in this quiet moment between chaos and decision...

Maybe the choice could wait.

CHAPTER TWENTY-NINE

The morning air was cooler, sharper, crisp enough to catch in your throat like the first breath after rain.

Ambry stood near the trunks of two Kavari trees, arms folded, eyes on the pale curve of the path ahead. Laz leant casually against a moss-covered stump, tapping at a compact metal device balanced in his palm. The casing was scuffed and etched with faint geometric lines, its edges threaded with fine wiring. Bits of polished crystal winked between the seams as the surface flickered with shifting light.

"So," Laz said, smirking, "are we finally admitting the forest girl's your weakness, or do I have to stage an intervention?"

Ambry shot him a look. "Careful."

Laz raised his hands. "Hey, I'm just glad you found someone who puts up with you. It's honestly impressive."

Light footsteps crunched on the path. Ivy stepped into the clearing, Gareth beside her.

"Is this him?" Gareth asked Ambry, nodding toward Laz.

"Unfortunately," Ambry muttered.

Laz straightened up and offered Ivy a salute. "Look who finally showed. You know, if you keep dragging Ambry out into the woods at night, people are going to talk."

Ivy rolled her eyes. "Good. Maybe then they'll stop asking if I'm lost and start admitting I'm the best entertainment this planet's had in decades."

"See? Trouble," Laz said, clearly delighted. "You'll need a logo. I do graphic design on weekends."

Gareth cleared his throat. "We don't have time for commentary." He stepped forward, offering a hand. "I'm Gareth. Ivy's uncle."

Laz took it, eyebrows raised. "Laz. Archives, sarcasm, and full-time pain in Ambry's ass."

Gareth let out a dry chuckle. "Good. We'll need someone like that." His eyes flicked to the device in Laz's hand. "Is that a datapad?"

"Datapad? Oh, sure, because it holds data. Real imaginative. Nah." Laz tapped the corner, and the screen faded to black. "It's a Tactis, short for tactical access. Lets you pull comms, maps, registry logs... whatever you've got clearance for."

Ivy nodded at the mess of wiring and crystal jutting from its casing. "And what's all that for?"

Laz grinned. "That's for everything you *don't* have clearance for."

Gareth chuckled. "Useful."

Then he turned serious again. "Laz, we need you to break into The Order's archive system."

Laz's eyebrows shot up. "Oh sure. Hack The Order's archive? Piece of cake. Want me to rewrite the suns while I'm at it?"

"Wish it was a joke, Laz. But it's not." Ivy said. "We found something. Something bad."

Ambry pulled out a small sketch Ivy had drawn. The console, the root system, the way the glyphs floated and moved. Laz studied it, expression shifting from amused to focused.

"Okay... maybe not the suns. But this? This I can try." He leant in, squinting at the sketch. "What does it do?"

"That's what we're trying to find out." Gareth looked at him evenly. "We'll need data. I can provide the distraction with David and Grace to get Ivy out for a few hours. Is there any way you can access The Order's databases?"

"Wait," Laz said, tilting his head. "We're talking about the archive system in Domaris? Not that thing from the drawing?"

Ambry nodded. "Yeah. Whatever that thing is, it's still running. But no one knows it exists. We need information before we go back. We think The Order's archive might hold records, something that explains what it is, or what it does."

"And we're betting they tucked it into some classified server and hoped no one would ever find it," Ivy added.

"So we need access to the Spire... the data hub." Laz clapped his hands. "Finally, something fun."

Gareth turned to him. "This won't be a full breach. Just get in, pull what you can on override systems, neural tech, any mention of the core structure. And stay quiet. We don't want them knowing anyone's sniffing around."

Laz gave a mock salute. "Quieter than Gareth on feelings day."

Gareth's eyes flicked toward him. That flat, unimpressed look that said *you're lucky we need you.*

Ivy looked between them, heart ticking fast in her chest. The next step was happening. And there was no turning back now. But one thing still gnawed at her.

She turned to Gareth. "The pendant, you said it was your mother's... but it's from here." Her eyes flicked toward Ambry and Laz. "This region, I mean."

"So... how did you get it? We've never exactly been out this way before."

Gareth hesitated. "She left it with me," he said. "A long time ago, before she died. I kept it because... it felt like a reminder. Of her, of what she believed in. I never imagined it meant anything more."

Laz gave a low whistle. "So you've been walking around with a secret key this whole time, and didn't even know?"

Gareth's mouth twitched into a half-smile. "I'm a slow learner."

Ivy met Gareth's eyes, holding his gaze. "Do you think it's strange, how it still took the scenic route back?"

Gareth met her eyes. "Maybe. Or maybe it just needed to get back home, any way it could." He held her gaze for a moment longer. "We'll talk, Ivy. I'll explain. When the time's right."

Ivy just looked at him, waiting.

The silence stretched. Long enough to turn uncomfortable before Laz gave a loud, pointed cough. "You know, I didn't bring enough snacks for this level of awkward."

Ambry came over and wrapped Ivy into a bear hug, his gaze flicking between the two of them. "We should go," he said. "We'll need time to plan, anyway."

Laz waved lazily behind him. "I'll start poking around. If there's a door, I'll find a way through."

Ambry pressed a kiss to the top of her head. "I'll write. Soon."

Ivy nodded, still tight-lipped, her emotions simmering just below the surface. Ambry hesitated, then gave her a crooked, meaningful smile, and turned to follow Laz. They disappeared into the trees, shadows folding around them like a promise.

"We should head back." Gareth gave her a quick glance, softer than before. "Long walk. And we've both got enough to think about."

Ivy nodded, falling into step beside him as they started toward the POD.

"So…" she said, turning slowly to Gareth. Arms folded. "Bit strange, huh? Having a magical key from Spero. On Earth. Before we even got here."

Gareth didn't answer immediately.

She raised an eyebrow. "Like… super weird. What gives, Gareth?"

He exhaled, slow and deliberate. "It's… complicated."

"Right. Because 'It's complicated' is basically our family motto at this point."

Gareth ran a hand through his hair as they walked. "I didn't lie. Not exactly. I just didn't tell you everything."

"Classic," Ivy muttered, folding her arms tighter.

He gave her a pointed look. "I was a kid, Ivy. I barely understood what was happening. All I knew was that the people who raised me, Toren and Mira, weren't my birth parents. They gave me bits and pieces of a story… probably too scared to say it out loud."

She softened, just a little. "Like what?"

"That I was born somewhere… important. Somewhere I couldn't go back to. They said I carried something valuable, something meant to stay hidden. The pendant. They didn't know what it did. Just that it had to be kept safe."

Ivy looked down at the pendant where it rested against her chest. "So you gave it to me?"

"I'd held onto it for years without knowing why. Then I saw the way you moved through the greenhouse, how the plants responded. You noticed things most of us would have missed. It reminded me of a story Mira used to tell, about how the Leafwings only ever showed themselves to people with a true connection. That story helped me remember why the pendant mattered. Why my mother passed it down."

Ivy's fingers brushed the pendant. "Wouldn't it make more sense for you to keep it?"

Gareth shook his head. "It was never about legacy. Or bloodlines. It's about who you are inside."

"So you just handed your whole family's story... to me? The girl who once broke your toothbrush?"

"Better than leaving it in a drawer."

Despite herself, she let out a short, startled laugh. "Is that why you came on this mission? Did you think the pendant was from here... or did you know?"

Gareth shook his head. "It wasn't about the mission, not exactly. Toren and Mira... they didn't even want me involved. Said it was too risky. Too close."

"Too close to what?" Ivy asked.

He hesitated, gaze flicking toward the trees. "To where I came from."

"You mean Earth?"

Gareth looked at her, calm and certain. "No. I was born here, Ivy. On Spero."

She stopped. The forest didn't. A breeze moved through the leaves above them, soft and unbothered, but everything inside her went still. "You're serious, aren't you?"

Gareth looked back, tipped his head gently forward, urging her to keep walking.

"Yes," he said. "I left as a kid. Too young to understand why. But I came back on purpose. The mission gave me a way to come home. To return to the place my roots were buried, even if I didn't understand them yet. Earth never fit quite right. But here, something in my bones remembered. And this pendant... my mother thought it mattered enough to pass it on. Toren and Mira made sure I understood the story behind it, so I wouldn't forget what it meant. What it might mean someday."

Ivy watched him for a long moment. Her mind spun, lining up memories. His quiet glances at the stars, his silence every time she asked about his childhood. It all made sense now, and yet somehow, none of it did.

"You were born here," she said, like she needed to hear it out loud. "That's wild."

Gareth gave a small smile. "You're not upset I kept it from you?"

She shook her head. "Nah. I was a kid, and you didn't owe me the truth about this. It was your story to tell. And geez, Gareth, what a story. I already knew you were cool, but this is next level."

He laughed. A real, surprised laugh that crinkled the corners of his eyes.

"Oh... the stories." Her eyes widened, a stunned laugh catching in her throat. "The butterfly lizards... the firefly birds. They were real."

Gareth's smile softened, something almost sad flickering behind it. "Yeah. They were real."

But Ivy's voice softened. "I'm sorry you had to go through all of this alone. I'm guessing my parents didn't know either?"

Gareth shook his head.

She exhaled, her gaze drifting to the stars above them. "I know what it's like. Not belonging, feeling like you don't have a home." Her eyes flicked back to him. "Wait... don't tell me. You grew up on a ship too?"

Gareth smiled. "Yeah. Six years old when they took me off Spero. I barely understood what was happening." He shifted a fallen branch aside as they walked, his voice low but even. "Toren and Mira... they saved me. Someone came for my family. That's how my parents died."

He paused, just for a second. "I still don't know why. It's what I've been trying to find out here. They got me on board just in time. The trip took twelve years. I was eighteen when we arrived."

"Wow, I'm sorry, Gareth," Ivy let out a slow breath. "That... must've been rough."

"I was very used to dehydrated lentils when we reached Earth." Gareth gave a faint smile. "By the time we got there... Toren and Mira weren't young anymore. They'd been in their fifties when we left Spero, and the journey pushed them into their sixties. I had some good years with them on Earth, but not enough. Age caught up fast, and eventually, I lost them too." He said it without bitterness, just fact.

"And you never told anyone?" Ivy glanced at him, her chest tight. "No one should have to carry that alone."

Gareth gave a small shrug. "Wasn't much choice."

Ivy pressed her lips together, falling quiet for a moment. "Lucky for you, I specialise in complicated." She gave his arm a nudge.

He snorted under his breath. "Lucky me."

She smirked. "And just so we're clear, I don't do exchanges."

He glanced at the pendant around her neck, his voice dropped. "When I was a kid... it used to open all the time. I thought it was just some clever trinket, something to keep me busy. It would hum in my hands, like it recognised me."

A flicker passed across Ivy's face. Not surprise, exactly. Something sharper. Like a thread pulling tight.

Beside her, Gareth kept walking, his steps slow and even. "But then... things got harder. The ship started breaking down, we didn't know how long the trip would take... every day felt like a countdown. We were counting rations, patching what we could. The AI back then wasn't like AURA, we fixed most systems by hand, half the time with no idea what we were even looking at. Just trying to make it another week. And I—" He drew a slow breath. "I went from a boy to a man faster than I should have. Worry crept in. Fear. I stopped thinking about anything beyond the next repair... the next ration."

He nudged a branch aside with his foot. "Then it stopped opening as much. Little by little... it went quiet." His voice lowered. "By the time I hit eighteen, by the time we reached Earth, it wasn't responding at all."

"And I stopped trying."

Ivy stared at him. At the forest behind him. At the world she was just discovering, one that had already turned its back on him. Her chest ached with something sharp and protective.

"Hey," she said, stepping closer. "You don't get to decide you're out of the story. Not when you carried this for so long."

She stopped and caught his arm, pulling him gently to a halt. "You've been carrying that longer than I've been alive. But you don't have to carry it alone, not anymore." Her fingers brushed the pendant. "We'll figure it out, Gareth. You and me. Whatever this system thing is... whatever the pendant does... we do it together."

Gareth met her eyes, giving a slow nod. The corner of his mouth lifted, not a full smile, but close. He wrapped an arm around her shoulders for a moment, gave a quiet squeeze, then let go and kept walking.

They reached the edge of the camp. Grace and David were hunched over a makeshift workbench, sorting through sample canisters and tapping notes into a datapad between them.

Ivy exhaled, glancing sideways. "But I have so many questions."

Gareth gave a quiet, knowing smile. "Later."

As they crossed into the clearing, Grace glanced up and caught sight of them. "Hey! There you two are. Don't forget to log those samples. If they degrade, I won't be happy."

Grace turned back to the datapad, flicking through readings with a practised hand, her sleeves rolled past her elbows. David leant in beside her, running a handheld scanner over the data stream, the two of them slipping right back into their usual rhythm.

Ivy barely had time to open her mouth before—

"Who," Grace asked, eyebrows high. "Logged a Pegasus into the mission records?!" She scrolled through the report, eyes narrowing.

David choked on his drink, coughing. "A Pegasus?"

AURA chimed in smoothly. "I believe that was Miss Virelli. I have the physical description on file, should you require it?"

Ivy buried her face in her hands. "We're really doing this?"

David gave her a look. "We are talking about a horse with wings... right?"

Chapter Thirty

The Lumenrail hummed underfoot. Silent, smooth, and unnervingly perfect. Ivy sat next to Ambry, fingers absently brushing the pendant at her neck. It was warm against her skin, hidden beneath the neckline of her shirt. Ambry reached for her hand and gave it a quiet squeeze.

The transport car glided along crystal-threaded tracks, the gold shine of the bioluminescent rails flashing silver as the twin suns struck them. During the day, solar panels on the roof absorbed sunslight, at night, the lunar-reactive strands powered everything with eerie precision.

Outside the panoramic windows, the outer rim of Domaris rose ahead of them. Perfect spirals of glass and metal, coiling upward like a flower frozen mid-bloom. It was beautiful in a way that felt... wrong. Every window glinted in sync. Every walkway curved just so.

Ivy gave a low whistle. "So this is what a control complex looks like when it's trying to impress the universe." She gestured at the huge metal spirals of glass outside. "What did they say at the festival? Technology woven gently with nature. Nailed it."

Ambry glanced out the window. "Funny how what they preach and what they build never quite match."

When the rail finally slowed, Ivy stood and followed him out onto the platform, their footsteps echoing slightly against polished stone. They stepped into a city that looked like it had been designed by symmetry itself. The trees were evenly spaced and identical. Their leaves didn't rustle. The wind was regulated. Ivy could feel it, the way the environment calibrated itself in real time. Light, temperature, airflow all shifting to maintain perfect comfort. No vines spilled freely. No animals darted by. Even the sky, locked in a pale midday glare between the spires, looked curated. Like a backdrop.

A small park sat to their right, and Ivy wandered toward it. Flowers bloomed in synchronised waves, opening and closing in rhythmic pulses. She crouched by a vine pressed to a sculpted wall. It didn't move when she touched it. Didn't reach for her fingers. It wasn't asleep. It wasn't aware. It was arranged. Back in the wild, nothing looked like this. Nothing felt like this. The forest moved in rhythm with her. Matched her silence. Echoed her pace. Here, the silence wasn't peaceful. It was obedient.

She straightened and caught Ambry watching her.

He offered a shrug. "I'll say it. I miss the bugs."

They moved deeper into the residential quarter, the symmetry pressing tighter with every turn. Each street a mirror of the last, every door perfectly aligned.

Ivy glanced around. "Does everything here come with matching instructions?"

Ambry gave a low snort. "Wouldn't surprise me."

They rounded another corner, and finally stopped at a low, unassuming house with a vine-laced arch over the door. Ambry knocked twice. They waited, long enough for Ivy to wonder if Laz was even home. Then the door slid open.

Laz stood there in a sharp-cut jacket over a simple tunic, sleeves pushed up. His eyebrows lifted. "Well, well. The forest fugitives return. Took you long enough."

"Why does everyone keep saying I am late?" Ivy said.

Laz grinned, stepping aside. "Get in before one of my neighbours reports your hair."

Ivy stepped over the threshold, and into something that felt like a memory sealed in glass. The home was quiet. Immaculate. Everything in its place. The walls were lined with soft-touch panels and diffused light, but it felt like no one actually lived there.

Laz closed the door behind them and gestured with a mock flourish. "Welcome to my state-sanctioned dream box. Shoes off. Questions later."

He led them through the entry hall, past a sitting room with a single couch and a crystal sculpture positioned as if it had never been touched. "Branik's idea of decorating," Laz muttered. "Minimalism with a touch of emotional suppression."

They passed the kitchen. Spotless, with one bowl drying on the rack, one cup on the shelf, a single place setting waiting on the table.

"He eats like clockwork," Laz said, voice lighter than it should've been. "Same chair. Same meal. Every single night."

He turned left into a hallway. The lights adjusted as they moved. Laz jerked his thumb toward a closed door on the right. "That's his room. Only go in there when you want to be asked about your efficiency."

Ivy wrinkled her nose. "Yeah, hard pass." She moved past it quickly and paused at the next door down. This one was slightly ajar. She peeked through the crack. The room was chaos. Wires, tools, and half-finished projects covered every surface.

"And that's mine," Laz said. "I like to think of it as organised rebellion."

Ivy nudged the door open and stepped inside. The room was bigger than she expected, not sprawling, but spacious enough to move without constantly bumping into things. It had the feel of a studio apartment, tucked into the curve of a city house. Which was good, because Laz's room had a *lot* of things.

A single bed was pushed against the wall beneath a narrow window, blankets half-kicked aside. A set of shelves ran along the opposite wall, stuffed with neatly folded clothes, spare tools, and whatever projects hadn't made it to the worktable yet. A climate system was built into the floor, humming faintly beneath her feet, a luxury compared to the fire-warmed forest homes. The air was cooler than she was used to. Not unpleasant, just... cleaner.

In the centre of the room sat a broad worktable cluttered with half-built circuits, cracked lenses, and a scattering of metal shards that looked suspiciously like they came from scrap. Tall stools stood crookedly on either side. It wasn't neat. It wasn't wild. It was Laz. Clever, stitched together, and somehow still warmer than it had any right to be.

"Yeah, sorry it's cold. I gave the Climeflow a little upgrade, and now it's punishing me with 'crisp'." Laz gestured vaguely toward the stools. "Sit. I'll find snacks. Or whatever passes for snacks in that emotionally repressed kitchen."

He disappeared into the hall, leaving Ivy and Ambry alone in the stillness.

Ivy stepped further in, eyes drifting around the room. A framed photo on the shelf caught her attention. Three figures, all shades of pink. A woman with salmon-coloured hair and soft rose-gold eyes.

A man with deeper tones, darker pink skin, near-crimson hair. And between them, a boy with magenta hair and a toothy grin, perched on the edge of a workbench, holding up a clunky circuit board like it was treasure. The warmth in the photo caught her off guard, all that colour, all that light. She didn't realise Laz had come back until he spoke from behind her.

"She left when I was eleven," he said, voice flat.

Ivy turned. Laz was looking at the photo, but not really seeing it, his eyes distant.

Then his gaze snapped back, and he straightened, tone suddenly lighter. "Anyway — found snacks."

— ✦ —

Later, the three of them squeezed onto battered stools around Laz's cluttered work table, half-empty cups and a bowl of solarbark crisps crammed between them. They'd been running through the plan for nearly half an hour, half-drunk cups and snack crumbs gathering between bursts of half-serious banter and frantic strategy.

"This is a terrible plan," Ivy said.

Laz grinned. "You say that like it's a bad thing."

"She hates me," Ivy pointed out. "I'm not even exaggerating. If I knock on her door, she'll probably yell, 'Release the hounds!' Only they'll be, like, elegant and violet and genetically engineered to judge me."

"But that's why you're the distraction... and I'm the one swiping her father's access pass."

"Wait — what?" Ivy spun to look at him. "How am I the distraction? Ambry's the one she has a crush on."

Ambry spluttered. "No she doesn't."

"Because," he said with a theatrical flourish, "you've got the drama, the tension, the ancient pendant of mystery. You're very distractable."

"That's not even a word."

"It is when you're holding the key to a planetary conspiracy."

Ambry gave her a look that was almost apologetic. "She's already expecting us. We just need five minutes. Enough for Laz to get into her dad's office while Nyra's talking to you."

"She won't talk to me," Ivy muttered. "She'll lecture me like I'm a glitch in her perfect system. And then have me archived."

Laz gave her a playful nudge. "Just do that thing where you dodge questions and act all mysterious. You're scarily good at it."

"You know what else I'm good at?" she shot back. "Detecting when I'm about to be thrown under a very symmetrical, moon-powered bus."

Ambry tried not to smile. "You're doing great already."

"Okay, okay," Ivy said, giving up. "If you're going to swipe the pass from Red Captain Planet, the least I can do is run distraction for you. I've got your back, partner."

Laz grinned, tapping two fingers to his temple in mock salute. "Knew I liked you."

"We should get moving," Ambry said. "Nyra's quarters are in the southern tower. She'll be expecting us. Let's go steal a pass and—"

But he didn't finish. A sound cut through the air, a hiss as the front door slid open. They all turned at the sound.

Heavy footsteps moved down the hall.

Laz stood up slowly, his whole posture shifting. Not scared, just tense. Like a cord drawn tight.

Ivy's heart thudded as the figure stepped into the room.

A uniformed guard. Tall. Broad. The quiet authority of someone who didn't need to speak to be obeyed.

Her fingers twitched toward the pendant. Ambry shifted like he was about to bolt.

They just stared, frozen for a second.

Laz's jaw tightened, just a flicker.

"Oh, hi, Dad."

CHAPTER THIRTY-ONE

The streets of Domaris curved around them in quiet spirals, gleaming under the soft afternoon light.

A vendor was starting to pack up his flatbread cart, steam drifting lazily from trays that were more empty than full. A breeze lifted the scent of warm herbs and fresh grain as Ivy walked between Laz and Ambry, her hands tucked into her sleeves. She folded her arms and kept pace, watching Laz stroll ahead with his usual easy swagger. Like it was any other day.

She waited until they were past the first tier of spiral towers before breaking the silence. "So…" she said casually. "Your dad's a guard?"

Laz didn't even flinch. "Mhm."

"As in, full badge, scary uniform, 'obey or we tranquilize you' kind of guard?"

"That's the one."

Her eyebrows lifted. "Is he… strict?"

Laz gave a crooked shrug. "Not really, I mean, not in the grounding-me kind of way. Technically, we coexist under the same roof. Not a lot of father–son bonding moments these days."

Ambry shot Laz a glance.

Laz waved a hand, brushing it off. "It's not a thing. He wasn't always like that."

Ivy tilted her head. "What do you mean?"

"Before he joined The Order, he was… different. Loud. Funny. The kind of guy who made weird voices at the dinner table just to make me choke on my soup. And he was always tinkering with junk tech he found in the recycling quarters. He used to build these dumb little bots that tripped over their own legs just to make me laugh."

"And now?"

"Now he makes tea at exactly the same time every day, reads the same schedule bulletins, and stares at the wall like it's personally offended him."

Ivy glanced at Ambry, who didn't speak.

"What changed?" she asked.

Laz hesitated, then shrugged. "He said he joined The Order for a better life. For me. Thought if he wore the uniform, followed the rules, we'd be protected. Safe. Respected."

"Are you?" Ivy asked quietly.

He didn't answer right away. "I don't know," Laz said finally. "I think I'd rather be unsafe and still have my dad."

They kept walking. Ivy didn't push further. Domaris shimmered ahead of them, all elegance and symmetry. A perfect city, built on silence. A group of schoolchildren passed on the other side of the lane, dressed in soft grey robes and walking in perfect rows. Their soft chatter floated between them, light, careful, too polite for kids their age.

Laz rolled his shoulders as if shaking something off and flashed Ivy a grin. "Anyway. You ready to charm a girl who may or may not be genetically designed to loathe you?"

"Born ready," Ivy muttered. "Do I have time to fake a new personality before we get there?"

Laz smirked. "Too late. We already submitted the morally smug version."

They reached the base of the south tower a few minutes later. It soared above them in gleaming tiers of glass and metal, every surface sharp-edged and spotless. The entrance was a perfect oval cut into the façade, rimmed with pale light. Ivy glanced up. The upper levels disappeared into the afternoon glare, spires stacked like circuit boards against the sky. The whole place hummed with quiet authority, like even the walls had clearance levels.

Chapter Thirty-Two

The lift doors slid open with a soft chime, revealing the top floor of Domaris's south tower. The kind of place that whispered wealth without ever raising its voice.

Ivy stepped out first, gaze sweeping across a long corridor lined with polished stone and glowing trim that pulsed in soft intervals, like a heartbeat engineered to impress. She felt the sudden, overwhelming urge to mess it up somehow. Maybe scuff the floor. Un-align a painting. Lick the wall.

They moved down the hall, footsteps muffled by carpet that looked engineered for silence. The walls were too smooth, too flawless, every painting perfectly spaced, every detail symmetrical. Ambry paused at a sleek panel beside Nyra's apartment door. "She's definitely home. The signal shows green."

"I could fake a seizure," Ivy offered. "Or die tragically right here in the foyer."

"Tempting," Laz said, tapping away at a small Tactis. "But if you die, I'm the one stuck letting Ambry crash at my place, and I've heard his snoring's an Order-approved torture device."

"Hey!" Ambry said, pressing the chime. "That's not true." He said to Ivy.

A pause, a soft click. Laz slid the Tactis out of view. Fast, silent, smooth.

The door slid open.

Nyra stood in the entryway barefoot, regal as always, wrapped in white and silver loungewear that looked too precise to actually lounge in. Her eyes flicked from Ambry to Ivy, then to the third figure standing behind them. "You brought both of them."

Ambry gave a small shrug. "Thought you wouldn't mind."

She didn't answer. She simply turned and walked inside.

Nyra's apartment was too perfect. Even from the hallway, Ivy could feel it. The unnatural stillness, the sterile beauty. The walls pulsed in cool violet, tuned to Nyra's biometrics. The scent of engineered lavender hung in the air, just enough to be calming, not enough to offend. It was harmony on display.

The apartment opened up like a gallery. Everything gleamed in various shades of white, from the polished floors to the seamless, luminous walls. A crescent-shaped lounge curved along one side of the room, upholstered in pale velvet and scattered with delicate cushions that looked like they'd never been sat on. A single bookcase broke the monotony, tall and minimal, each spine spaced with mathematical precision. Projected greenery shimmered across one wall, soft holographic vines trailing downward, flickering gently as the air shifted. Long curtains hung like draped art, crafted from white-dyed Kavari leaves, silvery-green at the edges, thick, and softly textured. The central stalk marks had been cut away entirely, the remaining panels trimmed into flawless rectangles. The entire space felt curated, quiet, and unnervingly perfect. Nothing breathed.

Except for the creature watching them.

It was curled on a velvet perch by the window, pure white fur catching the light like mist over snow. Its eyes glowed in deep, shifting opal, impossible to read. Long ears curled at the tips like ornamental tendrils, and its tail draped elegantly across its paws.

Ivy slowed. "What... is that?"

The creature blinked, unbothered.

"That's Asera," Nyra said. "My mother gave her to me when I passed the Arcanum Tier."

Ambry leant forward slightly. "She's a Velune, right? I've heard of them."

Nyra nodded. "They don't bond easily. But Asera... she senses intention."

Ivy frowned. "Intention?"

Nyra met her eyes. "What people mean. What they carry beneath their words. She's never been wrong."

Asera lifted her head and let out a low, singing sound that sat somewhere between a hum and a purr.

"I'll get the tea," Nyra said, stepping toward the kitchen with calm purpose.

Ambry leant close to Ivy. "Okay, we just need a few minutes."

"No problem," Ivy whispered, already halfway across the room. She crouched next to Asera like she was meeting royalty. "Hi there. You're perfect. Do you know that? You're the most perfect thing I've ever seen."

Ambry exhaled. "Ivy—"

"Just look at her little feet," Ivy whispered. "And her ears. And her eyes. I think I'm having a spiritual experience."

Laz and Ambry shared a glance, somewhere between concerned and resigned. Laz gave a low whistle. "Okay, plan's crumbling. That thing's stolen her brain."

Ivy didn't blink. "I'm fine. Everything is fine. This is the best day of my life."

Laz leant down, voice dropping. "Seriously. You might wanna blink before Nyra walks in and thinks you're proposing."

"I am not proposing," Ivy hissed. "I'm... admiring. Respectfully."

"Uh-huh." Laz smirked. "You want me to give you two a minute?"

"I'm good." Ivy gave Asera a soft scratch behind one ear. "We're good, aren't we, Princess Snugglepaws?"

Asera blinked slowly, entirely unimpressed.

"But you are supposed to distract Nyra," Laz whispered.

"I am!" Ivy said. "By being extremely lovable and bonding with her animal. This is a long game. A long, furry, sparkle-eyed game."

Asera yawned, then head-butted Ivy's hand with polite disinterest.

Ambry gave her a look. "Ivy... is this your idea of a distraction? Come on, what are you doing?"

Ivy rested her chin on her hands. "Kidnap. Adoration. Possibly soul bonding. Haven't decided yet."

Ambry sighed. "We've lost her." He looked to Laz. "Can you handle this on your own?"

Laz scoffed. "Wow. So much for 'I've got your back, partner.' That's not backup. That's full emotional betrayal by floof."

Ambry raised a brow.

"Fine," Laz muttered, "but I'm filing a betrayal report. With diagrams. And snacks. It's gonna be beautiful.."

Nyra returned just then, gliding in with a silver tray balanced perfectly between her hands. The tea set was exquisite. Delicate crystal cups etched with spiraling leaf patterns, their handles studded with tiny glowing beads. Even the steam rose in delicate spirals, as if the pot had been engineered for elegance. Ivy stared at the setup as if it might sing a lullaby.

"House blend," Nyra said, placing the tray on a low white table with a crystal top that caught the light like ice. "Infused with nightbloom, serenity root, and a few leaves from my mother's private grove."

"Of course it is," Ivy muttered.

Laz cleared his throat. "So... love what you've done with the place. Is it just you here, or are your terrifyingly powerful parents also lurking behind a kavari curtain?"

Nyra arched a brow. "They're not home. Order business. Likely a late night."

"Perfect. I mean — peaceful. Very... peaceful." Laz smiled too fast.

Ambry shot him a look that said, cool it, while Ivy absentmindedly braided a section of Asera's tail fluff like it was a sacred duty.

Laz's voice piped up too loud. "Bathroom? Where's the bathroom?"

Nyra gestured toward the hallway without turning around. "All the way down, last door on the left. Don't touch anything."

Laz squinted down the hallway. "If I disappear in there, tell Princess Snugglepaws I died bravely."

Nyra turned, frowning slightly. "I'm sorry — who?"

He slipped down the hallway like a man who thought he was being subtle.

Ivy lingered near Asera, who sat perfectly still and watching. The Velune stared at her with unsettling focus.

"Do you always stare like that?" Ivy whispered.

Asera blinked once. Then, tilted her head.

Ambry, watching from across the room, dragged a hand down his face and muttered something under his breath that sounded suspiciously like a plea to the Lightbringer for strength.

Nyra turned her attention to him with an amused smile. "Since when do you want to hang out in Domaris?"

"Ivy wanted to visit." Ambry forced a smile that could have cracked stone. "See how the other half lives."

Ivy, oblivious, was now trying to braid a second section of Asera's tail. "Do you think she'd mind if I made her a tiny flower crown? I feel like she'd really suit a flower crown."

Back down the hall, Laz found what he hoped was the office door. Locked. Seamless, no visible panel. He crouched.

A narrow band of etched blue shimmered at the edge of the door, almost hidden. Laz angled his Tactis toward it. He tapped the screen twice, then began typing fast, eyes locked on the interface. A faint shimmer rippled across the strip.

"Three pulses. Organic lock. Easy," he murmured. Click.

Inside, the office glowed like a living heart, pulsing light across the walls, data streams drifting like translucent veins. Laz scanned quickly, zeroed in, and plucked a slim crystal passkey from a recessed dock.

"Boom. Done."

He slipped it into his jacket and stepped out of the office, closing the door with exaggerated innocence. Just as Laz turned the corner, his Tactis slipped in his grip and knocked against the edge of a floating crystal shelf, a sharp clink of metal on glass echoing down the hall.

Asera lifted her head. Ivy tensed.

Nyra's brows drew together. "What was that?"

"Probably a breeze," Ivy said. "Or, you know, your tea set being emotionally resonant."

She turned toward the hall. "Laz, please tell me that noise wasn't you breaking something expensive."

Ambry stepped forward. "Wait, Nyra—"

Nyra paused. Ambry met her gaze with a half-smile, stepping smoothly into her path. "I was wondering something, actually," he said. "Do you still keep your books sorted by harmonic tone?"

She glanced at him. "Why would you—"

"You told me once. I always thought it was... elegant."

Nyra tilted her head slightly, eyes narrowing. "You remember that?"

"It's hard to forget anything you say."

Nyra arched an eyebrow. "Flattery? From you?"

"Just a thought," he said. "Some things are worth remembering."

Behind him, Ivy widened her eyes, hands flying up in a silent, *what are you doing?* When Nyra glanced over, Ivy abruptly turned it into an exaggerated yawn and pet Asera like she'd always meant to do that.

A moment later, Laz reappeared, drying his hands on his shirt. "All good. No death traps."

Nyra's eyes lingered on him a moment too long. "Right."

She turned toward the table. "The tea's getting cold."

Nyra turned toward the seating area, her steps smooth and practiced. Ambry followed, silent. Ivy lingered a moment longer, still crouched beside Asera. The Velune stared back, unblinking.

"I know," Ivy whispered. "This hurts me too." She gave Asara one last reluctant ear scratch, then stood with obvious regret and dragged herself toward the others.

They settled into the cushions, the tea set arranged on the crystal-topped table, all balance and ceremony, like everything else in the apartment. Ivy reached for her cup, and as she did, the pendant around her neck slipped into view.

Nyra's eyes tracked it instantly. "Nice pendant," she said. "New?"

"Old," Ivy replied, tucking it back beneath her shirt.

Asera stood. Uncurling like fog, she padded across the glass floor, soundless. Her opal eyes fixed on Ivy, or more precisely, the spot on her chest where the pendant hid beneath her shirt. She sniffed once, then let out a soft huff. Not disapproval, exactly. More like curiosity wrapped in silence. And then she turned away, tail flicking once behind her.

"She likes you," Nyra said. But her tone made it clear she didn't. She sipped her tea and gave Ivy a glance cold enough to frost glass.

"So, Ivy," Nyra said, tilting her head slightly. "What part of Spero did you say you were originally from?"

Ivy blinked. "Oh, you know. The, uh... tree-heavy part. Lots of bark. Big sky. Really — uh — bark-forward culture."

Ambry made a choking sound that he disguised as a cough.

"She means the western ridges," Laz chimed in smoothly. "They're known for their bark festivals."

Nyra gave him a flat look. "Fascinating."

"Very." Laz sipped his tea. "Last time I went, I saw someone juggle thornbulbs. Emotionally."

Ambry gave a low hum, almost like agreement. "Can't beat a good thornbulbs festival."

A long silence stretched between the group. Asera stared. Ivy melted. Nyra stirred her tea as if it were a diplomatic act.

Laz broke the silence. "So... is this the part where we politely pretend we're not all being judged by a sentient cloud puff?"

"She's not judging," Nyra said primly. "She's assessing."

"I don't mind," Ivy whispered. "Love being assessed. Especially by someone prettier than me."

Nyra didn't respond, but her eyebrow definitely had something to say.

Ambry tilted his head. "They're rare, right? Velune. I've never seen one outside the city."

She gave a small nod. "They're unique."

He glanced toward Asera. "So... where would someone even get one?"

Nyra's lips curved, but it wasn't quite a smile. "They're practically impossible to find. And even if you do... they almost never bond."

"I don't think that would be a problem."

Ivy caught the look Ambry gave Asera — quiet, thoughtful and something soft tugged at her chest. She smiled at Ambry when he met her eyes.

She finally snapped out of her haze. "We should probably get going. Big walk. Very important... walking."

Ambry stood. "Right. Thanks for the tea."

Nyra set down her teacup with a soft clink. "You don't have to go yet," she said, her tone a touch too casual. "I mean... Ivy and Laz clearly have somewhere to be, but you've only just gotten here."

He let his gaze drift around the group. "I'm pretty sure we all arrived at the same time."

She gave a small shrug, eyes dropping. "Still. You didn't even finish your tea."

He hesitated, glanced at Ivy, then back at Nyra. "Maybe next time."

Nyra didn't answer. She lifted her cup again, gaze fixed on Ambry, steady, unreadable. "Sure," she said, sharp as glass.

But her attention never drifted far from Ivy. Or more precisely, the spot where the pendant had vanished beneath her shirt.

As the door slid shut behind them, Nyra remained perfectly still. Her teacup rested in her hands, forgotten. Across the room, Asera let out a single, sharp exhale and returned to her perch.

Nyra's gaze stayed fixed on the door, jaw tight, eyes unreadable. Because that pendant hadn't just looked familiar.

It *was* familiar.

And as far as she knew… there was only one.

— ✦ —

As they stepped into the lift and the door slid shut behind them, Ambry leant against the wall and let out a slow breath. The soft hum of the ascent filled the quiet.

"That was almost a disaster."

"Was it?" Ivy asked dreamily. "Because I met a magical snow cloud who might be my soulmate."

"You forgot the part where you were absolutely no help and just… kept rubbing her ears."

"She liked it," Ivy said.

"Your soul straight-up left your body," Laz said. "Twice." He tipped his head back against the rail, a crooked grin playing at his mouth.

Ivy leant closer to Ambry and muttered, "Okay… but if we get through this? I want a Velune."

Ambry groaned.

Chapter Thirty-Three

The Vanta Spire looked like a sculpture designed to win awards for architectural smugness. Which, Ivy guessed, was exactly the point.

It rose from the heart of Domaris like a blade — tall, narrow, and impossibly dark. Its surface was a seamless fusion of black glass and brushed metal, stitched with the faintest silver lines that pulsed like a heartbeat. The panels glowed subtly, swallowing reflections rather than casting them. There were no signs, no visible entrance. Just a wall of polished silence, rising above the city like it had been lowered into place from somewhere else entirely.

Ivy stared up, heart thudding a little faster than she liked. The tower didn't shout. Didn't warn. It just stood there, silent and immaculate, daring anyone to come closer.

"Where's the door?" she asked.

Laz grinned beside her. "The Order doesn't do doors. It does… invitations."

Ambry pressed a hand to the panel. Nothing. "Then how do we get invited in?"

Laz stepped forward and slipped a small crystal pass from his pocket, the one he'd stolen from Nyra's house. "We ask nicely." He held it to a thin strip of etched silver glowing faintly along the side of the frame. A soft shimmer passed over the surface.

A pause. Then a faint chime. A seam appeared in the glass, vertical, precise. It opened like a breath. Cold air rolled out.

"See?" Laz said, smug. "Polite as ever."

The entry opened into a high corridor. Smooth, gleaming, and deliberately blank. Just pristine glass corridors bending softly around corners, leading deeper into the tower's hollow heart. The kind of place that was designed to disorient anyone who didn't belong.

"Hold up a sec," Laz said, crouching down and pulling out his Tactis. He tapped a command, and the device flared, projecting a tight ring of mini holograms that hovered just above its surface. Surveillance feeds flickering, crisp and silent.

"Cameras are in a loop," he said under his breath. "We've got about fifteen minutes before the system notices."

They followed Laz deeper into the tower, past branching corridors and mirrored walls that reflected nothing back but silence. Every surface gleamed, pristine and unmarked. Laz moved with purpose, checking his Tactis, muttering turns under his breath. Ambry stayed close behind, eyes scanning every corner, every curve. The deeper they went, the colder the air became, not in temperature exactly. Just sterile. Controlled.

They turned a corner, and Ivy slowed.

Set behind thick glass, a lab unfolded in two parts. The first lab stopped her cold. Dozens of flowers stood in perfect rows, each one perched in its own containment cradle. Their layered petals flared like crystallised flames, translucent and edged in soft opaline light. Silver-veined stems curled around slender supports, and at the heart of each bloom, a faint blue glow pulsed in slow, rhythmic light.

"Are those..." Her voice caught. "I've seen these before. In the palace."

They were the same bloom, only smaller. Replicated, tagged with numbers and wired into sensor arrays, clustered in cultivation trays. Not for display, but for harvest. Their core glow was dimmer than in the palace greenhouse, pulled inward, stored.

"They're growing them," she breathed. "Like crops."

Ambry stared through the glass, expression darkening. "What are they doing with them?" His eyes narrowed, he caught her arm. "Look."

In the adjoining room, the space changed, colder, clinical. Stark benches. Surgical tools. Vials glowing faint blue. Needles and scanners surrounded dissected blue cores, arranged with surgical precision, like anatomy samples on display. One fragment — the same bright blue as her pendant — floated inside a sealed case, fractured and half-harvested. Nearby systems pulsed with quiet function, steady and precise.

"Whatever this is... it's not natural." Ambry said, voice tight.

Laz checked the time on his Tactis, eyes narrowing. "We've got eleven minutes left on that loop." His voice dropped. Firm. "Whatever this is, we figure it out later. If we're getting that data, we go now."

They moved quickly, boots whispering on polished stone, until Laz found a hidden panel near a pulse-lit column. He tapped Solen's pass against the panel, and a faint pulse of silver light ran down the wall. A narrow seam appeared, then split, the panels sliding apart to reveal a small glass-walled lift. Its interior glowed faintly, light spilling across the polished floor. They stepped inside. The doors sealed without a sound, and the lift began a smooth vertical climb through the tower's hollow core. Light from the passing levels slid over the glass, reflections layering and shifting as they rose.

At the top, the doors parted to reveal the central chamber. The data hub.

The hub shimmered with layered data streams, lightforms spiralling through the air like slow-motion sparks. White walls arched inward, fluid and seamless, every surface alive with quiet motion. Pulses ran the curves — biometric locks, layered encryption, automated file audits — too fast to follow, but not to ignore. A faint hum pressed at Ivy's ears, the air sharp with the static tang of locked information.

"Peaceful utopias don't usually need this many servers," she muttered. "How do we even know what we're looking for?"

A central console rose from the floor like a monument. Tall, angular, matte black. Cold light spilled from narrow slits along its base, illuminating the banks of data streaming overhead. Thin layers of holo-screens spiralled around the core like stacked glass, each one alive with shifting code and classified logs.

Laz stepped forward, already scanning the console for access points. "That's why I'm here." He cracked his knuckles. "We take it all."

He moved fast, fingers flying across the holo-interface, files blooming around him in layered projections. Schematics. Memory indexes. Surveillance logs. A stream of secrets begging to be ripped wide open.

Ivy and Ambry stood guard, shifting uneasily. The silence wasn't peaceful. It was the kind that made your thoughts feel too loud.

Laz's hands moved in precise, practiced bursts across the holo-keys, tapping out sequences like a surgeon in a rush. Lines of code blinked, fractured, then reformed. The system held firm.

A flicker ran through the holograms. Ivy's heart jumped. "What was that?"

"Cipher Wall," Laz said. "It's not happy, but I've got Solen's pass. That should open everything."

He slid the crystal pass into the console. The system stalled, then unfurled with a soft chime. He muttered under his breath, brow pinching. "Come on... come on..."

Ambry's eyes flicked toward the lift. "How much time's left?"

Laz didn't look up. "Not enough."

"Then move. We're about to get caught."

"I know." Laz entered another command. The console chimed again. Locked. "Oh, think you're cute, do you?"

Ivy shifted her weight, every muscle wired tight. She scanned the walls, every surface too clean, too silent.

Ambry edged closer. "Laz. How much longer?"

"Almost there," Laz muttered, fingers still flying. "Just need thirty seconds."

Ivy pressed her palm against the cool console edge. Every second felt like a countdown she couldn't hear.

Then—

"Yes," Laz said, his shoulders easing. He pulled a data shard from his pocket and slid it into the port. Data unfurled across the console in shimmering streams — walls of code, layers of neural maps, dates, control logs.

Ambry leant in, his voice low. "What are we looking for? Schematics? Government records?"

Laz didn't glance up. "This isn't a 'figure out the secrets of The Order' mission," he said, fingers dancing across the data streams. "This is a smash-and-grab. We take everything and sort the nightmares later."

Ivy stepped closer as files began stacking, hundreds of them. Names, dates, memory suppression protocols. Emotional variance logs. One line caught her eye.

EOS 6 — MISSION LOGS.

She stepped closer, pulse spiking, but Laz was already moving.

He keyed the shutdown sequence, the projections collapsing inward in a ripple of light. "Got it," he said, sliding the shard into his jacket.

"Time to go," Ambry said.

They moved fast, crossing to the lift.

It dropped in silence, the glass walls reflecting pale streaks of light as they fell. They kept their eyes forward, letting the silence ride with them.

When the doors opened at the base level, the corridor was still. Empty.

They were clear.

Chapter Thirty-Four

The night air was warmer once they got to the village. Softer. The tension of the city began to ease from Ivy's shoulders as she walked through the forest. The sound of insects, the swaying hush of leaves overhead, the faint bioluminescent glow underfoot — it all grounded her, pulling her into herself again.

Ambry was walking her back, his hand wrapped around hers. He hadn't said much since they left the city, and Ivy wasn't sure if that was a good thing. They crested the last rise, the treetops opening to the stars above. Ivy paused, catching Gareth's silhouette up ahead, waiting in the stillness. Her gaze drifted to the moons, one silver, one gold, slowly pulling apart across the sky.

Ambry followed her gaze. "Do you think they miss each other?" he asked.

"What, the moons?"

He shrugged. "They're always pulling away. Always chasing, never catching."

She searched Ambry's face. "But they were close... the night of the Moonrise Pull."

His eyes stayed on the moons. "Yeah. Closer than they ever get." He exhaled slowly. "But once a year... doesn't feel like nearly enough." The light caught in the curve of his jaw, the quiet thoughtfulness in his eyes. Something inside her twisted.

"I hate this part," she said.

"What part?"

"The part where we leave each other."

His brow furrowed, but before he could answer, she caught his hands. They were strong, steady, warm. Her gaze lifted to his, soft with promise. "I'll try to get out more. When I can."

Ambry didn't answer right away. His thumbs brushed over her knuckles, slow. "I wish you didn't have to sneak around for that."

Ivy dropped her gaze. "It's complicated."

He gave a quiet nod, eyes fixed on their joined hands. "You're nearly eighteen, Ivy." The next words came low, almost breaking. "How long do you think we can keep pretending I'm just some… shadow you visit?"

Her heart sank. "It's… not like that."

He met her eyes, steady, hurting. "Then what is it?"

Her grip softened into something desperate, a plea not to let go. It was easier to hold on than to speak.

Ambry exhaled, a soft breath that sounded almost like surrender. "I know. I just…" He hesitated. "I want more than this."

Ivy felt a tight ache bloom in her chest, the words sat on the edge of her tongue. The truth, the real reason, everything. But she couldn't. "I know," she said. "I want that too."

They stood there, hands linked, the night pressing in softly around them.

He was quiet for a moment. "I keep thinking about the grove."

She tilted her head. "The one near your house?"

He nodded. "Yeah. Big clearing. Kavari trees thick enough to grow a house into. Space for a garden. Thinking I'll start shaping a place there soon, coax the trunks into walls, train the branches into a roof. Maybe have a Velune or two running around." His eyes searched hers. "It's quiet. Peaceful. Doesn't ask too much of you."

Ivy couldn't speak right away. Her throat felt too tight. With guilt, with longing, with something that might've been a promise if she'd dared to say it.

"I…" She stopped. Then smiled faintly. "That's a pretty terrible sales pitch. No maps, no weather reports, no planetary warranty?"

Ambry huffed a laugh. "Who needs forecasts? You'd be the storm, the sunshine… the whole atmosphere."

Despite herself, she laughed. When she spoke again, her voice was quieter, more serious. "Ambry… there's so much I haven't told you."

He turned to her, eyes searching. "Then tell me."

"I can't. Not yet."

He nodded slowly. "Okay. But when you do… I'll be here."

They stood like that for a while, fingers woven together, saying nothing. Just breathing. Just being.

Then Ivy looked up at him and smiled, soft, a little sad. "Don't forget to write in our book."

Ambry smirked. "Every dumb thought in my head. You'll regret it."

"I already do."

He leant in then, slow and careful, and kissed her. It wasn't like the first one, stolen and surprised. This one was deliberate. Anchored. The kind of kiss that says this matters. Her hands found his face. His arms circled her waist. And for one suspended moment, the world went silent.

When they finally pulled apart, Ambry touched his forehead to hers.

"I already miss you," she said.

"Me too," he whispered. "We'll meet at my place in a couple of days. Laz and Gareth. We'll figure it all out."

She hesitated a heartbeat longer, then leant in and kissed him again. Soft, slow, like a promise she wasn't ready to make. Then, she stepped back, fingers lingering against his before slipping away. She turned and walked into the trees, back toward where Gareth stood.

Ambry watched until the shadows swallowed her. And wondered how long he'd be waiting.

CHAPTER THIRTY-FIVE

Two days later, they gathered in Ambry's shed. Rough timber shelves and woven storage crates lined the walls, the air carrying the faint scent of sun-warmed wood and braided twine. Ivy leant against the far wall, while Laz fiddled with a hologram node on the bench. The walls were thick with dust, and sunslight leaked through in fractured beams. Outside, Ambry's family moved through morning chores, unaware of what was unfolding in the quiet behind the house.

"I told Grace we needed to collect water samples by the beach," Gareth said, arms folded as he watched the door. "She didn't even question it."

"Because she thinks we're doing science," Ivy said. "Not staging a miniature rebellion in a tool shed."

Laz clipped the node to the Tactis sitting on the bench, larger than his usual one, with reinforced casing and a faint Order crest etched near the hinge.

Ambry raised an eyebrow. "Where'd you get that?"

Laz shrugged. "My dad's. The Order gives them new ones every season cycle, wipes the old ones clean and reissues. He just brings them home and leaves them lying around."

The screen lit up, soft blue projections blinking to life across the bench.

"Okay," Laz said, tapping the Tactis. "Are we ready?"

Gareth gave a single nod. "Do it."

The hologram flared to life. A floating lattice of rotating glyphs, neural diagrams, and branching webs of code. Ivy leant in instinctively. The glyphs spun faster, translating line by line.

"Alright..." Laz muttered. "We've got neural data, activity logs... wait. This section's locked. Gimme a sec." He tapped rapidly. One of the threads unspooled. A new projection burst outward, darker, denser. Threads of light converged around pulse signals and layered overlays.

"Woah," Laz breathed. "Okay. This isn't just tracking. These are... emotional patterns."

Ambry frowned. "Patterns?"

"Maps of behaviour," Laz said. "Mood shifts, reactions, predictive protocols. They're not just watching how people feel, they're forecasting it." He swiped again. Layers peeled back.

The projections flickered. Directive protocols, emotional dampeners, neural pathways laced with control loops. A chill slid down Ivy's spine.

Ambry's hand cut through the projection, pausing on a single file. "What is that?"

Laz leant in. "Some kind of behavioural framework. E-rat response blocks, harm-neutrality directives..." His voice trailed. "These aren't readings. They're instructions."

"Instructions for what?" Ambry asked.

Laz hesitated, fingers frozen above the Tactis. "To shut down the parts of you they don't want," he said.

"How?" Ambry asked.

The words hung there, heavy, undeniable.

Ivy pointed at the left panel. "That. That's what we saw in the Core."

Gareth moved beside her. "Directive overlays. Identity regulation." His tone darkened. "This is it."

Laz's hands moved faster now. "Okay, wait... Found another thread. Chip logs. Calibration cycles. Something called 'emotive baselining'—" He froze. "Okay. Okay, no. This is messed up."

"What is it?" Ivy asked.

Laz stared at the data. "They're not just suppressing emotions. They're cutting them off, shutting them down at the source."

Ambry stepped forward. "Cutting them off?"

Laz gave a small, grim nod. "Yeah. Anything they don't like, any negative emotions. They just cut the wires."

"And leave what?" Ambry asked.

"Happiness," Laz said. "Just... calm. Manufactured harmony."

"I don't—" Ambry's brow furrowed. "I don't understand. How?"

Laz was already digging, fingers flying, glyphs flaring and collapsing across the hologram. Then he stopped cold. His hands hung there, motionless. When he finally looked up, his voice was low, stripped of its usual spark. "I found it." He swallowed hard. "They put chips in people. Control them... through a chip."

The air in the shed felt thinner. A faint breeze stirred the dust, raising the hairs on Ivy's neck.

"A chip?" Ambry echoed. "What do you mean, a chip? Where is it?"

Laz froze, eyes locked on the projection. Slowly, he looked up. "Ambry... we're chipped."

"What?"

Ivy glanced between them. Ambry's jaw tensed, like he was waiting for Laz to say he was joking.

"It's everyone."

"No..." Ambry shook his head. "No, check again. That can't be right."

"I've checked."

His jaw tightened. "No. You're wrong. We'd feel it. We'd know."

"We don't." Laz met his eyes. "That's the point."

Ambry looked between them, Ivy, Gareth, Laz, searching for something he wasn't finding. "You're saying... that we're all chipped. All of us? Me?"

Laz gave a single, slow nod. "All of us."

The words hung there, a weight neither of them could carry.

Across the room, Ivy caught Gareth's eye.

He stepped forward, fingers moving with calm precision as he filtered the projection. "It's more than a device," he said, pointing to the display as it narrowed to a dense weave of glowing nodes. "It's a distributed system, embedded through vaccines. Every person. Every region." He flicked his hand, glyphs scattering and reforming at his touch. "Nano-particles. Microscopic. Bio-reactive. Not engineered, harvested. Refined for control. The particles settle in the emotional centres of the brain."

He flicked his hand, pulling up another layer of text, stamped with what looked like the faded seal of the royal family. His jaw set, the silence around him taut. "Here. It was royal tech originally. Built to stop violence, a replacement for prison." His eyes stayed on the seal, steady but shadowed. "At least... that's how it began."

Ivy stared at the projection. "But someone changed it."

Gareth's eyes darkened, his words clipped. "The Order took it. Twisted it."

"They didn't just take it," Ivy said. "That's why the royals fell." She looked up. Then gently rested a hand on Gareth's arm, quieting him without a word.

They both glanced across the room.

Laz stood frozen beside the holograms. Ambry had turned away, jaw tight, shoulders set. Like holding still was the only thing keeping him upright.

Ambry's voice was barely above a whisper. "So, everyone on Spero..."

"Chipped," Gareth said gently. "Everyone."

"Wait — look at that." Ivy pointed at a hovering file in the hologram, its title flickering faintly. "What does it mean?"

"'Flagged emotional variance,'" Gareth read aloud. "If someone starts to resist... they have recalibration protocol."

Ambry went still. "That's what they were doing," he said. "I've seen it happen before."

Laz looked up. "What do you mean?"

Ambry's jaw tightened. "I've seen people taken. Then when I see them again, they are... quieter. Smiling too much. The edge gone."

The silence closed in again. Gareth swiped, logs filled the air. Names, timestamps, flagged incidents.

"And the guards?" Laz's voice barely rose above a whisper. "If they're chipped too... how can they do that to people?"

Gareth turned back, fingers moving fast. A new projection unfolded — branching signals, flickering red tags. "Wait... okay." He stared at the data, then looked up, his voice dropping. "Their chips are reversed. Same chip, different setting. It shuts down the positive."

Gareth met his eyes. "They're not there to protect you. They're there to hunt anomalies."

Laz exhaled sharply, shaking his head. "So... my dad." His eyes flicked back to the projection, his shoulders tense. "So that isn't really him." His voice cracked. "They stripped away everything good."

Ivy looked around. The weight of it was everywhere. In Laz's silence, in the set of Ambry's jaw. Her fingers curled around the edge of the bench. She didn't know how to fix this. But she couldn't just let them sit in it alone. Something pressed cool against Ivy's chest. The pendant.

She glanced down and absently ran her fingers along the folded leaves, tracing the edges without thinking. The metal was still. Quiet. "Okay. Now we know what it is. And we know where the core is." Her voice steadied. "All that's left is figuring out how to shut it down."

Gareth gave a slow nod, a flicker of something fierce in his eyes. "Laz?"

But Laz didn't answer. He stood rigid, staring at the data still hanging in the air. The chip maps, the recalibration logs, the guard protocols. His hands hung limply by his sides.

"Laz?" Ivy said again.

He shook his head once, silent. Processing.

Gareth placed a hand on his shoulder. His jaw clenched. "We need to move." He looked to Ivy. "Before someone notices this pull of data. We need to shut this down. Now."

Outside, the wind stirred the trees, a soft, restless shift. Inside, none of them moved.

"I need to get out of here," Ambry muttered. He turned and pushed through the door, the soft thud of it closing behind him.

Ivy stared after Ambry, one hand wrapped around the pendant at her chest.

The truth hung in the air. Heavy. Unmoving. Waiting.

Chapter Thirty-Six

They followed Ambry into the grove, light from the twin suns threading between the trees, scattering dappled gold across the ground. The quiet settled around them, full and complete, pressing in with the weight of what they'd uncovered.

The branches overhead shifted, stirred by the wind. Ambry and Ivy sat together on the bench beneath the Kavari trees. Laz lay stretched in a low-slung hammock, arms behind his head, staring up at the branches. Gareth stood a little apart, leaning against the trunk of a tree, Tactis in hand, scrolling slowly through lines of code. Small bugs floated through the grove, their colours fractured. Bursts of red, pulses of violet, others dark as soot. The air held them like suspended thoughts.

Ambry leaned forward on the bench, elbows braced to his knees, jaw clenched so hard the muscle flickered under his skin. He stared at the ground, eyes unfocused, like if he moved, the truth might get worse.

"They chipped everyone," Ambry said finally, voice low and ragged. "My parents... my brother... even Thess." His jaw twitched. "She doesn't even know what she's lost."

Ivy reached out and grabbed his hand, her voice quiet but steady. "We've got the pendant, we've seen the system, we know where the core is. And we still have Nyra's dad's pass. We can go back, get more data if we need to." She leant closer, willing him to believe her. "We can do this, Ambry. We just have to figure it out."

He nodded, just once. Then gave her hand a small squeeze, warm, quick, before pulling away again.

Laz hadn't moved. His eyes were fixed on the treetops, expression caught somewhere between dreamy and blank. If she didn't know better, she'd think he was bored. But it wasn't boredom.

It was that sick, hollow peace that came with the chip. Like the emotions had tried to bloom and gotten choked out halfway. She looked at Ambry again, wishing her words had helped, that she'd said the right thing, something that could actually reach him. But he was back to silence, carved still and unreadable. And he was chipped. What did that even mean? Could someone be saved from grief if they couldn't fully feel it? She looked down at her hands and realised they were shaking.

A quiet series of beeps broke the silence, soft and rhythmic. Gareth's thumbs moved quickly across the console, lines of code flashing beneath his hands.

Ivy pushed to her feet.

Gareth glanced up as her shadow brushed the edge of the Tactis. His eyes met hers, steady and sharp beneath a layer of exhaustion.

"Can I see it?" she asked softly.

He nodded and handed it over. It was warm, the screen still pulsing with lines of code and charts she only half understood. But Ivy didn't need to know the language. She just needed the shape of it, the logic. Something she could grab onto. Something she could do.

She started scrolling. Gareth watched over her shoulder, eyes sharp, as if searching alongside her, unwilling to miss a single detail. Most of it was dense, neural architecture maps, chip interaction overlays, notes tagged with half-decoded strings. But tucked between two data packets was something simpler. Older.

EOS 6 - MISSION LOGS

Her finger froze over the title. She tapped. The file opened with a hiss of compressed audio, a shaky voice recording warped by age. "...arrival complete. EOS 6 touch-down on Veritas-9 confirmed. Biosphere compatible. Initial scans reveal no major threats. Mission to proceed."

She skipped ahead. The logs grew darker.

"—disagreements with leadership. Ship's return protocol overridden. Commander Beckett insists the mission remain classified. Earth must not intervene. There is... potential here. Too much to give back."

Her brows pulled tight. She scrolled faster now, flicking past logs and mission fragments. Crew names, timestamps, scans of Spero's surface. What were Earth mission logs doing inside The Order's system? Not just stored. Integrated. These files weren't archived, they were linked, cross-tagged, buried deep in the network.

Her chest tightened. EOS 6 hadn't disappeared. It hadn't failed. It had landed.

And The Order had known. They'd known all along. It was all here — buried logs, suppressed protocols, the mission that never failed — laid out in front of her. Ivy scrolled, heart pounding.

Commander Beckett, the man who led the mission, had gone rogue. Instead of returning, he'd fallen in love with this planet and stayed. Stayed to build something of his own. "Why waste twelve years flying back to a burning corpse?" His words echoed through the old logs. He'd taught language, science, governance. Shared Earth's knowledge with a few trusted communities. Some called him the Skyfounder. The Lightbringer. The man from the stars. But over generations, his vision was reshaped, hardened into the structure known as The Order.

Ivy sat back, her whole body tight with shock.

"The Royal Family didn't fall by chance," Gareth said softly, still scanning the data. "The Order took control of the system. They seized the chip network, and the planet. The same tech meant to stop harm... they used it to strip away choice."

Ivy's stomach turned. "Earth did this. To Spero. To its people." Her pulse roared in her ears as the next log slid into place. An old personnel manifest blinked onto the screen, names, bios, old Earth security tags. And right there, tucked at the bottom... Her mouth went dry.

"Gareth..." she looked up at him, heart racing. "Did you come to Earth on the EOS 6?" She angled the Tactis toward him, her voice unsteady. "The logs, they show it was here. EOS 6 did reach Spero..."

"But it didn't stay. Gareth, it left again."

Gareth sighed, his gaze dropping to the ground between them. "Yes. I know." He took the Tactis gently from her hands, staring down at the screen like it confirmed something he'd carried alone for years. "That was the same ship that took me to Earth. I always suspected as much. The tech onboard... it was nothing like what Spero was capable of back then. It wasn't ours."

They stood for a moment in the quiet, the screen still glowing faintly in Gareth's hands.

"It's all too much." She leant against the tree, the weight of it sinking in.

"They didn't just land. They left fingerprints on everything. The chip system, the government structure, the control protocols. It's all Earth. All of this. It's all us."

Gareth touched her arm. "Ivy..." he said.

She straightened abruptly. "No. My parents lied," she said, voice rising. "They said the mission was about exploration. About hope. But Earth had already been here. They have already changed this place. And now we're back again, like some second wave of disaster."

Gareth straightened, his voice low but insistent. "Ivy—"

But she couldn't stop. She paced, short strides back and forth, like she was trying to outrun the weight pressing in. "So what happens when we go back and report on it? What happens when Earth sends more? When they find out there's a whole planet running on the control they always wanted. Perfect order, perfect obedience—" She broke off, voice cracking on the edge of fury and disbelief.

"They'll come," she said. "They'll come, and they'll take something else that glows... and destroy it."

Gareth moved then, stepping in, gripping her gently by both arms. His voice dropped, firm and low.

"Ivy." He glanced past her, a subtle shift of his chin. "Ambry."

Gareth's grip softened, but Ivy barely felt it. The silence had changed, charged now, pressing at her back.

"You lied to me."

Ivy flinched. The words struck like a slap. Ambry's voice didn't come from the bench. It came from behind her — sharp, cracked, and rising. She turned slowly, every movement pulled taut, as if her body needed time to catch up to what she'd just heard.

He was on his feet, every line of him alive, sparking like a match too close to dry leaves. "You're not from here," he said. "All this time... and you let me believe you were just some lost girl from the outer regions."

"Ambry, please. Let me explain," she said, voice low.

"You never said anything!" His voice cracked. "You let me talk about my family, my home, this planet. Like we had something in common. Like we were fighting the same fight."

"I am," she said, almost pleading. "Ambry, I am fighting it, I'm—"

"You're not even one of us!"

That hit harder than she expected. She took a step back, as if it physically knocked her. Gareth stepped up quietly, placing himself just behind Ivy. Silent, steady, close enough to remind anyone watching she wasn't alone.

Ambry's glare hardened. "You said your parents came here for research. You left out the part where they were from Earth. Where you're from Earth."

"I'm not from Earth," Ivy said. "I've never even seen it. I was born on the ship. I wasn't even part of the mission."

"Then why didn't you tell me?" His voice cracked again. "Why did I have to hear it like this? Like I was the outsider?" He drew a sharp breath, and when he spoke again, his voice had dropped, but it cut deeper.

"I let you in, Ivy. I trusted you. I brought you into my home... into my family. I defended you when people said you didn't belong. I thought—"

He stopped. His jaw clenched. The next words barely made it past his throat.

"I loved you."

The silence that followed wasn't soft. It was stunned. Splintered.

"And now I don't even know who you are," he said. "All this time, you've been sitting with us, smiling, listening, and every second you were collecting secrets. Like some Earth-born spy, pretending to care. Was any of it real? Or were you just waiting for your parents to tick us off, another sample bagged and boxed?"

His voice turned to venom. "Tell me, Ivy. When you looked at me, was it me you saw? Or just another entry in your family's perfect little report?"

"You think I lied?" Ivy's voice snapped like a wire under tension. "You think I've been spying on you this whole time? That I'm just walking around reporting back to Earth like some... some secret agent?" She knew she should stop. But the words came anyway.

"You think I faked all this?" Her hands balled into fists. "Without me, you'd still be sitting in the dark, smiling like idiots while the truth rotted under your feet."

Ambry flinched, but she didn't stop.

"And you," her voice wavered but didn't break, "you say you loved me? Please."

She stepped forward, eyes locked on his. "You want to talk about control, Ambry? You're chipped. The only reason you think you love me is because you don't know how to hate me."

That did it. His face went blank, too blank, like a door slamming shut behind his eyes. He turned and walked away. And with each step, something inside her cracked open, raw and spilling.

The hammock creaked. Laz shifted, dragging himself upright. He blinked, slow and groggy, like he was surfacing from something deep.

"Ambry... are you okay?"

Through the trees, Ambry disappeared into the shadows at the grove's edge.

"Ambry?" He swung his legs down. "Where are you going?"

The grove felt suddenly hollow.

And Ivy realised how wrong her words had been, and the weight of them pressed down hard.

— ✦ —

Nyra didn't move.

She stood behind the wide-barked Kavari tree, frozen, her back pressed to the trunk as if the rough bark could anchor her. Every word pressed in, sharp and unrelenting.

Ivy's origin. Gareth's, too. Earth.

The pendant. The override system. Old tech. Hidden, not lost. The betrayal curled in her gut like a sickness.

Her pulse thundered. Too loud, too close. Lumibugs spun in jittery loops above her, their pulsing red wings flickering like nerves exposed. She waved them off, but they kept circling, drawn to the rising tension in her chest.

They used me.

They came into her house. Stole from her father... the man who'd given everything to protect this city. They'd gone into his office and had taken his pass. His access. His trust.

Nyra swallowed hard, the weight of it pressing into her ribs. They hadn't just used her. They'd betrayed her family.

That thought struck first. Hot. Sharp. Ivy, the girl with mismatched colours and too many questions, had smiled at her. Shared meals. Walked through her home like they were equals. All while hiding something ancient and dangerous.

Nyra clenched her jaw, blinking fast.

You should turn them in. The thought came like muscle memory. Crisp, trained, instinctive. *Protect your father. Protect The Order.*

Ambry's silhouette moved ahead through the trees. Quick, steady, distant. And that, somehow, hurt the most. She'd thought they were friends.

She'd believed that. Believed that when he smiled at her across the learning grove, when they stayed too long after project rotations, when he'd eaten too many skyvine pods because she dared him. She'd thought of his family like her own. Mirae's laughter, Thess's sticky hands, even Riven's sharp, suspicious eyes, they'd felt like siblings in a way no one else ever had.

And Ambry hadn't thought twice. Lying to her face, stealing from her home.

Slowly, deliberately, she turned away. Chin high. Shoulders drawn back like armour.

The Lumibugs followed her like trailing sparks, their colours unsettled, flickering between indigo and scarlet, as if even the air couldn't keep up with the storm she carried.

CHAPTER THIRTY-SEVEN

The afternoon light cut through the trees in sharp lines as Gareth and Ivy followed the ridge trail. They hadn't spoken much since leaving the grove. Just kept to the trail, boots pressing into soft earth, the weight of everything they hadn't said crowding the space between them. Once, Gareth glanced her way, like he might speak... but his jaw locked, and the moment slid past. Ivy let her hand skim the edge of a fern that curled toward her fingers.

Ivy ached. Her body felt like a storm had passed through it, and her mind was still clearing the wreckage.

Gareth let out a slow breath. "Ivy... I know you've had more than enough for one day. But there's something else you should know."

She stopped and turned, eyebrow lifting. "Sure. By all means... pile it on."

He gave a small smile, but his eyes stayed steady. "My parents... were the king and queen of Spero."

Ivy gave a low, breathless whistle. Half disbelief, half 'of course they were.' She rubbed a hand over her face, then let it slip down with a sigh. "Wow." She didn't even try to wrap sarcasm around it. "That's... big."

For a second, she just stood there, letting it sink like a stone. Then she started walking, her eyes lifted to his. "You okay putting that out in the open?"

Gareth gave a small shrug. "Seemed fair that you knew."

They kept walking. Ivy's boots hit the path harder than usual, like each step was trying to ground her in a world that didn't quite feel solid anymore. "So," she said lightly, "do I have to call you 'Your Majesty' now?"

He snorted. "Don't push it."

She gave him a weak grin that faded just as fast. "Everything's changed, it's all different now."

"It's like something broke wide open. And no matter what I do, no matter how hard I try, it's never going to fit back together."

"The truth isn't meant to be easy," he said. "It's meant to show you what matters enough to fight for."

Ivy let her hand graze the leaves beside her, their soft edges grounding. "Did your parents ever try to contact you?" she asked.

He shook his head. "No. It wasn't like I could call home. The systems were all pre-programmed, automatic. In hindsight, the only reason we made it was because it defaulted to return to Earth. Toren and Mira didn't really know how the tech worked. They just knew they had to try. It was reckless, honestly. But it saved all three of us."

"So they knew the ship was from Earth, Mira and Toren?"

"Yes. They risked everything to get me away from The Order, to protect the legacy. They stole the EOS with help from other royal loyalists. Launched it during the chaos of the palace collapse."

"Did anyone follow?"

"Not that we know of. That was the only ship Earth had sent. As for whether The Order ever built more... I don't know. Maybe. Maybe not."

They kept walking, the quiet pressing around them. Ivy watched the path ahead for a moment, choosing her words carefully. "You told me you were born here."

Gareth nodded once, like that much was simple.

"So... why not tell me the rest? About your family."

He gave a small shrug. "It wasn't about trust. You were hanging around a lot of people, and I've lived a long time knowing how fast things slip when the wrong ears are close."

Ivy glanced at him. "You thought The Order would come for you?"

"I assume I'm the last of my line." The words were steady, but there was something brittle underneath. "If The Order found out... I wouldn't be the only one they'd hunt. I couldn't risk you being caught in it."

Ivy let the words settle. "Yeah... makes sense you kept it quiet."

"Seemed smart." Gareth met her eyes with a brief smile. "Besides... you stand out enough already. No point in making it worse."

Ivy snorted. "Wow. Deeply comforting."

"I try."

They kept walking, the quiet stretching between them.

"Did Toren and Mira tell you what happened? To your family?"

Gareth shook his head. "Not really. They were loyal, loyal as if it was stitched into them. Toren was head of The King's Shield, my father's right hand. And Mira, the Guardian of the Heir, or in Earth terms, my nanny."

Ivy gave a small laugh.

"But they didn't know what was happening, no one did. They told me stories... about Spero, about the creatures, about my parents. And they warned me about The Order. But details? They didn't have them. I would be surprised if even my parents had known what The Order was up to."

Ivy shook her head. "That's some plan. Sneak a prince into deep space and hope no one noticed."

"It was extreme," Gareth admitted. "But hiding me here wouldn't have worked. The Order was already closing in."

Ivy frowned. "So there was more at stake than just you."

"Yes." His gaze dropped briefly to the pendant at her neck. "It was about that too. The key. They couldn't risk it falling into The Order's hands."

Ivy let out a breath. "So... you escaped. And Earth just... happened?"

"We didn't plan that part. The ship's systems defaulted to a return path, pre-set from when it left Earth. Maybe Toren knew. Maybe he didn't. But once we launched... there was no changing course."

Ivy gave a low whistle. "That's... a hell of a plan."

Gareth gave a faint, wry smile. "It wasn't a plan. It was a last chance."

Ivy watched him. "They really loved you."

His eyes met hers, softening. "Yeah. They did. Loved me enough to never let me forget who I was... or why it mattered."

She held his gaze for a moment. "And now?"

"Now I know what they didn't." Gareth's voice dropped. "The Royals weren't overthrown. The Order made sure of that, they turned the people against them. Called them dangerous. A threat to peace."

Ivy frowned. "Because of the chip?"

He nodded. "The chip was royal tech. Criminal punishment instead of a cell. My parents kept it sealed. The Order wanted it, claimed it could keep Spero safe. Stop Earth's mistakes. But my parents... they wouldn't have given it up."

Ivy felt the chill work its way down her spine. "And that's when it started."

"That's when The Order made their move." Gareth's eyes stayed on the path ahead. "They took everything."

Ivy frowned, her gaze flicking to the pendant. "But... if you had the key. How did The Order get control of the system?"

Gareth shook his head slowly. "I don't know."

They moved on, the question hanging between them like a weight neither wanted to pick up.

Ivy sighed. "We're missing something."

"Yeah," Gareth said quietly. "Feels like there's a whole other chapter we didn't get handed."

A soft wind stirred the leaves above them. Gareth slowed. "I think it's time we told them."

Ivy stopped. "Tell who?"

"Grace and David. All of it. What we know. What we've seen."

Ivy hesitated. "You think that's smart?"

Gareth glanced her way. "They're not the enemy, Ivy."

"No... but they've been holding on to this mission for over twenty years." She wound a strand of hair around her finger. "They've sacrificed everything for it. Do we want to bring them into all this?"

He raised an eyebrow. "Do you think they can just keep collecting samples in peace for the next eight months? Especially if we are planning on shutting the chip down. And what if they're the only ones who can help us end this the right way?"

Ivy frowned. "But... does anything actually change if we tell them? The Order doesn't know we know. No one's breaking the system wide open, yet. We don't even know if it's the right thing to do."

Gareth studied her, silent, as if waiting for her to explain.

Ivy scuffed the toe of her boot against the dirt. "I've seen what they have done to Earth, what 'freedom' lets people do. Are we really the right people to be making this decision?"

"You want to... just do nothing?"

Ivy shrugged, "I don't know."

They stood there for a moment, the question hanging between them in the quiet.

"I'm not saying we wait forever to tell them," Ivy said. "But... can we just give it a few days? Let me get my head straight. After everything with Ambry... I just... I need time."

"And maybe I can delay the whole 'grounded for life' part."

Gareth's eyes softened. "Yeah. We can wait a few days."

She nodded slowly, but it didn't ease the pressure behind her ribs. "I messed it up," she said under her breath. "With Ambry."

"You were honest," Gareth said.

"No. I was cruel."

He didn't say anything, he didn't have to. The silence between them said enough. They moved on, the ridge sloping beneath their feet, the forest crowding the path on either side.

Ivy pressed her fingers to the pendant at her chest, the only thing still warm in a world that suddenly felt too cold.

CHAPTER THIRTY-EIGHT

The night air inside the POD was still. It seemed like Ivy had barely closed her eyes when she felt it, that charged stillness that meant someone was near.

Gareth's voice, low and steady, brushed against the edge of her sleep. "Pip. Get up."

She blinked, groggy, sitting up as his silhouette came into focus by the door. "What—"

"Come on," he said, already moving outside. "We've got a few hours before suns-rise."

She rubbed the sleep from her eyes, tugged on her boots, and followed without a word.

— ✦ —

The walk was silent. Moonlight sliced through the branches in silver and gold beams, catching on damp leaves and painting their path with moving shadow. Gareth didn't speak. He didn't need to. Ivy could feel it in his pace. Faster than usual, eyes sharp and searching. He didn't glance back once. Not even when she stumbled.

The ridge rose like a spine through the trees, its peak gleaming faintly in the night. As they reached the top, the castle unfolded below them. Not just stone, but memory, carved into the land itself. Its towers rose wild and untamed, reaching like fingers into the night.

Ivy tilted her head, breath catching. "Gareth... where are we going?"

"Do you remember how you and Ambry got into the castle?"

"Yeah," she said without hesitation.

"I need you to show me."

"Okay." She didn't ask why. It was Gareth. That was enough.

She moved quickly, leading him along the path she and Ambry had taken. The entrance still held, a section of fractured stone at the tower's base, a gap just wide enough to crawl through.

Gareth crouched beside the fractured wall, running a hand over the rough edge. His fingers stilled for a moment, then he nodded. They slipped through.

The air pressed close, cool and still, carrying the faint scent of stone and something older beneath. Ivy followed Gareth through the corridor, her steps falling into the same quiet rhythm she'd taken with Ambry days before. Back then, it had felt like trespassing. Now, with Gareth, it felt... different.

He moved slower, fingers brushing the stone as if reacquainting himself with something half-forgotten. His pace never faltered. His eyes never wandered. Light from the moons slipped through faded stain glass, painting soft patterns over the hallway as they moved past. Ivy half-expected him to turn left, the way she and Ambry had gone.

Gareth turned right.

She caught herself, quickening her pace to follow. The corridor narrowed, the air cooling as the walls pressed closer. Gareth said nothing. Ivy didn't ask, she just kept moving.

A soft sound escaped him. A word half-formed. Almost a name. The room was circular, tall columns lining the perimeter. At the far end, a high-arched window spilled faint light across a tall stone monument. Weathered by time but still clearly etched with the symbol Ivy had seen throughout the palace. Four wings, unfurled in motion.

The Leafwing.

Gareth moved to the stone carving, his gaze sweeping the wings. His hand followed its lines, fingers pausing over familiar curves worn soft with age. "I remember this," he murmured. "My mother used to bring me here, to the window there." He pointed to the high arch, its frame swallowed by vines. "She said this was where the light always found her."

He moved to one of the columns, crouching as his hand brushed the grooves near its base. "She used to hide things here," he said, almost to himself. "Little things... sweets, drawings. Stuff she said was just for me." A quiet breath slipped out, almost a laugh. "Mira never figured it out, how I was always eating solari cakes."

Ivy smiled, watching him.

He ran his fingers along the seams between two stones, working by touch more than sight. "I've been thinking about this since we landed," he said. "Kept telling myself if she ever... if there was ever a place she'd leave something for me..."

His hand slowed, palm flattening against the stone. "It'd be here."

Ivy held her breath.

Gareth pressed lightly against the panel. There was a soft click, and he eased it back, revealing a hollow space hidden in the wall. Inside, wrapped in faded cloth, lay a slim leather-bound journal. The cover was worn smooth, the Leafwing etched in delicate, repeating lines.

For a long second, Gareth didn't move.

Then he reached in, lifting it free with both hands, like he wasn't sure if it was real until he touched it. Gareth turned the journal slowly, fingers tracing the worn leather as though memorising its shape. When he opened it, the first page unfurled with inked sketches. Looping script, layered symbols, and the delicate pattern of woven threadwork. Gareth exhaled, voice steady. "I knew she'd leave something. She always planned further than anyone realised." He turned the next page. More ink sketches unfurled across the paper, curling vines, layered petals, a crystal core. These drawings were careful, deliberate, labelled in the same sure hand.

Liefen bloom. Native to the western highlands. Wild, untamed, and resonance-stable. Transported to the royal greenhouse under strict cultivation protocols. Rare beyond measure.

On the next page, a diagram showed the greenhouse, roots extending from a massive vine down into the earth.

Liefen blooms are the source. Only three have ever bloomed in captivity. Each one sacred.

One remains here, alive and whole. The other two were harvested. One forged into the core vessel, the other divided and refined into two pendants.

The pendants are keys, resonance-bound, created to interface with the chamber below.

Ivy leant in closer as Gareth turned another page. A sketch of the pendant took up half the sheet, the bronze wings folded over a glowing crystal centre.

Each pendant is formed from the Liefen bloom and aligned to the core through a shared signature. They respond only to coherence, never control.

Another diagram followed, this one of a stone chamber deep beneath the palace, with branching lines connecting it to the greenhouse and old tunnel systems.

The Core Chamber: designed by the High Order of Liefen Scholars. Not to punish, but to protect. A sanctuary for those overwhelmed by emotion, not a prison. The system draws imbalance back into alignment, offering relief. Access requires coherence. The chip system is marked as a proposal only, theoretical. Intended as a gentle aid, not mandatory.

Gareth's fingers lingered on the edge of the page.

Ivy's voice was soft. "And then The Order corrupted it."

Gareth didn't answer. He didn't have to. He turned another page, and there, inked in a steady hand, were words meant for him. He read aloud, his voice low, steady.

Gareth, my son.

They will take the palace. They will take us. And they will take the Liefen.

But I will not let them take you. I will protect you. Not so you may flee, not so you may forget, but so you may remember.

Remember who you are. And who we were before the silence came.

I have given Mira and Toran their orders. They will carry you beyond this world. They will keep you in orbit, beyond The Order's reach, until you are of age, until you are strong enough. Until you are ready.

Return then. Not to reclaim a throne... but to set this right.

Come find me, my son. My boy.

Even if they take my emotions, I will know you.

Find me. Find your father.

Beneath the palace lies the Core, the heart of the Liefen, the root of their control. When you return, the Core must be stilled.

I send you with my key. Only one who cultivates true harmony, who lives in flow with the natural order, may open it.

I hope you remember our lessons, Gareth. I hope they remain with you.

Your father's key is missing. We will find it.

We will fight.

I will always believe in you.

The words hung between them, sharp and alive in the quiet. Gareth stood motionless, thumb resting on the edge of the page, eyes tracing the lines she'd written, every curve burned into memory. Around them, everything settled. Only silence remained.

He closed the journal with care, thumb lingering on the edge, and stood. His eyes, shadowed with something older than grief, held to the leafwing crest carved into the stone. For a moment he said nothing, shoulders setting like armour sliding into place.

"She thought I'd come back when I was eighteen," he said. "When I'd be strong enough. Ready."

Ivy stepped closer. "And you did come back."

A quiet breath escaped him, almost a laugh, almost not. "Thirty-four years late." His jaw tightened. "I don't think this was the future she imagined."

Ivy met his eyes. "Doesn't mean it's too late."

Gareth gave a slow nod. "No. It doesn't." He reached out, brushing his hand across the leafwing crest. The carved lines caught the light, a soft gleam rolling over the stone. "The one who lives in true flow with the natural order," he murmured.

Ivy's hand found the pendant at her chest, its weight grounding her in a way she couldn't explain.

At last, Gareth turned toward her. And for a moment, there was nothing of the soldier. Nothing of the mechanic. Nothing of the guardian. "We were never meant to go to Earth," he said quietly. "I was supposed to stay in orbit. Wait, and then come back to save my family."

He shook his head, eyes fixed ahead, jaw clenched tight. "But I left. And I didn't come back."

Ivy stepped closer. "It wasn't your fault, Gareth. You were six."

One tear slipped down his cheek, tracking a slow, silent line along his face. He didn't move. Didn't wipe it away. He just stood there, shoulders set, gaze lost.

Ivy closed the last step between them and took his hands. Her voice was soft but steady, the kind that carried weight even in a whisper. "I know going to Earth may have cost you your family..." Her fingers tightened around his. "But coming back? You found one."

He didn't move. Didn't speak.

"This…" she said, reaching up, her thumb brushing the pendant at her chest. "It only opens because of you. Because of what you gave me." Her eyes searched his. "You think you lost your mother's teachings. But you didn't. You just passed them on."

"Everything you think you'd forgotten, you taught me. How to feel. How to think. How to listen." Her throat tightened. "You didn't just carry her legacy. You lived it. Even when you didn't know."

Gareth's eyes lifted at last, finding hers, like something inside him had steadied. His arms folded around her. Firm, certain, like the world could tilt and he wouldn't let go.

Ivy stepped in without a word, resting her head against his chest.

Gareth's arms gave the smallest shift. "I love you, Pip."

Ivy closed her eyes and leant in, holding him tighter. "I love you too."

They stood together, quiet, until he eased back just enough to meet her eyes. "Those other parts in the journal, about the blooms?"

Ivy nodded, fingers brushing the pendant at her chest. "The Liefen bloom."

Gareth's gaze flicked down to the journal in his hands. "One in the greenhouse. One forged into the console. And the pendants," he tapped the worn leather, "all carved from the same core."

"Ambry and I saw them the first time we found the greenhouse," Ivy said. "One of the blooms opened while I was standing there, like it recognised something." Her gaze dropped for a moment. "I thought it was the most beautiful thing I'd ever seen. I didn't know it was part of all this."

She looked back up, voice sharper now. "But in the Vanta Spire… I saw what The Order's doing. They're growing them. Dozens. Maybe hundreds. Not in greenhouses. In labs. Controlled. Harvested." Her fingers curled instinctively around the pendant. "They're not treating them like something sacred. They're treating them like power."

"Two keys…" Ivy said. "If this one was your mother's, where's your father's?"

Gareth nodded. "That's our missing puzzle piece."

Chapter Thirty-Nine

Nyra stood by the broad glass window in her father's office, arms folded tight, gaze locked on the city below. The words had already left her. Everything she'd seen. Everything she'd heard.

Solen sat at his desk, fingers poised above the light-paneled console, glyphs pulsing faintly beneath his hand, shadows stretching long across the floor. The recessed dock on his desktop still lay empty. He watched her for a long moment before speaking, voice low and even. "And you're certain?"

Nyra pressed her arms tighter. "I followed them. They didn't know." The words sat rough in her throat, cutting on the way out. "I heard them talking."

Solen reached for the stylus and turned it once between his fingers. A small gesture. Controlled. "And you say... they both came from Earth?"

She nodded once, voice tight. "Yes."

Solen's eyes flicked toward the window, calculating, the weight of strategy sharpening his stillness. "And this... Ivy," he said softly, tasting the name like a fault line. "She wears a pendant?"

Nyra swallowed. "Yes. Like the one Mother always wears."

Solen rose, smoothing a hand down the front of his robes, and crossed the room to her side. The window reflected both of them. Violet and crimson, shadow and flame.

"You've done well." His hand settled lightly on her shoulder.

Nyra didn't move. She wasn't sure she could. "What will you do?"

"We'll handle it," Solen said softly. "Quietly." He turned away, steps quiet against the polished floor.

Her gaze followed him, then shifted to the far corner of the room. There, seated in the high-backed chair beneath the wall of soft-lit panels, was her mother. Evara sat perfectly still. Back straight. Hands folded in her lap. Hair woven into a crown of muted indigo braids, pale skin catching the light with an icy sheen. Blue eyes soft, but vacant.

On her chest, a soft blue light pulsed.

"Why does she wear that?"

Solen's head tilted slightly, just enough to register the question.

"It keeps her balanced," he said, slow and deliberate. The softness in his voice returned, but with an edge beneath it.

Balanced.

"Is it the same as Ivy's?" Nyra's voice sharpened.

"We don't know yet." His tone stayed calm, but colder. "That's what we'll investigate."

Nyra's jaw tightened. "You have guards everywhere, Father. How did no one notice a girl with bright red hair and blue eyes?"

His eyes settled on her, cool, unreadable. "We noticed. But we've always known some of the early Order members defected. Left the city. Started families beyond our reach. We accounted for outliers." His fingers tapped once on the desk, deliberate. "We assumed she was one of them. A legacy child. Harmless."

He let the weight of that hang. "We won't make that mistake again."

Nyra looked at her mother.

Evara sat perfectly still, framed by the glow of the office light. For a moment, it was hard to tell if she'd moved at all, until her head tilted, just slightly. Their eyes met. A smile touched her lips. Gentle. Pleased.

"Nyra, darling," she said, voice soft as silk. "Stop bothering your father. He is doing what must be done. You should be proud."

No bite in the words. No tension. Just quiet certainty, as if she truly believed it.

Nyra's mouth opened, the question rising again, but it caught in her throat. She swallowed. "Yes, Mother."

Turning, she walked slowly toward the door. At the threshold, she glanced back.

Her mother sat flawless and still — like a portrait waiting for the artist who would never return.

Chapter Forty

It had been two days since the old palace.

Two days since Gareth had spoken more than a few words at a time. He hadn't mentioned his mother's journal again. Or the truth they'd uncovered. Or what they were supposed to do next. He'd gone quiet. And Ivy... wasn't handling the silence any better.

She sat cross-legged on the floor of her room, the datapad resting on her knees, its screen glowing faintly in the dim light. She wasn't really looking at it. The same mission log blinked. Irrelevant. Familiar. The kind of static that should've calmed her.

It didn't.

She hadn't touched the controls in over an hour. She'd tried. Tried to drown her thoughts in data, scans, logs, anything. But the memories kept coming. Fast. Sharp. Unforgiving.

Ambry's voice in the grove. His face when she said it. That awful flicker of something breaking behind his eyes.

'You only think you love me because you don't know how to hate me.'

The words slammed back into her chest like they'd been waiting in the dark. She pressed the heel of her palm to her forehead, bracing against the weight of it. What the hell was that? Who says that? She curled forward, elbows on her knees, trying to breathe through the tightness clawing up her throat. The guilt wouldn't back down. Neither would the silence he left behind.

She missed him. Not just the sound of his voice or the way he looked at her like she mattered, really mattered, but the feeling she got when he was near. Like she wasn't too much to hold. Like she wasn't a problem to solve. The way he'd catch her mid-spiral with a lopsided smile and a stupid line that somehow worked. How safe she'd felt. How free.

She remembered Gareth's voice months ago, just before the launch. *'You've never known pain. No bullying. No heartbreak. No fear. That's something, Pip.'*

He hadn't meant it as an accusation. More like a warning.

But now... now her heart felt cracked wide open. And somehow still beating. Which felt rude. Because all she was left with was pain. Not the sharp kind. The slow, sinking kind that settles deep and makes itself at home.

Was this what freedom really was? Not the wildness of stars or fresh air in her lungs, but this? The aftermath? Because this ache — this sharp, lonely wound — felt more real than anything she'd ever known.

The screen dimmed and shut off. She didn't move. Air cycled through the POD's vents, steady and familiar. Seventeen years of it. Routine, safe, predictable. And yet, nowhere had ever felt this hollow.

Footsteps passed outside the room. Gareth. She heard the soft creak of him stopping, then nothing. Waiting, maybe. Or giving her the space she hadn't asked for. She thought about going to him. About saying something. Anything.

But she didn't. She forced herself to her feet, legs stiff, like they didn't quite remember how to carry weight without him.

She passed Gareth in the corridor. He was crouched beside a storage crate, adjusting a worn strap on his bag. He looked up, just a flick of his eyes. She kept walking.

Grace and David stood at the lab bench, bent over mineral samples, scribbling notes. David muttered something under his breath, and Grace laughed, shaking her head before jotting another number. Business as usual. No one stopped her.

She stepped out of the pod and made her way across the clearing, the trees ahead steady in the light. The path to the hollow tree was one she didn't need to think about. Her feet knew. Her bones knew. The route carved itself beneath her like muscle memory. The tree waited where it always had, knotted, wide-trunked, half-swallowed by ivy. Their place.

The notebook rested in the crevice. She crouched and drew it out, fingertips skimming the etched cover before she began to unwrap it, slow and careful. Her heart thudded, sharp, restless, like it might bolt. The last page was still blank.

Her stomach dropped. "Cool," she muttered. "Really crushing the whole first heartbreak thing."

She sank down at the base of the tree, journal in her lap, arms locked around her knees. For a while, she just stared at the page.

Then, quietly — like the words didn't belong to her — she wrote, "*I didn't mean it.*"

And she hadn't. Not a single word.

But he was gone. The notebook stayed blank.

And so did the space he used to fill.

— ✦ —

The sun slipped behind the ridgeline as Ivy wove between the trees, making her way back to camp. The air shifted with the fading light, cooler, thicker.

She walked slowly, trailing her fingers along low branches as she passed. Leaves tilted toward her touch, a soft shiver of response. She wasn't in a hurry. The thought of stepping back into the POD, and everything waiting inside, felt heavier than the surrounding dusk. A soft rustle broke the silence behind her. Too slow for wind. Too steady for chance. Ivy kept moving, slow steps and a mind that was miles away.

The sound came again. Faint. Steady. Like footsteps laid over her own. A bird shot from a low branch ahead, wings flashing sharp as glass. Ivy jerked back a step, her heart spiking before she could catch it. "Geez," she said. "Watch it."

She sighed, dragging her mind back to the present. That's when she noticed it. The forest felt still around her. Not peaceful, but expectant. Her footsteps brushed through leaves, branches whispering against her jacket. Every step felt too loud. Too alone. Like something was off.

She expected to hear the familiar sounds of the forest at night, the soft hum of dusk-birds, the rustle of ground creatures finding cover. But the forest stayed still. Strangely quiet. Then, behind her, something shifted. A crack, low and quick, like weight pressed where it shouldn't.

Ivy stopped. Slowly turned. The path lay empty. Shadows, long and folded, stretched across the ground. For half a second, chest tightening, she thought...

"Ambry?" she whispered, the name catching slightly in her throat. Silence answered, thick and watching.

The hair on her arms lifted. She took a cautious step. Then another. Somewhere ahead, a leaf twitched. A branch dipped, slow, subtle. And the weight in her gut dropped, cold and heavy. Ivy stepped back, pulse kicking. Then she turned and moved. Faster now, cutting through the trees toward the clearing.

The sharp edges of the POD broke through the trees ahead, its panels catching faint streaks of fading light. Gareth sat beside the hatch, a worn camp chair leant back on two legs, eyes fixed on his datapad.

A little further on, Grace and David sat at the fold-out table, a soft lamp casting a pool of light over a weathered deck of cards spread between them. David leant forward, saying something under his breath that pulled a smile from Grace. One of those rare, private ones she didn't give out easily. As he reached for his next card, he dropped a quick kiss on her lips, casual, familiar, like they'd shared a hundred like it before.

She jogged the last few steps, feet skidding slightly on the soft earth.

Gareth looked up, the chair thunking forward as their eyes met. Steady, searching. "You okay?" he asked, voice low, gaze holding hers.

Ivy swallowed. Nodded. "Yeah. I... thought..." She trailed off, shook her head. "Nothing. Just the wind."

Gareth didn't look away. He was reading more than she'd said.

Ivy's gaze lingered at the edge of the clearing. The forest stood still.

She slipped into the POD without another word.

But the edge in her gut stayed sharp. Like she'd walked away from something that hadn't walked away from her.

Chapter Forty-One

The forest hadn't moved all night. Neither had she.

She lay curled on her mattress, blankets bunched close, the overhead panel casting a faint glow across the walls. The steady hum of the POD systems filled the quiet. She couldn't settle. Not with the weight pressed tight against her chest... and the forest pressing tighter outside. Her eyes kept drifting to the narrow window. The trees stood beyond the glass. Too still.

By the time dawn seeped through the trees, Ivy was sitting at the main console in the central chamber, staring out through the curved viewport.

"You planning on drilling a hole in that glass?"

Gareth's voice pulled her back. He leant against the corridor wall, arms folded, giving her that look. The one that said he wasn't buying it.

She sat slumped at the console, chin in her hand, gaze distant. "Couldn't sleep."

"Yeah," Gareth said. "Figured."

He nodded toward the hatch. "Come on. The water filtration's running low. Thought we'd grab a few canisters before your parents wake up."

She didn't move. Just kept staring out the window, as if the trees might shift if she looked long enough.

"Walk with me," he said. "Fresh air won't kill you."

"Fine," she muttered, like it was the most unreasonable request in the universe. Then peeled herself off the chair and trudged after him, shoulders slouched in protest. She snatched up her boots before ducking out the hatch.

They crossed into the clearing, then moved further out, weaving between broad trunks veined with silver bark and draped in trailing moss. Shafts of morning light filtered through the trees, catching on the fine mist that clung low to the forest floor. The hush between them stretched, filled only by the soft clink of canisters shifting in their packs and Gareth easing aside low branches with his hands.

After a while, Gareth's voice broke the quiet. "You holding up?"

Ivy shrugged. "I don't know. Maybe."

"Not your best lie."

She let out a soft huff. "I'm still... trying to make sense of it."

"Ambry?"

She nodded, watching her boots scuff through the undergrowth.

Gareth looked over at her. "You looked rattled when you came back from your walk yesterday. Something happen?"

Ivy shook her head. "No. I just... I think I'm starting to jump at my own shadows." But even as she said it, the memory pricked sharp. The faint sound behind her, the flicker of movement she'd almost believed was him.

"Probably need more sleep." Her fingers tightened on her strap. "There is one thing that keeps bothering me though... about Ambry."

"What's that?" Gareth asked.

"I just can't shake it. How angry he got at me." Her brows pulled together. "I mean, he got pretty angry. You know, for someone who's supposed to be chipped."

Gareth nodded, running a hand across the back of his neck. "True. That kind of reaction doesn't match what the chip's supposed to suppress."

"Yeah... I know..." Ivy shrugged, but the movement felt forced. "Doesn't make sense. None of this does."

The quiet stretched, broken only by the soft scuff of their boots and the distant murmur of water.

They reached a narrow stream, water running clear and quick over smooth stones set in the mossy ground. Ferns lined its banks, dew still clinging to their fronds. Ivy crouched near the edge, drawn by the glimmer dancing across the surface. Something shifted across the rocks, a ripple of colour too fluid to be stone.

Perched on a sunlit rock, a lizard no bigger than her hand blinked slowly. Its scales gleamed with soft iridescence, layered in shifting tones of rose-gold, amber, teal, and lilac — colours sliding over one another like oil spilled in moonlight. Each breath it took seemed to shimmer through a different colour. But what made her breath catch wasn't the colours, it was the sound.

Soft. Musical. Barely there. A faint chime, like wind through crystal. The lizard tilted its head, and the sound shifted, delicate and strange, as if its very movement strummed some hidden note in the air. She stayed frozen, listening. Wondering if she had imagined it. Then it darted, a flick of colour and sound, and slipped into the stream, leaving only ripples and silence behind.

She didn't say a word. Just stared at the rock, where the rainbow lizard had been.

Gareth stepped up beside her. "That's a Mirrascale," he said. "I used to see them all the time when I was a kid."

Ivy's breath caught at the beauty of it. It was a reminder that even with the weight pressing around her, the forest was still here.

Gareth crouched first, dipping one of the canisters into the flow. Ivy followed, kneeling beside him, the cool spray catching her fingers as she worked.

For a while, they filled canisters in silence. Just the rush of water and the low clink of metal against stone.

She didn't look at Gareth when she spoke. "I needed this. I didn't realise how much I'd stopped seeing it, the trees and the light. Everything." Her fingers brushed the surface of the water.

"Thanks," she said. "For getting me out of my own head. For showing me it's still beautiful out here. That it's still worth it."

Gareth knelt beside her, elbow resting on one knee. "You didn't stop seeing it," he said. "You just got buried under too much."

He picked up a smooth stone, turning it in his fingers. "You're not just surviving it, Ivy. You're part of it." He let the stone drop back into the water. "Come on," he said, rising. "Your parents are probably starting to wonder where we are."

The suns had lifted higher when they finally looped back toward camp. The path curved gently. Through the trees, they glimpsed the POD and the faint shift of movement around it. Looked like Grace and David were already up.

But Ivy felt it before she understood it. Gareth must've felt it too. His arm shot across her path, stopping her just before the treeline ended. The air pressed in, heavy and too still, like the forest was bracing for something.

"Stay here," Gareth said, his voice low but firm. His eyes stayed on the clearing, body held tense, alert.

She didn't.

They moved together. Quick, low, slipping between trunks until the POD came into full view. Ivy's chest clamped tight. The clearing looked wrong.

One of the chairs lay on its side, half-buried in the moss. A single pack slumped open nearby, contents strewn as if they'd been dropped mid-step. Grace's datapad was on the ground, screen dark. David's jacket hung from a branch. Not folded, not left, just... caught. Ivy's chest tightened. Something had happened here.

Then she stopped cold. The camp wasn't empty.

Figures moved near the POD, three of them, dressed in dark uniforms that cut hard against the morning light. Two stood by the hatch. The third crouched near the table, sifting through their gear like he had all the time in the world.

"Mum and Dad," she whispered, breath catching in her throat.

Gareth dropped into a crouch, easing back into the shadows. Ivy followed, pulse hammering.

"Those are Order guards," he said.

Her chest tightened. "But how? No one knew we were here."

Gareth didn't answer.

"Do you think... Ambry told them?"

"No," he said, but not fast enough.

She looked at Gareth. "He was upset. I shouldn't have said all that. I pushed too hard. What if..."

"Ivy." Gareth's voice softened. "That doesn't mean he betrayed you." His jaw tightened as he looked back toward the POD. "But someone did."

"What are we going to do?" Ivy's heart pounded in her chest. "We can't just leave them. We have to do something."

"We will," he said. "But first, we get somewhere safe."

"Then what?"

He turned back to the POD, steady as stone. "Then we bring them home."

The POD — their home, their escape — was no longer safe.

It was bait.

— ✦ —

They returned to their old campsite. The clearing lay quiet, undisturbed. Just trees and earth and the faint ring of ash where their fire pit had been.

Ivy dropped her pack onto the dirt and sank onto a log, hands pressed hard to her face. "Where have they taken them, Gareth?" Her voice broke on the words. "What if they're hurting them? What if—" She shook her head, breath catching. "You were right, we should've told them everything. We should've trusted them. I should've—"

Gareth crouched in front of her, his voice low, steady. "No. Don't do that. This isn't on you." He met her eyes. "We didn't know. And even if we had... there's no way to know if it would've changed anything."

"Is it safe here?" She asked, scanning the trees. "What if they come back?"

"If The Order had known about this place," Gareth said, "they'd be waiting for us."

She stared into the forest. "What now?"

Gareth exhaled, then sat beside her on the log, his hands resting on his knees. "Anyone I knew before I left... they're long gone. We're on our own out here." He glanced at her, voice low but firm. "But it's okay. We'll work on a plan. We'll figure this out together."

Ivy turned to him. "Did Toren and Mira leave you anything? A name? Somewhere to go if you ever came back?"

He shook his head. "They were focused on getting me out alive. And seeing as Earth wasn't even part of the plan... I don't think coming back ever crossed their minds."

Her throat tightened. "What are we going to do?"

Gareth sat beside her, his hand resting gently on her back. "We get through it... figure out a plan."

"Yeah." She tried to smile. Failed.

They sat there, the quiet pressing in, thick and close.

Then she whispered, "What about Ambry?"

Gareth's jaw shifted, his expression unreadable. "We have to be careful. He still might be the reason we're out here."

Her stomach twisted. "You said you didn't think he told them. I don't. I... I can't."

Gareth didn't answer right away.

And that's when the tears came. They slipped past before she could blink them back. Sharp, sudden, impossible to stop. She pressed her hands hard against her face, shaking her head as if that might hold them in. But the tears kept falling, silent and steady, a release she couldn't fight.

Gareth shifted beside her, his hand a solid weight on her back, something she could lean into without breaking apart.

When her breathing steadied, he reached into the pack beside them and pressed a water canister gently into her hand. Ivy pulled in a breath, rough and shaky, and took a sip.

He met her eyes. "I don't think Ambry betrayed you," he said. "But it's dangerous to assume he's on our side without knowing."

Ivy drew her knees up. "I know him. Not just the version he showed everyone. I know what's underneath." Her voice caught, a leftover crack of tears still rough in her throat.

Gareth reached into his jacket and handed her a folded cloth, simple, probably meant for gear.

She took it without a word, swiping it quickly across her face. "And if there's even a chance he'd help..."

"You're willing to risk it?"

"Yes."

He watched her for a moment, then sighed. "Then we find him. Quietly. Carefully."

Ivy looked up. "You mean it?"

"You're right. We don't have options. If we can get him alone... maybe he'll listen."

"Maybe," she said, her voice steadier now. "And if he does, he'll help us get them back."

Gareth didn't argue.

And somehow, that gave her hope.

Chapter Forty-Two

They crouched just beyond the market's edge, tucked between root-heavy trees where the stone path thinned into forest. Ivy kept low, her breath tight, heart thudding beneath her ribs. Beside her, Gareth stayed silent, eyes locked on the trading stands.

They'd made a small camp the night before. Nothing permanent, just a clear patch beneath the trees, a low fire, and packs for pillows. She'd taken Gareth to gather Kavari leaves, the same thick, soft ones Ambry had shown her that first night they'd camped in the woods.

But now, crouched in the fading afternoon light, they had only one hope. Ambry.

From here, Ivy could see the outer stalls, canopies stretched wide in patchwork colour, casting jewel-toned shadows across the crowd. She spotted Laz first, weaving between booths with something in one hand, grinning like he'd just bartered for treasure. He said something that made a vendor laugh. Then she saw him. His shoulders were hunched, movements slower than she remembered. He didn't smile at Laz. He barely looked up.

Her heart lurched, sharp and deep. She couldn't pull a full breath. She steadied herself against a low tree, the bark rough beneath her fingers, cool despite the thick air.

"We'll wait," she whispered. "Last time we were here… we headed back through the valley, toward the forest trail."

Gareth didn't speak, but she felt the shift in him, the way he went still when he was fully there, fully listening.

Ivy kept her eyes on Ambry. "There's a clearing near the turnoff. Just past the ridge. I'll talk to him there, away from the crowds."

He shifted beside her. "I don't like this," he muttered. "There are guards in the markets, and we're too exposed out here."

She followed his gaze. Two uniformed figures patrolled the far edge of the square, scanning the crowd as they moved. Not rushing, just present. Watching. Ivy turned to look at him. "We don't really have a choice," she said.

Gareth's eyes held hers, steady and unreadable. His hand shifted slightly. His fingers curled into his palm, a quiet reflex.

"Gareth," she said, quieter. "I trust him."

His eyes narrowed, not with suspicion, but something older. Deeper. "It's not him I doubt," he paused. "Is there another way? Another place?"

The question settled between them, real and heavy.

A breeze moved through the undergrowth, cool and dry. Ivy looked back the way they had come. The forest held still, but not quiet. Leaves hovered just slightly off rhythm. Shadows pooled beneath the roots, like something listening. She pressed a hand to her chest. Her heartbeat hadn't slowed. "No," she said. "It has to be him. And it has to be now. Unless you want to add stealing from the markets to the list of things the guards are chasing us for."

Gareth nodded once, then his hand squeezed hers. Quick, rough, grounding. "Are we sure?" he asked, voice low.

She returned the pressure, steady. "It's going to be okay," she said. "We've got this." She glanced back toward the market.

Ambry and Laz were leaving, slipping past the outer stalls, Laz still talking, Ambry quiet at his side. They were headed toward the ridge trail.

"We need to move," she said, already shifting low through the trees. "Further down, away from the markets."

Gareth followed, silent but close. The moment had shifted. No more questions, just steps. They looped wide around the ridge, slipping between moss-covered roots and tangled ferns until they'd pulled ahead. Ivy moved with care, boots sure on the uneven ground. She'd done this before, circled ahead to meet him. So much had happened since that first innocent night under the moons, when she'd stepped into his path like some half-wild mystery girl with red hair and too many questions.

She dropped lower behind a rise, eyes on the path. Ambry and Laz were still walking, not far behind now, their voices muffled by distance and leaves.

The clearing was just ahead. Ivy touched the pendant at her chest.

One more breath. One more step.

— ✦ —

The trail wound low through the trees, quiet but open. Light from the fading suns flickered through the trees as Laz walked backward up ahead, tossing a glowing fruit from hand to hand.

"Let me get this straight," he said, eyes narrowing. "You're spiralling because the girl you like might've been born in space?"

Ambry didn't respond. Just kept walking. Head down, steps steady.

Laz caught the fruit mid-air with a smirk. "Buddy. That's like the least weird thing about her."

Ambry let out a slow breath. "She lied."

"She didn't lie. She withheld. She's seventeen. That's basically a survival skill."

Ambry shot him a tired look. "She lied, Laz. You know, 'We're just travelling explorers,' ring any bells?"

Laz hopped up onto a low boulder beside the path, balancing easily. "Look, man. We were all raised chipped. Our parents smile the same way every day. Our neighbours treat grief like an awkward guest — ignore it till it leaves. We've lived in a fog and never questioned it. But Ivy? She's lightning in the middle of all this sleepwalking."

Still, Ambry didn't answer. His gaze stayed fixed ahead. Jaw set, shoulders tight, a storm still spinning quietly behind his golden eyes.

"So yeah, you got your heart bruised. But at least it's yours." Laz dropped down beside him.

"That sounded almost cynical for someone who's chipped."

Laz snorted. "You're one to talk. Pretty sure your chip's just running on dramatic sighs and unresolved feelings at this point."

The leaves around them rustled sharply. Ambry stopped. "Did you hear that?"

Laz stilled beside him, the fruit forgotten in his hand. Another rustle. Then a crunch.

Ambry straightened slowly, eyes scanning the trees. A figure stepped out.

Ivy.

She edged out of the forest, steps faltering, eyes searching for him before she found the courage to keep going. The weight of everything she'd left behind clung to her, but this was heavier, not knowing if he wanted her there.

Ambry's breath caught. "Ivy…"

"I… I didn't know where else to go," she said. Her voice was unsteady, like it might break if she spoke too loud.

Laz raised an eyebrow. Then he gave Ambry a small nod. "I'll meet you at yours."

He offered Ivy a brief glance, a flicker of something that said, *hope you're okay,* then turned and walked ahead, boots crunching lightly on the path.

Ambry took a step closer. "Are you alright? What happened?"

"They came." Her voice caught. "The guards. They took my parents. Just showed up and… dragged them out. And now they're looking for us." She swallowed. "I can't go back to the camp. It's not safe anymore. None of it is."

His shoulders tightened. "Gareth?"

"He's here." She tipped her chin toward the trees. "Not far."

Ambry nodded once, eyes shifting in that direction.

"I didn't know what to do," she said. "Where to go. We don't know anyone here."

"How did they find your camp?" Ambry's jaw tensed. "I swear, I didn't say anything. I've never even been near it."

Ivy stepped in. "I know," she said, quiet but certain. Her eyes held his. "If I thought you'd betrayed me, I wouldn't be standing here."

He hesitated. "I can help you… but we have to be careful. If they find out, they'll take them in for recalibration. Thess, Mirae…"

She nodded. "We'll be careful."

"We'll go to my house. It's quiet, and we know every way in and out. At least it gives us a head start." He glanced toward the trees. "Go get Gareth. We'll figure the rest out after."

Ivy managed a small smile. "Back soon." She started to turn, but Ambry's voice stopped her.

"Why'd you really come looking for me?"

She met his eyes. "Because when everything fell apart, you're the only person I wanted to find."

He didn't smile. But something in him softened.

Ivy stepped back toward the trees.

A flicker of movement cut through the undergrowth. Then, a sharp snap. Branches splitting apart as Gareth exploded from the shadows, slamming into a figure in a blur of motion. The figure stumbled sideways, crashing hard into the brush. Ivy saw the uniform catching the light. Guards.

"Gareth!" Ivy screamed.

More guards surged in. One drove a heavy elbow into Gareth's ribs. He staggered but stayed upright. Another blow struck his back. He dropped to one knee.

"Ivy!" he shouted, voice ragged. "Go!"

Ambry lunged forward, grabbing her arm. "We have to move!"

She twisted hard, wrenching free, eyes locked on Gareth.

The guards closed in, a swarm of black-clad bodies closing ranks. Gareth lunged first. His elbow slammed into the jaw of the nearest guard, snapping the man's head back with a crack. He pivoted fast, driving his knee into another's ribs, folding him sideways with a grunt.

He moved like a storm front, head low, brutal, every strike sharp and fast. Two more went down hard, one clutching his gut, the other staggering, gasping for breath. But the rest didn't stop.

One hit him hard in the side, knocking him off balance. Another crashed into his shoulder, dragging him down. Still, Gareth fought. Twisting hard, driving forward with sheer force, like a man with nothing left to lose.

Hands yanked his arms back. A knee slammed into his spine, forcing him forward. His breath jolted out in a sharp grunt. Another set of hands grabbed his wrists, snapping restraints tight against his skin.

He tried to push up. A last wild surge.

The hit caught him clean. A fist — fast, sharp — slammed across his jaw, snapping his head sideways. He hit the ground hard. And finally, with every muscle burning and his breath rasping shallow, he went still.

"Gareth!" she choked out, voice cracking.

"GO!" he roared, even as they dragged him away.

Ambry didn't wait for her to freeze. He yanked her back and ran, pulling her through the brush, branches clawing, leaves slicing. The trees pressed close around them. Even as they ran, she caught the flick of him looking back, his grip tightening at the heavy thud of boots pounding after them, the noise closing in.

Ambry stopped. Sudden. Sharp. He turned to her, eyes fierce beneath his furrowed brow. "Ivy, listen to me." His voice cut clean through the rush of branches. "They'll catch us both if we stay together."

"No—"

"Split up. I'll draw them off. You circle wide, cut east. The ridge trail. You know it."

"Ambry—"

He caught her chin, steadying her for a breath, bringing her eyes to his. "Go."

And then he was gone. Darting left, crashing through the underbrush loud enough to be heard for miles.

Ivy tore into the forest alone, feet hammering roots and rock. Her lungs ripped for air. A branch whipped her face, but she didn't stop. Behind her, shapes moved between the trees, sweeping closer in waves. The guards were tracking. Hunting.

She ran until her legs gave out, crashing hard into the dirt. For a breath, she stayed down, palms scraped, lungs heaving. Then shoved herself up and staggered forward. One step, then another. No choice but forward.

She didn't slow until the trees thickened around her. Dense enough to swallow the sound of pursuit.

— ✦ —

Ivy ran until her legs collapsed beneath her.

She hit the ground hard, breath torn from her lungs. She dragged herself forward, palms digging in, knees scraping bark and dirt. She forced herself up and kept moving. And then... she noticed the silence. The air had shifted with the fading dusk, shadows drawing longer, swallowing the last echoes of pursuit.

She stumbled forward and caught herself against the nearest tree. The bark was cool and firm beneath her palm. She stood in the hush, every thread that had once held her steady, unravelling. She sank to her knees, hands curling into the cool earth, the only solid thing left to hold on to.

Everyone she loved, vanished in a breath. And Ambry… she didn't even know. Had he run to protect her? Or just to run?

She stared at the dirt, her vision blurring. Mum had been right, she should've stayed in the damn POD. Control used to feel like a cage. Now it felt like safety. Predictable, survivable. All she'd wanted was one year. One real breath that belonged to her.

The grief didn't rise like a wave. It sank, slow and heavy, until it filled her completely, all at once. And somewhere in that weight… she broke. Sudden, graceless, like a branch torn down in a storm. The sobs hit before she could brace, raw and wrenching. She pressed her forehead to the ground, breath shuddering through anguish and shame. "I lost everything." The words broke out before she could stop them. She folded into the silence, sobs tearing through her chest.

Then. A sound. A crack of twigs, sharp against the night.

She froze, breath snagging, the sobs locking hard in her throat.

A sweep of pale light cut between the trees, slow, deliberate. Hunting. Bootsteps followed, a steady tick against roots and stone.

The guards. Still close. Still searching.

She couldn't keep running, couldn't even lift her head. Her body sank lower, curling in on itself, trying to vanish, too spent to flee and too raw to fight. Her cheek pushed against bark and soil. She pressed into the tree's base, its solid weight anchoring her as the world fell quiet. Her pulse tapped out a frantic rhythm, quiet but relentless, counting down in her chest.

Then… a flutter.

Soft.

Slow.

A wing brushed her arm. Another fluttered near her ankle and settled. Then more, drifting down like leaves on a soft wind.

Leafwings.

They settled gently, dozens of them, blanketing her in overlapping wings, each one a perfect echo of the forest. Her arms. Her back. The tangled mess of her hair. Her breath slowed — shallower, smaller — until it barely moved at all. She watched as her body vanished into the earth. Camouflaged, rewritten. Moss and wing and shadow folded over her until she matched the ground itself. The wings lay soft over her skin, holding utterly still.

She closed her eyes.

A branch cracked nearby. Light swept across the forest floor, sharp and fast. Grazing her hand, her back, her cheek. She didn't flinch. Footsteps landed hard. One. Two. Then stopped. The forest held its breath. A second passed. Then another.

The steps shifted again, slower now, fading into the dark. Silence crept back through the trees, heavier than before. As if even the forest didn't know what to do with what had just passed.

The Leafwings didn't move. They stayed. Dozens of them, wings layered like woven threads, their camouflage deepening until she was no longer girl or fugitive, just another shape in the undergrowth.

She stayed curled beneath them, too drained to move, too hollow to care.

Each breath felt borrowed. Each second stolen.

Their wings settled over her quietly, like ash after a fire, not saviours but companions, waiting until she could save herself.

Chapter Forty-Three

The curved walls shimmered in soft gradients of silver and lavender, pulsing slowly in time with the room's own engineered rhythm. Thin projections of flowering vines curled across the ceiling, delicate, symmetrical, caught forever in mid-bloom. A faint floral scent hung in the air, sweet and engineered. Soothing. Designed to fade into the background, the kind of aroma no one could object to.

The bed was sunken slightly into the floor, surrounded by light-etched panels and layered with silk throws in lilac and pearl, pillows piled high in matching hues. Like everything in this room, it was beautiful.

On the opposite wall, a dressing alcove unfolded like a gallery. Seamless panels parted to reveal a wardrobe arranged by colour, texture, and season. Ribbons, wraps, and finely stitched layers hovered on slow-turning display shelves, each piece suspended in soft light, like art behind glass. No clutter. No mess. Just choices. Elegant, curated, and quietly perfect.

Asera lay coiled on a velvet cushion near the window, tail tucked, glowing eyes half-lidded. The Velune didn't move when the door slid open. Neither did Nyra. She sat cross-legged on her bed, draped in a silk wrap, one shoulder bare. Her fingers flicked through layers of projected data with clinical grace.

Solen crossed the threshold. "You accessed the core files." He said, voice sharp.

Nyra didn't glance up. "Obviously."

He crossed the room slowly, every movement too measured, like he'd rehearsed calm and couldn't quite stick the landing. "You don't understand what you're seeing," he said.

She shrugged. "That's what people say when they're wrong and cornered."

Asera lifted her head from the cushion, ear tufts flicking like feathered fans as she watched, unimpressed.

Nyra gestured upward, and a translucent structure spiraled above her — chip schematics, core pathways, signal trees — rotating in soft light like an autopsy of obedience.

"It's all here," she said. "Every override. Every emotional suppression patch. Every system update." She tapped a node. "Did you know one of the earliest protocols was called Stillness Cascade? Poetic."

Solen's voice tightened. "Nyra, listen to me. What you're looking at... saved us. The chip saved this planet."

"Did it?" Her eyes rose, sharp now. "Or did it just make everything quiet?"

Solen stepped forward, still measured, but there was tension in the movement now, like the thread holding him together had started to pull. "You'll see," he said, heat threading beneath the words. "Peace only works if you take choice off the table. The Lightbringer showed us what happens when you don't. That was Earth's real lesson. You give people freedom, and they tear each other apart. Burn their own skies. Call it progress while everything dies."

"The Lightbringer?" Nyra repeated, voice smooth. She gave a theatrical pause. "Oh, you mean Commander Beckett. The Earth man. The one who helped his planet spiral into extinction?"

She met his eyes. "Wise leadership."

Solen's voice cut sharper, the edge creeping in. "Peace isn't a choice. It's a leash. And the second you loosen it, everything falls apart."

Her gaze didn't shift. When she spoke, her voice was even, deliberate. "And yet... Beckett never knew if the people of Spero would have done the same. He built his systems on assumptions, that his humans... and ours... were the same. Easier to call it inevitable than admit you were afraid of giving us the choice."

"If you wait to find out, you die wondering." Solen's voice hit the walls and bounced. "We took our stand, Nyra." The projection vines on the ceiling shuddered, then dimmed. Their artificial harmony destabilised.

Her voice dropped to a whisper. "You really believe that."

"I know it," he snapped. "They let people feel. Choose. Lead. And Earth decayed. Not in flames, but silence. Numbness so deep they didn't even notice they were dying." He stepped closer. "The Lightbringer saw the truth. He didn't want to rebuild Earth. He wanted to correct it."

"Until it collapses too." She stood, shoulders squaring toward him. "Because that's what you do. You build things you can't control... and then blame the wreckage."

A long silence. He looked tired. No, not tired. Hollowed.

"That decision was made long before I took this chair, Nyra. I've only maintained the harmony." He met her eyes, steady. "You see control. I see a gift. A world without anger. Without fear. No grief breaking people down. No greed ripping the planet apart. They get to live without hate, without pain. In harmony with each other. In balance with the planet."

Nyra's stare burned. 'Is that what you told yourself? When you chipped her?'

The words hit, and Solen stopped, breath held, fury coiled.

Asera stretched long against her cushion, fur rippling in the light, eyes locking on Solen.

"She's not like the others," Nyra said. "Even in the outer villages, the chipped still laugh, they share advice. They stumble, smile... love. But my mother?" Her words were quiet, but each one landed with precision. "She doesn't laugh. She doesn't engage. She doesn't even see me." Her eyes locked on his. "She's perfect. Polite. Empty. I've watched strangers share moments my own mother can't give me." Her voice dropped. "And you call that harmony."

"That's because she has to be," Solen said softly.

"Why?"

"When keeping the pendant active, the user must be completely in sync. Still. Controlled. Emotionless. The key only listens to a clear signal."

"So why wasn't the chip enough?" Nyra's voice grew colder. "Why did she have to lose everything?"

"It wasn't enough, Nyra. Not at that level of purity. Most chipped still carry interference. Attachments, fragments of emotion they can't let go of. The suppression dulls it, but it doesn't erase what clings beneath." He exhaled slowly. "But your mother... she allowed us to strengthen her chip. Adjust the protocol. Strip everything back. And that was enough. It forced her to let go of everything. Quieted her until there was nothing left to cloud the signal."

"We all have our chains… so she had to be built for it." Solen straightened, chin lifting as if the words alone vindicated him.

"So you silenced her completely… to keep your network alive."

"She volunteered."

"No," Nyra said, stepping closer. "She trusted you."

That hit harder than any wound. Solen took a step back. The light along the walls dimmed.

Asera rose and padded to Nyra's side, her white fur catching the dim light like silk. Her eyes glowed, sharp and aware.

"One more question," Nyra said. "How much control does it take… before there's nothing left worth controlling?"

Solen's silence pressed heavier than words.

"I see," Nyra said. She turned her back on him and sat on her bed, picking up her Tactis. The data spiraled around her like falling leaves. Asera sprang lightly onto the bed, curling against Nyra's side. Her opal eyes found Solen and held, a silent command that he was no longer needed.

Her voice stayed calm. "I understand now." She reached for the projections. "Thank you… for explaining."

Chapter Forty-Four

The morning mist drifted low through the trees, hushed and silver. High above, Tallwings moved through the branches, wings whispering, calls drifting down like wind chimes strung from glass.

Ivy stirred beneath a quilt of soft movement. Leafwings still covered her, rising and falling in time with her breath. They had formed a living cocoon through the night, shielding her from the cold and from the eyes that hunted her. As the first golden rays slipped between the trees, she opened her eyes.

"Hey," she whispered.

The Leafwings rustled faintly, like wind shifting through tall grass. She lifted a hand. They loosened their hold and drifted away... scattering like seeds on a breeze. A few hovered a moment longer before floating into the trees. Her body protested every movement. Stiff, sore, like she'd been wrung out and dropped. Breathing scraped down her throat, but she forced herself upright.

Birdsong rose through the mist. The forest moved on, unchanged. Like it didn't care if the world had broken overnight. Like it didn't care that the people she loved were gone. Or that they had trusted her. And now she was here. Useless. Alone. And maybe if she'd stayed inside the mission, followed the rules... she wouldn't be. They were taken because she couldn't sit still. Couldn't shut up. Couldn't leave it alone. She left safety behind and turned it into a disaster everyone else had to live with. It would've been easier. To let someone else steer. To follow the mission. The rules. To be a good daughter on a year-long science trip. But she hadn't. And now she was here. On the edge of something she couldn't go back from.

She curled forward, arms wrapped tight around her knees, and let the stillness press in. Even the air felt suspended, like the forest had taken a breath and forgotten how to exhale. She cried. Quiet at first, then harder. Until the sound blurred and her body just shook with it. Until there was nothing left but breath and a raw ache behind her eyes. Not broken. Just scraped empty.

She drew in a breath and lifted her head. High above, something moved, a flicker in the branches. A single Leafwing drifted down through the mist, its wings slow and steady, catching the light like moving glass. It circled once, then landed lightly on her shoulder. With delicate steps, it made its way along her collarbone and paused at the pendant, wings folding in as if it belonged there.

The pendant — the legacy Gareth had placed in her hands — caught the morning light, its bronze wings curled tight around the crystal core. Still. Silent. Waiting.

Ivy stared at it, a quiet ache pressing beneath her ribs. It didn't soothe. It didn't beckon. Just weight, and memory. A reminder. She lifted her hand, steady. The Leafwing stepped onto her finger, its weight barely there.

"Okay," she whispered. "Maybe I don't have the answers. But I'll get them."

The pendant gave a quiet pulse, soft, blue, and sure. The Leafwing lingered a moment, then slipped into the air — silent, weightless — and vanished into the trees.

Ivy drew in a slow breath. No more waiting. No more hoping someone stronger would step in.

She stood. Unsteady, but upright. Not ready. But willing.

There was nothing left to think through.

Her feet were already moving.

CHAPTER FORTY-FIVE

Ivy crept through the forest with quiet steps, using every ounce of caution Gareth had drilled into her. Her goal wasn't the POD, not at first. She needed food. Water. Supplies. Her mind had already started mapping the risks, weighing distances. It wasn't just survival anymore. It was strategy.

She moved like someone trained to obey. Shaped by Gareth's survival routines, her mother's precision, her father's quiet expectations. Quiet. Careful. Invisible. The clearing opened ahead, and there it was. The POD, smooth and sharp against the wild quiet of the trees. She paused. Breath held. Waiting.

Movement in the light, just shadows stretching with the dawn. Her hand rested on the trunk of a Kavari tree. She could do this. Just grab what she needed and go. And then she'd head back to camp, the one she'd shared with Gareth. If it was still there. If The Order hadn't found it yet. Then she'd be alone. Truly alone.

Because Ambry wasn't an option. Not anymore. She didn't even know if he was safe. If he cared. If he had ever really cared. The chip made everything uncertain. Every word, every kiss, every promise. It hurt too much to wonder. So she didn't. She made herself keep going.

Then she saw it. Curly black hair. A profile turned toward the ramp. Her breath caught. "Mum?"

It was Grace. Solid, real.

Relief slammed into Ivy like a tidal wave. She stumbled into the clearing without thinking, feet moving faster than her thoughts. "Mum!" she choked, rushing forward. "I thought they took you. I didn't know. Gareth's gone…" She flung herself into Grace's arms, the warmth of her mother's embrace almost enough to quiet the shaking in her chest.

Grace wrapped her arms around her, calm and steady. "Ivy... you're back," she said, voice low and soothing. "You're safe."

Ivy buried her face in her shoulder. "I'm so sorry. I messed everything up. I shouldn't have left the POD. I shouldn't have dragged anyone into this."

"It's alright," Grace murmured. "You're back where you belong."

Ivy pulled back slightly. "Wait. How did they let you go? Did you escape?"

"They just wanted to talk," Grace said, her voice unnervingly calm. "They explained the structure, the purpose. It's all logical, really." She smiled. "It's not what we expected... but it makes sense. It feels right, Ivy. You'll see."

Something cold slithered down Ivy's spine. That didn't sound like her mother. That sounded... programmed. "You're not angry?" She asked, her voice small. "Not even a little?"

"There's nothing to be angry about," Grace said lightly. "You made a mistake. But you came back. That's what matters."

Too soft. Her mother was many things, but gentle forgiveness was not one of them.

David appeared at the top of the ramp. "Ivy... I'm so glad you're here," he said, stepping down toward them. "And I'm glad you're safe."

No questions. Just calm acceptance. And a little too glad...

Ivy stepped back fully now, her gaze darting between them. "What did they do to you?"

"I don't know what you mean, Ivy." Grace's voice stayed even. "No one did anything to us. We just... understand things more clearly now." Grace's gaze dropped to Ivy's chest, where the pendant rested against her shirt.

"The pendant," Grace said. "They identified it as unstable. You need to hand it over so we can keep you safe."

Ivy's stomach turned. "You want me to give it to them?"

David's voice was level, his smile kind. "Yes Ivy. It's a hazard. It shouldn't be in circulation."

Her hands closed over the pendant instinctively, the cool metal grounding her for a heartbeat as panic surged in her chest. This wasn't a reunion. It was a retrieval. And she was the package.

She looked at them. Too still, too smooth, their calm just a little too perfect. And she knew.

They were chipped.

Her parents — the ones who taught her, pushed her, protected her — weren't standing there anymore. Not gone. But only half the people they once were. "I don't—" she began, but her voice cracked. She took a step back. "The chip…"

"Ivy!"

She spun. Ambry broke through the treeline, eyes wide, panic etched across his face. Laz skidded in behind him, already looking for exits.

"They got to them," Ambry gasped. "We have to go. Now."

Ivy turned back. Grace and David were still smiling. Still perfect. Still waiting.

She hesitated, fingers trembling against the pendant. Her mother's voice in her head. Her father's quiet nod. The weight of always needing to do the right thing pulsing through her. Now she had to choose.

"Ivy, let's go!" Ambry called, eyes scanning the trees. "The guards are seconds away!"

"I'm sorry," she whispered.

Then she ran.

— ✦ —

They ran fast and low, weaving through the trees as the clearing vanished behind them. Ivy's breath came sharp, her legs aching, but she didn't slow. Not yet. Not until they were deep enough that mist curled between the trunks and the air felt still again.

Ivy stumbled into a clearing and dropped to her knees, breath hitching hard in her throat. She didn't cry. Not this time. Her lungs just pulled in air as if it was the only thing left keeping her upright.

Ambry stood over her, chest heaving, sweat clinging to the edge of his jaw. He didn't say anything. Not yet.

Laz hung back, pacing like a caged animal, eyes scanning the trees.

Ivy looked up. Ambry met her eyes. And everything she'd told herself — all the reasons she couldn't trust him, shouldn't trust him — cracked. She surged to her feet and threw her arms around him. It wasn't graceful. It wasn't clever. But it was real.

He caught her instantly. His arms wrapped tight around her, one hand bracing the back of her head, holding her like he thought she might shatter.

"I thought you were gone," she said into his shoulder, voice hoarse.

"I couldn't just leave you," he whispered back.

She pulled back just enough to see his face. "I shouldn't have said that to you. About your feelings for me. I didn't mean it—"

Ambry shook his head. "I deserved it. I was so angry you didn't tell me about Earth. About the mission. But I get it now."

"I'm sorry," she whispered.

"Me too."

Ambry gave a broken laugh. "I didn't know if I should find you. Or if you'd even want—"

"I do," she said, without letting him finish. "Always."

He pulled her close and kissed her, fierce and certain, fingers tightening at her waist like he needed the feel of her to believe any of this was real. Every thought in her head went quiet, doubt silenced by the heat of him, the pull of everything unsaid. And when he finally broke away, he held her tighter, like maybe he wouldn't let go again.

Behind them, Laz coughed. "Okay, lovebirds. Not to ruin the moment, but can we please keep moving before we all die?"

Ivy stepped back, a shaky smile forming. "Right. Because that is pretty important too."

Ambry's fingers closed around hers, steady and firm. "Let's get you safe."

Ivy nodded, fingers curling around his. They turned into the forest together, still catching their breath, still piecing it all together... but side by side.

And for the first time in days, the path ahead didn't feel impossible.

Chapter Forty-Six

Nyra stepped into her mother's quarters and let the door seal behind her with a soft hiss. Her boots clicked on polished stone, all shine, no softness. Near the far wall, two white lounge chairs curved toward each other across a small round table. A tall glass vase stood to one side, holding three long-stemmed blooms with pearl-edged petals, symmetrical as a diagram. Against the back wall, a low bookcase cradled a dozen pale-bound volumes, arranged so evenly it looked like no one had ever touched them. The ceiling panels glowed with engineered balance, casting a soft, perfect sheen across the room.

Evara stood at the open glass wall, spine straight, gaze locked on Domaris. The city stretched below in perfect symmetry, every glowing curve too flawless to feel real. Her indigo hair fell sleek down her back, not a strand out of place. At her throat, the bronze pendant pulsed softly, steady as a heartbeat.

"Mother?"

Evara didn't move. Just stood there, silent, still, as if the city held her more than the voice behind her. "Nyra," she said, her voice calm. "What are you doing here?"

Nyra stepped forward. "I just wanted to see you. Just a moment." She hesitated. Her eyes flicked to the pendant.

"Do you know what that pendant does?" She asked, her voice low. "The Order implants chips to control people. To force peace. To suppress emotions so they can't rebel. And that's what they did to you."

Her mother kept her gaze on the city below. "Yes, Nyra. Of course I know what the chip does," she said, voice smooth. "It maintains peace and harmony, so we can thrive without fear. Without conflict."

Nyra's fingers curled at her sides. "Why did you let him do this to you?" she whispered. "Why did you let Father chip you so far you can't even... feel anymore?"

Evara's tone softened, almost fond. "Nyra, your father is a great man. A wise man. He knew some answers cost too much. We chose not to keep asking."

"And you really believe that..." Nyra murmured. She stepped in beside her, close enough to touch, but her mother didn't move. Her gaze stayed fixed on the city below.

"Mum, I have to know," she said. "Are you still you behind all of this... perfection?"

"Nyra," she said gently, "I am me. I'm just... confused about what you're talking about."

"You don't see me!" The words tore out, too loud, too sharp, like something cracked wide open. She straightened, cleared her throat, and forced her voice steady. "You don't even look at me."

A silence stretched. Nyra smoothed her hands against her dress, slow and steady. "Come sit with me," she said softly, reaching for her mother's hand. "Please."

For the first time, Evara looked at her daughter, slow and serene, and let Nyra guide her across the room.

They sat in twin lounge chairs upholstered in a lush, snowy fabric. Between them, a small round table gleamed like cut glass, small, pale jewels set into the surface like frozen drops of rain.She tried to smile. "Do you remember our trip to the Singing Groves? I was ten. We made up silly songs and sang them like we were the choir of Domaris. We danced in the stream until our feet went numb. And then we drank sunberry pulp straight from the husks, sticky and cold and too sweet to be good for us. We laughed, really laughed. Do you remember that, Mum?"

The pendant on her mother's throat gave a faint pulse. Then steadied again. Evara's face didn't change. "I do not remember laughter," she said. "But the Groves were a productive expedition."

Nyra's eyes flickered closed, just for a second. Then she drew in a breath and held it, steady and sharp. She reached out, resting her hand gently on her mother's arm, hoping for something — a flinch, a flicker, even the smallest tremble of recognition. But Evara didn't stir. Her skin was warm, her posture perfect. Like Nyra hadn't touched her at all.

"They're suppressing you," Nyra said. "Keeping you locked down, so the pendant stays active."

Evara met her eyes and smiled. "My service supports the greater balance."

Nyra let her hand slip free, slow and deliberate, then rested it against her leg. Her jaw tightened. And then, quietly, she rose. "You would've fought for me."

She turned before the tears could reach her voice, spine straight, eyes forward. "Then I'll fight for you," she whispered.

Behind her, Evara didn't answer.

Nyra walked out without looking back, leaving only the steady pulse of the pendant behind.

CHAPTER FORTY-SEVEN

Ambry's home rose from the base of the Kavari trees, its walls formed between living trunks and supported by broad wooden beams, shaped to match the land's quiet curves.

He pushed open the door, and warm air met them like a wall. The glow of the fire lit the room in soft golds and browns. Worn, lived-in, safe. Light filtered through open window slats, framed with carved shutters that swung wide to the forest beyond. The floors were timber-panelled, worn smooth by time and softened with thick woven mats in warm, earthy tones.

The main room was wide and open, centred around a stone hearth that held a crackling fire. A stack of split logs rested beside it, and plush, well-worn lounge chairs circled the warmth, one patched at the arm, another draped with a handmade quilt. Shelves lined the walls, carved directly into the support beams, crammed with books, seed jars, and half-finished tools. Dried herbs hung from the rafters above, brushing the air with a scent that smelled like mint and lemon. Fresh, sharp, and grounding. A wooden staircase curved up one side of the room, leading to a modest upper level nestled beneath a gently arched roof, shaped by the living curves of the Kavari trees. High above, simple lanterns hung from the rafters, flickering, tangled with loops of dried vine. Near the doorway, boots were scattered across the floor and cloaks hung from peg rails. Nothing matched, but everything felt placed with care. It wasn't fancy. It wasn't polished. But it was honest. And Ivy could feel the weight of it — the history, the love, the effort — in every quiet detail. She stepped inside, boots sinking into thick rugs, the scent of herbs and roasted roots wrapping close.

Laz charged past her with a groan of relief. "Please tell me that tastes as good as it smells."

From the kitchen nook, a soft laugh answered. "Roasted roots and flatcakes. Can you stay for lunch?"

Laz was already halfway to the kitchen. "Only if there's enough. Ambry said he's not that hungry."

Ambry raised his voice toward the kitchen. "Mum, I did not say that!"

Riven lounged in one of the patched armchairs, a carved wooden puzzle turning slowly in his hands as he twisted the pieces with calm focus. "You look like you lost a fight," he said. "With gravity."

Laz didn't miss a beat. "I've been in the forest with two emotionally volatile rebels. What's your excuse?"

Ambry's mum glanced out from the kitchen nook, her golden skin catching the firelight, a soft, sunlit yellow that seemed to warm the room around her. Butter-hued curls were pinned back with a carved wooden clasp, loose strands brushing her cheek as she stirred the pot in slow, steady circles, one hand resting lightly on the bench. A faint smile played at her lips.

"Ambry," she called, voice light. "Lunch will be ready soon."

"Mum," Ambry said with a small nod. "Meet Ivy. Ivy, this is Avenya."

Avenya's eyes met Ivy's. "Welcome," she said gently, before turning back to the pot.

The back door creaked open, and Ambry's dad stepped in with his arms full of firewood. His blue-toned skin caught the light as he crossed to the hearth, sleeves pushed high, bark clinging to his forearms. He gave Ivy a brief nod, then set the logs down with a quiet thud.

"Kaelen, leave your boots by the door," Avenya called. "I just swept."

Ambry met Ivy's eyes and gave a slight shrug, like this was normal.

Ivy leant closer, her voice low. "Should I tell them I'm from some faraway planet, here to corrupt their son with all the terrible habits of Earth folk? See if it short-circuits their programming?"

Ambry huffed a soft laugh. "Might as well. You're already halfway there."

She met his eyes. "They're still them. Just like you're still you… and Laz is still Laz."

His smile tilted, a little crooked. "Yeah. They love us. And sometimes... that's all you need."

"You know what? You're pretty great," Ivy said. "And you're chipped. But maybe that didn't matter. Maybe you never had anything in you the chip could shut down."

His eyes didn't move from hers. "You really believe that?"

Ivy's smile lingered. "Of course I do." Ambry's mouth curved in answer, a quiet grin meant only for her, before he nudged her further inside. She noticed the table then, wood-grained and slightly uneven, like it had been made by hand. Plates were already laid out. Nothing matched, but every piece seemed like it belonged. Flatcakes were stacked high beside roasted roots drizzled with something golden. A bowl of glistening sunberries sat next to a plain jug of water, cool and clear.

Avenya set the last dish down, her yellow-toned skin catching the light as she moved with quiet ease. "Help yourselves."

Laz was already reaching. "If I'm chewing, I'm not causing trouble," he said, grabbing two flatcakes and stacking them. "It's a public service, really."

Kaelen gave a dry laugh. "Then don't stop chewing. Ever."

Avenya smiled at Ivy. "There's plenty. Sit."

Ivy slid into a chair beside Ambry, the fire's glow brushing her shoulders. The scent of warm flatcakes and roasted roots rose up to meet her, sharp, rich, overwhelming. Her stomach twisted, uncertain how to react after nearly a day of eating nothing. Her fingers hovered at the edge of the plate.

Ambry nudged her. "They're good. I promise."

She didn't answer but took one, biting down. The taste bloomed slow, soft and earthy, with a hint of spice that caught the back of her throat.

Laz was already on his third. "If we die tomorrow, I want this to be my last meal. And maybe another flatcake for the road."

Kaelen raised a brow. "You planning on dying somewhere specific?"

"Just keeping my options open," Laz said through a mouthful.

The table shifted with quiet movement, spoons scraping, water pouring, the quiet rhythm of people who knew how to be together.

Ivy watched them, this family who joked and teased like nothing had ever been taken from them. Who still had nicknames and inside stories. She didn't join in. Just sat there, letting the warmth soak into her skin like something she wasn't sure she was allowed to feel.

— ✦ —

They stood from the table together, the clatter of bowls and scrape of chairs replacing conversation. Ivy reached for the nearest dish without thinking.

"You don't have to do that," Avenya said, gathering plates from the table.

"It's okay," Ivy replied, stacking them. "Happy to help."

Ambry met her at the basin, rinsing while she dried. The water ran warm, spilling from a curved, leaf-shaped spout.

"Wait, hot water?" Ivy asked.

"Heatstone," Kaelen said, stacking cups behind her. "Line the pipes right and it holds warmth all day." He glanced at Ivy. "What do they use where you're from?"

Ivy hesitated, then gave a quick shrug. "Oh... same."

Ambry shot her a sideways look but didn't say anything.

They moved in quiet rhythm. Wash, rinse, dry, stack. The kind of task that didn't need words. At the final bowl, Ivy dried it carefully, setting it down with a soft clink.

Avenya paused beside her, watching. "You've got careful hands."

Ivy glanced up. "I grew up around plants. And equipment. Breaking things was... not encouraged."

She reached out, a light press to Ivy's elbow, warm and steady. "I hope you know you're always welcome here."

Ivy nodded, too quick, too automatic. But her throat tightened anyway.

"Thanks," she said softly. "For lunch. For all of it."

Avenya gave her a quiet nod.

Ambry touched Ivy's shoulder. "Come on. Let's go upstairs."

They crossed the main room toward the staircase, passing Laz sprawled sideways across one of the couches, his head tipped back dramatically, a bowl still balanced on his stomach. Riven sat curled at the other end, content and glassy-eyed, half-listening to something Kaelen was saying from the kitchen.

"Hey," Ambry called, "we're heading up to talk."

Laz raised a single hand without opening his eyes. "I can't stand, so... go without me. I'll die here. Tell my story."

Ambry tapped him on the shoulder as he passed. "Come up when you've mourned your stomach."

Laz groaned. "How did you let me eat that much?"

Ambry rolled his eyes and kept walking. Ivy followed him up the stairs, Laz's dramatic moans trailing behind them.

Ambry's room was round, tucked into the upper level of the house, with smooth wooden walls that curved gently inward beneath the sloping roof. A single round window sat low in the wall, letting the afternoon sun spill in warm, golden bands stretching across the floor. The bed was handmade. Raw-edged timber sanded to a soft, worn finish, layered with soft Kavari blankets, each marked at the centre with the faint round scar where the stalk had once been, and a scatter of mismatched pillows. A fire crackled in the hearth, casting gentle shadows across smooth floorboards softened by woven mats and layered rugs. Shelves carved straight into the wood held salvaged tech, folded blankets, and a few softly glowing light-stones. In here, the world outside felt quieter. Further away.

Ivy rubbed at a smudge of dirt on her arm, only smearing it further. Her hair was tangled, her clothes stiff with dried sweat and forest grit.

Ambry noticed. "Want to wash up?" he asked softly, nodding toward the pale wood panel between the bookcases. "Shower's through there."

"I don't have anything clean," she said.

He crossed the room, opened a drawer near the bed, and pulled out a folded shirt and a pair of soft linen pants. He held out the bundle. "Now you do."

She gave him a look, half amused, half grateful. "I'm going to owe you forever, aren't I?"

Ambry smiled. "If that's what it takes to keep you around."

Ivy stepped closer without thinking.

His smile dimmed, not lost but softened, like he was holding space, waiting to see what she needed. She just stepped in and curled her fingers into the front of his shirt.

Ambry met her halfway, his mouth finding hers like it had always been waiting. His hands settled at her waist, steady and sure.

Ivy's fingers slid behind his neck, her body answering before her mind could catch up.

When they finally broke apart, she stayed close, forehead resting lightly against his chest. "I needed that," she said.

Ambry's voice caught low. "Me too."

She gave him another quick kiss before slipping through the curved doorway, sliding it closed behind her.

The bathroom was carved directly into the heart of the rock, smoothed by water and time.

A copper spout curved from the wall above a wide basin. The air held the scent of crushed herbs and a flower Ivy couldn't name, something sweet and sharp and vibrant in a way she couldn't explain.

Beside her, a small carved shelf held a few of Ambry's things. An old soapstone comb, a worn cloth bundle that smelled faintly of juniper, and a chipped cup that looked suspiciously like it had once belonged to a toolkit. A dark green towel was slung carelessly over a hook, the edges frayed from years of use. A smooth dish of washing stones sat at the edge of the basin, each one rounded by use and dappled with pale mineral streaks.

She hesitated, her hand brushing the towel. The space was simple, but it was his. She felt it in the way everything sat, casual and unhidden, like this was Ambry's space and he'd never cared who saw it.

Slipping off her clothes, she folded them into a neat pile on the bench near the wall. Her fingers lingered at the pendant still hanging around her neck. After a moment, she unclasped it and set it gently on top.

She crossed the warm stone floor, the air was already humid, heat rising from the pipes hidden behind the walls. A soft glow radiated from the stone itself, gentle and steady, enough to see by without casting hard shadows.

The alcove waited in the far wall, smooth stone beneath her feet, a simple copper ring overhead. When she turned the handle, water poured from above in a clean, steady stream, warm and quiet. Steam drifted upward, curling along the stone floor and softening the edges of the room.

Heat rolled over her as she stepped beneath the stream. Dirt loosened from her skin in slow spirals. Her hair clung to her face until the water dragged it back. Tilting her head, eyes closed, she let herself vanish into it. She braced her hands against the stone wall, shoulders dropping as warmth settled deep into her muscles. She was used to sterile showers aboard the ship, the kind that sprayed in rationed bursts, cleaned efficiently, and left no time to feel anything. Even here, it had been quick river dips with Gareth while they camped, cold and quiet and practical.

But this... this was something else.

This felt almost sacred.

CHAPTER FORTY-EIGHT

Ivy stepped out of the bathroom, her bare feet quiet against the layered rugs. The suns had dipped low, casting only a faint wash of light through the window, the rest of the room lit by the steady flicker of the fire.

Ambry's borrowed clothes hung loose on her frame — a sleeveless tunic dyed in worn shades of rust-red and faded amber, paired with drawstring pants woven from something that felt like silk but breathed like cotton. Spero fabric. Soft, lived-in. She shifted the tunic against her shoulder, the scent catching her, woodsmoke and something warm and mineral, like sun on stone.

Laz sat cross-legged near the fireplace, the flicker of a holo-display dancing across his features. His usual spark was dimmed, replaced by something quieter, watchful, weary. Brax curled beside him, head on Laz's thigh, sleeping quietly. He stayed focused on the Tactis, not looking up until her footsteps drew close, soft across the rugs. Then his eyes lifted, tracking her carefully.

"You look like hell," he said gently. "But, you know. Still statistically more attractive than Ambry."

Ivy snorted. "I just stepped out of a shower sent by the gods, and you still rank me below shipwreck chic? Rude."

She sank down beside him, drawing her knees in close, arms resting lightly across them. A flicker of a smile played on her lips, brief and tired. The silence that settled between them was the kind that knew too much, familiar, but weighted now. Heavy with everything they hadn't said yet. She looked over at him. "Thank you," she whispered. "For helping me get out."

Laz shrugged one shoulder, trying for casual but not quite pulling it off. "Please. If The Order had taken you, Ambry would've brooded even harder. And we don't need that level of drama in the house."

"They took my parents," she said eventually, her voice barely audible. "And Gareth... I don't know what happened to him. I saw him fighting. Then he was gone."

Laz looked down at his Tactis. "We found something in the files, a missing royal, six years old when the Sweep hit. His name was Gareth. That's not a coincidence. I don't think he even knew how much he mattered."

Just then, the door creaked open, and Ambry stepped inside, his arms full of food stacked on a woven tray. Steam curled from a bowl of spiced root stew, and something that looked suspiciously like solarbread was balanced on top. "I figured we'd all feel braver with full stomachs," he said.

Ivy looked at the tray. "But we just had lunch."

Laz snorted. "Yeah, and you were in the shower for, like, a small geological era."

Ambry grinned. "He's not wrong."

Heat crept up her neck. "Oh."

Ambry laughed. "It's fed from a natural spring, and with the heatstones, it never runs out. It's okay, you're allowed to enjoy it."

He set the tray down between them and moved to sit next to her. He handed her a bowl of soup, warm and fragrant in her hands. "Were you talking about Gareth?" he asked gently, catching the tail end of the conversation. "I think he knew something. He always knew more than he said."

Ivy nodded slowly, her fingers tightening around the bowl. "He did. He knew everything. His parents... they were the king and queen of Spero."

Ambry's head jerked up. "What?"

Laz actually choked on the sip of broth he'd just taken. "I'm sorry. Did you just say, king and queen? Like actual royal royalty?"

She held their gaze. "Yeah. All this time... he's been searching for answers, trying to find out what happened to his family. He's the last of them."

Ambry let out a slow breath, shaking his head. "And we've been walking him around Domaris like he's nobody."

Laz leant back on his hands, eyebrows raised. "Well. That explains the 'constantly carrying the fate of the world' vibe."

Ivy gave a faint, shaky smile. "He used to tell me stories when I was a kid. About a boy who lived on a planet that glows. About protectors with wings." She laughed softly, more breath than sound. "I thought they were just bedtime stories. Fairy tales to help me sleep."

Laz shook his head, quieter now. "Maybe they were. Or maybe... he was preparing you."

There was a long pause. The fire cracked and flared.

"He's royalty," Ivy said, as if the words would settle the spinning in her head. "He's royalty. And now he's gone."

Ambry's voice was quiet but firm. "Then we find him. And we finish what the royals died fighting for, to keep this world free."

Laz looked at both of them, his eyes darker than usual. "You know this doesn't end small, right? If Gareth was royal, and you're... whatever you are... this doesn't end with just rescuing your parents. This ends with tearing the whole damn system down."

Ivy stared into the fire, her voice hollow. "Then we burn it."

The room went still again, her words settling like ash. Outside, the last of the light slipped away, leaving only the quiet flicker of the fire, steady and low.

Ambry glanced toward Laz. "Then we need to know where to strike."

Laz exhaled and reached for the Tactis. "Right. Okay, let's see what we are dealing with." He spun the schematic into view, the projection casting faint light against the wall. "Here's what I found. The chip doesn't just suppress emotion randomly, it targets specific neural patterns. Grief, unrest, violence. People can still laugh, still smile and live normal lives. But they can't snap. Can't rage. Can't lash out, even if they wanted to."

He let out a low whistle. "And I'd probably be pretty angry about that... but you know. Chipped." He tapped a point on the projection. "The core beneath Domaris holds the original logic. That's where it all runs from. But the core doesn't adapt or update. It's static. Old tech. Ancient, really. It was meant for something gentler."

Ivy leant in. "Yeah... Gareth told me the royals used it for criminals. Instead of locking them away, they stripped their right to feel certain emotions. It was a way to keep their freedom but remove them as a threat.

Ambry leant forward. "How old is this system anyway?"

Laz tapped the edge of the projection. "The original chip tech? Over eighty years. But the real control? That came later. But as far as I can tell... the mass chipping didn't start until about forty-five years ago."

Ambry's jaw tightened. "When The Order took over?"

Laz gave a grim nod. "That's when it shifted from justice... to control."

Silence fell between them.

"And if we shut it down?" Ambry asked at last.

Laz shrugged. "We don't know. Could be peace. Could be chaos. Depends on whether people remember how to feel without losing control."

Before anyone could speak again, a knock echoed against the doorframe.

Ambry stood slowly, tension flickering behind his eyes. He moved toward the door but didn't open it. "Who is it?"

"It's me," a familiar voice cut through the quiet. "Your dad let me in." Nyra.

The door creaked open, spilling golden firelight across the landing. Nyra stepped through the threshold, every inch of her coiled elegance in place. But there was something different in her posture. Something stripped down.

Ambry didn't move. His eyes stayed on hers, too steady. "It was you." Silence stretched between them. "You told them."

Something in Ivy's chest tightened. Of course. Of course it was her. The realisation hit like a slap — sudden, shameful. How had she not seen it before? Nyra, always watching, always circling. The way she looked at the pendant. The timing of the arrest. The silence that followed. It all lined up.

Ivy stood slowly. Not out of fear. Out of fury. "It was you," she said.

Nyra didn't deny it. "I saw the pendant when you were in my apartment. I thought you'd stolen my mother's. So I went to Ambry's to confront him. And I overheard... how much you were hurting him, where you were from, what you had done. Maybe I jumped to conclusions, but at the time, I truly believed I was doing the right thing."

Ivy's hands clenched. "What, and now you want to apologise? After what it cost?"

Nyra's eyes flashed. "Ivy, you came into my house, looked me in the eye, and stole my father's pass to The Order's archives. You used me."

"And you handed my family over like they were nothing," Ivy snapped. "You stood there in your perfect house with your perfect parents and played the victim. You don't get to stand here and say 'I was wrong' like it's a band-aid on a severed arm."

Nyra paled but didn't back down.

"Ivy," Ambry said quietly.

She cut him off with a sharp look. "You have no idea what it's like, to watch your whole family disappear right in front of you. To be left with nothing. No one." Her voice dropped, tight with fury. "Gareth's gone. My parents... chipped, Nyra. Chipped. Some ancient biotech in their heads doing god knows what." She held Nyra's gaze, every word cutting sharper. "And you gave them up. Not because you were scared. Because it was easier."

Brax lifted his head from Laz's lap and growled, low, almost protective.

Nyra didn't flinch. "You came to my planet, into my life. And you were hurting my friends. I thought I was protecting something that mattered."

"You were protecting power," Ivy said coldly. "And now you've seen what it costs. Congratulations."

The room went quiet. Firelight danced across the walls. Brax gave a soft huff, his head settling back against Laz's leg, like even he'd decided to wait.

"I came to help," Nyra said at last. "Not to be forgiven. Just to help."

Laz didn't look up, still tapping away at the Tactis. "Funny how people only switch sides when their own house starts burning," he muttered.

Nyra turned to Ivy. "That pendant. My mother wears one too, always has. I used to think it was just a family heirloom." Her voice dropped. "But when I pulled the records... I found out the truth. It's a key. And to keep it active, the wearer has to hold a perfect emotional frequency, something The Order forces on my mother through extreme chip suppression."

"She's wearing the king's key," Ivy said, her fingers brushing the pendant at her chest. "And this one is the queen's."

Nyra's jaw tightened. "I started watching her. She's still. Perfect. Polite. Empty. And the pendant keeps on pulsing."

Laz's face shifted, serious now. "If her pendant's always active, it means she's in a forced state of 'harmony.' It's fake. Artificial. And your father's using her to force open the key, to control the chip's core."

Ivy's eyes locked on Nyra. "And you want to help bring this whole chip system down?"

Nyra met her gaze without flinching. "I want to free her. I want to know if there's anything of my mother left. Before there's nothing left at all."

The silence stretched long.

Ivy's expression didn't shift. "I don't trust you."

"I know," Nyra said softly. "I'm not asking you to trust me. Just... let me fight for her."

The moment hung heavy. Then Ambry stepped in, voice quiet but firm. "She's telling the truth."

"She told the truth before," Ivy snapped. "Right before she sold me out."

Laz rubbed a hand across his mouth. "You're not wrong. But... we need her. Not just because of the pendant. She knows Domaris from the inside. She knows how her father thinks. That gives us an edge."

"I'm not asking you to forgive her," Ambry said. "I'm asking you to let her fight with us. We need every edge we've got."

Ivy's eyes flicked from Ambry to Laz, then back to Nyra. The fury was still there, sharp as ever. But beneath it, something else moved. Tiredness, grief, the sheer weight of everything they still had to do. Ivy looked away, jaw tight.

Ambry spoke up again. "At least let her try."

Laz raised both eyebrows. "If we say no, she'll probably come back with a battle bot and a lecture, and my ears still hurt from the last one."

There was a pause. Silence stretching just long enough to feel loaded.

Ivy stared Nyra down, then tilted her head. "Alright. You can help, but only because Asara would've wanted me to be the bigger person."

Nyra arched a brow. "If it helps, she's also mad at me." She shrugged. "I changed my shampoo."

Ivy considered it. "Well, she has excellent judgment. And yes, that helps." She glanced at Ambry and Laz. "Fine. She can stay." She looked to the three of them. Her voice was calm, but commanding. "We prep tomorrow. At midnight, we move. We breach the archive. We shut down the core. We end this."

No one argued.

For the first time, Ivy wasn't standing on the outside, waiting, wondering where she fit.

She wasn't just part of the plan, she was leading it.

— ✦ —

Later that night, when the house had gone quiet and the fires had burned low inside, Ivy sat beside Ambry on the porch steps. The air was cool on her skin, tinged with the earthy sweetness of flowering vines and damp stone. Moonlight spilled over the wooden planks, casting soft shadows as the trees swayed above, whispering secrets through their leaves. The quiet settled around them, broken only by the rustle of leaves and the distant call of a nightbird.

Ambry's fingers brushed against hers, then slowly threaded between them. His thumb traced a line along the inside of her wrist — light, steady, grounding. "There's something else I want to tell you." He hesitated, then met her eyes. "It turns out... I'm not chipped."

Ivy turned to him sharply. "Wait, what?"

"It's true," Laz said, stepping out onto the porch with Nyra close behind. "I dug through everything I could find. No registry. No neural imprint. Nothing. He's clean."

Ivy blinked. Her heart was already racing. She looked back at Laz. "And you?"

He grinned. "Oh, I'm totally chipped. But I'm charming enough to compensate."

A breath escaped her, part laugh, part disbelief. Her gaze drifted to Nyra.

Nyra rolled her eyes, arms folded, lips tugging into a wry smile. "Please. My father wouldn't let anyone near my head with a needle. I'm a prodigy, not a prototype."

"Of course," Ivy said dryly. "Should've guessed."

Nyra glanced at Laz. "Walk with me to the Lumenrail?"

He gave a small bow. "Wouldn't miss it."

Ivy stood and crossed to them, wrapping Laz in a quick, impulsive hug. "Thank you," she whispered.

"Anytime," he said, squeezing her shoulder.

She turned to Nyra, the warmth slipping from her face. Ivy gave a small nod. Nyra's reply came just as brief, just as sharp. Not anger, but the edge of what still hung between them.

"See you in the morning," Ambry said.

They disappeared into the trees, their silhouettes dissolving into the darkness.

Ambry caught Ivy's hand as she turned. His fingers curled around hers, tugging her gently back down beside him.

"See?" he murmured, the corner of his mouth twitching. "I can hate you."

Ivy stared. "What?"

He smiled. Real. Mischievous. Alive.

She studied his face, the glint in his eyes, the curve of his mouth. Then, softly, "Do you?" Her voice barely carried. "Hate me, I mean. Because I said some awful things to you. Things I didn't mean."

Ambry's smile softened. "I did too," he said. "But where you were born doesn't change who you are. Or what colour you are. Or that you're mismatched. None of that matters." He paused, then met her eyes fully. "I wasn't forced. Not nudged. Not programmed to like you. I chose you, Ivy. Every time."

The world tilted.

Ambry's smile faded. His gaze dropped to their hands. "You don't have to say you love me," he said softly. "Or that you're staying. You don't have to say anything. But Ivy…"

He looked at her again. No teasing now. "You have to let me love you. That's mine. This feeling. This choice. You don't get to take it from me."

Her throat tightened. It was a lot — not in a bad way, just… full. Like her whole chest had been cracked open and filled with something warm and unfamiliar and terrifying.

But his hand stayed in hers, his fingers gently tightening like an anchor, like he could steady her with nothing but touch. Their palms pressed together, deliberate and intentional. Chosen.

Ivy swallowed hard, her eyes stinging. "I love you too," she whispered. "I didn't know how to say it. I still don't. But I do."

She leant into him slowly, resting her head on his shoulder. His breath left him as if he'd been holding it for weeks. His arm slid around her, firm and sure, pulling her in, not like he was holding her together, but like he needed her there to hold himself steady. The world slipped back. Just his arms. Her heart. And the silent vow in the way he held her, like letting go wasn't even an option. Around them, the branches swayed. Stars blinked through the trees, and the wind lifted the moment gently into the night. The silence finally felt shared. Like a promise.

Ambry let out a slow breath. Then, gently, "Come on. We should get some sleep."

Ivy nodded, the motion small, like anything louder might shatter what they'd just built between them.

He stood first, then gently pulled her up, their fingers still tangled. They crossed the porch and stepped back into the quiet house, the worn rugs soft beneath their feet. The fire in the hearth had burned to a low glow, casting the main room in shades of gold and shadow. Brax padded along behind them, nails tapping lightly on the boards where the rugs gave way.

Ambry didn't say much as they moved through the house. He didn't need to. The quiet between them had shifted, steady now, and warm. Just full. When they reached his room, he pushed open the door and stepped aside to let her in first.

The fire crackled low in the hearth, soft light curling against the stone walls. It wasn't just warmth that filled the room, it was the quiet imprint of Ambry's life woven into every edge. The worn rugs, the faint scent of smoke in the air. Like the space had never been meant for anyone but him. She stepped inside, the quiet settling around her like a welcome. Brax immediately curled up near the fire, flopping down with a grunt and a soft puff of mossy-scented fur.

Ambry closed the door behind them. "My mum washed your clothes," he said, scratching the back of his neck. "They should be dry by the morning."

Ivy smiled faintly. "Thank you." She glanced toward the bed, then back at him. "Are you sure she is okay with me staying here? Doesn't think it's… I don't know. Inappropriate?"

Ambry gave a crooked half-smile. "Maybe a little."

That didn't exactly reassure her.

"But," he added, stepping further into the room, "I'm eighteen. She trusts me."

She crossed to the bed and brushed her fingers over the blankets, then glanced at him, one eyebrow lifted. "So… where do I sleep?"

He laughed under his breath, moving to the opposite side. "Wherever you want. I'll take the floor if you're more comfortable."

Ivy sat down slowly, hands curling in the blanket. Her voice was barely above a murmur. "I just… I don't want to be alone."

He climbed in beside her and pulled the blankets over them both. The fire cracked softly, warming the air. She shifted instinctively, finding his shoulder with her cheek. His arm curled around her without hesitation, like it had always known how.

"Is the fire warm enough?" he asked quietly.

She nodded. "Perfect."

For a while, neither of them spoke. The quiet stretched, not awkward but full, like the room had expanded to fit all the things they couldn't say yet.

Then Ivy whispered, "Ambry?" She leant into him, her voice low. "Thank you… for choosing me. Even when I gave you every reason not to."

Ambry didn't speak right away, just pressed his lips to her temple, his arm curling around her, steady and sure.

Then, softly, he murmured into her hair, "I never needed a reason. I only needed you."

The fire popped once, low and soft. Ivy closed her eyes. And for the first time in what felt like days, maybe longer, she didn't brace for sleep. She didn't curl in tight, or keep one foot on the floor, or lie with her thoughts spinning like orbit maps behind her eyes.

She just breathed.

Held. Safe.

Somewhere nearby, Brax let out a low snore, all soft growl and contentment.

And Ivy let herself drift, the heat of the fire and the rhythm of Ambry's breathing pulling her under. Not into darkness, but something quieter. Something that felt like home.

CHAPTER FORTY-NINE

The next day, the grove buzzed with life. Sunslight filtered through the treetops in warm, flickering shafts. Birds called overhead, leaves shimmered in the breeze, and one of Ambry's sisters let out a laugh that rang through the trees like wind chimes daring the wind to chase them. Everything felt awake.

Ivy sat at the edge of the clearing, her fingers brushing over the stem of a low plant crowned with yellow-orange blooms. The petals tilted toward her touch, soft, almost warm. Very impressive... if the plan involved defeating The Order with flower arranging. She let her hand rest there a moment longer, watching the bloom lean closer. Until the moment came to unlock the core, she wasn't sure how much help she really was.

Across the grove, Ambry knelt over a flat stone, his paper notebook spread across it, pencil moving in sharp, steady lines as he mapped trail routes and fallback points. His jaw was set, expression unreadable. It was the same look he wore when patching a broken toy for Mirae or carrying Thess to bed, half-asleep — quiet, determined, like the whole thing was already done in his mind. She watched a moment too long, a small smile forming before she caught herself and looked away.

A few metres off, Laz sat cross-legged in one of the hammocks, a tangle of scavenged tech in his lap that sparked every time he touched it. He smacked it with the heel of his hand. It sparked again. Then stopped. "Fixed," he called. "Probably..."

Ambry didn't even look up. "Don't say 'probably' when it's connected to the comm relay."

"But," Laz said, holding up a finger, "I said it with confidence."

Nyra sat with her back against the big Kavari trunk, the living bench curving beneath her like it had been shaped for this exact purpose. An expensive-looking silver Tactis rested on her knees, fingers gliding across the surface with quiet precision. Data flickered across the screen, soft pulses of light, fast and constant. Her face held steady, beauty caught in place like a statue warmed by sunlight.

Ivy drifted toward her, hands shoved into her pockets. "So... we're doomed, or?"

Nyra didn't look up. "Well, you *are* the one leading."

Ivy smirked. "Ouch. Confidence boost, thanks."

Nyra gave a small almost-smile. "Anytime." It wasn't warm. But it wasn't cold either. Ivy counted it as a win.

Still, the day unfolded in quiet pieces. Everyone had something to do. Ambry's hands and instincts, Laz's tech, Nyra's mind. Ivy helped where she could, but mostly just got in the way. She was the key, literally. But until the system core was in reach, she was just an extra pair of hands. Ones that didn't quite fit.

By late afternoon, Ambry's mum arrived with a bundle of wrapped parcels. "Glowbread dumplings, stuffed with mashed talli fruit and herb paste." She set them down on a flat rock and gave Nyra a nod. "Thank you for bringing those city spices. They made all the difference."

Nyra gave a polite dip of her head. "Glad they're useful."

"Thanks, Mrs. A," Laz called, flashing a grin.

She gave a small wave, already turning back toward the house.

Ivy took one, unwrapping the cloth. The bread was warm and soft, its edges crisped golden from the fire. It smelled like honey and woodsmoke and something citrusy she couldn't place. Her first bite was hesitant. It was... strange. Sweet, with an earthy undertone. The centre was soft, the mash whipped to something airy, but the chunks of talli gave it texture, a surprising bite. The flavours didn't land all at once. They unfolded, slow and indecisive, like they hadn't quite agreed on what they were meant to be.

"Oh," she said quietly.

Ambry glanced over.

"It tastes like..." She paused. "Like honey and fresh bread and... something I didn't know I was missing."

Ambry snorted. "That's what you're going with?"

Ivy grinned. "Hey, I don't have the vocabulary for food that tastes like a hug, okay?"

He smiled and took a bite of his own.

She took another bite, chewing thoughtfully. "This is the same fruit you gave me. The morning we went to the singing grove."

Ambry looked over, surprised. "Yeah, can't believe you remembered that."

She shrugged, trying to play it off, but her smile lingered.

Ambry's dad showed up not long after, lugging tent supports and a roll of Kavari blankets. "Can't have a camp without a camp expert," he said, puffing out his chest as he dumped the gear down. He clasped Laz's hand in greeting, then nodded toward Ambry as he reached for the first pole. "Bet he remembers. How about you, Laz? Branik still take you out, or you need a hand?"

"Not as much," Laz said. "Was kinda hoping you'd do all the hard parts."

Kalen huffed a laugh and got to work.

By dusk, the camp was set. Kavari blankets stretched over poles for shelter, more layered beneath for bedding, fire crackling low, and the last of the dumplings warming on a flat stone.

Ivy sat cross-legged under the shelter, wrapped in a Kavari blanket, the fabric warm and oddly fragrant, like pine and rain. She'd never just hung out like this before, not with friends, not under the stars, not in the easy kind of night she'd always imagined teenagers were supposed to have.

Ambry dropped beside her, lifting the edge of her blanket to slip in like it was the most natural thing in the world. He passed her a dumpling, their hands brushing in a quiet, familiar touch. She leant in and he shifted closer, fitting easily into the space beside her. He pressed a soft kiss to the top of her head, steady and certain. Just... them. The fire popped. A breeze swept through the treetops, rustling silver-green leaves against the deepening twilight. Laz scooted closer to the centre, a half-eaten dumpling in one hand and an unmistakable glint in his eye.

"All right," he said, brushing crumbs off his shirt. "You want to understand the override? Time for a Laz-led educational experience."

Nyra rolled her eyes. "Do we get flashcards?"

"You get full genius," he replied, mouth full. "You're welcome."

Ambry smirked. "Go on."

Laz leant forward, suddenly all focus. "The chips run on bio-linked nanotech, microscopic particles made from bloom crystal. It's the same material as the pendant, just ground down and coded to bond with neural pathways. They inject it through vaccines. Once it's in, it settles near the amygdala, prefrontal cortex, motor pathways — anywhere emotions flare up. It dulls the surges, keeps people chilled but still functioning. No zombies. Just smoothed out, like someone sanded down all the sharp edges."

Ivy looked down at her pendant. "When Ambry and I came across that bloom crystal in the greenhouse, we didn't even know what it was. Just thought it was some kind of rare plant. It wasn't until Gareth got the journal from his mother that it all came together."

Laz gave a cheeky half-grin. "Well, turns out your rare plant is the emotional leash for half the planet."

Ivy frowned, eyes on the fire. "But they're not gone. They laugh, they hug, they say all the right things... but something's holding them back. Like their emotions are running on rails."

Laz's grin faded. "Yeah. My dad used to hum when he cooked. Tell the worst jokes. Now he just... makes the food and leaves the room."

She turned toward him. "Laz, I—"

He held up a hand, flashing a bright smile. "It's fine. I tell myself he's just tired. That one day he'll yawn, stretch, and say something completely inappropriate in front of Nyra's mum, like the old days."

Nyra gave a quiet snort.

Ivy's voice softened. "We'll get him back."

Laz glanced over, and for a second, the firelight caught something raw behind his usual charm. Then he smirked. "Yeah. And when we do, he owes me at least three hugs, a proper apology, and his best stew recipe. In that order."

She smiled. "You're chipped too. And you're amazing, Laz. Truly."

Laz gave a mock bow, hand to chest. "Yeah, well. Not everyone can be a fabulous emotional disaster like me."

Nyra folded her arms. "Focus, sparkle-brain."

"Right. So. The chip core, the one in the palace vault, doesn't micromanage the particles. It just anchors them. It maintains the programming signal. That's why it's so hard to trace, it's passive. Doesn't emit much. But if we shut down the core, the signal stops. And once the signal stops..."

"The particles die?" Ivy asked.

"They unravel," Laz said, clearly proud. "They're programmed to degrade without a constant link. I confirmed it with a test rig. Fake signal, cut it off, total destabilisation. Within hours, the body starts flushing them out."

Ambry tilted his head. "So the people don't even know it's happening?"

"Not until the emotions hit," Laz said with a grin. "It's like pulling the plug on a full bathtub, everything rushing out at once."

Nyra looked wary. "And they can't just restart the core after?"

"They can try," Laz said. "But with no active particles in the body, there's nothing left to control. The core can't rewrite what isn't there. It's a one-way flush."

Ivy frowned. "Couldn't they re-chip everyone?"

"They'd have to inject every person all over again," Laz said. "No instant updates, no system overrides. It's back to syringes, lies, forced consent. And good luck doing that once people know what was done to them. Once they can feel again."

"Now for our hero's moment." He leant back, reached into his pack, and pulled out a folded scrap of paper, the edges smudged and dog-eared. "Wrote it all down. Glyph sequence, trigger protocol, backup paths. But don't get lazy, memorise it." He handed it to Ambry. "I figured you'd rather run through it now?"

Ambry gave a single nod. He unfolded the paper, eyes skimming the tight pencil marks across the page. "You could've at least drawn it like a treasure map."

"Sure," Laz said. "Next time the fate of emotional freedom rests on our shoulders, I'll add doodles." He reached forward, snatching the paper back from Ambry and flattening it between them. "Okay… start here. Root-layer glyph. That opens the base." He tapped the next symbol hard. "Then the override, but only after the pulse drops. That's the pendant syncing. If you press early, the system won't recognise it."

His finger shifted. "Then it's top-left, centre, and the glyph that mirrors the root one. That's the shutdown sequence." He looked up. "Three glyphs. One clean shot. If you pause too long or screw up the order, it resets. And if it resets twice… you're locked out for good." He slid the paper back to Ambry, eyes steady. "Your turn to save the world."

Ambry nodded, already focused. "I've got it."

Ivy shifted beside him. "And if it resets?"

"Then you panic artfully," Laz said, straight-faced. "But I tested it. Mock setup, multiple times. Sequence is solid. This'll work." He hesitated. "Just... don't let it reset twice."

Ambry looked up. "Why?"

Laz shrugged. "Because then you need a masterkey. Or a royal gene-seal. Or recite an old Order oath backwards while balancing on one foot, I don't know. I don't make the rules. The console locks out. Permanently."

Ambry folded the paper and slid it into his jacket. "I'll remember it."

"You better," Laz said, tapping the side of his head. "I'm not just the brains of this operation. I'm also the emotional support."

Ivy leant forward slightly. "How did you find all this?"

Laz smirked. "It was all there in the data we hauled from Domaris. Turns out Nyra's dad really is top-tier, full access, buried gold. Sorry again about borrowing his pass." He flashed Nyra a sheepish look. "Purely in the name of emotional liberation."

"Next time, just ask," Nyra muttered.

Laz: "Noted. Will forge a polite request form next time."

"Also," he tapped his temple. "I'm brilliant and emotionally neglected. Gives you lots of free time."

Ivy snorted.

Then he flopped back onto his blankets with a satisfied sigh. "Now if you'll excuse me, I have to mentally prepare for tomorrow's heroics. Maybe visualise a statue."

Ambry snorted. "You'll be lucky to get a plaque."

"I'll take it," Laz said. "But make it shiny."

The fire popped again. Ivy tucked herself deeper under her blanket, her fingers finding Ambry's. "You ever think we're not ready for this?" she asked.

Ambry met her eyes. "Every second."

Nyra shifted by the fire, setting the Tactis aside and folding her legs beneath her. "While not quite the genius spectacle of that," she said, tipping her head toward Laz, "I did comb through every log my access allowed. There's no mention of a breach at the core. No alerts. No trace. They never even knew you were there. And as for the Domaris data haul..." Her tone stayed calm, almost amused. "They don't know about that either. My father did notice his pass was missing and made it very clear he knew I used it. But he hasn't reported it. Not yet."

Laz gave a low whistle. "So no guards at the palace?"

"Minimal. Most will be concentrated in the city. The core isn't under active surveillance, they'll assume no one's foolish enough to try." She looked directly at Ivy. "They won't expect anyone to be that stupid."

Ivy gave a soft laugh and nodded her head slowly.

Silence folded around them again. Softer now, warmer. Ivy leant back against Ambry and watched the flames. After a while, she nudged his arm. "How did you avoid it? The chip?"

Ambry dropped his gaze to the fire. "I didn't even know it existed. I used to think I was a problem, too different. Like I felt too much, or cared too hard. My parents... they laughed, told stories, made everything seem fine. We had this little Muruun Kippa. Powder-blue, half the size of Brax, always in trouble." A subtle smile played at the edge of his mouth before fading. "When he got old and passed... I was fourteen, I cried for days. Couldn't stop. They just buried him. Smiled, laughed like it was nothing."

Ivy's fingers trailed slowly up his arm before curling gently around it. "Gareth told me once I was lucky in some ways," she said. "Growing up on the ship, away from heartbreak and bullying." Her voice dipped, thoughtful. "I didn't really get it at the time. But maybe he was right. Your sisters grieving something they loved... maybe being sheltered wasn't the worst thing."

Ambry glanced down at her, and some of the weight in his eyes eased. "Maybe? I spent years thinking I had to be like that. Keep it light. Keep it easy. Pretend nothing got in too deep." He drew in a slow breath. "And then I saw kids who felt like me, kids who couldn't hold it in. And instead of it feeling good, like maybe I wasn't alone... I watched them get hauled off by the guards. I thought maybe they were being punished. I was young." He exhaled, eyes on the fire. "After that, I got good at it."

Laz let out a low breath. "Wow. That's... cheerful." He gave a crooked grin, voice light. "Remind me not to ask you for bedtime stories."

Nyra leant forward, resting her elbows on her knees. "I didn't know about the chip either. I mean... I always knew I was different from the forest kids. But come on, look at us. I grew up in an apartment made of glass, and they grew up in… trees." She gave a small shrug, glancing at Laz and Ambry. "No offence."

Laz flicked his hand in a lazy wave. "None taken."

She gave a small smile. "I never really thought about it. I guess… I was jealous. How happy everyone seemed out here, I think that's why I liked being with you two." Her fingers traced the edge of her knee, slow and deliberate. "There were other Order kids like me, bratty, entitled… yes, I said it. But I think Order families get certain privileges. Maybe they get a say in who gets chipped, or when? And maybe I slipped through because of that."

She let out a soft breath, the words coming slower now. "But my mother… as far as I know, she was always chipped. Only… she wasn't like this. Not at first. She loved hard. She laughed. She spent time with me like I was the most important thing in her world." Nyra's hand found the hem of her sleeve, fingers curling into the fabric, a small, steady hold. "And then, when I was about twelve… something changed. She changed. Like someone flipped a switch. The laughing stopped. The warmth… gone. I just want her back."

Ivy met her eyes across the fire, her voice low but certain. "And we will. I promise."

They both turned to Laz. He was halfway through a mouthful of dumpling, chewing like this was any other night. It took him a second to notice the sudden silence and the fact that everyone was staring at him.

He froze mid-bite. "What? Emotional heart-sharing and staring contests? You guys really know how to make a guy feel special." He grinned. "No backstory for me. I got the chip like everyone else. Standard issue government-sponsored harmony."

Ivy frowned. "Do you feel it? Like right now?"

He tilted his head. "I dunno. It's like living with the volume knob turned down. Most days you don't notice, until someone shows you what loud feels like."

There was a pause. Long enough to settle.

Then Laz's voice dropped, softer than before. "Sometimes I wonder…"

They looked over.

He stared at the fire, his usual grin nowhere in sight. "What if I'm not… good without it?"

Ivy sat up, her brows pulling together. "What do you mean?"

Laz gave a slow shrug, but his eyes stayed locked on the flames. "What if the chip didn't just dull me down? What if it stopped me from being... worse?" He let out a soft huff, almost a laugh, but not really. "What if I'm the kind of person they made it for? The ones who snap. The ones who... hurt people. What if we shut it off and find out I'm exactly what they were afraid of?"

For a moment, no one spoke.

Ambry was the one who finally answered. His voice was quiet but sure. "I know you, Laz. I've known you my whole life. You've got this spark, this lightness, like you're made of mischief and heart. No chip could ever change that. You're still going to be you."

Laz sat silent for a long moment, picking at the dumpling in his hand. Then he shoved it into his mouth and grinned. "Guess we'll find out. Can't wait to see if I'm a baby-kicker."

Ambry let out a laugh and shook his head. "You're impossible."

Laz flashed him a grin. "Yeah, but at least I'm a charming kind of impossible."

Ivy's gaze shifted between them, Nyra, Laz. "We'll bring them both home. Your mum. Your dad."

Laz shot her a grin. "Yeah, I can't wait to get my dad back. This whole reverse-chipped thing is wild."

The fire cracked. Somewhere overhead, a prism-winged insect flicked through the dark, its belly pulsing soft green. Ivy leant forward, voice low but fierce. "And then we get Gareth out while The Order's still scrambling. Hit them before they even know what's happening."

She looked up, her gaze fierce. "We're not just breaking the core. We're tearing the whole damn system down. And we're taking everyone back."

CHAPTER FIFTY

Night fell in waves. Domaris sank into shadow and glassy light, its layered tiers catching the moons light in sharp, unnatural lines. From afar, it looked like a dream. From here, watching from the edge of the forest, it looked like a fortress.

Before boarding the Lumenrail, they'd swung past the POD, just long enough to grab comms. Ivy had paused outside her parents' alcove, one hand resting on the sealed door. The signs of life around the POD — blankets shifted, cups left drying — told her they were safe. Relief pressed tight against her ribs, sharp with longing. It would have to be enough. For now. "Perfect," Laz had muttered, fiddling with his earpiece. "I get Ambry in high definition. All my nightmares coming true at once."

Now, from the edge of the forest, they stood in silence, eyes on the city ahead. Just four of them. Different pasts, the same stakes.

Ivy turned the pendant over in her hand, watching it catch the flicker of moonlight. "This is it," she said, glancing up. "You run distraction. We shut the chip down."

Nyra didn't flinch. "And if you don't, we'll have front-row seats to a public execution."

Laz snorted. "Wow. You really know how to fire up a team."

Nyra offered a shrug. "Realism is a gift."

"Is that what we're calling chronic pessimism now?" he shot back. "Or is that just the default setting when your sarcasm chip malfunctions?"

Ambry smirked, but his gaze never left the gleaming city. "Two teams. Nyra, you get us into the system. Laz, jam what you can once her signal's live." He glanced at Ivy. "We move on the core."

She nodded, fastening the pendant at her neck before tucking it into her top. "And keep an eye out for any sign of Gareth. The second this is all down, we make our move."

"They'll be watching for that," Nyra added. "It's what they'd be expecting." She glanced at Ivy, something flickering behind her eyes. "And you'll go where they don't expect."

Ambry's fingers brushed Ivy's wrist. "Ready?"

She nodded. "Let's bring it all down."

They moved in pairs. Nyra and Laz slipped into the city first, shadows brushing past glassstone walls and echoing steps. A few blocks in, Laz peeled off down a narrow access route, grinning as he turned. "Don't get sentimental if I explode," he said. "Just remember me with dramatic music."

Nyra raised a brow. "You assume I'd remember you at all."

"Cruel," he said with a grin. "But fair."

She rolled her eyes and turned, her long, dark coat catching the breeze as she headed toward the shadowed corridors of the outer tier. The city loomed around her, all sharp lines and gleaming restraint, each step taking her deeper. In her earpiece, Ambry's voice came low and steady. "Everyone in position?"

"Ready and scrambling," Laz answered. "Just waiting on Nyra to get me in."

Nyra didn't respond. She didn't need to. Her silence was the answer. She moved like someone who expected to be watched but refused to perform. Every step deliberate, soundless, purposeful.

The streets narrowed the closer she got to the heart of Domaris, buildings sharpening into lines and shadows. Up ahead, the Vanta Spire loomed, tall and ruthless, its mirrored black surface swallowing every light it passed. It didn't look like a data centre. It looked like a punishment.

Nyra crossed the empty plaza without hesitation, coat drawn close, the access pass warm in her palm. She found the faint silver etching along the side of the frame, barely visible, almost decorative. She pressed the pass against it. A shimmer passed over the surface. Then a faint chime, a narrow seam cut down the glass, straight and sharp. The panels parted with a soft exhale, cold air rolled out. She stepped inside. The door sealed shut behind her.

"Interference running," Laz crackled. "You've got five minutes before the city figures out I'm charmingly illegal."

"Copy that," she murmured.

Nyra moved quickly, each step precise. She knew these corridors. Efficient, exact, never designed for wandering. She didn't need to guess. She remembered the path. She turned left, then right, navigating the Spire's familiar geometry. Every sound seemed sharper here, the faint click of her boots, the swing of her ponytail with each precise step. Just a little farther.

She rounded the last corner and stopped.

Solen blocked the corridor ahead, perfectly still. Black robes, the red emblem of The Order blazed sharp against his chest, hands clasped behind his back. His eyes locked on hers, steady, empty.

For a moment, everything in her locked too. Something in his gaze was colder. More clinical. Like she wasn't his daughter. Just another variable gone rogue.

"Did you really think I wouldn't notice?" he asked, voice like ice across metal.

She didn't answer. Just watched, calculating. Guards stepped from the shadows, movements smooth and silent. She turned, two more behind her. A trap, perfectly laid.

Her comm crackled. "Nyra? Are you okay? Was that your dad's voice?" Ambry's tone was low, tight with alarm.

She didn't reply. Couldn't. The walls felt too close.

Solen stepped forward and, with a flick of his wrist, took the access pass from her hand. He held it like a relic. Then, snapped it in half.

Nyra met his eyes. "Dramatic," she said, sharp with a mocking edge. Then she stepped closer, her face inches from his, words quiet but cutting. "You always said loyalty was the highest virtue."

He squared his shoulders, but the set of them shifted.

"Then watch me live by it." She walked past him. Past the guards, shoving through without a word. If they wanted to stop her, they'd have to drag her. But she wasn't begging. It wasn't her style.

One of the guards turned to Solen. "Directive, sir? Do you want her detained?"

He didn't turn. "Leave her. She can't do any harm now."

Nyra kept walking until she reached the curve near the inner column, and there it was, the faint silver pulse down the polished wall. The lift panel. Hidden unless you knew where to look. She slipped her pass from her pocket, holding it up for a beat before pressing it to the panel. The wall split with a soft chime, panels sliding aside to reveal the glass-walled lift. The floor lit beneath her boots as she stepped in, then turned slowly to face them.

The guards looked up. Solen turned at the movement, his gaze narrowing.

Nyra raised her hand and fluttered her fingers in a slow, exaggerated wave, every inch of it pure mockery. The lift doors began to close.

Solen's jaw twitched. The guards hesitated. "Well?" he snapped. "Go after her, you idiots."

The lift hummed beneath her boots, rising smooth and silent through the Vanta Spire. A soft crackle in her earpiece. "Nyra? You good?" Laz's voice, low and cautious.

She smiled, adjusting her coat. "Guess who just lost admin privileges?"

A pause. "What did you do?"

"I tried to give him back his pass," she said, all false innocence. "But he didn't seem to want it."

A short silence. Then a grin in Laz's voice. "Nyra, I could kiss you."

"File it under fantasy," she said. The lift eased open with a quiet sigh. Nyra stepped into the core chamber, her pace unhurried, coat trailing behind her like she had all the clearance in the world. Cold light spilled from the base of the central console, a monolith of matte black and flickering screens. The holopanels spiralled upward, alive with shifting code and streams of encrypted data.

She crossed to it without hesitation and held her pass to a glowing strip embedded in the base. A shimmer ran across the console's surface. Lights flared to life. The holoscreens unfurled one by one, layers of data spiralling upward. She pulled Laz's data shard from her pocket. "This better work," she muttered, slotting it into the nearest input.

A sharp chime answered. The holoscreens blinked, then settled into a steady pulse. "I'm in," she said into the comm. "Datahub is yours."

"Signal's live," came Laz's voice in her ear, already focused. "You're a genius."

"I know," she said, brushing imaginary dust off her coat. "Now go break something."

The lift chimed. Two guards rushed out.

Nyra stood smoothly and turned toward them, holding the pass up like it was nothing. "Oh. You came for this?"

No answer. Just blank stares.

She sighed, crossing the distance in smooth, deliberate steps. "Fine. Take it." She pressed the pass into one guard's hand and, without another glance, walked to the lift.

— ✦ —

Across the city, Laz crouched in a narrow maintenance bay tucked behind a sealed service panel. The walls buzzed faintly with current, wires coiled like veins across the ceiling.

He'd patched a makeshift Tactis straight into the pulse grid. His fingers flew, sweat slicking his temple, expression locked in. No time to blink. No room to mess it up. The code was shifting fast, and he had to be faster. A sharp pulse echoed through the grid. Something was coming. Several signatures converging fast. Too fast.

"That's not terrifying at all." He said under his breath. "Okay, okay, Plan B. Panic edition. Let's go." He hit the disruptor. For a second, the lights in the outer corridors flickered, then dimmed to darkness, the steady hum of the city's power fading into eerie silence. The silence didn't last. Boots started moving. The kind that weren't rushing, just organised. Confident. Close.

"Nyra's down," he whispered into the comm, voice low but urgent. "I'm buying you five minutes. Make it count." He yanked the Tactis from its port, shoved it into the side pocket of his pack, and bolted for the back exit.

A brutal blow slammed into his ribs as a guard lunged from the shadows. He hit the floor hard. "Easy! I bruise like a Lumibug," Laz wheezed. The guard reached for his collar. Laz scrambled — not exactly fighting back, more like slippery flopping — and managed to twist out from under him. Another guard lunged. Laz ducked.

"I'm chipped, you idiots!" he shouted as he pushed to his feet. "I can't fight, just flail and pray!" He staggered behind a support pillar, gasping, one hand pressed to his side. For a heartbeat, he stayed there, breath shallow, ribs screaming. Then he pushed off the wall and lunged for the exit, his shoulder slammed into the control panel.

The door stuttered open with a groan of metal. Laz shoved through it and didn't look back.

His heart thudded like it hadn't signed off on this plan. Fast, overreacting, entirely unhelpful. The chip held steady, no panic spike, no fight reflex, just that eerie calm of a body outmatched and unable to fight back. But his thoughts were screaming behind it.

Another voice crackled through the comm. "Laz? You still there?"

"I'm still here. My ribs would like a word, though," he said. "Now move. Before they figure out you guys are not here." Something hit the ground behind him — solid and heavy, very much his cue to leave. The guards were sweeping, methodical and silent.

Laz closed his eyes for half a second, muttered, "Spero help me," then bolted again. Arms pumping, heart racing, sprinting straight into the dark like a very sarcastic deer. Pain stabbed through his ribs. Every breath dragged fire. But his feet kept moving, not from panic, not even urgency. Just the flat, stubborn rhythm of survival, glitching past the chip's control. He tore around the corner—

And stopped cold. A guard stepped into view. Taller than the rest. Too familiar.

Pink eyes. Same as his.

"Dad," he whispered.

The man didn't respond. Just stood there. Expression blank, eyes empty.

"Dad?" Laz stepped forward, chest tight.

Branik didn't speak, but his jaw shifted, a twitch, barely enough to call a flinch. Then he stepped forward, his hands reaching out for Laz in perfect, unnatural sync.

"It's me," Laz whispered. "Dad, it's me. Look at me."

His reach faltered for a second, only a flicker, before resetting. Then his arms stretched toward Laz again with empty precision.

They stood locked in place — same eyes, same stance, same blood — with a lifetime of something unspoken wedged between them. Then Branik moved. Not toward Laz. Just a shift. Weight to the right, chin angled left. A break in the sweep behind him.

Laz's eyes flicked to it, then back to his father.

Branik didn't follow. Didn't block. His mouth opened just enough for the words to slip out, flat and familiar. "Go home. Clean up. Dinner's waiting." The words didn't make sense. His hands twitched, like he was trying to stop... and couldn't. Branik looked away.

Laz didn't wait. He bolted. The sound of his own breath filled his ears, sharp, fast, too loud. He spotted a hatch panel and slammed his hand onto it. Locked. "Really?" he hissed. "You'd think being a good little citizen with a perfectly compliant chip would count for something."

No answer from the panel. Behind him, the sound of boots picked up fast, deliberate. They knew where he was.

Laz glanced up, spotting an open vent grid high on the wall, just above a narrow polished support brace that looked about one breath away from buckling. He gave it exactly one second of consideration before grabbing hold. The metal flexed under his weight, groaning in protest. His boot slipped, jolting his ribs with a flare of pain as he fought for balance. He shoved higher, reaching for the edge of the vent... caught it. Barely. The chip offered no objection, just a flat sense of logistical apathy. If he survived, great. If not... well, at least it'd be quick.

He clambered up, body protesting, fingers scraping metal. His hand caught the ledge just as a guard shouted below.

"Initiate lockdown!"

"Oh, that's rude," Laz muttered, hauling himself into the shaft with the grace of a dying beetle. He kicked the vent shut behind him and lay there in the narrow crawlspace, chest heaving, vision fuzzing. The chip finally kicked in — synthetic calm smoothing the edges. Like handing him a paper fan in a burning building.

Laz blinked up at the metal ceiling. "Ten out of ten escape attempt. Would not recommend."

Silence. At last. At least for now.

CHAPTER FIFTY-ONE

Far from the glittering towers of Domaris, beneath a sweep of smooth stone and stained glass filtered with light, Ivy and Ambry slipped through the palace like ghosts.

The halls curved with quiet precision, arches rising in perfect balance, their edges softened by climbing ivy. Mosaic ceilings scattered moonlight into shifting patterns across the tiled floor. It was history held still, the royal heart of Spero, waiting in silence. Their boots moved soundlessly over stone warmed by centuries. No shadows trailed behind them, no voices stirred the air. Only the mission, and the silence.

Ivy glanced at Ambry. "How are they doing?"

He didn't need to ask who she meant. "Nyra's father caught her. She's under watch, sitting in the Council Chamber like a model citizen. Laz is hiding in a maintenance shaft above the archives. He'll stay there until we give the signal."

She swallowed. "And if we fail?"

"They both have exit plans. But they won't work until the guards are free of the chip."

Ivy nodded, then hesitated. "Anything about Gareth?"

Ambry's jaw shifted. "Nothing yet. But if he's there... we'll find him."

Then she nodded. Barely. But it was enough.

He squeezed her hand. "Come on, let's go." And together, they ran.

Ambry led without hesitation, turning left through the lower corridor, the same path they'd taken days ago. Ivy followed, steps matching his. As they passed the greenhouse entrance, her gaze flicked sideways. The bloom was still there, its leaves curled inward, light pulsing faintly beneath the surface. She didn't slow. Just kept moving.

The corridor narrowed, that quiet charge settling over them again. Ivy's gaze skimmed the walls, still marked with shallow carvings, the same scattered crests she hadn't been able to recognise before. Leafwings. Warnings, maybe. Or memory.

Two guards stood at the mouth of the vault corridor. One pacing a slow line along the wall, the other posted firm at the entrance, arms braced, jaw set. Different faces, maybe. But Ivy felt the same weight settle in her chest. Same uniforms, same position. Like the last time had never ended.

"Did you hear the broadcast?" one asked, voice low. "They're saying Solen's daughter took him down, and some kid crashed half the central systems. Total blackout."

The other gave a short, humourless snort. "Glad we pulled vault duty. Let the elites scramble in the dark for once."

"Still." The first one adjusted his stance, eyes scanning the far wall. "You think it's real? Solen compromised?"

"Doesn't matter," came the reply. "Orders haven't changed."

Ivy and Ambry kept low, skirting the perimeter until they reached the narrow passage they'd used before, tucked off the main junction, its entrance easy to miss if you didn't know the way. The air here was warmer again, pulsing faintly beneath the stone. Ivy's pendant pulsed once. Blue light threaded through the bronze wings, steady and even.

Ambry moved ahead without hesitation, his fingers trailing along the wall until they landed in the right place. "It's here," he said quietly, gaze fixed on a smooth stretch of stone just recessed enough to catch the eye if you knew where to look.

Ivy moved beside him, eyes tracing the outline of the hidden panel. She reached for the chain at her neck, unclipping it with steady fingers, then slid the pendant free. It settled into her palm, wings already unfolding, the core pulsing with quiet blue light.

She pressed it into the waiting hollow. The fit was perfect, like it had always belonged there. A soft click followed, then silence.

Then, a low vibration rolled through the wall. The panel clicked, then slid aside, edges retracting with clean precision. A narrow gap opened. Ambry's hand brushed hers, a silent check-in. Ivy gave the faintest nod, then moved first. He followed.

Inside, the chamber still felt suspended in time, roots coiling along the walls, old light slanting through fractures in the ceiling. Her pendant pulsed the second they entered. For a moment, she stood there, holding it in her palm, watching the way the light caught along its bronze edge. The wings had folded closed again, hiding the glowing core beneath smooth bronze.

"Ambry," she whispered, "are we doing the right thing? What if this makes it worse? What if we trade control for chaos, destruction, Earth all over again?"

He paused beside her, his eyes drawn to the pendant resting in her hand. "I've thought about that too," he said. "Every day since we found out about the chip."

"Spero's perfect," she murmured. "The forests, the air, the balance. I've felt it. What if that's only true because of the chip? What if we destroy the one thing Earth couldn't keep? Harmony with nature?"

Ambry's gaze met hers, steady. "Spero was in balance with its people long before the chip," he said. "It was The Order who got lost. This control, it's not harmony. It's silence. Manufactured peace."

"But maybe peace is protection," she said, quieter now. "What if the chip is the reason Spero never fell the way Earth did?"

He shook his head. "It's a lie. A beautiful one, maybe. But no one gets to choose peace for someone else. Not like this. Not by cutting out their feelings and calling it order."

"And if we're wrong?" She asked. "If taking it down unravels everything?"

The answer came low. Certain. "Then we face it. Together. But not with our minds caged. Not pretending this isn't a choice. Nyra's mum, Laz's dad... they deserve to feel again. Even if it hurts."

Ivy's fingers tightened around the pendant. "Even if it ruins everything?"

"Especially then." He looked at her. "Because at least it'll be real."

Ivy gave a small nod, the words settling deep in her chest. She drew in a slow breath, met Ambry's eyes, and found nothing but quiet certainty staring back. She looked down at the pendant, turning it gently, fingers tracing the groove between the folded leaves. The wings shifted open in her hand, smooth and certain, blue light threading through every etched vein. Light from the pendant spilled across her fingers as she moved toward the console. The core beneath glowed steadily, layered and alive, casting a faint shimmer across her face. She turned to Ambry, her hand hovering above the panel. "Do you remember what Laz told you?"

He gave a single nod. "Every word."

She lifted the pendant, its weight felt strangely right. She drew a breath and lowered it to the socket. It shifted in her hand, falling into perfect alignment, and settled into place with a soft click.

A low, harmonic tone vibrated through the chamber. Not loud, but deep, like the stone itself had shifted. Glyphs shimmered to life. Vines along the wall flexed, their golden veins lighting in sequence... then fading. One by one. As if the tension had drained from the air.

Ambry stepped forward, heart steady. The console waited. Still, clean, pulsing faintly beneath the light.

"Root-layer glyph," he murmured, brushing the panel. The marking flared in response.

He pressed the override. The pulse hadn't quite faded, but he didn't pause.

"Top-left. Centre." His fingers moved fast, sure.

"The final glyph, near the base."

He stepped back.

Silence.

The console just... sat there. Waiting.

Ambry frowned. "That... that was it."

Then a warning tone burst from the console — sharp, single-note, enough to rattle the air. The chamber pulsed red in time with the sound, light flaring across the walls in harsh, rhythmic flashes.

SEQUENCE INVALID — SYNC NOT DETECTED

Ambry stepped back, eyes locked on the console. "Something's wrong."

Ivy glanced at him. "What just happened?"

"I don't know." His voice came thin. Tight. "It should've worked."

She stepped closer, scanning the glyphs. "You followed Laz's sequence, right?"

"I think so." He ran a hand through his hair. "Yeah. I mean... I thought I did."

Ivy's chest tightened. "How many tries did he say we had?"

A pause.

"Two." His voice landed steady, but his eyes were too wide.

Ivy moved quickly to the squared-off doorway at the far end of the chamber, leaning just far enough to glimpse the corridor. The guards were still posted, one tapping something into his wristband, the other speaking low under his breath. His head tilted toward the chamber, his gaze locked on the vault door. The other followed, eyes narrowing.

Their posture shifted. They'd seen the pulse. Heard the sound.

"Ambry—" Ivy stepped back fast, breath caught.

"They heard it," she said, voice low but urgent. "They're coming." She crossed back to Ambry's side, pulse thudding. "We need to get this right."

Ambry's shoulders tensed, hands braced on either side of the console. "I thought I did," he muttered. "I followed the sequence. Everything Laz said—"

"Okay, well… maybe you panicked?" Ivy offered. "Or hit something too fast. Or didn't sync first. Or—"

"I did sync." The words snapped out, sharp, unfiltered.

She flinched, but only a little. "Alright. But something glitched. But we still have the paper, right? Laz gave it to you."

Ambry drew a steadying breath. "Right. The sheet. He wrote it down."

She shot him a look. "So? Where is it?"

Ambry yanked open his jacket, rummaging through the inner lining. His breath caught sharp, shoulders tight, before he forced it steady again. "Dammit," he breathed. "It's not here." His gaze darted to the floor. To the cluster of roots near the wall.

"I had it. It was in my jacket. I must've dropped it." He spun around, scanning the floor.

Ivy moved with him. "Well, un-drop it. Those guards heard the noise. They'll be checking it out any second."

Their eyes swept the floor. Smooth, spotless. No crumpled sheet. No backup. They both froze. A steady rhythm of boots struck the stone outside, the guards were coming.

She stepped in close to Ambry, eyes locked on his. "Okay. Think."

Ambry tensed, chest rising fast.

"Ambry." She grabbed his shoulders, firm. Steady. "What did Laz say? Exactly."

Her voice cut through the static.

Ambry drew a shaky breath. Closed his eyes.

"Start with the root-layer glyph," he murmured. "Wait for access to pulse through. Then hit the override. After the sync, not before. Then the three-glyph sequence."

He opened his eyes. "I jumped the sync. Didn't wait."

She gave a nod. "Then you've got one shot left. Make it count."

From inside the chamber, the shift was subtle, just a flicker of movement through the small square window in the door. One of the guards had stepped into view. Then another.

A sharp voice rang out. "Inside!"

Ivy's breath caught. A faint click echoed as the locking mechanism engaged. Then stopped.

Another click. Louder this time. The door held. Outside, one of them muttered something sharp. A code not working. A key misread.

They were trying to open it, but fumbling. Seconds. That's all they had.

Ambry's hand hovered over the console. He exhaled. Slow. Steady. Fingers flexing as he stepped back to the console. The surface waited, humming faintly, almost like it remembered him.

"Root-layer glyph," he whispered, pressing the mark. A soft pulse spread out from his touch. Slow, deliberate.

This time, he waited.

When the light faded, he pressed the override. The panel shifted, mechanical clicks unlocking deep in the system. Glyphs slid into view.

"Top-left," he breathed. "Centre..."

His hand hovered. Just a second. Then—

"Root." The glyph lit beneath his touch.

For a moment, nothing.

Then the console flared.

A deep tone ripped through the floor. Low, resonant. Across the wall, vines flexed. Glyphs snapped out of alignment. Light stuttered, flickering like it couldn't decide whether to vanish or fight.

Ambry stepped back from the console. He reached for Ivy and pulled her in tight, her back to his chest, holding her. They watched as the golden veins faded. Not darkened, just eased out, like warmth retreating from the surface. Then the quiet pressed in. Thick, charged, alive beneath the surface.

Ivy looked up at Ambry. Her chest felt weightless. "Did it work?" she whispered.

"I don't know," he said, his arm still tight around her, breath shallow and unsteady.

The chamber door cracked open beside them. Ambry turned, releasing her, but caught her hand fast, holding on as they backed up together. The two guards stepped into the chamber, slower now, their movements off-kilter, like they were walking out of a dream.

One of them winced, pressing a hand to the side of his head. The other stumbled, steadying himself against the wall. Their breathing came uneven, then steadied, like systems sparking back online. Their eyes flicked around the chamber, sharper now. Present.

One of them let out a shaky breath. "Why was I always so pissed off?"

The other blinked, as if coming out of a fog. "Yeah. Everything got under my skin."

"I thought it was just me. Like... I was just miserable or something."

The second one shook his head slowly. "No. I felt the same too, just annoyed at the world. All the time." He stared at the floor. "The orders they gave us... the things they had us do..."

His jaw clenched. "We took people in. You remember that?"

Silence stretched between them.

"God." His voice was barely above a whisper. "What the hell did we do?"

Ambry didn't move. His breath came slow and measured, eyes fixed on the space where the guards stood.

Ivy reached for his arm, fingers gentle. "It worked," she said quietly.

He looked at her, really looked, and finally exhaled.

— ✦ —

Across Domaris, everything paused. A hush swept the city, like the moment before a storm. A heartbeat held.

Then it broke.

Chipped citizens froze mid-step. Eyes widened. Breaths caught, a sharp jolt, like waking from a dream you didn't know you were having. And then, all at once, the flood came. Some gasped. Others pressed hands to their hearts. A few simply stood still, blinking as if the world had sharpened around them.

Across the city, sound returned. Soft laughter, sharp cries, voices rising in half-sobbed wonder. Mothers scooped up children, hugging tight, cheek to cheek. Partners clutched each other, laughing, crying, arguing. Strangers no longer, but something deeper, something real. The harmony they'd worn like a second skin cracked open... and they didn't fall apart. They came alive.

From hollow spaces, emotionless, untouched, something stirred. Leafwings. First by the dozens... then by the hundreds. They emerged from vents, walls, cracks in Domaris' flawless order. Winged and waiting, breathless with purpose. One by one, they rose into the air.

A silent storm. Gold and green, alive and rising.

They swept through the domes, flooded the courtyards, circled the spires. No longer hiding. No longer still. Some landed on shoulders. Some on outstretched hands. Others hovered in the light, wings casting shimmering shadows that flickered like fire. And with the Leafwings came the feeling.

A woman suddenly laughed, full-belly, wild. Then burst into tears, hugging a stranger and apologising for stepping on their foot... six years ago.

An elderly man collapsed against a wall, clutching his head. "Too loud," he murmured. Then, shook a fist as two kids went racing past. "Slow down, you little menaces!" The children screamed with laughter, chasing Leafwings. "Kids these days," he muttered.

One little girl stood still. "Why do I feel weird inside?" Their older sister hugged them tight. "I don't know... but I think something good just happened."

A man stormed into a bakery and yelled, "YOUR SOLARBREAD IS TERRIBLE!" And then immediately gasped, horrified, slapping a hand over his mouth. The baker burst out laughing, hurled flour at him, and they both dissolved into laughs.

Two old women sat quietly on a bench. One turned to the other. "I hate your harmony chimes."

"Good. I hate your meditation crystals." They nodded solemnly and held hands.

For a moment, the city held itself open, wide and wild and breathing. The sound of it swelled. Laughter, tears, footsteps, the flutter of wings. Nothing measured. Nothing clean. Just life, messy and loud and theirs.

High above, on a balcony overlooking the chaos below, Solen stood motionless. Hands clasped behind his back, spine straight, his gaze swept the streets. Crowds churned beneath him. The Leafwings flooded the city like a living storm, weaving between buildings, sweeping low over the plazas. A single Leafwing broke from the swarm and drifted toward him. It hovered near his face... circled once... then again.

Solen's mouth pressed into a hard line. He lifted a hand, flicking it aside with a sharp, dismissive gesture. The movement was precise. Controlled. The gesture of a man who expected to be obeyed.

The Leafwing floated sideways, unfazed. Then, with deliberate slowness, settled squarely on his head.

A muscle jumped in his cheek. His hand snapped up, faster this time, swatting it aside.

The Leafwing lifted... and circled back.

Chapter Fifty-Two

Nyra rose to her feet, spine straight, head high. Around her, the Council Chamber churned with motion, guards exchanging confused glances, citizens murmuring like they'd woken mid-dream.

No one moved to stop her.

She walked forward, calm, unhurried. An Order steward wavered into her path, eyes unfocused. Without slowing, Nyra plucked the access pass clean from his belt. She kept her eyes ahead, moving with quiet purpose as the outer doors came into view. With a swipe of the pass, the lock gave a soft click. She didn't pause, didn't glance back. Just stepped through the open door and kept walking.

Around her, chipped citizens blinked, as if waking from something half-remembered. Some reached for their faces. Others clutched their chests like they were bracing for impact. The air surged with sound, voices rising, laughter breaking, arguments starting mid-sentence. It was loud. Messy. Real.

Nyra moved through the crowd without pause, cutting a path toward her apartment. The city stirred around her, cracks splintering through the Order's silence. Windows banged open, voices clashed in the alleys, laughter rose where it hadn't in years. Nyra walked steady through it all, the tide of sound swelling at her back.

She stepped into the small courtyard outside their door, a quiet terrace carved into the base of the south tower. Pale tiles lined the ground, warm from the morning sun. A low stone bench curved along one wall, half-shaded by flowering vines that spilled from the planter above. Evara stood outside, steady, her face tilted to the morning light, soaking it in like it was something new. The stillness was gone. Her expression had shifted, not composed, not serene. Just, real. And a little lost.

"Nyra?" Evara's voice cracked. Not the practiced calm of a Council wife. Just a raw, human sound.

Nyra was running before she realised, crossing the space between them. She didn't hesitate. Didn't analyse. Just threw her arms around her mother and held on like she was thirteen again, trying to wake the woman behind the chip.

Evara trembled. Then, hesitantly, she hugged back. Her arms tight, her warmth unmistakable. For a moment, they held each other in the middle of the waking city, wrapped in something too raw for words.

"I'm sorry, Mum," Nyra whispered. "I'm so sorry it took me this long."

Evara pulled back, hands lifting to Nyra's face. Her thumbs trembled as they traced her cheeks, slow, reverent, like she couldn't believe she was real. Tears spilled freely now, no effort to hide them. "I'm sorry, too," she said. "I thought I could carry it. I thought it wouldn't change who I was. I didn't realise how much it would take away."

Tears spilled down Nyra's cheeks. "I had to be. I couldn't just sit there and watch you disappear."

Her mother nodded, the motion tight, like something fragile was splintering beneath it. "You held on to me. Even when I couldn't hold on to myself."

Nyra leant in, their foreheads touching. Her voice cracked. "I missed you, Mum. Every day. Even when you were right in front of me."

Evara pulled her in — sudden, fierce. Her arms locked around Nyra like the world would fall apart if she let go. "I missed you too," she said. "Even when I couldn't feel it."

Nyra hugged her back, face tucked into her mother's shoulder, eyes squeezed shut. She didn't say anything, just held on.

Then, a voice cut through the haze.

"Well, you told me to break things," Laz said, grinning like he hadn't just limped through a full-blown government collapse. His hair stuck up in wild clumps, dirt smeared across his face, lip split in two places. Like he'd head-butted a wall and then apologised to it.

Nyra turned, brushing the tears from her cheeks with quiet grace. "You look like the aftermath of a failed science experiment."

"Yeah, well, you try dodging guards, eating a few punches, and swan-diving through maintenance shafts. See how your hair holds up." He winced as he eased himself down onto the edge of a low stone bench.

She snorted. Just a little.

He stretched his legs out in front of him, still catching his breath. "Is it bad that I actually enjoy blowing up government systems? Like, I'm pretty sure that's a red flag. Possibly several."

Nyra's gaze drifted to her mother, surrounded by Leafwings. Awake. Whole.

"She's free," she whispered. "For the first time in years, she's really free." Her gaze shifted to Laz, something tender breaking through. "And so are you."

Nyra met his eyes, a slow smirk curling at the corner of her mouth. "So... feel like kicking any babies yet?"

Laz gave a crooked grin. "Nah. Might cry at a sunrise, though. Real dangerous stuff."

Without thinking, Nyra leant down and pulled him into a quick, fierce hug. "Don't get used to that," she said as she stepped back, her voice still raw.

"What, emotional vulnerability? Gross. I'm deleting that memory immediately." He flashed a grin.

— ✦ —

They slipped through the side hall, feet light on ancient stone. No alarms chased them. No voices called out. Just the soft echo of their footsteps and slow exhale of a stronghold that had held its breath too long. The corridor curved gently, its walls lined with faded glyphs and shallow recesses that glowed faintly as they passed. Sunslight poured through the high mosaic windows, breaking across the floor in fractured colour. Ivy glimpsed rooms tucked behind stone arches, undisturbed, dust-soft, like no one had walked them in decades.

Ambry walked beside her, their hands linked. His grip was loose, easy. Not guiding, just there, steady. There was nothing left to plan. Nothing left to run from. Only the walk back into a world that had already started shifting.

Just before the outer hall, Ivy slowed. A side room opened onto a broad terrace, sunlight spilling across the floor. She pulled Ambry toward it without a word.

Stone tiles stretched outward in soft patterns, weathered by time but still smooth underfoot. Stone planters lined the edges, overflowing with green and gold leaves that caught the light like coins. She let go of Ambry's hand, drawn toward the edge where the view reached all the way to the city. She could picture it easily. Royals standing here long ago, sipping from leaf-etched cups, watching The Order rise through the streets below, never knowing it would one day unseat them.

Domaris gleamed in the morning light. From this height, the city looked almost gentle, spires catching sun, streets pulsing with movement. Small figures stepped into the day, untamed and restless. Messy. Alive.

Ambry stepped up beside her, his shoulder warm against hers, solid and grounding.

Ivy stared at the city. "I thought it would feel like a win," she said. "Like a moment I'd want to hold on to." She shook her head softly. "But it just feels like... a beginning."

Ambry's fingers found hers again. They stood together, watching the city below.

After a moment, Ivy's voice dropped. "Do you think we did the right thing?"

Ambry's eyes didn't leave the city. "I think freedom always comes with risk. But people deserve the choice."

She nodded slowly. "I'm scared we broke too much," Ivy said.

"We didn't break it," Ambry said. "We opened it. Now they get to decide what comes next."

She didn't know what came next. But standing here beside him, after everything, felt like its own kind of answer.

"And I'd do it again," he said softly.

Ivy glanced at him. His profile was steady, eyes sharp in the morning light. For the first time, she saw a future in him, someone to choose tomorrow with. It felt like a beginning. She squeezed his hand. A breeze caught the edges of her hair, the pendant at her chest pulsing faintly as Domaris stirred below.

And for once, the city didn't feel like a monument. Not perfect. Not peaceful.

But free.

Chapter Fifty-Three

They pushed up the last slope. Trees thinned. Light filtered through Kavari branches onto ground packed hard from countless steps. And there it was.

The POD sat low in the centre. Sleek, sealed, out of place. Its hull caught the suns like it didn't belong here, a piece of another world that didn't quite fit. Ivy slowed, her breath uneven. The vents were still active, humming low. It looked... unchanged. Like her parents might step out any second, asking for soil readings and water logs, like none of it had happened. Just past the edge, her hammock was still strung between the two silver-leaved trees, tight and empty. Her space. Her mornings before all of this.

"They're here," she said as they crossed the clearing toward the POD, her voice tight. But that didn't mean they were safe.

Ambry's hand pressed lightly against her back, a touch that steadied her.

Ivy reached for the hatch, fingers brushing the sensor. It hissed open on command. She stepped inside first, heart thudding. Ambry followed close behind. The air hit sterile. Cool, familiar. Soft light hummed through the walls. And there, beside the command panel, stood her parents.

Grace spun from the console. "Ivy—" She crossed the room in two strides and pulled her in, arms wrapping tight around her shoulders, breath catching hard against Ivy's neck. "You're alright," she whispered. The words came hoarse. She held on a second longer, then stepped back, hands gripping Ivy's shoulders like she wasn't ready to let go.

"Where have you been?" Grace demanded. "We've been trying to track you for days." She glanced toward David, then back at Ivy, jaw tight. "We were worried sick. Do you have any idea what you put us through? You could've gotten a message to us," she said, sharp and measured. "That was reckless, Ivy, completely irresponsible."

Ivy exhaled, then looked at Ambry with a grin she couldn't hold back. "Yep. That's my mum. Definitely not chipped."

David stepped around the console, a little slower than Grace. His hand found her shoulder, steadying her, before he turned to Ivy. His voice was gentle. "Your mother's right... but geez, we missed you, sweetheart."

Ivy stepped into him without hesitation, wrapping her arms around his middle. His arms came around her, strong and steady, holding on like he'd been bracing for the worst and only now believed it was over.

"Hi, Dad," she said, voice muffled against his shoulder. "I missed you too."

He pulled back just enough to see her face. "I'm just glad you're alright." David's gaze moved past Ivy, settling on Ambry. He hadn't seemed to notice him until now. "And who's this?"

Grace followed the movement, eyes narrowing.

Ambry hesitated. Then gave a polite, steady nod. "Hi."

Ivy stepped back slightly, her hand brushing Ambry's. "Mum... Dad... this is Ambry." Her voice stayed light. "He's from one of the villages near here. Remember? The one you told me to stay away from?" She gave a quick shrug. "Yeah. Funny, isn't it?"

No one interrupted. So of course, she kept going. "He's been helping me. A lot, since the beginning, really. He really knows this place better than anyone else. And... and he's with me."

That last part landed quieter. More real. The tension didn't snap, it stretched. Grace's silence burned. David stared at Ambry, unblinking.

Grace stiffened, eyes narrowing. "Ivy Eleanor Virelli. You made contact?!"

"It's okay, Mum," Ivy said quickly. "I know. I'm sorry. You can ground me later. I promise to endure twelve years of lectures on the way home." She took a breath, words tumbling faster now. "You can start with protocol violations and work your way through emotional recklessness, I'll even take notes. But right now I need your help."

"Gareth's been taken." She stepped forward. "We think he's still in Domaris, maybe at Order headquarters. If we're going to get him out, it has to be now. While everything's still," she waved a hand toward the world outside, "in chaos."

A crackle of static flared in Ambry's ear. He touched his comm instinctively, voice low. "Laz?"

David tilted his head, brow furrowing. "Is that one of our comm units?"

A crackle of static answered. Ambry's brow furrowed as he listened. "They're okay," he said, glancing at Ivy. "Nyra's with him." Another burst of static flared. He nodded. "We're meeting at Nyra's mother's grove."

Ivy turned back to her parents. "I want you to come. Please." Her gaze locked on Grace. "For him. For me. I'm not leaving this planet without him."

For a moment, Grace didn't answer. She just stared at her daughter. The same girl she'd raised in silence and steel, now standing with red hair tangled and eyes too bright, asking them to follow her.

David looked at Ivy, voice dry. "And where do you think they're keeping Gareth?"

Ivy didn't hesitate. "One of the council chambers, probably."

He raised an eyebrow. "And where exactly are those?"

Ivy crossed to the lockers by the airlock, flipping one open by feel. Her voice didn't pause. "The city. Domaris." As she spoke, she shrugged out of her jacket and grabbed a fresh one from the stack. Grey, fitted, familiar in all the right ways.

David nodded. "Right... the city."

Grace gave a sharp laugh. "Unbelievable." She turned to Ivy, eyes narrowing. "So all this time... when you said you were collecting samples. The camping with Gareth?"

Ivy lifted a shoulder. "Technically true." She kicked off her boots and grabbed her old pair from under the bench, scuffed, solid, already moulded to her step. She dragged them on, fast but focused.

"Technically—?" Grace's voice sharpened. "You've been sneaking into cities? Making contact with locals? For months?"

Ivy didn't flinch. "I didn't plan it that way. But... yeah."

Grace let out a short breath, more disbelief than rage. "You lied to us."

Ivy's throat tightened. "I didn't know how to tell you. And once I started... I couldn't stop."

Grace looked like she might combust.

Ambry met her eyes, a flicker she felt more than saw. Then he tipped his head toward the hatch, his voice was low. "Ivy... we need to go. Everyone's waiting."

But Ivy didn't follow right away. She turned to Grace. "I'm so sorry." Her voice was steady this time. Not defensive, not rushed. Just true. "I should've told you everything. And I will once we get Gareth back. I'll sit down and explain all of it. I promise."

She hesitated, then added, quieter, "But I can't do this alone. Please, Mum... please come with me."

Grace's eyes didn't soften. Silence stretched, heavy in the space between them. She looked at David. Then at Ambry. And finally, back to Ivy. Ivy's stomach knotted. A breath slipped from Grace, more surrender than agreement. She nodded. Once. Sharp. She turned to David and reached out her hand. He took it without hesitation, fingers closing tight around hers.

Ivy turned and moved toward the hatch, her parents close behind. Together, they followed their daughter, stepping out of the sterile safety of the POD and into something real.

Chapter Fifty-Four

They crossed into the grove through a narrow, vine-draped archway, and Ivy stopped short.

It was... stunning. Technically, it was a private garden, but it felt older than the city, like the walls had grown up around it and never quite won. The trees rose in soft curves, their trunks twisting in silver-gleamed spirals beneath a veil of delicate flowering vines. Skyvines curled lazily from high branches, their pods swaying faintly in the warm air. Pale blossoms blanketed the lower hedges in soft layers of colour — lavender, soft gold, deep blue.

At the heart of it all stood a single, slender Velmiir tree. Smaller than the wild ones Ivy had seen, but glowing with faint silver veins across its bark. Two hive clusters clung to its lower branches, and the air hummed with the faint, low buzz of Velmiir bees drifting between blooms. Near its base, a lounge spread outward, the seats curved like petals, shaped from polished pale wood that caught the light like water. Their cushions shimmered faintly. Layered, silk-soft, and too perfect to be handmade. They framed a central stone table, half-sunk into flowering moss.

And waiting among them... were the people Ivy never thought she'd see together.

Nyra sat beside her mother on one of the low couches, their posture near identical. Straight-backed, composed, with their hands were gently clasped between them. Nyra leant in slightly, saying something low, and her mother gave the smallest smile in return. The warmth between them softened the space more than any light could. Laz was crouched beside his father near the central table, their heads bowed over a flickering Tactis, Branik pointing something out with a broad finger while Laz grinned like he was getting away with something. And overhead, stretched across a curved branch like she owned the place, was Asara, Nyra's Velune. Tail flicking lazily, eyes half-lidded and watching everything with regal disinterest.

Ambry moved first, crossing to Laz with a grin and pulling him into a quick hug.

"Finally." Laz grinned. "Thought you were going to make me rescue Gareth myself."

Branik stood, arms out. "Ambry!" He pulled him into a bear hug before he could protest. "Look at you. Leading missions, breaking into cities. Weren't you climbing trees just yesterday?"

"Still am, some days." Ambry smirked. "Good to see you, Branik."

"I should hope so," Branik said cheerfully. "You're family, after all. Even if you do keep showing up with trouble on your heels."

Nyra rose then, tugging gently on her mother's hand as she crossed the clearing, stopping in front of Ivy. "Mother," she said, eyes warm. "This is the girl I told you about." She turned slightly. "Ivy, this is my mother, Evara."

Ivy smiled at her, then looked back at her parents. "Mum, Dad. This is Nyra and Evara." She caught her parents' expressions, and couldn't help the flicker of smug satisfaction that rose in her chest.

Nyra and Evara stood side by side, calm and composed, but their presence landed like royalty. Nyra's amethyst skin glowed where the light touched it, her posture effortlessly elegant. Beside her, Evara stood just as poised, her pale blue skin catching the sun in a faint icy sheen, indigo braids coiled into a crown.

Grace blinked once, then again, like her brain had short-circuited somewhere between who they were and how they looked. "You're..." Her voice caught. "You're both stunning."

David let out a breath, barely audible. "Wow."

Evara's lips curved. "And you must be Ivy's parents."

David nodded. "David Virelli. This is Grace."

"Welcome," Evara said, with a voice like silk. "I want you to know you'll be safe here."

Grace's gaze swept over the soft blooms and delicate branches. "This garden... it's beautiful."

Evara's gaze softened. "My mother planted the first vines here. It's always been a sanctuary." She gave a small smile. "Would you like me to show you around?"

Grace nodded, her voice barely a whisper. "I'd like that."

The two women drifted toward a shaded bench beneath the flowering branches, voices low as they moved together through the hush. One woman born into power, the other shaped by the systems it left behind.

Near the centre table, Ivy glanced at Ambry, then at Laz and Branik, who were already setting up the Tactis between them.

Ivy turned to David and touched his arm. "Alright, Dad," she said. "Let's make a plan." As Ivy stepped forward, Nyra moved with her, slipping into stride like they'd done this a hundred times before.

Laz tipped his chin toward Ivy. "Nice to see the family resemblance."

Ivy gave him a flat look. "Behave." She turned to her father. "Dad, this is Laz. And his father, Branik."

David nodded, still taking it all in. "I'm David. Nice to meet you."

Laz beamed. "Pleasure's mine. Ivy didn't tell us much about you, just that you're brilliant with bioscans and apparently fine with your daughter dating my best friend."

David's eyebrows lifted. "She said what?"

Ivy groaned. "Laz."

Utterly unfazed, Branik chuckled. "He means well. Just never learned to say it quietly."

David glanced at Ivy, one brow still raised. "We'll circle back to that."

Without ceremony, Nyra pressed a slim, gleaming Tactis into Laz's hand. "This one's scrubbed. Encrypted. Don't lose it."

He lifted it with a low whistle. "I love you."

Nyra arched a brow. "I'm not above slapping you in front of your father."

Laz grinned, then angled his Tactis toward Branik. "All yours, Dad."

Branik leant forward, fingers moving with silent precision as he tapped into the feed. A series of glowing glyphs pulsed to life across the Tactis. City schematics, patrol loops, internal access logs. "Here," he said, zooming in on a quadrant beneath the Council chambers, part of the Sanctum Tier. "Holding cells. Deep level. Reinforced doors, minimal access points." He swiped again, and red lines flickered into view, slow-moving loops and checkpoint markers rotating through corridors.

"They've pulled most of the guards," Branik continued. "Order sent them to the outer villages. People are finding out the truth, and The Order's losing control. That means minimal coverage near the cells." A faint smile tugged at the corner of his mouth as he reached into his coat and pulled out a slim black command tag. He set it on the stone table with a soft click. "This," he said, tapping it once, "will get you through every access gate in the city. Guard wings. Labs. Holding blocks. But don't stall, the patrols reset every fifteen minutes. Miss the window, and you'll trip an alert."

He looked up, meeting Ambry's eyes. "One shot. In and out."

Ambry gave a single nod, steady. "We won't miss it."

Laz leant in, flipping his own Tactis around. "I'm piggybacking their comms net. Still scrambled, but I can patch our team's signals to a clean channel. No cross-traffic, no flagging." He grinned. "Also... I may have borrowed a tower diagnostic script that'll loop your IDs for twenty minutes. They'll read you as environmental techs doing sensor recalibration."

Ivy squinted at him. "You what?"

Laz shrugged, like it was nothing. "Hey, you spend enough time dodging rules, you learn to rewrite them."

Ivy smothered a grin as Nyra turned and pressed a folded bundle of soft fabric into her hands. "They're mine," Nyra said simply. "Put them on, they'll blend in."

Ivy ran her fingers over the material, soft, muted, and nothing like the fitted gear she was used to. "You're sure?"

Nyra met her gaze, level. "Don't act invisible. Act like you belong."

Ivy gave a quiet nod. "Thank you."

Grace and Evara crossed back toward the group, their voices low but steady. Whatever walls had been up earlier, they seemed softer now, two mothers from opposite worlds, walking in quiet step.

Grace met Ivy's eyes, a flicker of resolve behind her calm. "Is the plan set?"

David exchanged a glance with Grace, a look Ivy couldn't quite read, then gave her a quiet nod. But Grace's focus had already shifted. "Good. So... who's going in?"

There was a pause.

Ambry said, "Ivy and I."

Grace raised an eyebrow. "Sorry, what?"

The conversation around the table dimmed, and Ivy quickly stepped closer, lowering her voice. "Mum, it has to be me."

"In what universe—" Grace cut herself off, glancing around the garden. Her voice dropped to a sharp whisper. "You think I'm letting you walk into a government facility? Are you out of your mind?"

Ivy didn't flinch. "We're just getting in and out. We have a pass. We've studied the timing, the layout—"

"That's not the point," Grace hissed. "Can't someone else go?"

"Mum, it's Gareth. I'm going in," Ivy said, steady now. "I can do this. You have to trust me."

Grace looked to David, but he only pressed his lips together. Torn, but silent.

"I'm not asking for permission," Ivy added. "I'm asking you to believe in me."

Ambry straightened beside her, checking his gear. "Ready?"

Ivy exhaled, her hand brushing over the pendant beneath her shirt. She grabbed the folded clothes Nyra had given her, tucking them under her arm. "Ready."

Nyra gave her a look. "Stay sharp. Domaris won't give you a second chance."

"Get in, get Gareth, get out." Laz's voice carried like an order. "And grab snacks if you see any. Sweet, salty, I'm not picky. Surprise me."

Ambry cracked half a smile. "Can't make promises."

Ivy turned back to her parents. Grace looked like she wanted to pull her back, to stall just a few more minutes, but she didn't. David stepped in first, wrapping his arms around Ivy tight. Grace joined a heartbeat later, holding on like she wasn't ready to let go just yet.

"I love you both," Ivy said. "I'll be back. I promise."

Grace kissed the side of her head. "You'd better."

David's voice was low. "Be smart. Be fast. And come home."

She nodded, then stepped back beside Ambry. They moved out together, into a city unravelling by the minute.

Perfect conditions, really, if your plan involved rescuing someone from a high-security lockup.

— ✦ —

The city pressed in around them — noise, colour, movement.

Ivy stayed close to Ambry's shoulder as the crowd folded and shifted like a living tide. Voices clashed in sharp bursts, angry shouts, urgent questions, the clipped commands of Order guards trying to restore control.

Ambry moved through it with quiet precision, a hand at Ivy's wrist, guiding her past pockets of civilians. His eyes tracked the current of bodies, searching for gaps before they opened. Ivy kept her head low, the soft hood of Nyra's borrowed clothes shadowing her face. The soft weave blurred her sharp edges, masking the boldness of her mismatched skin and eyes.

They passed two guards at a corner. One tapped quickly at a forearm Tactis, the other murmured into a comm, scanning the crowd with bored detachment. Neither spared Ivy or Ambry a glance. As they neared the outer plaza, Ambry slowed, eyes locked on the sleek, glass-paneled structure ahead. The holding sector. Half-sunken into the stone beneath the Council chambers. Minimal guards, Domaris didn't expect break-ins. He let go of her wrist and took her hand instead, fingers lacing through hers in a quiet anchor.

He stepped forward, sliding the command tag across the scanner. The panel flicked green. The doors parted without a sound, glass sliding open. They stepped in. The air inside was cooler, quieter. Too quiet, like the silence had been installed along with the wiring.

They moved fast, boots silent against the polished floor as the outer doors slid shut behind them. A short corridor stretched ahead, ending at another sealed door, bulkier than the rest, framed in reinforced alloy with a glass panel running through the upper half. Ambry stepped up, scanning the tag again. A soft chime. The door lit green, then slid open in two precise halves. They passed through.

Inside the holding wing felt more like a biotech lab than a prison, smooth walls, soft lighting, sound dampeners built into the floors. The air was still, almost too still, like the whole place had been scrubbed of conflict. They moved down the corridor, scanning the cells as they passed, one at a time.

The first cell was crammed with storage crates, neatly stacked, some still marked with faded Order inventory codes. Whatever this wing had once been for, it hadn't seen prisoners in a long time. The next was empty. So was the one after that.

Ivy's pulse quickened. "Where is he?"

Ambry checked the Tactis Branik had loaded, frowning. "He should be in this wing," he muttered.

Then—

A flicker of movement. Fifth cell down, left side.

Gareth.

He sat on the narrow bench, shoulders tense, eyes locked on the far wall. Then he looked up. His face cracked with relief. "Ivy."

Ambry swiped the tag. The lock blinked. The door slid open.

Ivy crossed the space quickly and wrapped her arms around him. Gareth held her tight.

He stepped back, then pulled Ambry into a brief hug too. "Good to see you, Ambry."

Ambry smiled. "You too." He threw a glance over his shoulder. "We should move."

They slipped back into the corridor, Gareth falling into step beside them. The reinforced door was ahead, its glass panel catching the light as they approached. Ambry swiped the tag.

Nothing.

He tried again, slower this time. The reader blinked red.

Ivy's breath hitched. "Ambry—?"

"I know." His mouth pressed into a hard line as he stepped back, eyes scanning the panel like he could will it to change. He tried the tag once more, angling it carefully, but the reader stayed red, unblinking.

Ivy turned toward him, voice sharp with urgency. "What's happening?"

Ambry's shoulders shifted, calculating. "The systems locking us out."

A low alarm buzzed through the walls, faint, but rising.

Gareth stepped forward, tense. "Let me try."

Ambry handed him the command tag. Gareth swiped it across the reader, slow, steady, like the extra second might change the outcome.

The panel blinked red.

Footsteps approached, sharp and deliberate.

Gareth stepped back, motioning them toward the wall, eyes scanning for exits that didn't exist. "Guards. Brace."

A guard rounded the far corner. Through the glass, he locked eyes with Gareth... and raised both hands, palms open. Ivy froze. Ambry stepped in front of her, but the guard kept his pace calm, steady. He reached up, tugging back the edge of his uniform. A faint shimmer of bronze embroidery caught the light. A Leafwing.

Gareth inhaled sharply. Recognition passed between them. Quiet, steady, certain. Just two men who knew exactly what they were seeing.

The guard swiped his tag across the door. It slid open with a quiet hiss.

He held Gareth's gaze. "You've been gone a long time."

Gareth nodded once. "Not by choice."

The guard stepped back, clearing the way. "Let's get you out of here."

He turned, already moving. And they followed. None of them speaking, but all of them had seen it. The symbol. The stitch. The past coming back in thread and silence.

— ✦ —

The air inside the POD carried a different kind of quiet, not the hush of tension, but the kind that comes after holding your breath for too long.

Ivy sat at the central table, one leg tucked beneath her, a warm bowl of root broth cradled in both hands. The herbal steam curled upward, familiar and grounding. Across from her, Gareth leant back against the built-in bench, tearing a wedge of solarbread into uneven pieces. Ambry sat nearby, elbow braced on the table's edge, his bowl beside him. Laz had claimed the corner of the lab bench, one foot propped on a lower drawer, eating with one hand while idly scrolling his Tactis with the other.

Grace moved through the compact kitchen, her steps precise. The food had been prepared under Branik's watch, but still her movements carried the wary precision of someone who hadn't yet decided if she trusted it. She poured the last of the tea blend Nyra's mother had given her. She hesitated at Gareth's cup, a flicker of something unreadable crossing her face, before she tipped the pot, careful and quiet. She looked at him. "You okay? Need anything else?"

Gareth met her eyes. "Bit tired," he said quietly. "But, thanks."

Grace nodded, a simple acknowledgment, and poured the next cup.

Ambry leant in close, voice low near Ivy's ear. "She's not at all like you made her out to be."

Ivy gave him a dry look. "That's because she's in front of company. I'll get all the questions once you lot leave." It still jarred, her mother in the POD kitchen, pouring tea and ladling out the food Branik had prepared. For months, Grace had warned against contamination, drilled every protocol into Ivy's head. And now she was eating it. Serving it. Like the rules had been rewritten overnight.

Ivy nodded toward Gareth. "Although I'm not sure who's going to cop it worse, rebel Ivy or Prince Gareth from Spero."

Ambry smirked. "Tough call."

They laughed, quiet, but real. The kind of shared moment that softened the air around them, even here.

Outside, near the window, David's voice drifted in, low and steady, explaining something to Branik as they stood in the clearing beside the solar panels.

Grace settled beside Ivy and poured herself a cup of tea.

For a few heartbeats, the only sounds were spoons tapping and bowls shifting.

Then Laz leant back with a satisfied sigh. "Cosy. Who had 'quiet meal with a rogue scientist and a royal fugitive' on their apocalypse bingo card?"

Ambry snorted. "You did."

"Fair. I hedge my bets."

Ivy smiled into her bowl. "It was good to see Nyra happy."

Ambry nodded. "She hasn't looked like that in years. Not since before..." He stopped, shaking his head slightly. "It suits her."

A pause followed. Not heavy. Just full.

Ivy glanced around the table. "So... what's next?"

"Sleep," Gareth said without missing a beat. "Lots of sleep."

Laz raised his cup. "Finally, someone with a sensible plan."

A soft tone chimed from the wall console.

"System scan complete. Atmospheric conditions remain within safe variance. Hydration levels optimal."

Laz flinched like he'd been shot. "SORRY? Was that your datapad thing? No, seriously, did it just growl at me? I knew this place had too many buttons." He looked around, wide-eyed. "Is this how I die? Taken out by something with the world's most boring name?"

Ivy smothered a laugh. "That's AURA. Ship's AI. He's been monitoring the POD since we landed. Environmental systems, vitals, comms, all of it." She glanced toward the central console. "You could've said hi sooner."

"You were rather occupied," AURA replied, unbothered. "Though I assume housekeeping has been permanently downgraded."

Laz stared at the console. "Did... did we just get insulted by the air conditioning?"

David stepped back into the POD, Branik trailing behind with a curious glance around the space.

"Showed him the equipment," David said, reaching for a mug. "Branik's got a few ideas to improve the filtration system."

Branik gave a small nod. "Your condenser's clean but underpowered. I can reinforce the vent plates and reroute the heat bleed, smooth things out."

David poured his tea, then leant down to press a quick kiss to Grace's temple. "Just scientists on a research mission, hey Grace?"

Grace didn't miss a beat. "We are. We just have a broader data set than expected."

That earned a quiet chuckle. Ivy caught her mother's eye, and this time, Grace's smile was warm and real.

Gareth lifted his tea. "To that."

Cups clinked. Soft, imperfect, honest.

Ambry leant forward, gaze finding Ivy's across the table. She looked up and smiled. No words. Just a promise, quietly shared.

And for one small night, in an overcrowded POD with too little space and too much history, they let themselves be human — together.

CHAPTER FIFTY-FIVE

Three weeks had passed since the collapse of the chip network.

Domaris pulsed with new life. Messy, unpredictable, loud life. Laughter rang through courtyards where silence once ruled, and native creatures crept back into the open. Ivy had seen them slipping across rooftops, sleek-bodied and soft-footed, curling along warm stone ledges as if the city already belonged to them again. A Tallwing perched on an arch above the gardens. Its prism-feathered wings catching the morning light as it watched the streets below, like it too, was still trying to understand this new version of the world.

Grace and David had started venturing beyond the POD more often. They drifted through winding paths and village groves, where wary glances turned curious, and cautious warmth met them halfway. Grace spent hours in the garden beds, sharing datapads and sketches with a village herbalist, her sleeves often dusted with soil and pollen. David worked beside a gardener bundling Kavari leaves for mat-weaving, their soft, mossy texture clinging to his hands like fleece.

"We used to engineer polymers for this," he'd said once, quiet with awe.

The gardener had only nodded, steady hands tucking each leaf with quiet care.

They lingered in open courtyards, trading questions with children eager to hear about stars they'd only seen in storylights. They laughed. Not politely, not professionally, but freely. Like something had been unlocked. Some days, Grace joined music-sharing games with children who tried to mimic Earth's old symphonies using wind-bent leaves and harmonic stones. On other days, David found himself surrounded by young teenagers, trying to teach them how to whistle. They were awkward, overwhelmed, but always grinning. They saw it now, not just the beauty, but the rhythm beneath it. The way people moved together, not in perfect unison, but in quiet understanding. And it unsettled something in them. Not because it was wrong, but because it wasn't. Because soon, they'd be expected to explain this place. And they still didn't have the right words.

Inside the POD, the air was too still. Too final. Grace moved between compartments with tight, practiced motions, coiling cables, sealing ration packs. David crouched near the floor storage hatch, sliding medical crates into position with careful precision. The familiar hiss of the seals echoed softly as each one locked into place.

Ivy stood near the central console, arms crossed, the leafwing pendant glinting faintly against her chest. Her gaze tracked their movements, calm and unwavering. "I need you to say it's uninhabitable," she said, voice calm and clear.

Grace didn't pause. "But that's not true."

"I know." Ivy watched her mother fold a thermal blanket and press it flat. "That's the point."

David straightened, wiping his hands on his pants. "Ivy... do you understand what you're asking?"

"I'm asking you to protect what you came here to find," she said. "A living world. Harmony. Balance. You said you wanted to learn, not conquer. Well, learn this, Earth can't have Spero."

Grace zipped a supply case and placed it by the hatch. "We can't just lie."

"You already have." Ivy's gaze didn't waver. "You hid my birth. For seventeen years, you lied to Earth. Not for the mission, but for me. Do it again."

The soft hum of the console filled the silence. Ivy hesitated, then shifted her approach. She reached for something else. Something softer. "Then stay," she said. "Let's build a life here. You don't have to go back. Not to the missions, not to the silence. We don't have to run through the same loop again."

She looked between them, a thread of warmth rising. "We could choose something new." She let her words settle in. "You've seen this place, the beauty, the joy. You're not just surviving here. You're smiling. Laughing. When was the last time Earth felt like that for you?"

Grace's hands slowed. David looked up, and for a moment, their eyes met. Not surprise. Not disagreement. Like the question had already been asked, and left unanswered. And in their gaze, just for a second, Ivy saw it. The temptation of peace.

Then, it was gone.

"Even if we try…" David exhaled, stepping around the med crate. "If we don't return, they'll assume the worst. They'll send another mission, military this time. Not scientists. Our silence might make things worse."

"Then be clever," Ivy said, still steady. "Send the ship back. Empty. No signs of life, no crew, no hope. Make Spero look toxic. Dangerous. Make it look dead."

Grace's voice cracked, just slightly. "And if they call our bluff? If they send drones, weapons, scans we can't intercept?"

Ivy's voice didn't rise. "You said Earth called EOS 11 the final mission. So what makes you think they'll send anything at all?"

David rubbed his thumb along the edge of a case lid. "It didn't work for EOS 6. They tried to disappear too, stay hidden and live quietly. But Earth was desperate then. It's worse now. EOS 11 wasn't just the last. It was their last hope. And they think this planet has it."

He looked at Ivy. "They weren't wrong."

"Exactly." Ivy nodded. "That's why you have to do it right this time. EOS 6 vanished. No message. No warning. Earth filled that silence with fear, and plans."

"We don't have to vanish. We can tell a different story, one that makes them stay away."

Grace stopped mid-motion, a medical scanner loose in her hands. "We left Earth to find hope, Ivy. We can't give up on the people still there."

"This is hope." Ivy took a step forward. "Right here. Living and breathing and just wanting to live their lives in peace. If you hand this over to Earth, you're not giving them hope. You're handing them a blueprint for colonisation."

David stood still for a moment. "We could slant the report. Emphasise instability. Suggest biosignatures but not intelligence. Enough red flags to delay a follow-up. It's not the lie you want… but it's something."

Ivy shook her head, calm but certain. "That's not enough. You have to pick a side. Spero… or Earth."

Grace finally looked at her, really looked. "I can't abandon everyone we left behind."

"I'm not asking you to save everyone," Ivy said. "I'm asking you to protect something better. Earth destroyed itself. That's not Spero's burden to carry."

The silence hung heavy. Ivy didn't fill it. She let it stretch. Let the weight of it settle on their shoulders. Then, with everything she had left, she said it. "Then I'm staying. Even if you don't."

Grace spun around like she'd been struck. "Absolutely not. I am not leaving my daughter alone on an alien planet!" Her voice rang sharp, too sharp, against the quiet walls. "You have a life waiting for you on Earth, Ivy. A future."

Ivy's eyes didn't flinch. "A life?" she said. "Twelve years on a ship, alone. Watching you and Dad like some permanent third wheel. No friends. No Gareth, because he found his home before I even had the chance to know mine." She crossed her arms, not in defiance, but grounding. "Then what? I'm supposed to land on Earth at thirty, marry some middle-aged stranger, and breathe filtered air outside?" Her voice didn't rise. It sharpened. "That's not a life. That's a sentence."

Grace's breath caught, but her voice hardened. "Ivy, you're my daughter. And I am not letting you throw your life away on some wild planet... just because you've lost your head over a boy."

David stepped in gently, his hand brushing Grace's shoulder. She didn't shrug him off, but she didn't relax either.

He turned to Ivy. "This isn't just your decision."

Ivy held his gaze. "It's my life, Dad. And for the first time... it actually feels like mine." Her voice cracked, but she didn't look away.

"You taught me to think for myself. To question. To protect what matters. Well, this matters. Spero matters. Ambry, Gareth. The kids in the singing grove. The way this world feels alive in a way I finally understand. I belong here. I've never belonged anywhere before."

Grace had gone still. Her hands had curled into the sleeves of her jacket.

"You said I was born in the silence between worlds," Ivy went on. "That silence raised me. It taught me how to listen." She looked around the POD. The clean edges, the silent systems, the legacy of every choice made before she had one. "I used to think silence meant safety. But this... this is different." She met their eyes. "Now I can hear what matters."

"I don't want to spend another twelve years on a ship, retracing decisions I never got to make. You chose this life, thirty years in space, chasing something new. I didn't. I'm done living with the weight of choices I wasn't part of." She held her ground.

David opened his mouth, but nothing came out. He looked at her like he was seeing something new.

Ivy's voice softened. "Let me stay with Gareth."

Grace flinched. "Ivy... no."

"No?" The word landed cold and clean. "Why not? You trust him. You said it yourself, he understands this world better than any of us."

"That's exactly why." Grace's voice was quiet now, but firm. "Gareth's part of this world in ways we don't even understand. You're part of Earth. That's where you belong."

"I'm not." Her voice stayed calm, but there was something raw behind it. "I was born without a home."

Grace faltered, shoulders falling as her arms folded in tight. "I don't want to lose you, Ivy. I don't want to lose our family."

"I'm not asking you to lose me," Ivy said. "But I am asking you to let me choose."

David cleared his throat, eyes on Grace. "If she comes with us... we'll do it. Not just a slant. A full rewrite. Collapse the biosphere, trace toxins, unstable atmosphere. Enough to keep Earth away." He looked at Ivy. "But we only do it if you come home with us."

Grace's head snapped toward David. "You're serious?" Her voice was sharp again, but cracking at the edges. "We give up everything? We erase thirty years of our lives?"

David didn't flinch. "For something that matters."

She shook her head, voice tight. "We trained for this. We fought for this. We left everything behind. And now we're supposed to do what? Go back and lie to their faces?"

David stepped forward. "Grace... she's our daughter. What in the world, what in the entire universe, matters more than that?"

Grace's arms dropped. The scanner in her hand clattered softly onto the bench. "This isn't how it was supposed to end," she said.

David's voice was quiet. "We came all this way for hope. And now we know what hope really looks like."

Grace laughed, bitter, soft. She turned to Ivy, eyes shining.

"Okay," she said. "We'll do it. We'll give Earth a reason to turn back." She held Ivy's gaze. "But I'm doing this for you. Not for them."

Ivy didn't answer right away. She nodded, slow and careful. Like she knew exactly what this moment meant.

"How are you going to explain me to Earth, anyway? You never reported my birth. As far as they know, I don't exist. What happens when they find out you've been hiding a child born in deep space? Do I get studied? Tested? Do you get thrown in prison for it?"

David stepped closer. "I don't care what Earth thinks. We'll figure it out. We'll face whatever comes together. There's a whole life waiting for you back there."

"That was never really my life to begin with. I was raised by silence and metal walls." Her voice dropped. "The ship. Space. That's what I know." She glanced toward the hatch and drew a slow breath, like she was locking something away. "All right. We do it. For the right reasons."

Grace didn't reply. She just nodded, shoulders slack, eyes full.

For the first time, there were no orders. No mission.

Just a mother and her daughter, standing on the same side of a choice.

Chapter Fifty-Six

I vy sat on the porch steps outside of Ambry's home, the weight of everything she wasn't saying pressing against her chest. Ambry sat beside her, silent, turning a stone over in his hand, just like he had for the past ten minutes. The hush between them wasn't awkward. It was worse.

Then— "Ivy!"

Thess barrelled out of the doorway, flinging herself down beside Ivy with a wide grin. Mirae followed close behind, quieter but no less determined, her bare feet padding softly over the porch boards.

"You're going already?" Thess demanded, crowding in so close Ivy had to shift closer to Ambry. Mirae hovered just behind her, a soft smile on her face.

Ambry gave a low exhale and stood. "I'll go wait for Laz and Nyra in the grove."

His voice was quiet, but Ivy caught the weight beneath it. He gave her a soft look, then ruffled Thess's hair on the way past.

Thess scowled and ducked. "Hey!"

Ambry didn't look back. Ivy watched him go until Thess tugged at her sleeve. "You weren't gonna leave without saying goodbye, were you?" She leant in, hands on her hips, looking like a tiny guard dog.

Ivy smirked. "I was hoping to escape unnoticed. Clearly, I forgot who I'm dealing with."

Mirae settled quietly on Ivy's other side. "You'll come back, right?" she asked softly.

Ivy met her gaze and felt the words catch in her throat. She forced a smile and reached for the pendant instead. "You want to see something cool before I go?"

Mirae hesitated, then nodded.

Ivy unclasped the chain and let it slide free. Then she held it out, the bronze wings catching the light as they swung gently in her grip, curled tight around the core. She placed it gently in Mirae's hands. Her fingers closed around it, brushing the edge. The bronze wings unfurled with a quiet precision, slow and deliberate, revealing the crystal core beneath. A soft blue light flared to life, veins of light running outward like circuitry waking up. Mirae gasped. "Oh cool, it's alive."

Ivy stared at it, heart thudding against her ribs. "Or maybe… you're magic."

Thess spun off the porch and cartwheeled across the grass, arms flailing. "I'm magic too! Look! I've got wings!" Then she flopped dramatically.

Ivy snorted. "Perfect. We'll form a club."

Mirae held the pendant carefully in her hands, the soft glow casting faint lines across her skin. Then, as slowly as it had opened, the wings folded closed again, the light dimming to a quiet hum against her palms. She turned the pendant over once, then held it out with both hands. Ivy reached for it slowly, her fingers brushing Mirae's as she took it back. The metal was still warm, a soft hum beneath her touch. She clasped the chain back around her neck, eyes lingering on Mirae, a flicker of wonder softening her gaze.

"I think you'll come back," Mirae said with a small smile.

Ivy swallowed, then nudged her gently. "Well, you two can annoy Ambry for me while I'm gone, keep him busy."

Thess bounded back up the steps and pressed into Ivy's side. "Easy!"

Ivy laughed and pulled them both into a hug. Tight, fierce, and quick before either could see the tears in her eyes. "Look after each other, okay?"

Mirae nodded against her shoulder. "We will."

When Ivy pulled back, she caught Mirae watching her with that soft, knowing look, the kind that said too much without saying a word.

Ivy gave her a wink, then stood slowly. "Be good, okay?"

She turned and stepped off the porch, her boots catching briefly on the wood. Then she made her way toward the grove, before either of them could ask her to promise what she already knew she couldn't.

— ✦ —

The twin suns hung high, casting dappled light across the ground as Ivy moved deeper down the warn path. The air held an easy warmth, a light breeze stirring the branches as shifting shadows danced along the ground. Ahead, the arch came into view, woven vines tangled with pale blossoms, shifting gently in the light. Ivy slowed. Beyond it, the grove waited, the one that had become theirs over quiet moments and shared days. Lantern orbs swayed between the trees, catching sunlight in lazy flickers. Hammocks hung like forgotten sighs. This was where she'd chosen to end her story. This was freedom. This was home.

And now... it was goodbye.

Ambry, Laz, and Nyra stood waiting. Laz had his arms crossed, an expression halfway between a scowl and a smirk as Ivy approached. "I was going to say something cutting and memorable. Something you'd replay while floating off into the void. But..." He shrugged. "You already know I'll miss you, figured I'd spare us both the awkwardness."

Ivy laughed, tears catching in her throat. "That was very nearly sweet."

"Don't get used to it," he muttered. "Are you sure you have to leave now?" he asked, frowning. "There's still time on the clock, right? You said your mission was meant to last a full year."

"It was," Ivy said. "But it's already been five months. And the chip might be gone, but The Order isn't. And if they knew what our true mission was, I don't think they would be very willing to let us leave, even though we have agreed to falsify the reports.

Laz's expression darkened. "True, The Order still has control, but now people are asking questions. About freedom, about emotion, about what was done to them. That makes things... unstable."

A rough edge cut into Nyra's voice. "They're scrambling to maintain the illusion of control. People are waking up, but the leadership is pretending like nothing's changed. That tension won't hold forever."

"Exactly," Ivy said. "We're cutting the mission short to protect what we've done. The less time Earth thinks we spent here, the easier it is to deceive the reports. To convince them there's nothing to come back for."

"Well. That's one way to dodge interplanetary war." Laz said.

Ivy tried to smile. It didn't quite reach her eyes. Then, without warning, he pulled her into a hug. Fast and tight, like letting go too soon would be a mistake. "I'll miss you," he said. "And he won't say it, but losing you might break him."

Ivy dropped her gaze, her throat tightened. "Take care of him for me?"

Laz's grin was faint but fierce. "Don't worry. I've been Ambry's emotional support disaster since childhood."

She managed a soft laugh. "I'm glad you're still you, Laz."

He gave a mock bow. "Some of us were just born awesome."

Nyra stepped forward, silver-lavender eyes gentler than Ivy had ever seen. "We spent half our time fighting and the other half proving we weren't friends. Maybe we could've been."

"We still could be." Ivy smiled, small but real.

A quiet laugh slipped from Nyra. "What? I'll call you?"

"You're paying the long-distance bill." Ivy smirked.

Her mouth twitched. "If I'd known then how much you'd end up meaning to Ambry..." A pause, then a shrug. "Yeah, no. I still would've given you the third degree. Maybe harder."

Ivy laughed, choked and honest. "Glad to know some things are consistent."

"Someone had to test you." She hesitated, voice softening. "If you stay... I mean, for Ambry... I'll get you your own Velune. One that's just as stubborn as you. Red-furred, so you match."

Ivy's brows lifted. "You'd really do that?"

A tiny shrug. "I'm elite. We specialise in impossible things. Like making friends."

Warmth threaded through the ache as Ivy smiled. "Thank you for everything."

Nyra surprised her then, stepping forward and wrapping her in a hug. Not stiff or formal, but real. Grateful.

While the others spoke, Ambry had stood a few steps back. Silent, unmoving, arms crossed, eyes on the ground. Like if he stayed still enough, the moment might pass without shattering him. She walked to him as if it hurt to move, like every step was one she'd never get back. He didn't speak at first. Just held her gaze, like memorizing her. Like blinking might erase her.

Nyra turned to Laz and nudged him lightly. "Come on. Let's give them a minute."

Laz opened his mouth like he might argue, then caught Nyra's look and nodded. The two of them drifted back toward the trees, their footsteps soft on the grass, until the leaves closed behind them.

"I wanted to say goodbye here. This is where I let myself feel safe. Where I started to understand what home could be."

Ambry's voice cracked. "Don't."

She flinched. Not because he raised his voice, he hadn't. But because it sounded like speaking physically hurt him.

"Don't say goodbye like it's the end," he said. "Don't walk away like this is just a memory."

"I don't want to," Ivy whispered. "But I have to. To protect this place. To protect you, all of you. It's the only way."

Ambry stepped in, closing his hands around hers. "Let them come," he said, voice raw. "We'll handle it, we'll prepare. Please, Ivy, stay. We'll find another way. Any way. Just... don't leave."

Her eyes closed. For a moment, she let herself imagine it, staying. Choosing him. Letting someone else carry the weight. "I want to," she said, barely a breath. "More than anything."

She opened her eyes, and the look she gave him shattered something between them. "But look what happened last time people from Earth invaded Spero. If I don't go... everything I love here could be taken apart. You. Your family. This world. Everything we fought for could be destroyed before it ever really begins."

Ambry's hands closed around hers. "Then let me say it, even if it breaks me. One last time, so it stays with you, even when I can't."

"I love you." His voice caught on the edges, pressing into her until her chest ached. The words sank deep, final and infinite all at once. He drew her hands to his chest, clutching them tight against the quick thud of his heart, as though sheer will could keep her here. "Not the way it's said in passing, but the way the ocean meets the shore, again and again, no matter how many times it's pulled away. Through every storm, through every fading star, I will love you."

Ivy didn't answer right away. A knot tightened in her throat. For a moment, she just looked at him, like saying the words might shatter her grip.

Then she leant in, pressed her forehead to his, and her voice cracked open. "I love you." Her voice shook. Fierce. Unfiltered. "Ambry, I love you. So much it hurts to breathe."

He kissed her slowly, like it hurt. His hands framed her face, thumbs brushing the tears she hadn't noticed falling. Then he pulled her closer, deepening the kiss, his hands finding her waist, her hair, like he couldn't hold enough of her at once. Ivy pressed in, fingers curling at the back of his neck. Kissing him like a promise she couldn't keep, like if she held him tight enough, maybe she wouldn't have to let go.

When they finally pulled apart, he leant down, resting his forehead gently against hers. Her breath trembled in the space between them. She didn't wipe the tears. Didn't try to hide the way she was breaking.

He already knew. A tear slid down his cheek. Silent, unwilling, like it had betrayed him just by falling. He didn't wipe it away.

"I'll come with you," he said suddenly. "I'll go to Earth. I'll help from there... just don't leave me behind."

Her heart cracked wide open. For a second, she wanted to say yes. But then she thought of Riven, Mirae, Thess. The woods and the wildness. Ambry's laugh by the fire, the way he carried other people's burdens like they were his own. She reached up and touched his face, wiping the tear he wouldn't. "You can't," she whispered. "Your family needs you. Spero needs you."

The thought of Ambry in a ship, a metal box hurtling through silence, broke her. He was made for the wildness, not walls. For forests and starlight and little sisters who believed in magic. "Besides," she said softly, "you belong here. And I couldn't stand to watch you become someone you're not."

Then she kissed him again. Fierce. Desperate. Like she was carving him into her bones. Like part of her would stay here, even if the rest had to go. Her hands cupped his face, their tears mingling. When they finally broke apart, she whispered, "I love you, Ambry."

Ambry pulled her into his arms and held her. Not like goodbye, but like breaking. His whole body shook, and then he couldn't hold it in anymore. He sobbed into her shoulder, raw and unguarded. The kind of sob that sounded like something tearing from the centre of him.

Ivy clung to him, her own tears falling faster now. "Please, Ambry," she whispered.

He nodded against her neck, shattered. She stepped back slowly, like detaching from gravity itself. Then she turned.

The sound of his sobs cracked through the air like thunder. Like grief given shape. It didn't just hurt, it ruined. It stripped her bare.

Still, she walked. Each step, a betrayal.

And she didn't look back.

Because if she did... she'd fall apart. And the piece of her that still had the strength to leave would be gone.

CHAPTER FIFTY-SEVEN

The twin suns sank low, casting long, amber shadows as Ivy slipped away.

She didn't go far, just beyond the edge of the camp, to the quiet slope where the trees thinned and the clearing opened out beneath her. The ground fell into a wide, grassy ledge, ringed by silverbark trunks and soft with wind-brushed moss. It felt held somehow, like the forest had pulled back just enough to let the sky in. Five months ago she'd stood here, taking her first real look at Spero. Back then, it had been wonder. A world waiting. Now... it was goodbye.

At the far side of the ledge, the space narrowed, the ring of trees pressing closer. She lowered herself onto the slope and pulled off her boots, toes sinking into the soil. Cool. Damp. Alive beneath her skin. A soft breeze wound around her shoulders like a shawl. Overhead, the leaves gave a low, sighing rustle, as though in greeting. Dozens of small creatures blinked into view, their stained-glass wings catching the light. Ivy had called them hummingbird fireflies at first. She knew better now.

"Lumibugs," Ambry's mum had told her. "They glow to match what you're feeling. You can't hide your true self with one of those around." One of them hovered close, its wings fanning the air in a slow, whispering hum. The glow along its feather-lined abdomen shimmered faintly. A dull violet, tinged with gold.

A soft rustle overhead, then a Tallwing dropped from the branches, landing in front of her. With two quick hops, it settled on her knee. She reached into her pocket and pulled out a few glowvine seeds and held them out. The bird pecked at them delicately, then paused as she stroked its head.

When it finally lifted off, its iridescent wings caught the sunlight, scattering prisms of colour in its wake. A parting gift, like a blessing.

Nearby, a Muruun padded from the brush, a cloud of pink and white, two small cubs tumbling at her heels. She settled beside Ivy with a soft huff, her moss-laced fur catching the fading light — pink brushed gold, every strand threaded with dusk. Ivy reached out, brushing a hand gently over the mother's head. "Hey, troublemaker," she murmured. "Brought the whole family this time?" One of the cubs flopped onto Ivy's foot with a soft chirp.

She slipped her hand into her pouch and pulled out a Talli fruit, dappled skin glowing soft gold in the fading light. She held it out, palm steady. The mother Muruun leant in, nose twitching, and took the fruit delicately between her teeth. Ivy stroked her mossy fur as she chewed, slow and content.

The two cubs nosed forward with soft, hopeful chirps. Ivy smiled and pulled another fruit from her pouch, splitting it carefully between them. They snuffled at her hands, tiny teeth nibbling at the sweet flesh, tails flicking as they pressed close.

"You'll have to get your own Talli fruit from now on," Ivy whispered, her voice low. "I have to go home tomorrow." She hesitated. "Wherever that even is."

"A planet I've never seen... or maybe it's the ship. Maybe that's the only home I get."

One of the cubs nudged her hand, tiny teeth catching gently on her fingers as it finished the last bite of fruit. Ivy let out a soft breath, almost a laugh, except it caught halfway. "I'll miss you too, little one."

She exhaled, her fingers brushing the mother's soft fur. "I wish I could stay. But some goodbyes... you don't get to choose." The mother nudged her gently, bioluminescent freckles pulsing faintly along her fur, as if offering comfort.

The trees shifted, leaves whispering in a soft, gentle rhythm. "I don't know what to do," she said. "I know I'm supposed to go. That's how I keep everyone safe. But all I want is to stay." A single leaf drifted down, spiralling slowly through the air, not from wind, but weight. As if the forest had exhaled.

"I don't want to live in a cage again. I want this. I want to live." She lay back in the grass, arms flung wide, breath caught somewhere between desire and ache. The pressure behind her ribs bloomed sharp and full, like something breaking open. The ridge held her. Not as a visitor. But as part of its story. And the wild, quiet and endless, held what she couldn't say. A sound behind her, slow footsteps, quiet on the moss. Ivy didn't move, just stayed where she was, arms wide in the grass.

David stood at the edge of the clearing, hands tucked into his pockets, gaze following the quiet swirl of Lumibugs and the Muruuns pressed close beside Ivy. When his eyes settled on her, something in his expression shifted. The sharp lines of logic eased, the scientist fell away, and there was only a father. A man watching something he couldn't explain, and couldn't deny.

He hesitated a moment longer, then cleared his throat gently. "Dinner's up," he said. "We're waiting for you."

He turned to go, but his gaze lingered. Not on the creatures, not on the clearing, but on her. The way she moved here... as if the place already knew her. A flicker crossed his face. Wonder, maybe. Or something heavier. Then he walked away, his steps fading into the trees.

Ivy waited a moment longer before pushing to her feet. By the time she reached the camp, the fire was already crackling low, casting a soft, flickering light over the group. Flatbreads and root stew, a gift from Ambry's mum, sat warming by the flames, their spices curling into the air like a quiet promise of comfort.

They ate in a loose, easy quiet, the kind that only came when the world outside was too loud. Ivy sat close, her gaze fixed on the fire, her half-eaten flatbread crumbling in her fingers.

Grace glanced across at Gareth. "I still can't believe it," she said, shaking her head. "You came back... on EOS 6. That's—"

"Unbelievable," David finished. "How did you even blend in on Earth? Grey might pass on an old man, but you were eighteen."

Gareth gave a soft snort, eyes flicking toward the flames. "Wasn't that hard. I stayed off-grid. Changed my look. Worked for food. People stopped noticing once they figured I could fix things."

Grace leant in. "Changed your look?"

He shrugged. "Dyed my hair. Used some tone-masking pills. Nano-tech capsules, pigment-adaptive. Shift your skin tone for a few hours, longer if you stack the dose. They sold it as personal freedom. 'Be whoever you want to be.'" He tore off a piece of flatbread and bit down, chewing slowly. "Big trend for a couple of years... until it stopped feeling edgy. By the time I left, it was just holo-theatre, cosmetic mods... or safe tanning. You know, the important things."

David let out a short breath. "Seriously?"

He glanced toward the fire. "It didn't take long before I stopped bothering with the pills. Earth got so politically correct, no one dared question anyone's skin colour anyway."

Grace gave a soft laugh. "I always thought you looked a bit... grey."

"Blending in's overrated. Hiding in plain sight worked fine," Gareth said.

She studied him. "Wait. Didn't they find albino markers in your bloodwork at some stage? Actually... how did you avoid the medicals?"

Gareth gave a low shrug. "I added the markers myself, slipped them into my record when people started getting curious."

David's brow lifted. "You hacked the system?"

Gareth shot him a look. "You remember the security on that 'final' EOS mission? I could've registered as a sentient houseplant and no one would've noticed."

David let out a quiet snort. "Yeah, true... explains a lot." He gave him a look, half impressed, half disbelieving. "And Toren and Mira? They were with you the whole time?"

Gareth nodded. "They just wanted a quiet life. Stayed home mostly. Ordered everything in. You could get anything delivered... anywhere... anytime. That suited them fine."

Grace tilted her head. "And you lived... where?"

"We settled in the fringe districts, not far from the city, but far enough no one cared. The kind of place the government ignored because fixing it wasn't worth the effort, too few votes to win, too many problems to bother. We found a half-standing house, good bones, stripped bare. Fixed it up. Grew what we could in the greenhouse." His eyes dropped to the flames. "Mira and Toren loved tending that greenhouse. Called it their little world. The air wasn't great, Skyfilters didn't make it out that far. They both ended up with chronic coughs."

Gareth leant back slightly, voice low. 'But they were happy.'

"Then I found someone willing to sell me papers, licenses, the works. Took a job with the ASA... and the rest is history."

A soft hush settled around the fire.

Ivy stayed quiet, arms folded tight. With every word, Earth felt less like a destination... and more like a warning.

Gareth shifted back toward the fire, settling cross-legged beside the flames. He reached into the pack at his side and pulled out a small bundle. Thin leaves folded tight around something soft and round. He set them on the rocks at the fire's edge, unwrapping one with practiced fingers.

The sweet, sharp scent hit Ivy first. Warm, spiced, touched with smoke. She blinked. "Is that...?"

"Solari cakes," Gareth said. "Ambry got them for us." Placing each one carefully onto a flat plate. "I figured if I'm dying tonight, might as well have dessert first."

Ivy's eyes flicked to the plate, then dropped. Ambry's name hit sharper than she'd expected, a twist low in her chest. She folded her arms tighter around her knees, staring at the fire until the blur passed.

David smirked, tapping his datapad beside the fire. "Technically, you'll be listed as drowned in a tragic waterfall accident."

Gareth didn't miss a beat. "Was it at least a respectable waterfall?"

"Fifty metres," David noted. "Steep drop. Very heroic."

Gareth gave a slow nod. "Nice. Think I screamed on the way down?"

"I logged it as a silent fall," David said. "Dignified."

For a moment, it almost felt normal. A quiet meal. A bad joke. The family they'd made, holding space together.

David's fingers hovered over the datapad. His voice dropped. "Ready?"

Gareth gave a slow nod.

David tapped the screen. "It's done."

Gareth's name flickered once on the display. Then shifted to: Deceased.

Ivy stared at the datapad. One word. Final. It wasn't a death. Not really. But it still felt like losing something.

Gareth caught her eye across the flames. He gave a small, almost invisible nod. I'm here.

She managed a faint smile back. I know.

But underneath it, the ache stayed. This was goodbye.

Then the ache cracked, sharp and sudden. Before she could stop it, Ivy's breath hitched, and then broke.

She folded forward, pulling her knees tight to her chest as the first tears tore loose. It wasn't loud. It wasn't graceful. It just… happened.

Across the fire, Grace and David exchanged a glance, something tight flickering between them. Neither moved.

But Gareth did.

He crossed the space quietly, dropped into a crouch beside her, and wrapped an arm around her shoulders. Solid, warm, steady.

"It'll be okay, Pip," he murmured. "You've got this. You always have."

She didn't answer. Didn't try. Just pressed her face into his jacket and let the weight of it all fall out in jagged, uneven sobs.

No one tried to stop her.

They just stayed, close, silent. Letting her fall apart before she had to put herself back together.

Chapter Fifty-Eight

The ship vanished into the sky, a silver whisper swallowed by morning light.

Ambry stood at the edge of the clearing behind his house, shoulders rigid, eyes on the sky. The glow from the launch had almost vanished, but he hadn't looked away. The silence left behind wasn't peaceful, it was hollow. A gnawing space where something living had once been.

Laz stood beside him, chewing on the stem of a skyvine pod. He didn't speak. Just offered Ambry one, like maybe that would be enough.

It wasn't.

Ambry's shoulders squared, then he stepped away. He didn't look back as he walked off.

The shed welcomed him like muscle memory — the scent of woodsmoke, the clutter of tools, the faint hum of something unfinished. He moved on instinct. Pulled out bags. Gathered parts. His satchel lay open on the bench, gear spilling out in tangled loops. Half-buried beneath it was Ivy's notebook, the one they'd hidden at the base of the Kavari tree. Its waxed cover was smudged with dirt, the edges curled. He turned the pages slowly, mind racing. Inside, on the last page, her handwriting curved steady and fast, like she'd written it all in one breath.

I've seen the pendant respond to Mirae. If anything happens and you need the key, tell Gareth. She might be able to open it. Be gentle with her. She doesn't know what it is. Or what it can do.

He held the notebook a moment longer, thumb brushing the faint spiral inked beside her name, then folded it closed and slipped it into the satchel. The weight settled over him, not sharp, but slow and crushing, pressing from every side. His jaw clenched. No sound, only breath, sharp and fast. He kept moving, one hand after another, as if stopping would let it all collapse.

Laz appeared in the doorway, arms crossed. "Whatcha doing, buddy?"

Ambry didn't look up. "I'm going to steal a ship."

Laz tilted his head. "Okay... why?"

"I'm going to follow her."

"Yeah, nice," Laz nodded. "Follow her to... Earth?"

Ambry shook his head once, sharp. "To wherever she is." He swallowed hard, hands tightening on the strap of his satchel. "I can't let her just vanish. I don't know how to live in a world that doesn't have her in it."

Laz didn't say anything at first. Just stood there, hands shoved in his pockets, eyes tight. "Do you even know how to fly a ship?"

"Nope."

"Do you even know if there are ships to steal?"

"Nope."

"Solid plan," he said. "I'll start digging our graves now. Want matching headstones or nah?"

Ambry yanked open a drawer too hard, tools clattered to the floor.

"Whoa, calm down," Laz said, reaching out to steady Ambry with a hand on his shoulder.

"Calm down?" Ambry looked his best friend in the eye. "Tell my chest to calm down. Tell the crushing pain to calm down. And please, someone tell my stupid heart to stop loving her. Because it sure as hell isn't listening to me." His voice broke. "Please, Laz. I have to do something. I can't bear this."

Laz looked at his best friend, really looked. Ambry wasn't just hurting. He was unraveling. "Okay, okay. I'll help you break into a heavily secured facility so you can steal a ship that may or may not exist, and chase your true love through the unbreaking darkness of space."

Ambry gave a small grin. "You truly are the greatest of all friends, Laz."

"Yeah, yeah, flattery will get you everywhere." Laz picked up a duffle bag and started to gather some tools. "You know we'll probably get caught, right?"

Ambry picked up a broken Tactis panel, not looking at his friend. "It's a possibility."

"And you do know that if there is a ship there, it'll be basically impossible to get it out of that place, yeah?"

Ambry sighed. "Basically impossible is not the same as impossible. And you know, you are a little negative now you're not chipped, just saying."

"Wow," Laz said. "Rude." He thought for a moment, then huffed a laugh and threw up his hands. "Fine. Let's go break the universe."

They packed in silence. Steady hands. Set jaws. Ambry's hands worked without thinking, coiling old charge cables, keeping busy while his mind ran wild.

Behind them, the door creaked open, slow, weighted.

They turned.

Ivy stood in the doorway, like she hadn't planned to. Like her body had arrived before her mind caught up. Boots scuffed, curls wild, leaves in her hair. Her eyes found Ambry, and for a second, she didn't say anything. She looked like she'd walked through a storm and hadn't quite made it out.

"I couldn't do it," she blurted, brushing wind-tangled curls from her eyes. "I tried, I really did. I got to the ship, and my parents were like, 'Come on, Ivy,' and I swear, for a second, I thought they were gonna physically lift me and just... fling me up the ramp." She gestured vaguely. "But I couldn't move. I just stood there like, cool, yep, this is happening, goodbye forever, no big deal. Except it was a big deal, and then I panicked... actually I think it was a panic attack."

"And now my parents are gone," her voice cracked, "and I don't even know where I'd go or what I'd do, and, and I'm—"

She broke off, tears filling her eyes. "Ambry, I couldn't get on the ship."

Ambry moved without thinking. He rushed forward, wrapping his arms around her, burying his face in her hair.

"Ivy," he whispered. Her face pressed against his shoulder. His hands curled at her back, anchoring her, steadying himself.

He shut his eyes and let it sink in. The feel of her, the truth of her.

Not gone. Not imagined. Just Ivy. In his arms.

And for the first time in days, everything made sense.

She was here. She was home.

CHAPTER FIFTY-NINE

As the suns dipped low, the grove settled into a hush. The lantern orbs drifted between the trees, their soft glow tangled in the branches like caught starlight. Ivy lay stretched in a hammock braided from silken vines, its gentle sway cradling her in the soft breeze. A few paces away, Ambry rocked in his own, one foot hooked over the edge, keeping a slow, easy rhythm — his free hand tangled with Ivy's between them.

The air carried the hush of leaves and the faint sweetness of something warm and blooming in the dusk. Softwoven mats lined the ground below, scattered with folded blankets and the remains of their dinner. A shared plate of glowfruit slices and a few crumbs of Solari cake left between them.

"I miss them already," Ivy said softly.

Ambry didn't shift, but his fingers curled a little tighter around hers.

Ivy traced her thumb over his. "You should've heard the things they were saying about Earth... no nature, artificial air filters instead of trees. Every waterway treated with chemicals, rivers, oceans, everything. Like they're keeping the planet on life support."

Ambry let out a low breath. "How do they even live like that?"

Ivy sat up a little, her movements slow, thoughtful. "I know I made the right choice. This is where I'm meant to be. But they're still my parents. I love them, I do." She let the words slip out, barely a whisper. "And they love me... in the way they know how."

Ambry sat up slowly, their hands still linked, and met her eyes. "You think they'll be okay?"

Ivy swung her legs over the side of her hammock and slipped into Ambry's, curling in beside him as it swayed gently beneath them. She leant her head against his shoulder.

"Yes," she said quietly. "They've been inseparable since the day they met. Mum was eighteen. Dad... twenty, I think. And it was just... them. They found something in each other that nothing else could touch. Not distance, not danger, not even a mission halfway across the galaxy."

She pushed up slightly, resting her weight on one hand as she looked at him. "They've always been this... unit. Like they move through the world as one, same thought, same heartbeat. From the moment they met right to the very end... all they'll ever need is each other." She let out a soft breath. "And I'm okay with that. I'm happy they have that."

She lay back down, tucking herself into his arms, letting the sway of the hammock hold them both.

Ambry wrapped his arms around her, firm and certain, like he wasn't ready to trust the space between them. Like some part of him still remembered how it felt to lose her... and was still putting the pieces back together.

They fell into silence again, the kind that didn't need filling.

Laz's voice drifted from the house, loud enough to reach the grove, something about escaping kitchen duty again. Ivy smiled. Home didn't feel like a place anymore. It felt like this. Like people. Like choices.

Ambry shifted beside her. "How did they let you stay, Ivy? I thought Grace would fight it to the end."

Ivy sat up, pulling her legs beneath her, the hammock swaying unevenly. "I just stood there... looking at that ship. At my future. And I couldn't move. I physically couldn't take the steps it would've taken to get on board. I just... stood there. Staring."

She gave a soft breath. "Dad came down first. Then Mum. They... had a bit of an argument. But this time... Dad stood up for me. He told her I wasn't a mission report. I was their daughter." Her voice thinned, softer. "They stood there for ages, arguing, like if they found the right words, it wouldn't end this way. But it always came back to the same thing. They couldn't make me go." She pressed her lips together. "So in the end... they agreed I could stay. With Gareth. It was either that... or pick me up and drag me onto that ship."

Ambry brushed a curl from her face. "So... they'll amend the records? Lie for you?"

Ivy held his gaze. "It's not just about the planet anymore. It's about me. They hid me for seventeen years... what's the rest of my life compared to that?" Her voice dropped, steady. "They know if Earth ever comes for Spero, it comes for me."

Ambry tilted his head, a slow smile edging onto his face. "Do you know where you're going to stay yet?"

Ivy's whole expression lit up, like the question cracked something wide open. "Gareth said we can get a little house, in one of the outer villages. Apparently, with him being royal, and everyone knowing it, The Order can't touch him. So people are actually helping us."

She gave a soft, breathless laugh. "Ambry. A house. With a door. And a yard. And everything." She shook her head like she still couldn't believe it. "Can you imagine?"

Ambry watched her, the way her eyes sparked over something so simple. Like it was the first good thing she'd let herself picture. He smiled, quiet and soft. "Only you," he murmured. "Only you would get that excited over a door."

She looked at Ambry, the boy who taught her how to listen to the wind, who stood beside her when everything fell apart. "I'm staying," she whispered, as if she finally believed it. "I'm really staying."

He brought her hand to his lips, kissing the knuckles with reverence. "Good. Because I so wasn't dramatic about you leaving, not like I was going to steal a ship to chase you through space or anything."

"Liar."

He grinned. "Total liar."

And as the last light spilled through the trees and the breeze lifted her hair, Ivy leant into his shoulder, into the quiet rhythm of a world that had waited for her — and finally, finally, welcomed her home.

She turned to Ambry. "So, about that Velune."

Acknowledgements

To write a book is one thing. To finish one is another. To survive four rounds of edits without hurling your laptop into the sun? That's pure madness — and I didn't do it alone.

First, to my incredible boys, Charlie and Logan, and my husband Ben, thank you for surviving on toast and patience while I lived half in Spero and half on this planet. Your love and support gave me the time and space to bring this story to life.

To my best friend Elza and my sister Tamara, who listened to endless years of "I'm writing a book!" and never once doubted me — you showed up for me and kept me laughing when I wanted to cry. And to my friends and family I didn't tell, because self-doubt whispered, "If you tell them, they'll know…" SURPRISE! I wrote a book.

To my beta readers, especially my father-in-law Craig, who was brave enough to dive into messy drafts and generous enough to tell me the truth: you made this story sharper and more alive. And the debates about whether jeans would still exist in a thousand years were invaluable.

And to my Dad, who is a true gentleman, a pure soul and the reason I am who I am today: determined, strong and damn funny with those one-liners. Your support means the world to me. Thank you for the hype speeches, and for reminding me that no book will ever be perfect. The real courage is in being brave enough to share it anyway. This book would not exist without you.

Finally, to you — the reader. You chose to pick up this story, step into Spero, and walk with Ivy through the cracks in perfection. That choice means everything to me. Thank you for believing in this journey.

— Monique

P.S. If the cover's upside down, pretend it's a metaphor.